MORE BY THE AUTHOR

SPECIAL AGENT KIM KUPAR

Jade Eyes
They
The Why Files

THE TSCHAAA INFESTATION

Book 1: The Gathering Storm
Book 2: The Tsunami
Book 3: Typhoon of Steel
Free Range Protocol: Tales of the Tschaaa
Beyond the Great Compromise: Tales of the Tschaaa
Survivors: Escaping the Tschaaa

ANTHOLOGIES

Monstrosity (Unnerving Anthology)
Descent (Unnerving Anthology)
Wicked (Unnerving Anthology)
Nightfall (Unnerving Anthology)
The Mighty Pen
Unconditional
Cascadia
Tales of the Slug
Super: Unexpected Heroes Arise

COLLECTED WORKS & MORE

Inhumanity: A Year of Stories
The Island (The Haunting of Orchard House)
Shane (Angels of Anarchy)

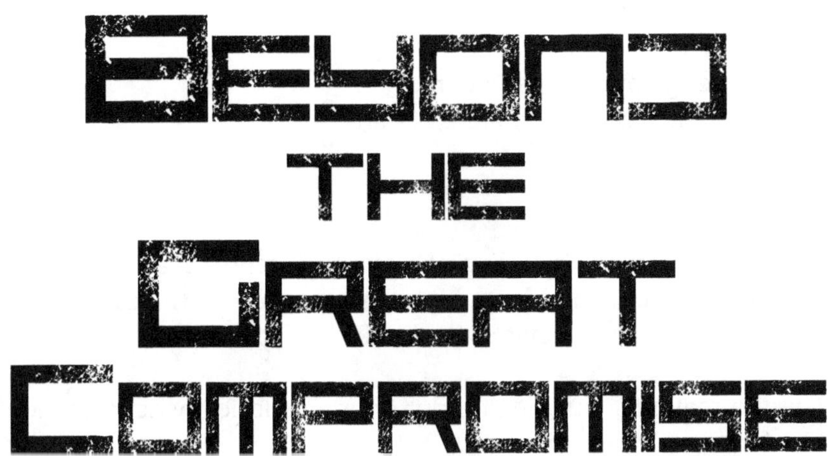

TALES OF THE TSCHAAA

MARSHALL MILLER

BLUE FORGE PRESS
Port Orchard, Washington

Beyond the Great Compromise
Copyright 2020, 2022
by Marshall Miller

First eBook Edition May 2020
First Print Edition May 2020
Second eBook Edition April 2022
Second Print Edition April 2022

Interior design by Brianne DiMarco
Cover art and design by Brianne DiMarco

ISBN 978-1-59092-973-5

For information about film, reprint or other subsidiary rights, contact: blueforgegroup@gmail.com

Blue Forge Press is the print division of the volunteer-run, federal 501(c)3 nonprofit company, Blue Forge Group, founded in 1989 and dedicated to bringing light to the shadows and voice to the silence. We strive to empower storytellers across all walks of life with our four divisions: Blue Forge Press, Blue Forge Films, Blue Forge Gaming, and Blue Forge Records. Find out more at www.BlueForgeGroup.org

Blue Forge Press
7419 Ebbert Drive Southeast
Port Orchard, Washington 98367
blueforgepress@gmail.com
360-550-2071 ph.txt

DEDICATION

I would like to once again dedicate this book to my loving wife, Sheri, and our Four-Legged Furry Family for putting up with my late-night forays in creating weird and wonderful worlds from my imagination.

Table of Contents

Beyond the Great Compromise

TALES OF THE TSCHAAA

MARSHALL MILLER

REMNANTS

Colonel Bettie Bardun stared at the tiles covered with the detritus of what was a type of laboratory. The problem was she had seen the horror this lab represented once before. Among the shattered equipment, beakers and flasks sat a series of ceramic tanks, now burned black from the flames. Bettie had seen these types of human body sized tubs previously. As the memories of that incident flooded back into her conscious mind, she began to shake. The tall and slender Colonel did not realize she was emanating a keening sound from her mouth until strong and familiar male hands held and guided her towards the exit door.

"Out of the way, people," her husband Colonel Cliff Hunter commanded. "Colonel needs some air."

With her love propelling her as well as supporting her, Bettie just made it outside the door before she lost everything had eaten that day. Cliff kept her from falling into her own vomit as she retched and retched, soon reduced to dry heaves. Luckily Bettie's hair was tied up in a bun as per military grooming regulations, or it would fall into the line of her projectile vomiting at the beginning of her being sick. Finally, she managed to stop the revolt of her stomach. A handkerchief appeared in front of her tear-blurred eyes magically as she tried to straighten up. She used the proffered cloth to wipe first her eyes, then her mouth and nose.

"Well, that handkerchief is trashed," Bettie mumbled.

"I've some others, dearest." Cliff had that sure voice and demeanor of the fighter pilot he had been for some twenty years, over seven of them during the Tschaaa Alien Infestation. With overly broad shoulders and chest which seemed to end in a too narrow waist, the joke was he had the physique of a cartoon hero character from before the attack from space. Bettie, somewhat composed, performed an unladylike spit onto the ground.

"Well, Cliff. At least this time there is no dead body of a psychotic bitch for me to puke on. Although I dream of killing her again."

"Come on, Bettie. Short walk to the car for that thermos of coffee I always carry. Use it to rinse out your mouth."

"I don't think I like scrambled eggs coming up for a rechew, Cliff," said Bettie. She frowned. "Trained Doctor, Exo-Biologist, and the woman who developed a WMD for use against the Squids, and I now have a weak stomach. That's just great."

Bettie held her husband's arm as they walked to the government sedan. Bettie did not realize how shakey she still was until Cliff helped her sit in the back seat. She suddenly felt weak all over. From seeming nowhere, Cliff produced a cold medical compress and placed on the back of her neck. As Bettie blinked back tears, she pressed her hand over her husband's as he held the compress.

"I don't... know what I would do without you, love," she said. "I am one hot mess."

"Oh, Christ, Bettie," responded her husband. "You a trained doctor don't understand PTSD? My God, I've lost count how many times something suddenly climbed out of my memory and sent me shaking. Even puked once or twice."

Cliff took her face in his hands and kissed her.

"My mouth tastes like vomit, Cliff. How can you kiss me?" Bettie asked as she touched his face.

"Because I love the holy Hell out of you, my dear. We help each other through the bad times. Remember?"

Bettie blinked back tears once again as she smiled at her one and true love. For some six years, she had thought he was dead, killed during the early part of the Tschaaa invasion. Then, magically, he was alive on the orbital Platform One of the Tschaaa Lord known in English as The Wizard. The thought of where they had met made Bettie remember it was on that former Earth International Space Station where she had seen similar horrors to the ones in the nearby lab. Only then, the remnants had not been burned and dead. They had been alive.

"You're looking green around the gills again, Babe," Cliff said. "I think we need to call it a day."

"NO!" Bettie did not mean to snap at Cliff. She quickly took his hands in her own.

"Darling, I know you want to protect me. But I have to deal with this. Only you and I saw closeup what those sick bastards were doing to what were once human beings, babies on Platform One. We have to certify that... this is the same. And help to find the bastards that are creating that evil once again."

Cliff paused for a moment, then answered.

"Okay. We'll help our resident Shield Maiden and Federal Investigator Brynhildr Knudson in locating and convicting the sick assholes who are doing this. Only, with one condition."

"What's that?" Bettie asked with a quizzical look.

"This time my dear, if necessary, I do the killing and puking on the bodies, not you."

The military couple made their way back into the building and the concealed laboratory. The area of the alleged experiments was now primarily a burnt shell. However, as often happens in a building fire, the arcane 'fire spirits' turned some items into piles of ash while leaving others scorched but still identifiable. It was the second class of objects which Bettie and Cliff had to examine.

Supervisory Special Agent Brynhildr Knudson, maiden name Jorgenson, met them as they reentered the crime scene. For initial examinations did show that crimes against humanity and nature had occurred.

"You wish to continue, Bettie?" the statuesque New Viking blonde asked. "We could take photographs, then show them later."

"Thank You, but no thank you. I need to see all this close up. There are some items that only I will know are important."

Brynhidr had known Bettie and Cliff since the final days of the Infestation. Bettie Bardun had helped organize the surveillance and recording of a fateful meeting between the Females of the two warring species. It was a secret meeting between the late President Sarah Paul and the senior Breeder known as Elizabeth. Without that meeting, there would have been no Great Compromise. Madam President would have used the MWD Bettie Bardun had developed. There would have been no morning after for billions.

"Okay, Bettie," replied the Special Agent. "Please tell my forensic personnel what to photograph, what to collect. There is no reason to hurry now."

Bettie stood still and looked at Brynhidr. Then she spoke with icy tones.

"Yes, there is a need to hurry. For if we don't, both new

victims and new… monsters will be created."

It was late at night when the two Colonels arrived back home. They had Senior Officer Quarters on Malmstrom Armed Forces Base, which meant a large house made for military officers with children. No sooner had they arrived, than Bettie began to kiss her beloved hungrily. Cliff returned the passion, and thus they did not even make it to their bed. On the plush sofa in their living room, the two survivors made passionate love. Not just once, but repeatedly did they become as one. They fell asleep in each other's arms.

They woke just before dawn. Cliff spooned up against Bettie's firm ass with his arms around her, holding her hands. Bettie moved her head and kissed his muscular bicep.

"I think I just seduced you, Cliff."

"I think it was mutual, Bettie."

The slender but shapely brunette shifted her body, so she was facing her love.

"I know I am not supposed to be able to tell this so soon, but… I think you just knocked me up. I think that is the term is in the street vernacular."

"I kind of figured that was what you wanted," replied the fighter pilot.

"You're not mad? I didn't exactly ask you, Cliff."

Her husband kissed her long and passionately.

"Does that answer that question? With all this… death we have been privy to, some we have caused, I can see no better act but to bring new life into the world. And do it the way Homo sapiens have done it for millions of years."

Bettie looked into Cliffs eyes as hers teared up.

"I do so love you, Cliff."

"And I you, Bettie. So, another round, so to speak? I think a part of me is waking up."

"Hmm. I think you are right. Kiss me. Now."

Hours later, the two Colonels met the Supervisory Special Agent in a forensic laboratory at the Federal Law Enforcement Building in Great Falls, Montana. The entire series of rooms were filled with the items and photographic evidence collected at the hidden laboratory. Someone had tipped the former lab occupants that 'the Cops were coming,' thus the attempt to destroy the contents by fire. The mistake the users made was they did not stay around long enough to ensure the job was done. Thus the clues left to track them were numerous.

Bettie walked over to a sizeable recovered vat containing mammalian remains.

"Brynhildr, these are the remains of anencephalic fetuses developed in these cloning vats, just like..." Before the Exo-biologist could complete her sentence, memories slammed into her consciousness: *A zaftig blonde Susan Smith is spinning and screaming, life's blood spurting from around the scalpels Bettie had plunged into neck and eye socket. Bettie then opened the Doctors neck with a bone saw.*

Things went black for a moment, and then Cliff was holding her tight.

"Deep breaths, Babe. They are just memories. They can't hurt you now."

"Bettie, please. We can—" Brynhildr was cut off by a loud cry from Bettie Bardun.

"NO!" Bettie slowly untangled herself from Cliff's hug. She stood up straight and walked back to the vat.

"These remnants are at the exact stage of those Cliff, and I saw on Platform One. Just before I... sent Susan Smith to Hell."

Bettie quickly turned her head towards the Federal Agent.

"What happened to Robert Smith, her husband."

"That is a good question," a frowning Brynhildr answered.

"He was part of this abomination. He supported his wife's efforts, was proud of it. And he has the same expertise." Bettie waved her hands to encapsulate the entire room.

"All this has his fingerprints all over it, even if they were burnt up. Only he would have a reason to continue this... sickness."

Bettie strode over to another recovered vat.

"And here we have an attempt to turn a human form into... something else. Too many arms, too many legs."

Bettie looked up at Cliff, Brynhildr, and the other personnel.

"Now you see why time is of the essence? This makes the Frankenstein story look like a child's nursery rhyme. The idea is to develop deformed and nonviable human offspring for not only spare parts, but also for the beginning stages of creating... things."

"What kind of things?" Brynhildr asked. "For what purpose would someone modify human young to such an extreme?"

"You were there during Hell Day. When Hell Spawn attacked Malmstrom Armed Forces Base. Including the Hospital Maternity Ward."

Brynhildr's mouth dropped open a bit. Then she began to curse in Norwegian, then spoke.

"They would turn our babies, our children into Hellspawn, Beasts, to kill us all?"

"Krakens would. Helped by a Tschaaa or two still angry about not being on the apex of the social order."

"And Robert Smith is such a person," added Cliff.

"Then the search begins today," stated Brynhildr. "The entire resources of the Federal Government will be at our disposal."

"I hope it is enough," said Bettie.

"It will be. I swear by Thor's Hammer. Our children will be protected."

Doctor Robert Smith checked off each crate, box, and piece of equipment as they were brought into the cavernous basement of the former mansion. Abandoned after its millionaire owner had died during the Infestation, a year after the signing of the Great Compromise it was still vacant. The trappings of wealth were just not as crucial to a populace who had barely avoided being eaten. Thus, rogue Tschaaa funds, as well as Kraken resources, were more than enough to purchase the house and property outright.

Smith had lost weight but still looked like Santa Clause with his white hair and beard added to his height. A muscular Kraken with a non-tattooed face but with a full Cthulu tattoo on his chest named Cross walked up to the Doctor.

"Everything showing up, Doc?"

"Yes, Mister Cross. I do not know how you did it, but that warning you received gave us enough time to transport most of the equipment before that raid." Smith sighed. "Too bad we did not have one more day. Then we would not have had to burn so many biological samples."

"Well, Doc, we do have that one large refrigeration unit with some of the most complete examples which were saved."

"Yes, Mister Cross. Can you have your people move it into that corner area over there? There is a two-twenty volt outlet in that wall I do believe."

"Will do, Doc." Cross walked up the direct access ramp to the basement and began to bark out orders.

"So close," Smith mumbled to himself. "Dearest, I was so close to achieving what you wanted. We'll have our revenge, Susan. I promise."

Smith looked up in time to see the before-mentioned refrigeration unit being wheeled down the ramp. The Doctor smiled as he approached to direct the workers where to position it.

A circular object came skittering down the ramp, nearly hitting the feet of one of the workers.

"What..." Smith said as the flash-bang exploded. The Doctor screamed, but could not hear as the flash-bang had both blinded and deafened him. Thus stunned, he was oblivious to the Federal Tactical Unit which flowed down the ramp with practiced ease. They only had to shoot two of the Kraken Minions. The others, including Cross, were taken to the ground not so gently and put in chains. As Smith managed to focus his eyes, he was staring into the face of a statuesque blonde woman in full tactical gear and holding a Viking battle ax.

"I know you are deafened, Doctor," said Brynhildr, "but I wanted the pleasure of telling you that you are under arrest for a list of crimes so long I will not tell you here. But I will have the pleasure of twisting your arms behind you as I handcuff you and you scream like a little girl, you sick son of a bitch."

The trial was short and brutal. Both Smith and Cross received the death penalty. There was no explaining away the physical remains of babies developed in the artificial wombs of the Tschaaa cloning tanks with no brains, just the bodies, and a partially formed skull. Next, there were the multi-limbed monsters that had once been human but were then made into... something horrific.

"It was for the advancement of science," explained Robert Smith. Cross tried the "I was just following orders defense," but then said "Fuck You all! You Mud People! Cthulu comes!"

As the two were loaded into a prison transport, Cliff and Bettie were escorted up to the van by Brynhildr.

"Remember us, Robert?" Bettie asked. The former Doctor's eyes widened as he answered.

"You! You killed Susan, my wife. I loved her."

"I killed a sick piece of shit, just like you. I just wanted to say 'so long.'. By the way, there will be no firing squad for you two."

"Why not?" Cross spat out.

"Because the Tschaaa likes their meat fresh."

The prison escort officers slammed the van doors as Smith began to howl. Brynhildr motioned for the vehicle to be on its journey. As it drove away, Brynhildr turned to Bettie and asked, "Is that a baby bump I see?"

"I'm starting to show, I guess."

"Yes, Bettie. And it looks good on you." Brynhildr patted her own stomach.

"Think I will look good pregnant also? "

"Yes, I do."

"If a lowly man may have an opinion," interjected Cliff.

"Go ahead, Dearest," replied Bettie.

"After all this death the past few years, signs of life in the form of pregnant women is a very nice change."

Brynhildr nodded her head in agreement.

"Your husband is quite smart and perceptive, Bettie."

"Think I'd let just any old fool knock me up?"

The three friends began to laugh as they walked away from the courthouse. Life always finds a way.

DUTY

John Patrick flipped the buffalo burgers on the large barbecue grill with practiced ease. Before he had joined the United States Air Force, he had been a short order cook in his family's restaurant. John had purposefully not shared that information with the Recruiter, as John did not want to be a cook. He wanted to be a Security Force Member. He wanted to see combat in Iraq or Afghanistan, anywhere the U.S. Military was, just like a couple of his older cousins. The thought of his two cousins, now long dead, brought a frown to his face. Two small bundles of energy brought a smile back to his face.

"Daddy! Is the food ready yet? We're hungry," John Junior, the male half of the fraternal twins, asked with a forceful bluntness that was all from his Russian mother, Afanasi 'Fanny' Koslov. The dark skinned, brown-haired six-year-old John Junior took after the Patrick side of the family as much as his sister took after the Koslov side. Their daughter Lilya, named after a famous Russian female pilot from World War Two, took after her mother, with natural blonde hair. The daughter soon echoed her brother's complaint.

"Children, did I not tell you we have guests coming?" Fanny's forceful comments made both children turn to her and answer in harmony.

"Yes, Mother."

"And did I not say we had to wait for their arrival before we could eat?"

"But they are late." Once again, there was the unnerving ability to answer simultaneously.

"Then your father will slow down on his cooking, and you will still have to wait."

At that moment, the doorbell rang.

"Saved by the bell," said John. As Fanny went to answer the door, John looked at his two children. Once again he realized how blessed he was to have a family. By all rights, he should be dead due to radiation poisoning from being in the general area of the Hanford Nuclear Storage Area Explosion during the Tschaaa Alien Invasion. Instead, some six years after the signing of the Great Compromise, ending the conflict between the Tschaaa Squid Aliens and humanity, John had a loving wife, a house in Great Falls, Montana, and two precocious twins. He was perfectly happy to be the 'stay at home Dad' while Fanny still worked for the New Federal Government, though no longer as an intelligence operative, the fancy word for spy.

As the kids ran to meet the guests with a gregarious nature, John no longer possessed. In his own private thoughts, he often wondered if a high level of natural socialization had ever been part of his makeup. He put those thoughts out of his mind as he put some chicken and hot dogs on the grill. John always made sure visitors were well fed, just as his parents had done in a different life.

Fanny had invited some young newly minted officers and their partners. There were even a few children as some of the officers were 'Mustangs,' those with enlisted service. John had been medically retired as a Captain, but his promotion to officer status had been a so-called battlefield promotion, though it happened away from a battlefield. He still thought of himself as an E-4 basic NCO. As one of the labeled Russian Three Sisters, former spies now put to use in other areas, Fanny was an excellent Administrative Officer for the ever-expanding Training Division. This was why she took it upon herself to invite new officers to their home for a little rest and relaxation. Fanny knew everyone was trying to adjust in this new world of working with an Alien species that used to look at humans as food, plus the losses in family members for almost the entire population of Earth.

Over an hour later, the children were burning calories from the food they ate with various games as the adults sat in the large back yard. John had demanded an oversized backyard and a house with large rooms, high ceilings when he and Fanny had looked for a home.

"I was cooped up for most of six years," he had said. "I and mine will never go through that again."

Since he had six years of unspent back military pay plus interest to buy the house outright, his was the majority opinion. Besides, Fanny planned on staying in America after meeting John, so a big house was okay with her.

As the parents and couples sat drinking adult beverages, John noticed one young female Lieutenant seemed to be summoning up the courage to say something to him. He sat as he knew she would eventually comment. John had the concept of patience forced on him years ago.

"Sir, begging your pardon," the young brunette started her

comment, and John stopped her.

"No, 'Sir.' Just John. I'm a civilian now."

"Then please call me Joan. I just wanted to say my older brother Don was at the Customs Port of Entry on the Idaho-Montana border when you walked up. He told me I had to tell you that what you did was one of the bravest things he had ever seen." John paused for a moment, then answered.

"No bravery in just doing your duty. Lots of other men and women were braver than I was. Take my wife Fanny here…"

"Now, John," interjected his wife, "Lieutenant Whitehead is just passing on a compliment from her brother."

"You did more than I did, Fanny. You and your fellow Russians. I just sat still."

"My brother said you did more than that, John," said Joan Whitehead. "He said…"

"I just did my duty. Like any good soldier." John suddenly stood up and walked away. Joan looked worriedly at Fanny.

"I'm sorry, Colonel if I said something…"

"No need to apologize. Excuse me for a moment." Fanny rose and followed her husband into their home. She found him in the basement recreation room, staring at a photograph of the former Fairchild Air Force Base before the Tschaaa had trashed it during the initial invasion. She walked up and put her hand on his arm.

"My love, please. Come back to the guests. Joan Whitehead did not mean to offend…"

"I did my duty. Nothing more. I could have retreated to Malmstrom Air Force Base. I could have become part of the attempts at killing the Director while he worked for the Tschaaa Lords. All while the Squids killed and ate people. Instead, as other the people around me died, I found a place to hide, stay behind, because I had to do my duty, follow my orders, stay until relieved."

"Dearest, it is the past…"

"The past is never really past." John stared at the photograph as the past became the present.

The first Space Rock hit at 9:13 AM, Eastern Standard Time. Rocks/ meteors struck from the East Coast to the West Coast as they also struck around the world. Two basketball sized projectiles smashed into Fairchild Air Force Base, destroying air refueling tanker aircraft stationed there. The airfields were trashed as aviation fuel was spread by the explosive force of the rock strikes. Later in the day, a larger piece of space debris broke apart, sending small pieces like a shotgun blast over the base housing area. As fires spread, order and discipline collapsed.

John had worked a graveyard shift as a Security Policeman. When he was done, he went off base to his girlfriend's home and had some early morning delight. Jeanine worked a late night shift also so spending time in bed during the early morning hours was an enjoyable activity. Especially with the man she loved.

If the explosions had not woken John and Jeanine up, Central Security Control communication via his cell phone a total Base Recall would have. As he threw his uniform on, Jeanine made him a sandwich and coffee as they watched the breaking television news.

"You stay inside, Jeanine," he told her. "This meteor shower may get worse instead of better." Jeanine kissed him.

"You watch your light chocolate colored ass yourself, and come back to me, John."

"Of course. Being careful is my middle name."

John made it to the base in record time even with all the craziness due to the damage and panic. He and many of the arriving Security Forces were sent to cordon off the airfield area. As additional pieces of rocks struck the housing area, personnel were dispatched to help. Everything was treated as part of a natural disaster of biblical proportions.

Twelve hours in, the Tschaaa alien craft showed up. Delta Fighters began to strafe military bases and major cities. As they arrived, the immense Harvester Arks appeared. They disgorged the Harvester Robots which started collecting humans for slaughter. Then the Falcon battle cruisers showed up, piloted by the cyborgs soon to be called Robocops. The entire world now knew that the space rocks were not natural, but part of an Invasion. So began the Tschaaa infestation.

John was grabbing a few moments of shut-eye in the back of a van when two Deltas began strafing Fairchild AFB. He scrambled out of the vehicle, grabbed his weapon and went towards the sound of gunfire. He saw a Delta zip overhead and knew someone was attacking. A couple of Security Force members were trying to bring a Stinger shoulder-launched missile to bear on the Deltas but seemed to have trouble with the self-contained radar and sensor system. John dashed up and took over.

"Here. I scored expert with this at Red Flag."

The second Delta was making another pass when John heard the audio tone which told him the weapon system was locked on. John fired the Stinger and watched it accelerate towards the alien aircraft. The pilot apparently had no clue of Earth weapons as he/she did not even notice the threat until after it struck. There occurred a satisfactory explosion and one of the soon to be identified Scramjet engines fell to the tarmac. A cheer went up at the sight of the vulnerability of the unknown enemy. The damaged Delta started to climb but the pilot must have been injured in the attack as the enemy aircraft flipped upside down and went nose first into a base administrative office.

The other Delta zipped by, setting off the shock wave of a

sonic boom. Intact building windows within the affected area were shattered by the sonic wave. John tried to round up as many Security Police as he could in some kind of organized response force. He appeared to be the only NCO around.

As John formed a two squad force, a deep rumbling came from the sky, At first, the personnel thought it was some kind of thunderstorm. Then they saw the gigantic Harvester Ark. Its oversized landing rockets lit up the entire area as it maneuvered to land on the damaged base runways.

"Perimeter! Form a three sixty degrees perimeter around that son of a bitch," John yelled out as the Ark settled to earth. A sizeable forward access ramp dropped, and the first of many six-wheeled Harvester Robs accelerated from the bowels of the alien butcher craft. The Security Forces put up a valiant fight, their automatic fire turning at least a dozen of the ATVs with a ball turret into sparking heaps of metal.

Then the Falcon came.

Blue beams flashed out, and various pieces of human anatomy were burnt or sliced off. The surviving Security Force personnel ran. They had nothing to use to deal with this new threat.

John found himself crouching in the ruins of the Base Theater, watching as the remaining Harvester Robs used ball turrets mounted with extremely bright floodlights to blind and sometimes burn their human prey. Humans knocked down or staggering around were grabbed by metal tentacles which zipped out from six-wheeled 'bots. The humans were then dragged or carried back into the Ark.

John knew he could do nothing on his own. He needed to find other armed individuals to mount some form of defense. Slowly and carefully, the Senior Airman crawled around the ruins of Fairchild Air Force Base. Another vibrating rumbling thunder cascaded around the area, and John watched the Harvester Ark lift off, apparently heading for greener prey pastures.

Somehow, John found himself in an undamaged maintenance double-hangar on the flight line. Inside were a couple of F-22s interceptors which appeared to have been undergoing some form of maintenance when the first space rocks hit. Crammed in as afterthoughts were some four A-10 'Warthogs.' John did a tactical sweep of the area, found he was alone, and took cover behind a large maintenance cart.

"Now what?" he said to himself. Was he the only survivor? If he was, he would have to make the decision if he was going to bug out, and then to where. As he stayed hidden, he heard a couple of voices. He crouched lower.

"What are we going to do, Captain?" It was a female voice.

"I don't know, Chief." Another female voice. "If we could get one of the F-22s up and running, I could fly it out of here. We could jam the two of us in the cockpit I think."

"They are both down for maintenance, Captain Lockhart. Then we would have to find fuel for them."

"I guess I could fly an A-10 in a pinch. These have two seats. But again, fuel is a problem."

Just then, John stood up and approached them.

"Ma'am, Chief, don't shoot. Senior Airman Patrick," John had called as he did not know what weapons they may have. As he neared the two, he saw the Chief, a late twenties brunette aircraft crew chief, had an assault rifle in her hands. The redheaded Captain Lockhart had her assigned pistol.

"Been here long, Patrick?" the Captain asked.

"About fifteen minutes. Ma'am. My Squad and I tried fighting, then that damn big disc-shaped craft showed up. It blew the hell off of everything."

"Well, Sergeant Maverick here found this M-4 on the tarmac.

Might be one of your Squads."

John shrugged. If the weapon was loose, the owner was probably being drug off to be butchered.

"If you can use it, you're welcome to it. The question, Captain, is what do you want to do? I think you are the ranking person around."

The three stood in silence. John knew pilots were an independent lot, were more concerned about flying than commanding. However, like it or not, due to her rank Captain Lockhart just had command responsibility forced on her.

"Well, Airman, we were discussing the possibility of flying out of here," said the Captain. "But getting an aircraft fueled is the problem. The thought of leaving all this hardware behind for the Aliens is not my idea on how to fight a war. Which is what this is, sure as shit."

"So, do we destroy everything, Captain?" the crew chief asked.

"There has got to be another way..."

"I could stay, guard them while you two look for help," interjected John. "Or transport. There might be some civilian truckers still alive we could convince to help us."

"That is not a bad idea, Patrick. We can chain the hangar doors shut."

"Captain, there is an old Cold War bomb shelter under this hangar,' said Sergeant Maverick. "Maintenance uses it for storage."

"Okay. We have a plan." Lockhart looked at Patrick. "It may take us a while to arrange transport."

"I'll stay until relieved, Ma'am. Just like my general orders. It's my duty."

The three USAF personnel quickly put their plan into motion. They went to the former bomb shelter and found a cornucopia of material. Chains and locks were found, and within a half hour, all doors were locked from the inside. There was a couple of small personnel access doors on the side on the side and rear of the oversized hangar. The doors had turn bolt locks on them. Thus, someone inside could easily safeguard the area yet have quick egress. The access hatch to the old bomb shelter was near a back corner of the hangar. A person could secure the building, then retreat to the underground bunker.

In the now storage room they also found some emergency rations that someone had forgotten existed. There were also some flares, a battery radio with all the emergency broadcast bands one could ever want, first aid supplies and some old musty blankets from a bygone era. The three cleared out a bunch of spare aircraft parts to give Patrick some room if he chose to stay there. A careful reconnaissance outside resulted in finding a bloody tactical vest with some extra loaded magazines. John transferred the ammunition to his own tactical equipment and placed the tattered vest in a corner.

"Someone died defending Fairchild," he said.

"A lot of people did, Patrick," replied the Captain. "Now, you stay here until we get back."

"Ma'am, I'll stay here until relieved. Find some fuel and pilots, and we can give those Aliens some payback." He came to attention and saluted Lockhart. "It's a pleasure to serve with you."

The Captain smiled as she returned the salute. "Same here. See you soon."

John Patrick never saw the two women again.

Patrick stayed inside the hangar and away from the doors. He turned the multi-band radio on and listened to whatever channel he could pick up. Everything was hit and miss. What he did glean was that the Aliens were cephalopods and thus were soon given the moniker of

"Squids." He thought he caught the word "Tschaaa" as the name the invaders gave themselves. John also heard of renegade humans who were helping theses Squids in attacking humanity. The world was falling apart.

On the Fifth Day, everything went to Hell. The Hanford Nuclear Storage Area achieved critical mass.

There was a deep rumbling sound that shook the hangar. John took the chance and looked out one of the personnel access doors. As he looked towards the southwest, he saw an ever-expanding plume of smoke forming into a well know the mushroom shape.

"My God! Hanford!"

Everyone at Fairchild was briefed on Hanford because of all the nuclear waste and material. Theoretically, U.S. A. F Security Forces would respond to help support the Department of Energy Security if something drastic like a terrorist attack happened. The situation was well past that. John also knew what the plume meant. Radiation is coming from some one hundred forty miles away, blown by some of the same high altitude wind currents which had spread the Mount St Helens ash plume. However, that volcanic explosion so many years ago was not radioactive.

John Patrick's training took over. He secured the door, ran around the hangar and checked all the locks and chains. Everything was as locked up as things could be in the rapidly disintegrating environment. He beat feet to the bomb shelter access door and then down the stairs. John shut and bolted the lead-lined door, next went looking for a specific item hanging in a small closet in the back. Someone had hung up two 1980's style radiation and HAZMAT suits and forgotten about them. John had already brushed the accumulated dust off days before. Now, he hoped they still had some integrity when it came to stopping radioactive fallout.

After zipping up the suit. John tried to get some reports on the radio. What he heard was hit and miss, the explosion or explosions interfering with radio transmissions. What he did understand was that there had been a nuclear explosion. And now the cloud of radioactive fallout was headed his way. The Senior Airman knew the old bomb shelter would have some protective capabilities due to its design. However, as he put the suit's helmet on, John knew that with radioactive contamination, it was better safe than sorry. John Wayne was killed by radioactive dirt particles logging in his lungs after filming in the Nevada Test Site, resulting in reoccurring cancer. John Patrick wanted to live just as long as he could.

John sat in the near dark, a small flashlight illuminating the room around him. He had turned the radio off to conserve the batteries even though it had a small charging handle. How long would he have to stay underground? His training told him two weeks to start with, a month would be better.

"I hope the Captain and Sergeant made it out," he said to himself. He knew that was a fantasy after he voiced it. As he turned off the flashlight and laid down on his makeshift bed to try and sleep inside the protective suit, he said a short prayer.

"Lord, if I ever needed help, it's now. Amen."

A month and innumerable games of Solitaire interspaced with meals of survival crackers and cheese, John breached the bomb shelter door. He had the full protective suit on as well as his assault rifle in his hands. People could be driven mad from the results of radiation poisoning, not to mention some of the before said human renegades could be snooping around. There was a light covering of dust on the stored aircraft, blown through the cracks of the hangar doors. John would have to sweep all the dirt up and push it out of the hangar as the Geiger counter he had put into operation still pointed to above than normal levels of radiation, although not the worst the manual with it suggested.

John peeked out the back personnel access door. The vegetation looked normal, In fact, there were some signs of recent rain, which could be good or bad news depending if the rain brought fallout down from the atmosphere, or washed it away from the hangar. Holding the Geiger counter in front of him, John walked around the hangar. Again, the results were a little higher than usual, but not off the scale he was expecting. There was a possibility most of the fallout was blown past Spokane, WA into Idaho. That would be good news for him, bad for the residents of Idaho.

Just as he was about to enter the double hangar once more, he heard someone call out.

"Hey, Spaceman! Hold up!"

John glanced around, his protective helmet restricting his vision. He finally saw the source of the yell. Two scruffy looking men were walking towards him, both with hands behind their backs. Some seventy yards away, he called at them to stop and show their hands. He set the Geiger counter on a ledge just inside the door and stepped further outside.

"What you got in there?" one called out, not stopping his approach. Both of the strangers still had hands concealed behind their backs. In one smooth action, John performed the Security Rock move. He grabbed the butt of the rifle slung on his right shoulder, pulling it out and up so as the assault rifle rotated off his body. It was in his hands pointed to the threat, ready to rock.

"Halt!" John yelled. Hands came from behind the backs and fired pistols. Even as the rounds hit John's concealed body armor, he was shooting. One miscreant's head exploded like a dropped watermelon on the Fourth of July, his blood and brains splattering his partner. John screamed a curse from the impacts of the bullets as he stumbled back, still shooting. The second stranger went down with several hits in the chest.

John managed to stay standing, stood up and screamed: "You Fucker! Why'd you shoot me? You holed my HAZMAT suit."

He stomped up to the fallen shooter and stepped on the man's gun hand as he pointed his rifle at his face. Some body armor on the man's chest had partially deflected John's bullets, so he was still alive. In a rage, John yanked his protective helmet off and yelled at the man.

"Why'd you shoot me? What are you doing on the Fairchild Flightline? This is a controlled area!"

The scruffy man stared up as his mouth formed into an evil grin as he saw John without his helmet on. "Why, lookie here. A nigger."

John stomped on his face. As the man screamed in pain, John kicked the pistol out of reach. "You see a surviving human, and you call him that? Are you nuts?!"

Holding his broken nose, the man sputtered up at John. "Didn't you get the word? You're Dark Meat! The Squids love you darkies! They think you taste the best!"

"What's that got to do with you and me?" growled John.

"We help find you for them," came the reply. "And you are as good as dead. My friends will be here soon when I don't check in. Another nig—"

John blew his brains out.

John spent the next few minutes dragging the bodies over to a dumpster. Strength fueled with rage, and he had little trouble boosting both dead men into the trash. John Patrick took the two pistols and stashed them in the hangar. Next, he closed and locked everything up. John stripped off his holed protective suit and shoved it into a trash can behind one of the jets.

"If I get radiation poisoning..." he cursed, then realized since the miscreants were already dead, he couldn't hurt them more. John swore and cursed even more at that thought. The Airman went back down into his protective den, locked the access door, and sat in the dark.

"Alien Squids are eating us, and we still are a bunch of racist fucks." John was talking more and more to himself as there had been no one else to speak with. Now, the first two people he had a conversation with and he wound up killing them.

"This world sucks," John said, Then he crawled to his bed and closed his eyes.

A year after John killed the two strangers he went out scrounging for food. He was on his guard after learning they were Krakens, minions of the Alien Tschaaa, the Squids. Plus, due to his darker skin, John was on the Squids menu as the main course. Well, he would not go without a fight.

John found some odds and ends in the abandoned buildings and vehicles which were not burned up or trashed. Then he saw the two gigantic rats. The Airman was afraid to think about how what they ate to grow so large, but John did not hesitate to shoot them. Back to the hangar and he used the Geiger on them. Their contamination was within limits, so John skinned and then roasted them.

John had no razors left, so he was getting scraggly looking. His BDUs were looking worn also.

"I'll have to try and make it to the BX and the uniform store," John said out loud. "I have to look like the E-4 that I am. Gotta respect my rank."

He listened to the radio for a few minutes. He was hearing about some guy called the Director in the Florida Keys who was working with the Squids to keep "non-Dark Meat" humans alive. Also, some people were trying to save some Mid West States functioning as a reduced United States. He snorted.

"Why doesn't anyone want to visit me, Senior Airman Patrick? Why not?" He took a swig of liberated whiskey, then turned off the radio. He had only so many batteries to use. He pulled out an old magazine he had found and leafed through it.

"Have to make plans for tomorrow," he mumbled to himself. "Need to go shopping."

John was up with the Sun and headed towards the Base Exchange. Thanks to the clouds from the Hanford Explosion, the Spokane area was a ghost town. Apparently, even the Squids were afraid of radiation. The Geiger counter told John the contamination was not as bad as everyone thought.

"Just like Chernobyl," he mumbled to himself. "Mother Nature bounces back while men are afraid."

John managed to find a few odds and ends that had not been looted, to include some snacks, vitamins, and some BDUs, plus some underwear. He wrote an I.O.U. at the check out stand and headed out the main door pulling a kids wagon that people had somehow overlooked. John sipped at a lone beer he had found. He looked up and saw the deer.

John froze as the deer looked at him, then slowly started walking away.

"Thanks, Mother Nature," John mumbled as he shot the deer.

John made a foray the third year to the on-base liquor store. He had decided he did not have anything else to do, so why not? John had found an old chess and checker set and was playing a series of games against Bobby Fisher who periodically visited when John felt an urge to play. The Senior Airman dusted off the aircraft as best he could, kept an eye out for Krakens and feral humans. Stay Until Relieved. So far, there was no relief. Only Bobby Fisher visited, and he was not Air Force so he could not relieve him, could he?

The liquor store was a big surprise. A locked room in back contained cases of beer, some wine, even some hard stuff. People must have really panicked and ran to leave all this behind, he thought. Their mistake, his gain.

It took him three trips with the little red wagon, but he got everything. He was standing out back of the hangar when the Ferals showed up.

There were three men and a woman, all looking like they had seen better days. John had a pistol stuck in his belt left over from the Kraken as the four humans approached.

"Stop right there," John called out. "Restricted Area. Authorized Personnel Only."

"Well, look at the tin soldier," the woman sneered. "Whatcha got in that building?"

"Classified," John replied.

"Hell, how about sharing it, buddy?" one of the men said as a rifle was produced.

"He's just a tin soldier," the woman sneered again. "Come on. Give it…"

John emptied the pistol at all four. Three went down, the fourth, a man, ran. John went back into the hangar and locked the door.

Bobby Fisher stopped coming after John started talking about the broadcasts from the Unoccupied States of America. The shit hit the fan when after John had heard about the attack on Key West, the heroes involved, a call from this Madam President for help, for Allies.

"I have these military resources, Bobby. They could help… .

No, I won't get killed. I will come back, and we can play... Well, if you are going to get nasty about it, just go fuck yourself!"

A week later, John Patrick locked up the hangar as best he could. Word must have gotten around a Crazy Man was guarding the airfield as no one else came by after shooting that woman and two men. The radiation threat seemed to keep the Squids away.

"Time to move," John said. He had stopped drinking after Bobby Fisher left. Now, it was time to see if he had the guts to make it to the Unoccupied States.

"I'll be back, my aircraft friends," John called out. He came to attention, saluted, about-faced, and, marched off.

At a new Port of Entry on the Idaho-Montana Border, a skinny man with a chocolate complexion wearing a faded and ragged set of fatigues had come marching up to the Customs Official and announced, "Senior Airman John Patrick Reporting, Sir. I need to talk to the President or Commanding General on a matter of extreme importance."

After asking him nicely to put his assault rifle down, the Federal Customs Officials had escorted him to a back holding area. They at first were about to write him off as a Feral who had spent too much time sucking in radiation in the Eastern Washington/Idaho area after the Hanford Disaster. He then produced a couple of instant camera photos and managed to bring up a picture on his old cell telephone. The photographs appeared to show some military aircraft stored in a hanger on an Air Force Base.

"Been trying to protect them for the last six years. Heard the broadcasts about the Nuke at Key West, the Pits in Great Falls. I guess you're the closest thing to the United States Air Force in existence. I need to turn these resources over to you. Sir. Ma'am."

They had a chopper fly him to Malmstrom where Captain

Afanasi 'Fanny' Koslov, the blond member of the Russian Three Sisters, used her interrogation skills on him. All he could do initially was to stare at her. Finally, he spoke.

"Sorry, Captain. Ma'am. Never seen a good looking Russian woman officer on an Air Force Base before. Also, you're the first woman I've been this close to, talked to in six years. Ma'am."

"Well, Airman, what were you doing for the six years, besides not talking to women?" Fanny had smiled at him, seeing that a little female friendliness would go a long way with him.

"Eating rats, emergency food rations, melting snow for water. I was in an old Civil Defense bomb shelter underground of the double hangar. The base personnel used it for storage. Owe the Air Force for some.223 ammo I expended. I figured they can take it out of my last paycheck. Had to shoot two big ass rats, a deer, and some people trying to steal the jets and other stuff. ."

"Jets? Aircraft? What kind of aircraft?"

The Senior Airman had shown her the faded photos, the cell phone images. Fanny had flashed him a big smile

"I bet you could use a nice steak, baked potato, and a cold beer right now. Am I right?"

Patrick had stuttered a bit. "I, I, I, don't know, Ma'am. I'm still on duty, no one has relieved me from my post. I just came here because I didn't want something to happen to my aircraft if I got sick, died. My General Orders say..."

Fanny had reached across the table and grabbed his hand. "How about if I had General Reed, Senior Allied Commander, have someone relieve you, take over your post at the Air Base? Would that do?"

"Ma'am, I'd have to see his I.D., Line Badge, check to see if he is who he says he is. It could be a Standboard or I.G. trick, test, to get me to leave. Or maybe you're spies." The young man was becoming agitated. He was getting sensory overload after years of being alone, with just his Duty.

Fanny kept smiling. "I was a spy. For Russia. Now I work for General Reed, fighting Squids. We are all on the same side, my friend. Now, I am going to get that steak dinner, my treat. And the General will want to talk to you, I just know it." Fanny had taken the photos and cell phone.

"I will bring these right back after I call General Reed. I promise. Okay?"

The Airman had stopped, stared off into space for a minute.

"Okay. If you bring back the General, I'll let someone relieve me from my post."

Fanny had patted his hand. "Be right back."

General Reed's driver SSGT. Pasqual had gotten him to the Intelligence Office in record time. Then he was sent off to get as much food and drink as he could find, including steak and some beer.

General Reed had walked into the room, handed Patrick an old Air Combat Command Restricted Area Badge.

"Permission to enter and approach your post, Senior Airman Patrick."

Years of practice came rushing back as the former U.S. Air Force Security Force Member. He flipped the I.D. over, then again, looked at the photo, at General Reed. He handed the badge back to the General. He snapped to attention. "Sir, I recognize the General. You are cleared to enter the restricted area." He performed a snappy salute.

The General returned it. "At Ease, Troop." He then stuck his hand out. "Welcome Home, Son. And it would be an honor to shake the hand of a Security Force member who kept his post for over six years, did his duty."

Patrick took the proffered hand and shook it.

"Just doing my Duty, Sir. Just like anyone else would."

General Reed knew the young man had some mental issues from being alone for six years. But he would, by damn, make sure he was well taken care of. Patrick had watched over some much-needed aircraft for six years, probably ate some radiation during that time. A mission to the former Fairchild Air Force Base would be mounted ASAP to recover what looked like some A-10s and a couple of F-22s. In the background of one of the photos seemed to be a couple of air to air missiles, as well as a belt of 30 Millimeter GAU cannon rounds. This Senior Airman was a Godsend.

"Well. Will you do me the honor of dining with me here, with my driver and Captain Koslov? I'd like to talk to you about Fairchild. I haven't been there for years. And yes, you are at this moment officially relieved of your Security Post. Job well done."

"Thank You. Sir." With that, Patrick began to twitch, then sat down with a thump. Fanny suddenly went over and put her arm around him.

"It is okay, Airman. Your mission was successful. You did your job." He began to sob. The General slipped out the door, figuring a good looking woman would be a better comforter that a General ever would be.

The General walked down the hall, some Military Police Officers awaiting his orders if need be, with some medical personnel and a gurney nearby. He addressed the small group.

"Ladies and Gentlemen, in that room is an example of someone who took Duty, Honor, and Country to heart. I expect him to be treated with the utmost respect. He has been through a special kind of Hell but completed his mission. Understand?"

"Yes Sir" rang out.

"Good. Now, hopefully, Sergeant Pasquale will be back soon with some good grub. And I guess I need to get a hold of the Base

Commander and have Clothing Sales opened to get the new Second Lieutenant some new uniforms and rank insignia. Plus some underwear, socks, sweat suits. And a barber."

General Reed looked at the door to the interrogation room. "Give me a thousand troops with his stubborn belief in duty, and the Squids won't have a chance."

Peter "Pappy" Gunn, former U.S. Army Chief Warrant Officer, and current scrounger for the Allied Forces had gotten the task of arranging the recovery mission to Fairchild Air Force Base. He quickly rounded up enough protective gear for radiation exposure, as he had no idea how much crap from Hanford had reached Spokane, Washington. Pappy had shanghaied Colonel Clifton Hunter of the Space Plane escape into the retrieval mission. His aircraft expertise would help in determining what could be salvaged.

A couple of squads of Russian Spetsnaz, half a dozen Japanese technicians, and some of Pappy's own staff took some flatbed trucks, Humvees, SUVs, and an ex-Army Deuce and a Half on the trip to Spokane, Washington. A very cleaned up new Second Lieutenant Patrick was the guide as they retraced his steps from Fairchild AFB to the Montana Border. In addition to his new rank, Patrick had been given all of his back pay also. Six years' worth, ninety-five percent of it now sitting in savings and precious metals.

A week of some TLC from a particular Russian Intelligence Officer had done wonders. War and conflict created some odd bedfellows.

The salvage mission had gone surprisingly smooth and quick. A few Ferals had taken a look at the combined firepower of the detail, had quickly disappeared. Padlocked and chained hangars had revealed six A-10 attack craft and two F-22s.

Colonel Hunter's face had busted into a broad grin at the sight of the aircraft and equipment. "We're in business now. Like people used to say, cooking with gas on all four burners." He had turned to the new Second Lieutenant. "Why'd you stay when everyone else bugged out when Hanford blew, the radiation came?"

"Never left my post until relieved, Sir. Wasn't about to start bad habits."

One of the SPETSNAZ troops said something. Pappy had asked him to translate.

"He'd make a good Russian. Never give up. Fight the Fascists to the end."

"Well, it's the Squids who are the problem now," Pappy said. "Now, let's get moving. We have a lot of work to do as long as the cloud overcast stays. Don't need the ole Eye in the Sky watching us, getting nervous."

"Yeah" replied Cliff. "Thank God the Tschaaa depend so much on their eagle-like eyesight enhanced by those Eye in the Sky, space telescopes. If they ever figured out real aerial surveillance, we'd be stewed, screwed, and tattooed."

Twenty-four hours later, they were loaded up, the aircraft all in good shape by having been kept out of the elements. The radiation levels had not been high either. And the winter cloud cover held, with not too much snow. No snooping Deltas or Falcons appeared.

A day later, they were all back at Malmstrom, being refitted, re-conditioned. John Patrick was learning what it was to be an officer, thanks to a former Russian Spy who seemed to love him to death.

"John, please." His wife's voice and loving touch brought him back to the present. He turned at looked at her.

"Why me, Fanny? Why just I survived? Why wasn't I harvested as Dark Meat as all my friends, relatives, comrades in arms were? Why?!"

Fanny hugged him as hard as she could, then kissed him.

Fanny looked him in the eye.

"Because it was meant to be. We were meant to meet. I was meant to fall in love with you. Now we have two beautiful children, after all that worry about radiation. Please, Dearest. Accept the happiness we have. Look forward to the happiness our children will have."

John Patrick looked at his Russian wife, took a deep breath, let it out, then kissed her. The kiss was a long one, but no one complained. As they finally parted their embrace, John spoke.

"I guess I still feel these… ghosts around. I did my Duty, but so many others also did. And they are not here to share in the happiness. My life changed. Their lives ended."

"We all lost someone, dearest. Now we have each other. We must make the best of it in honor of all those who have passed on."

"My intelligent Russian philosopher," John said with a grin. "Why you married a dummy like me I'll never know."

"Because my dearest husband, you are not dumb, and you are the best man I know, I have ever known. Accept it."

John sighed. "Okay, I'll accept it. Now, I guess it's time to face the real present."

The couple rejoined the party. When LT. Whitehead tried to apologize, John waved it off.

"No need, young lady. Just some ghosts in the machine. Hopefully, you'll never have any. Here, let me freshen your drink."

As John was at the wet bar, he looked up and saw Bobby Fisher in the mirror behind it. John sneered as he mumbled.

"Go away, Bobby. We don't need no ghosts. I did my duty. I have love now. That is all I need."

Man's Best Friend

The man in camouflaged fatigues yelled and cursed at the War Dog. He jerked and yanked at the long and thick leather leash.

"You God-damned mutt! Mind me!"

The large K-9 growled, then snapped at the abusive holder of the leash. The Military Dog Handler's eyes widened with anger and fear. He pulled a collapsible baton from his duty belt and snapped it to extend the striking metal end.

"I'll teach you, you son of a misbegotten bitch," the man cursed as he raised the baton to strike. Before he could land a blow, he was picked up by what seemed to be an elemental force and thrown across the grassy training field. The handler fell with an impact sufficient to see stars. When his eyes focused, he saw the person who had tossed him like a rag doll.

In front of him stood a massive man with the muscular build of an Adonis. The individual locked his steely gray eyes on the fallen person.

"Sergeant," said the individual who is known to all as Dogman. "You don't beat on your dog. If you resort to that, you have done something wrong."

Dogman fixed his stare on the baton still in Sergeant Dicks hand.

"And you don't beat them with that."

Sergeant Dicks was not a small man. In fact, he was close to two meters in height, although not as massive as Dogman. Dicks was also embarrassed, angry and scared. He was humiliated in front of his fellow Handlers, and thus motivated to take the next unwise step.

The sergeant sprang to his feet with the baton still in his hand.

"No one lays hands on me like that!" he bellowed as he went for Dogman.

It was all over in a flash, except for the bleeding and pain. A massive hand caught the baton, while an equally massive fist smashed into Dicks' face. Blood spurted from his broken nose. The force of the blow sprawled Dicks out, and he lay still.

"Shit," one of the other handlers said. "Is he dead?"

"No," replied Dogman. He then walked over to the now loose K-9. The War Dog knew Dogman but was scared and agitated. He showed his teeth in a defensive gesture of 'don't hurt me, I bite' as the K-9 crouched to flee or fight. Dogman stopped and looked at the K-9.

"Hey, Bullet. Nothing in my hands. See?"

He turned his head slightly but kept the dog Bullet in his peripheral vision.

"Patrolman Green. Come to me, please."

Cathy Green, a police officer from the newly created Portland, Oregon Police Department, walked towards Dogman. As well as being the youngest in the training class, she was also the smallest. Five foot two, eyes a blue, she still had strong shoulders and wiry strength.

"Sir, I mean Dogman."

Dogman was adamant about being addressed with just his name, nothing else. Actually, used as his assumed name, as his real name was Romanian. Everyone knew him as Dogman, except his niece, the Avenging Angel, Abigail Yamamoto. To her, he would always be Uncle Buck.

"Okay, people." Dogman's voice resonated over the training area. "Teaching moment as my wife would say. Green, let me have your dog, Thunder. Now, take command of Bullet."

Cathy Green slowly approached the large K-9, still showing teeth. Bullet in his K-9 brain did not know if he wanted to be a subservient pack member at this moment of both fear and rage, so he snapped at her. He missed the proffered hand of friendship. Before Bullet could make another attempt, the Police Officer had a vise grip on the fur and flesh around the long-haired K-9 throat.

"OUT!" Green yelled as she twisted the fur and flesh, using her weight and the surprise move to force the dog's head towards the ground. Bullet gave little resistance as the command voice, and the grip suddenly reminded him of his place in the world. He went to the grass, his paws up but not scratching.

"Excellent, Green." Dogman then addressed the other trainees.

"Mother dogs discipline their pups by nipping, or grabbing the pups in her jaws and forcing the pup down, in a subservient position." He walked around to the far side of Green and Bullet. K-9 Thunder kept glancing at Dogman with a "Hey, why is my human wrestling with that other dog?" expression on her face. Dogman gave an ear a reassuring scratch and continued.

"We are not designed to be nipping or using our jaws to hold a

K-9 down. So, we use our hands and powerful command. Okay, Green. Let him up, and I'll swap dogs with you."

In a moment Green was scratching Thunders ears as Dogman put Bullet on a short lease, then knelt down and began to talk with the K-9 in low tones. Within moments, Dogman had Bullet on his back and scratched the dog's chest. Once the K-9 Trainer could feel and see the tension begin to leave, Dogman had Bullet heel. Now, Dogman would have to find a new and decent human for him. Until then, he'd give the War Dog some structure and a little TLC. But not too much TLC. He was a War Dog, after all.

"Dogs are actually better people than we are," Dogman told the group. "They are more honest with their actions and feelings. Dogs won't lie to you. They will die for you. War Dogs are our Partners, our comrades. Don't abuse their love and loyalty."

Dogman had the eleven remaining trainees take their War Dogs and run them through the obstacle course, as they were en route to when Sergeant Dicks had his meltdown. Dicks was beginning to moan when the onsite EMTs showed up. Dogman knew there would be a report, a complaint from the unit Dicks belonged to. The K-9 Trainer did not care. The worse they could do would be to fire him, then he would train other peoples dogs, not just for the government.

An hour later, the EMTs transported Dicks to the local hospital at The Dalles, Oregon and the Trainees secured the War Dogs in the large kennel complex. Dogman walked to his sizable residence on the edge of the first War Dog Training Academy. The Academy was his and his wife's creation. Mary Lou Spencer, once the Sister Wife of the now dead Director Adam Lloyd of the infamous Selected Survival Protocol, was now Dogman's love of his life. Along with four children, two the offspring of Dogman and Mary and the older two the family of Mary and the Director, Dogman finally had a life full of the love of other humans, not just dogs.

He had helped save Mary Lou from being slaughtered by the Krakens, human minions of the Tschaaa Squid aliens, almost three years prior. While transporting her and the two young girls, Kathleen and Marian, to safety during the hectic days before the signing of the Great Compromise ending the Tschaaa/Human War, something clicked between him and Mary. They fell madly in love, a first for Dogman. Many a woman had seen this Adonis and desired to be Dogman's wife, but none came close to that reality. That was until Mary came along. Mary had asked her husband if they could name the boy and girl after her children from her first husband, all lost during the first part of the Tschaaa Infestation. Thus, Johnathan and Susan were the newest members of the family as fraternal twins.

He entered the spacious house through the side door which led into the kitchen and was immediately tackled by two four going on five-years-old twin girls, Kathleen and Marian. Actually, they attempted to grab their father, but all the two sisters could do were wrap arms and legs around Dogman's muscular legs and hang on as he strode around the kitchen. This was a game repeated almost every day.

"Someday, girls, you will be too big to do that to your father," Mary stated as she walked in with the younger Johnathan and Susan in tow. Dogman smiled at the black haired beauty, then kissed his love.

"I saw the EMTs transporting someone, Dear," said Mary. "Dog bite?"

"No. Broken nose."

"Broken nose? How did that happen."

"The former trainee tried to hit Bullet with a baton. Then he tried to hit me."

Mary knew her husband did not suffer idiots well. Especially if someone tried to harm a K-9. So his typical short explanation was enough for her to see the situation was handled as efficiently as Dogman did everything.

"Well, dearest, how about you walk those two girls over to their places at the table. We have non-radioactive Columbia River giant catfish stew, fresh corn on the cob, rice and strawberry shortcake for dessert. By the way, it's your turn to say grace."

Over an hour later and all six humans were in a sizable recreation room helping with the socialization of six new War Dog puppies. The proud mother, Portia from the Sergeant Fuzz bloodline, laid on the floor next to Dogman. She was quite content for her humans to keep the six soon to be weaned puppies occupied as she obtained some deserved rest. Like all of the Fuzz bloodlines, they had German Shepherd fur but with a head a bit more massive as in a Great Dane, and ears that flopped over at the top. Plus, they were already twenty percent larger than other large breed puppies at that age. Not to mention the increased intelligence.

"Ladies, and Gentlemen, it is nearing time for bed," said Mary. "Let's all go upstairs and wash up."

All four children started to make 'do we have to' sounds until Dogman commanded: "Do as your Mother says." With that, one by one they kissed and hugged their father and went upstairs with Mary. Dogman helped Portia corral her pups and put them behind some interior fencing. All the K-9s were soon fast asleep.

He met his wife at their master bedroom and knew she had something on her mind when she stripped her clothes off and hugged him, then kissed him long and luxuriously. He was already down to his underwear when Mary did this, so it became quickly evident he was responding to her affection.

"I think, based on your body's reaction, that I have my

husband's full attention," Mary said with a mischievous smile.

"You always have my attention," Dogman replied.

"Even around your War Dogs?" Mary asked.

"Well, usually you win out, dearest."

"Such Flattery, husband! Now come here and love me, you oversized jerk."

Early in the morning hours. Dogman silently sat and gazed at his sleeping wife, She was a dead ringer for one Bettie Page, 1950's era Pin-Up. However, her looks were not the reason he loved her. As he had told her and others before, something had "clicked" within hours of first meeting her. Just as dogs picked their humans as humans thought they were adopting a pet, Dogman had seen in her the love of his life. Luckily, she had soon seen the same in him. Had she not, honor would have prevented him from forcing himself on to Mary. He had done many a wrong act in his life, to include killing some people who did not deserve death. However, he had never forced himself on a woman.

His love resulted in him raising four loving children, two not even his own. General Torbin Bender, Hero of the Resistance during the Infestation, had asked him once why he was raising two children fathered by the now dead Director, a one time supporter of the Tschaaa lord who had occupied North America.

"I love and take care of puppies, who are not only not related to me but are of an entirely different species," he answered. "So, why cannot I do the same with human children, our 'pups'? They all need love, help in growing. What is the difference?"

Dogman would never know, but with that answer, Torbin Bender had realized the Hercules looking person standing there was so very much more complicated than most people could ever imagine. Of course, Mary had ascertained that early on.

"So Kathleen and Marian. You accept them as your own?" she had asked him the day they had consummated their love as they lay in the afterglow.

"I love you. Mary," Dogman had replied "You love your children. Thus, I will love them. Case closed."

Dogman had demonstrated this love through actions rather than words, for he was much more a man of action than verbal assurances. Thus, Dogman was "Daddy" to all.

His Cellphone beeped, and he grabbed it before it woke Mary. He stood and slid out of the master bedroom with a grace that belied his massiveness.

"Dogman here," he answered in low tones. "You almost woke my wife."

Everyone who worked with Dogman knew he did not want his family disturbed.

"Uncle Buck, it's Emily Anders," said the voice on the phone. With the name and the recognition of the speaker, Dogman's irritation dissipated. If the Veterinarian and good friend Emily called at that hour, the subject must be urgent.

"What's up, as the American's say, Emily."

There was a pause on the other end, and Dogman could sense a dread about the subject of the telephone call.

"We have another Dog Beast."

The Sun's rays were beginning to peak over the Rocky Mountains as Dogman finished the preparations of the oversized metal connex. He had modified the former seagoing container to meet his special needs. The needs included the ability to restrain a near-prehistoric creature. For both Emily Anders and Uncle Buck Vladu, AKA Dogman considered all the poor animals turned into Beasts, known to some as Hell Beasts, were oft time closer to some long lost fauna of the Earths ancient history than today's wildlife. *JURRASIC PARK* had nothing on what Dogman and the Vet had seen and treated.

Disgusting humans working with Tschaaa biological science had warped and mutated natural Earth fauna into... Things. These things called Beasts had been used not only for the amusement of the Tschaaa minions named Krakens in Pit Fights but also as weapons of terror and death. The worst use of them was during Hell Day, the attack on Malmstrom Armed Forces Base. Not only was President Sandra Paul targeted by these monstrous Beasts, but also infants in the Hospital Maternity Ward. Some actions could never really be forgiven. Krakens found to have been involved in the use or creation of such beasts were often summarily executed in the months following Hell Day. Because the Beasts were once Earth creatures, some saw them as worse than the alien introduced Eaters.

As Dogman checked the thick chains used to secure the enclosure, he sensed someone approaching behind him.

"Mary, I wished you would stay in the house with the children."

"I will," said Mary "after I make sure you will be safe with this new arrival."

Dogman turned and walked to her. They clinched in a bearhug, and Mary kissed him.

"I wish you weren't so goddamned hardheaded, Buck. There must be someone... "

"No, dearest, there is no 'someone else' who can do this. I built some of this compound on the Columbia River because I need to handle these problems. I, Dogman. I can do this. I need to do this."

Mary looked up at him.

"I think you have paid enough penance, my love."

Dogman looked into her eyes. "You are the best thing that has happened to me since coming to America all those years ago. But I must do this. I was part of the Kraken sickness. I must help fix what it broke."

"Just don't let it break you, my Hercules. Please remember your family needs you."

"I will always remember, my love. I can never forget."

A semi truck and trailer pulled into the far driveway, the driver blowing its air horn in a short blast to alert Dogman.

"Mary, if you could please stay inside with the children as we unload our new… guest."

"Of course, my love. You just be careful."

"Always."

A large black SUV with tinted windows followed the tractor-trailer in, then peeled off and drove towards Dogman. It stopped and disgorged two passengers well known by Dogman.

"Doctor Anders, Commissioner Miller. Welcome to the War Dog Training Academy."

The brown haired veterinarian smiled as she approached her friend and hugged him. Dogman had met her through his niece Abigail, and they had become fast friends for they both loved and respected dogs. Her husband, Federal Law Enforcement Commissioner Paul Miller, walked up and shook hands. There was mutual respect between the two men, but not real friendship. Paul would always have a problem with Dogmans violent past with the Tschaaa's Kraken minions.

"I'm here strictly to keep my wife here out of trouble, Dogman," Paul stated. "Nothing official."

"You know what they say about bullshitting a bullshitter," Dogman said with a slight smirk. "It just makes you both messier."

"Oh all right," the Commissioner said with a grin. "I wanted to see what all the government funds have bought. I have not been here since you broke ground… how long ago was it?"

"Coming up on three years."

"Damn. Time flies Dogman." Paul Miller turned and looked over what he could see of the mile square training facility. "You have made something special."

"Give a lot of credit to Mary," replied Dogman. "She has the brains to organize all this. I just train the dogs and their humans."

Armed guards from the SUV and a small sedan were out and backing the truck up to the oversized metal connex that was a supercage. As they did, something big inside the trailer hit the near side of it with a loud thump.

"She awake?" asked Dogman.

"I guess so," the Vet said with a frown. "I thought I had given her enough sedative. I guess not."

"She's pregnant, right?"

"Yes, Dogman. Which is why I was being careful with the amount of the sedative. I don't want it to lead to any lost pups."

The creature inside the trailer slammed into the side once again, this time with enough force to shake the entire back of the truck. Emily swore and strode to the end of the SUV. In moments she had a long gun case out. Dogman watched as she quickly assembled a large capture rifle.

"Let me try and get her in without that," stated Dogman.

"How're you going to do that?" asked the lawman. "Trust me, she is huge even for a Beast. Bigger than even the bear creatures we saw at the Pits."

"I set that containment building up just for this," replied Dogman. "Oversized ocean shipping connex I modified to offload any and all animals directly from the truck. Watch this."

Dogman strode over to the rear of the semi-trailer. As he had requested, the back of the van had a large roll-up door which locked at the bottom. Emily tossed him a key for the oversized hasp as she stood by with the capture rifle and its sedative dart. Dogman stood still for a moment, then unlocked the high-security hasp as quietly as possible. With ease for someone his size, Dogman climbed to the top of the trailer cage. He signaled, and the truck was backed up, so that bare inches separated the trailer and the oversized containment structure he had built. Like the Hercules, some said he resembled, the Romanian grabbed the top of the roll down door and pulled it up as if he did this every day. The creature inside the mobile cage had been waiting for a moment to grab freedom and exploded from the semi-trailer. It went into the containment structure, looking for another exit. In a series of smooth moves, Dogman let the roll-up door slam down. He lept to the top of the local cage and released the equally massive sliding door. It slammed down, and a bolt slid into place.

The Beast, seeing there was no back exit, slammed into the now closed entrance. The force of the impact almost dislodged Dogman from his perch. The door held. A loud howling growl emanated from within the supercage as Dogman dismounted from the top. He motioned the driver to pull away from the new home for the Breast. Dogman stepped in front of the supercage so the strange creature could see who was the one to imprison her once again. Through vision slits, Dogman saw eyes glaring at him which told him what he needed to know.

"What do you think?" Emily Anders asked from behind him.

"Windows into the soul," replied Dogman.

"Come again?"

"Dog eyes. She looks at me with eyes from a canine. I have seen enough of them to know deep inside her is the soul of a dog."

"So, you think you can do something… for her?"

Dogman turned and looked at the Vet.

"I will free her dog soul. For it is trapped in a body not of her doing."

A couple of hours later, after Emily. Paul and the others had lunch provided by Mary, and the transport group was preparing to leave, Dogman stood in front of the supercage. As soon as he approached, the Beast had fixed him with her eyes. She let a rumbling growl issue from her throat to give the man notice that she saw him. And that she did not trust this man.

"You need a human name, lady," Dogman said in a low tone. "A name you will come to recognize as we take this journey together."

He stood silent, as the Beast examined him and the area beyond him. The dark furred Beast would escape if given a chance.

"Catherine the Great. A Russian ruler was known for her strength, intelligence, and toughness." Dogman smiled as he said the name. "I can respect Russians even if I do not like what they did to Romania,"

"Dogman!" May called out his name. "Come and say goodbye to our guests."

"I'll be back with some more food and water for you, Catherine. As befitting a Queen."

Dogman walked back to say goodbye.

"Think you can handle her?" Paul Miller asked as Dogman approached.

"She is close to the size of a polar bear, but she is still basically a dog," answered the trainer. "I have never met a dog, a canine who I could not deal with. It is about mutual trust. Also, love and loyalty help."

"Betty Bardun our resident exobiologist says someone spliced some hyena DNA in her genome," Emily said. "That and everything else they did to her, I question how much real 'dog' we have there."

"She is Dog. Trust me."

Mary stepped up and looped her arm around his massive bicep.

"I have learned that when my Buck says to trust him, you can take what he says to the bank."

"If anything goes wrong..."

"You will be the first to know, Emily. But nothing will. I am Dogman. Remember?" He ended his comment with a rare smile.

Dogman approached the supercage with a huge bucket full of water and a second equally massive bucket with raw Buffalo Meat. One positive thing that had resulted from the Tschaaa Infestation was herds of wild Buffalo. Not only were the native creatures a source of excellent lean meat, but American Bison were death on alien Eaters. Bull bison took the existence of an Eater near a herd as a personal affront and would run it to ground even on the Buff's short legs.

The Romanian knew Catherine the Great was watching his every move. Given a chance, this first day of captivity at the War Dog Training Academy would be her last.

"You are highly intelligent, Catherine," he said in his native Romanian. He planned to train and communicate with the creature in his native language. Thus, as time went by, she would look to him for communication and direction. Or so he hoped.

Dogman slowly approached the sliding access slot for the food and water. Catherine's nose was working so he knew she was hungry. The statuesque man slid the access aperture open and slipped a large piece of raw meat through it.

"Here, Catherine. This meat has some added vitamins and antibiotics."

It was her first feeding after the trip so the beastie must be hungry. However, the dark-furred Beast sniffed the meat, then stared at Dogman through the visor above the feeding aperture. The trainer smiled.

"Don't trust the odd smell from the medicine, huh? You were drugged once before with food and remember."

Dogma pulled the medicated meat out and replaced it with virgin flesh. This twenty-pound piece of Buffalo Catherine eagerly grabbed and backed towards the dark rear. Her massive jaws and teeth made quick work of the food as Dogman watched her with a night vision monocular. He allowed the added security Catherine felt in the dark until at least she was more comfortable.

The she-beast finished and approached the front of the supercage again.

"Oh, so you want more? Why should I give it to you? "

Catherine the Great fixed him with a stare that in some humans would either make them run or piss their pants. All Dogman did was chuckle.

"Another Apex Predator I see. Well, watch."

Dogman held the other twenty-pound piece of meat up and bit into it. He tore off a small portion of raw flesh, chewed and swallowed it. Catherine never once relaxed her surveillance. Dogman placed the meat in the feeding aperture once again and slid it towards the Beast. This time, she grabbed it without pause, and once again went to her dark, safe stop. Dogman had placed some old Army blankets in the cage and Catherine had readily made a nest out of them. She had the instincts of any pregnant canine, would want a secure place to give birth. Whenever that would occur. Dogman slid the deep pan of water into the supercage and stepped back.

"Take a nap, Catherine," he said. "Let your food digest. This has been a stressful day." Then he laughed. "More stressful on the transport team of humans than you, I bet."

Dogman knew that had she woke early on the trip, there would have been Hell to pay. Catherine had massive jaws and teeth and may have been able to chew the way out of the tractor-trailer. If that had happened, she might have been shot.

"No one will shoot you here, Catherine," Dogman stated. "Not if I have any say. Which I do."

Dogman turned and walked the one hundred yards to his house. Mary was waiting for him at the back door.

"Watching me and Catherine the Great?" he asked as he kissed her cheek.

"I wanted to make sure that great Beast did not try to snack on a piece of you."

The Romanian turned at looked at the supercage.

"She is intelligent. Not only is she enhanced in size, but also in her mental faculties. She knows I am not threat."

"But she would still run over you to escape," added Mary.

"Yes, dear wife. I just have to make sure she does not."

The Beast slept through the night and did not stir until Dogman brought her breakfast at sunrise. He figured Catherine would be near exhaustion due to the stress of being drugged, then transported to a strange place. Emily Anders had said they only captured her the day before she had called Dogman. The Beast had been found when it had broken loose from a clandestine Pit Fight operation in Southern Idaho. Had Catherine not escaped, killing some of her Kraken scum captors, the Pit would have remained hidden. Years after the Great Compromise and the former minions of the Tschaaa still would not abandon their obscene ways. Luckily, Emily and Paul Miller responded with the necessary capture gear so that they did not have to kill Catherine the Great.

A short whistle woke up Catherine. She produced a deep rumbling warning growl that meant "go away," then stopped as she caught the scent of Dogman and food.

"Come, my beauty," he said in Romanian. "I have four fried eggs on another huge Buffalo steak. It is going to take me a while to figure out how much protein you need."

Catherine was up near the feeding slot before Dogman even noticed her movement. He chuckled.

"You can move as silent as a Bengal Tiger," Dogman said. "I'll have to remember that. I cannot afford you sneaking up on me until I know we are friends. Or at least respected pack mates."

Dogman slid the large food tray into the supercage. Catherine was on the food in a flash, inhaled it into her mouth. The trainer heard some quick chewing, then silence. A broad black muzzle poked through the feeding aperture, an oversized dark red tongue probing for more food.

"I will get you more food, Catherine," he said in Romanian. "But first, let me get a better look at you."

Dogman walked to the side of the supercage and slid a heavy metal cover back from a window of armored glass. He had planned to look at her and see the correct length, but she had other ideas. Large grey-tinted blue eyes stared back at Dogman, Catherines nose working a mile a minute to smell him and the area around the window. Dogman laughed.

"You are an alert beastie! I'll have to remember that. You are not someone who likes to be snuck up on."

If he were dealing with a standard canine, he would have tried to approach and presented a hand for inspection. Then, maybe a light ear scratch. But Catherine was not a typical canine.

"Your eyes suggest some Siberian Husky in you. The rest of you..." Dogman tried to look down the side of the Beast, and see its tail. As if Catherine sensed what he wanted, the Dog Beast made a complete three hundred and sixty-degree turn in place. Dogman saw black and brown thick matted fur, then a massive tail. In a moment,

Catherine the Great was staring into Dogman's eyes once again.

"You are a beauty. But you will need some grooming. Only after I know you are safe to let out."

Just then sounds came from across the Training Academy grounds. The Trainees were completing the morning feeding, with the War Dogs greeting their humans. The supercage walls and the area around them shook with a growling bark. The War Dogs heard the voice of the new animal, and some began to bark and howl in response until their humans quieted them. Dogman grinned as he looked at his latest four-legged ward.

"Well, my lady. They now know there is a new four-legged Alpha Female in their midst."

Catherine gave a low coughing bark as she and Dogman looked at each other.

"But, when will you accept me as the Alpha Male?" said Dogman. "That is the vital question.

The next few days involved Dogman developing mutual trust between himself and the unusual type of canine creature. The second day of Catherine's residency, Dogman found a used large truck tire for a toy befitting an animal with massive jaws. He had also noticed two incisors that were almost as long as Sabre Tooth Cat fangs of old. Thus, Catherine needed something to chew that would not be demolished in minutes. A good scrubbing, the insides filled with meat and blackberry jam for flavor, and Dogman climbed on the top of the supercage as quietly as possible. When he opened a large ceiling hatch to drop the treat in surreptitiously, he found Catherine sitting and looking up at him with a "have something for me" look. He grunted.

"I forget how smart and observant you are. Here. A toy for you."

He dropped the tire prize, and Catherine caught it with her jaws in mid-air. Dogman thought he saw a bit of a twinkle in Catherine's eyes, but it may have been his imagination. Once again, Catherine retreated to her dark den. Dogman shut and secured the hatch with the high-security lock, then climbed back down to the ground. A half hour later, he had a massive meal and fresh water for his charge. Catherine approached him with a new air of confidence about her. The Romanian smiled as the Beast took the steak and once again started to retreat. Halfway turned, she stopped and turned back. Catherine the Great fixed Dogman with a piercing gaze.

"Still trying to figure me out, Catherine?" asked Dogman.

The magnificent creature managed a 'gruff" response around the meat in her mouth. To Dogman, it sounded like a 'yes' answer. He smiled at her, watched as she slowly turned back around and went back to her darkened den corner.

"You're coming around, Catherine. Good."

Dogman turned and walked towards the Academy Training Area. The current class was down to the last two weeks. He had some field exercises planned, but based on the caliber of dogs and humans who remained, they would be more of a formality than a necessary test. The Canidae and the Homo sapiens had all bonded quite nicely. Although in human culture the man or woman must be seen as the Alpha pack member, Dogman knew that in actuality it became a true partnership over time. On a special Wall of Honor, Dogman had listed all the four-legged and two-legged people who had given the ultimate sacrifice for their partners, their family. Recorded at the top was Sergeant Fuzz, he who saved Dogman's niece Abigail, the Avenging Angel and First Banshee to some. So many of the K-9s at the Academy was of his lineage, were true War Dogs.

Dogman stopped at looked back at the supercage. Would or could Catherine the Great become a particular type of Fuzz, the beginning of another unique line from genetic tampering by humans and aliens? He hoped so. The thought that dogs could be so abused and then be destroyed because of it infuriated the canine trainer. Dogs would never do that to humans. In that, they were better than Dogman's brothers and sisters.

The sounds of the War Dogs forming up on the exercise field pulled Dogman's mind back to the here and now. Time to do his job.

On Days Three and Four of Catherine the Great's residency Dogman was a little closer each to each day. He fed her, found him some other 'toys' for her to try and destroy. Every time he spent time with her, she stayed in the light near the front of the supercage for a more extended period, examining the human who fed her and talked with her. It was to the point that as he left his house and walked across the field to the what was once seen as a Beast but now to Dogman as a Giant Canid, Catherine was always waiting for him well before he arrived at the supercage.

"I think we may just be friends someday, Catherine. What say you?"

The large canid examined him with her piercing gaze. She moved closer and stuck her great snout up to the feeding slot. Dogman slowly moved his hand to within an inch of Catherine. He knew that if she wanted to, the large canid could amputate his hand in the blink of an eye. But his gut told him she would not.

An oversized dog tongue flicked out and tasted his hand. Then Catherine backed up from the front of the supercage. A small 'ruff,' and the canid turned slowly and walked back to her dark corner.

"Next time, my lady," said Dogman. "You will stay in the light for me."

Day Five in the evening and Dogman stood on the back porch, looking at the supercage. Mary stepped through the back door and put her arm around her large husband.

"Penny for your thoughts, love," she said.

"I have seen her soul, Mary. And I hope she can see mine. Catherine needs the chance to be a dog, not an 'it' that Man screwed with."

"If anyone can save Catherine from being caged forever, or destroyed, it is you, Boian."

Dogman looked into his wife's eyes. She was one of the very few people who knew or used his Romanian Christian name. When Mary said it, he knew she was speaking from her heart.

"When you say it, then I know it must be the truth, my love." Dogman, Boian, kissed her. Mary and their children were the only ones who ever saw the 'softer' side of the man who looked and acted like a modern Hercules. The man knew that Mary made him whole, a person worthy of living among others.

"Now, let me check the grounds one more time. Then to bed."

"Promises," Mary replied with a mischievous smile.

The next morning, Day Six, Dogman carried the oversized breakfast to the supercage. Catherine was already up and sitting near the cage front. The trainer smiled as he spoke.

"Good morning, my lady. You know I bring you food for those pups in your belly."

Dogman did not expect what happened next. He would tell the story years later that he had underestimated Catherine's intelligence and perception. To himself, he said he had become sloppy and careless.

As he opened the food aperture and began to slide the sizeable flat pan into the supercage, a paw closer to the size of a grizzly bear's than any dog pinned the hand with the pan to the bottom of the cage. Dogman froze. He knew that if Catherine wished, she could separate his appendage from his body in the blink of an eye. Without looking into Catherine's eyes, he spoke in a calm and low voice.

"Offering me the Paw of Friendship, Catherine?"

Dogman knew that if he suddenly met the dog creature's gaze, such an action could be taken as a challenge. Thus, he let Catherine decide the next move.

The trainer was unsure as to the time he spent frozen in place, but it seemed like long minutes rather than seconds. As quickly as the paw appeared, the canid removed it. The huge muzzle then pushed forward, and the oversized tongue caressed the once trapped hand. Slowly, Dogman turned his hand over, then began to scratch the underside of the canine jaw. Within moments, Catherine was giving small groans of pleasure.

Dogman moved closer and crouched down next to the food slot.

"Ear scratch?" he asked the great Beast. The massive body was suddenly pressed up against the supercage front. Dogman began to scratch whatever piece of dog body he could reach through small slats in the cage front. Catherine had somewhat friendly communications with humans before but was only now admitting to it through her actions. Then those humans had tried to turn her into an "it" rather than a friend of humanity. Catherine's last memories were almost certainly not pleasant.

The two mammals stayed in physical contact for some ten minutes. Then Catherine the Great stepped back from the cage wall, 'ruffed' and picked up the food pan in her jaws. She turned and went back to her dark den corner.

"You're welcome, my lady," Dogman said as he stood up, turned and walked back to his house. He met Mary in the kitchen as she prepared breakfast for the children. Dogman walked up behind her and nuzzled her neck.

"Morning, dear. How is the big beastie?" Mary asked.

"Fine. Just Fine."

The morning of the Seventh Day saw Dogman walk out to the back of the supercage. He slid a metal shutter back from a hidden window. Catherine was up and looking at him through the armored glass. What Dogman was about to do he wanted it to be a secret from all others for the time being.

The Romanian undid some heavy latches, and the glass swung up like the back hatch on an SUV. The now open window was not large enough for Catherine to escape through, but she could get her head through the window opening. A quick moment of inspection and Catherine had her head through. Dogman whispered words of encouragement in Romanian as he scratched her ears, massive jaws, and head. Catherine slurped him with a gigantic doggy kiss, then butted him with her head.

"OOF! Easy. You almost flattened me, young lady."

Dogman managed to move her head from the window and then convinced her to place her left side against the opening. With careful hands, the trainer felt the female's stomach and abdomen. Then he stepped back.

"You're pups are definitely coming along, Catherine," Dogman said. "Due to your size and development, when they are due is a bit hazy. Especially due to the damnable modifications some assholes tried on you."

Catherine stuck her head through the window opening once more. Dogman spent minutes scratching her ears and neck, then patted her.

"Sorry, my lady. You can't come out yet. A few days after I

have had time to explain to everyone... then we will figure out where you will live. "

The Romanian gave his four-legged friend a couple of small steaks as treats, and she stepped back so he could resecure the security window. As Dogman walked back towards the house, his mouth formed in a somewhat unfamiliar shape.

Dogman soon sported a broad, toothy grin.

An intrusion alarm sounded, then shut down in a mid-howl. It operated long enough to wake Dogman, who grabbed the .500 Nitro Express Double he had obtained years ago for Beasts. Mary woke up, and her husband called to her as he headed down the stairs from the upstairs bedrooms.

"You and the kids, into the safe room, Now!"

Mary had learned long ago that when her husband pointed to safety, it was best to follow his direction. She moved.

Dogman ran out the back of the house buck naked, with just the elephant gun and his short handled battle ax. The gun was for Catherine if she had suddenly gone rogue and was trying to break out. His battle ax was for smaller animals.

A flashlight bobbed from the Academy Kennels, which told Dogman the Charge of Quarters for the training area was responding to the interrupted alarm. The system being cut off that way meant to Dogman human involvement. Thus he could use some backup. He heard a voice yell out the CQ Cathy Green's name, so another Trainee was awake also. Both being 'Cops' Dogman knew they would be armed.

Cathy Green caught up to Dogman at that moment, and he motioned for her to take the left side, and he would take the right. He glanced back and saw a large human which he identified in the dim security lighting as Asmund Nyberg, a new Viking. Leave it to a

Norskie to rush into harm's way.

As Dogman rounded the right corner of the supercage, someone started shooting from the left side. A gunfight ensued as Green began trading shots with some unknown person. As the Romanian rounded the back right corner, someone stepped from the dark and struck at him. Dogman went into a running forward roll as the assailant missed with a crackling cattle prod. He turned with battle axed raised to throw when the attacker screamed. A long broadhead hunting arrow had pinned the man's legs together, and he fell to the ground. Asmund had brought a bow to a gun fight, but the New Vikings always were different.

Dogman saw that someone had used a large cutting tool to knock down the back of the supercage. As Catherine had not howled, the intruders must have sedated her somehow. This was a highly planned operation. At that moment, Cathy rounded the back corner and saw the trainer.

"One shot, dead. Sorry, no information," Cathy said between breaths.

"Mine still lives," Asmund's voice boomed out.

"Good," said Dogman as he strode over to the figure on the ground. With no hesitation, the Romanian reached over and began to twist on the arrow struck through the man's legs. The intruder started to scream like a little girl.

"Where are they going with my Beast?" Dogman asked. The shots and screams were now waking up all the other humans and dogs. As Dogman began to twist on the arrow some more, the man with no name blurted out.

"The River! They have a barge."

The Acadamy was with a mile and a half of the Columbia River, an old stomping grounds of Dogman before the Great Compromise. No doubt the intruders had some electric powered vehicles for near silent travel. The Tschaaa 'Squids' had some excellent electrical power systems which were adapted for all types of cars, ever since the Harvester Robots. The trainer turned to the others.

"Take him back. Set up a response with the others. I'll run ahead and slow them down."

The two Cops knew arguing with their Trainer would gain nothing. Asmund slung the wounded man over his shoulder and began moving towards the barracks. Already, more flashlights were bobbing around as people responded towards the supercage. Dogman turned and took off running, fast for a man of his size. He hoped Catherine's size would slow the previous 'owners' down. Dogman knew that only people with some past connection with Catherine would go to all this trouble to obtain her. Now Dogman knew the Beast was something extraordinary.

The Romanian's stride ate up the distance. About ten minutes later, he heard cursing and splashing ahead. As he surmised, the thieves had underestimated the difficulties. He swung wide, came in from the opposite side than his approach.

"Goddamnit, can't you two work that derrick any better than that?" an angry voice called out.

"Boss, she's a lot heavier than she looks. And we are down two men."

"Well, Pete, whose fault is that? Next time hire someone who actually knows alarms systems. That should never have gone off."

Dogman moved up into a clump of dark and looked at Catherine. She was in a heavy sling, with four humans trying to maneuver the animal onto the barge, but were not experienced, stevedores. He watched for a few more moments, then called out from his hiding place.

"I suggest you let her down. While you can with no pain."

The men trying to load Catherine froze in place. Dogman saw the man called the "Boss" step forward with a gun in hand.

"I thought you were dead, Dogman," the Boss said.

"You know me?" Dogman replied.

"Remember that day with Sparks and Talbot, trying to round up that Dark Meat that was trying to get away from Cattle Country? When you slit the throat of the black boy because they killed your dog?"

"I remember it," replied Dogman.

"I was there. Seems like ancient history, but I remember you."

"Well, I don't remember you, Boss."

"Yeah? Well, we have more gunmen coming. And I wonder if all your new people know your background. You might want to let sleeping dogs lay."

Dogman stood silent for a moment. Then he responded.

"Penance. I am paying penance. So, sleeping dogs or Beasts are not going to lay still." With that, he put his fingers to his mouth and let out a shrill whistle.

"Protect," Dogman bellowed out in Romanian.

Catherine the Great was not a sleeping dog. The sling snapped in two as the huge beast lunged towards the shore. The Boss started to raise his gun, and Dogman blew him apart with the Nitro Express. Then he was charging into the midst of the thieves, battle ax in hand as Catherine began to bite, slash, and tear.

Some dozen law enforcement officers with K-9s were approaching the area of the shot when a large shape seemed to rise from the mist around the shores of the Columbia River. The War Dogs began to growl and snap, to be answered by a much more massive growl. Guns came up, and then a familiar voice called out.

"Anybody shoots in my and Catherine the Great's direction,

and their firearm will be put where the Sun don't shine."

"You okay," Cathy Green called out.

"Fine. Just a Man and his Dog out for a walk."

The next day additional law enforcement types responded and helped clean up the bodies and capture another group of the retrograde Krakens. The miscreant with the arrow in his legs sang like a bird, so rounding up people was pretty simple. Colonel Bettie Bardun, the exobiologist, responded and told Dogman what he already knew.

"They wanted her back as she is the first of a type of Beast they want to breed true. Bigger, smarter, nastier if they have their way."

"Sick Bastards," said Dogman. "She's my dog now."

Bettie and Emily, the Vet, looked at each other.

"Ah, Dogman," Emily said. "She is really not all dog…"

"She has the soul of a dog. She picked me to be her human also. Case closed."

"Ladies, from the voice of experience," said Mary, "once he has his mind made up, you'll need a tactical nuke to change it."

"Just received special dispensation from President Williams," Paul Miller interjected. "Dogman is the senior official War Dog Trainer for North America. And has a Special Commission to handle crimes involving the Beasts. So, as long as he keeps Catherine the Great under control, she stays with him."

The Law Enforcement Commissioner looked at Dogman.

"You will keep her secured."

"Of course, Commissioner."

"So what is next for this huge beast, my large friend?"

"She stays here. Catherine the Great is a member of my pack, my family, now." He turned and faced the Commissioner.

"It is not her fault that she was created, was not allowed to develop as a normal dog. But she has the soul of one." Dogman glanced at the supercage, knew that Catherine was watching him as all canines watch their pack members. As he would protect her, she would protect him from all threats and enemies. She had proven that. It had been that way for millennia, dogs and humans joined at the hip.

"She is Man's Best Friend, just like in the old saying. Sergeant Fuzz and all the War Dogs in his lineage know that. They will die for us. As we will die for them."

"Now, Commissioner, if you will excuse me. My newest family member wants some quality time with her human."

Dogman walked towards the supercage. A small smile graced his mouth as he talked to Catherine, the first in a new lineage.

"I wonder what the Lawman would have said if he knew this cage is unlocked?"

Catherine imparted a huffing canine laugh as she turned her head for a good ear scratch.

Golden Halos

anette Jamison turned the power switch to "on" and watched the two Golden Halos light up. The halos were the signature sign of this business venture she had created and organized. Soon, this restaurant, which Janette marketed as a Fast Food Eatery Plus, would be alive and filled with customers. Great Falls Montana was growing like the proverbial bad weed some three years after the signing of the Great Compromise with the Alien Squids called the Tschaaa. Humanity was working at getting back to normal since being in danger of being served up as dinner to an alien species originating in the outer reaches of the Universe. One thing humans loved to do was to eat together. Janette had striven to make this location a place where the new families could come, relax, have good food, and regale in being safe from being killed and eaten.

Janette had come up with this business idea a year prior. She was fast friends with the person who it was claimed had a halo or two hovering around her. Abigail Yamamoto, the Avenging Angel, and her War Dog Sergeant Fuzz had saved Janette and her two children, Timothy, and Lori from the fate of being eaten by the human minions of the Tschaaa known as Krakens. Fuzz had eventually given his life for his human, Abigail, after ensuring Janette, Timothy and Tina had reached safety. Janette had traveled to Malmstrom Armed Forces Base for the Sergeant Fuzz memorial and stayed. Abigail helped her find a home and a job.

"We are all one big family, all of us touched by Fuzz," the Avenging Angel had said. "Thus we help each other and pass it on."

Janette had taken the statement to heart. From that day she had striven to pass it on, to make it a bit better for the survivors of the Tschaaa Infestation,

It seemed like just yesterday she had seen a bunch of people standing around a boarded up Bar and Grill a mile from the main gate of Malmstrom AFB. She approached the group and struck up a conversation. She asked the dozen people why they were standing outside the boarded up building.

"This used to be a community hang out," a gray-haired and beefy man called Pops answered. "Entire families came here, rubbed shoulders with the military base people, ate good food, watched football, just had fun living." The man's face clouded over. "Then the Squids came, we started freezing and starving... and hiding."

"Memories," the grandson of Pops, John, chimed in. "I was just a teenager, but I remember the parties and fundraisers the owners used to have." John sighed. "The Samuelsons are long gone. They died during the Long Winter, thanks to all the crap thrown into the sky due to Squid bombs and rocks."

"Anybody thought of buying it and reopening?" asked Janette.

"You know how to run a restaurant, Lady?" someone asked.

"Why, yes. I do. My family had one in Wyoming. Before…" Everyone knew 'before.'

That had got Janette thinking. What better to help rebuild her new home community but to recreate a landmark of good memories? And, Hell, she HAD run the family business even after she had married. Then the Squids and the Kraken came, her husband Frank was killed. She was saved in a quick baptism of blood by Sergeant Fuzz and Abigail. Now was time to wash away the blood and bad memories.

Janette made sure the doors were unlocked and her morning staff was ready to go. Her day manager was John Pohl, Pops grandson. And, of course, Pops was a regular.

"The Fuzz Room is all set up for the birthday party, Boss," informed John.

"Good. K-9 balloons and all?" asked Janette.

"Yes, Ma'am."

Janette had set up a former meeting room as the Sergeant Fuzz Memorial Party Room. She had commissioned a copy of the famous American Viking carved memorial statue of Fuzz the First War Dog, which sat in the entrance of the Banshee Barracks on the base. Larger than life-size, a huge Great Dane/German Shepherd mix, tail erect with a searching gaze, it caught the essence of Sergeant Fuzz in life. With her copy, kids could climb all over it, laugh, play, imagine that Fuzz was in the room with them. Late at night, Janette could swear she heard and felt a dog brush by her. Rumors and stories from the Cheyenne were that a Spirit Dog visited those he still cared for and loved. Janette believed it.

"Just passed our first anniversary, Fuzz," she told the statue as she wiped it down. No matter how clean it was, Janette always wiped the figure down at the beginning of the day. She also always talked to it. Janette knew it was a conduit to Sergeant Fuzz in the hereafter. And even if it were not, it made her feel better.

"Busy day today. A kids birthday party, some club meetings, then the regular sports crowd tonight. Help us keep an eye on the kiddies, Fuzz. Like you did for Tim and Tina."

"Hey, Boss," John called out. "Got a guy up front. Said he'd like to talk to you."

"Be right there," Janette called back. She glanced around to make sure no one was watching. Then she kissed 'Fuzz' on the nose. "See you later, my friend."

Janette went up to the front of the restaurant. She saw two men she did not recognize gazing at the memorabilia on the walls, as well the as the printed menus. They were both in new looking suits, still reasonably rare some three years out from the end of the War. The shorter of the two with slicked-back hair and a tightly trimmed goatee, Janette immediately made as to the person in charge. The other was a towering hulk of a man, beardless but with the same slicked back hair. Janette grabbed a serving towel and wiped her hands as she approached.

"Hello, I understand someone wanted to speak with me? I'm the owner, Janette Jamison."

The short man smiled and stepped forward. He gave a short bow, then proffered his right hand to shake. Janette noticed his fingernails were manicured and had a slight gloss indicating possible clear polish.

"I am David Michaels," he said as he gave Janette a firm handshake and a professional smile. "I was told to look for an attractive brunette, and I guess the instructions were correct."

Janette smiled. As a businesswoman, she was used to people trying to disarm her with flattery. Funny how almost being killed and eaten put such minor irritants into perspective.

"I accept the compliment, Mister Micheals. But I don't think that is why you are here. Or am I wrong?"

Michaels chuckled, then answered. "A perceptive businesswoman. Well then. This will go quickly." The man motioned with his hands to include the entire restaurant.

"You have done an excellent job in taking a closed and aging bar and grill and turning it into one of the most popular dining establishments. I especially like your 'Golden Halos.' A nice take off on a well-known chain that has yet to re-establish itself in today's world, post-Great Compromise. However, I have an offer to take your business to the next level in profitability and success."

This was not the first time someone had approached Janette after she had done all the hard work with an offer she should not refuse. Her question was always, where were they a year ago when she was looking for investment money?

"Well, Sir, I guess I'll bite," Janette replied. "If for no reason it has been a month since the last offer. Someone's success seems to attract people like new spring flowers do attract bees."

Michaels laughed. The laugh seemed genuine to Janette, but she also knew some people were adept actors.

"An apt comparison, Ma'am. But I think I have honey to attract you, not the other way around."

"Well, Mister Michaels, shoot. I'm all ears. At least right now."

"I have a series of properties and businesses stretching from the West Coast to rebuilding Chicago. My interests also include-arrangements I have made with our multi tentacle friends the Tschaaa. These arrangements help me to provide the necessary products an establishment such as this to expand past just a single location."

"And these products are?" interjected Janette.

"Freshly harvested seafood. The Squids are the best ocean fisherman on Earth because they originated in an ocean environment. Add this to a transport system second to none, and I can easily see you have three restaurants in a year. You have the unique footprint already with the Golden Halos attached to your friend, the Avenging Angel. People think of Halos, they think of Abigail Yamamoto. And of course, her late War Dog Sergeant Fuzz."

Janette stood silently in thought. Proposals similar to what Michaels had just made had been floating around for some time. The human species in the U.S. was trying to rebuild its economy and social structure severely damaged during the Tschaaa Infestation. With the Government trying to rebuild also, there was a bit of the old Wild West flavor as areas bare of inhabitants were restored and repopulated. Thus, buyer beware was an oft-heard moto.

"I appreciate the offer, Sir. However, right now I am enjoying getting this location up and running to its full potential."

"Spoken like a genuine business person, Ma'am. But I assure you, my assistance would ensure that result in record time."

Janette smiled as she replied.

"Again, I appreciate your offer. Mister Michaels. Right now, I think I have all the assistance I need from my local partners. So I will have to reject your kind offer."

Michaels flashed what was once referred to as a Hollywood Smile.

"Well, I hope you don't mind if I stop by once in a while to see if you might change your mind. Things sometimes take a turn for the worse. I am always ready to lend a helping hand to those in need. Please, take this business card with my direct phone number on it."

"Thank You again. Sir. I will keep that in mind. Can I offer you something on the house? I don't want you to feel slighted due to my rejection of your offer."

Michaels looked at his wrist and a very high-end Pre-Infestation watch.

"Thank You, Ms. Jamison. However, I see I can just make

another meeting before Noon. May I have a raincheck?"

"Of course. Come back and ask for me when you can."

Janette shook hands with Michaels and his 'silent partner', who fixed her with a penetrating gaze as his large appendage engulfed hers. Something told her that the man was not just all muscle, that he was appraising her for... something.

As the two men left, John approached her.

"Another offer?" he asked.

"Yes. First one this month."

"Did you take it?"

Janette gave John her best 'Are You Kidding' look.

"No."

"Hey, boss. Had to ask to see if I need to look for another job?"

"No such luck, John. Now, time to get cracking like my Grandma used to say."

A week after, things took a turn for the worse. First, deliveries which had previously been smooth and timely were interrupted. It seemed delivery vehicles began to have mechanical problems. Regular orders were mysteriously canceled or sent to the wrong addresses. One supplier was suddenly bought out and then shut down for 're-organization.' Through all this, Janette somehow kept the customers happy and the food orders filled.

Then, at the end of the second week, The Golden Halos' power was shut off for a half hour. The power company claimed someone hacked the grid and caused the shutdown. Odd that it was only the one business that suffered. It was also unusual that she received a voice mail from David Michaels, asking if she had thought about his offer. Janette did not return the phone call.

Next, the water service was interrupted by a burst line which fed directly into the restaurant. Close friends of Pops Pohl rushed in with a backhoe, found the burst line and repaired it. The City Water Department complained about permits etc., then backed off when Pops made a few telephone calls to some more friends. It helped when you became a local landmark and favorite spot for the local Base personnel. It looked like the worst was past when late one evening two large strangers entered the restaurant. As one was seated, his partner made a beeline to the Men's Room. Within minutes, the restroom was flooded as the last user exited and complained loudly.

"What kind of place are you running?" Stranger Two yelled. "Can't even take a crap without being soaked."

"That has got to be a health violation," Stranger One chimed in. "How can you eat with turds floating by?"

John Pohl tried to brace the two men.

"What did you do to the toilets?" he demanded. "They were working just…"

A sock full of coins smacked John in the back of his head, and he went down. Janette rushed forward, and the cooks came from the rear area.

"Hey! What in the Hell do you think you are doing?" she called out.

"He insulted us, Lady," Stranger One sneered. "Do you want to be sued for making false allegations?"

"I suggest you back off, Honey, or you'll get some…" Stranger Two was unable to finish his statement when booted foot slammed into the side of his head. He collapsed like a sack of potatoes. Stranger One turned, and a figure in a blur of motion took him to the floor. Within seconds a Banshee Blade was pressed against his throat.

"Move, Cabron," Banshee Captain Lupe Pena growled at her

victim. "I dare ya."

"Don't kill him, Battle Buddy," cautioned her fellow Banshee Dagan McDowell as she made sure Stranger One was down for the count from her kick. Janette approached the two Original Banshees, survivors and instigators of the Great Salinas Kansas Rout.

"What are you two ladies doing here this late?" Janette asked.

"I have a cousin coming up from El Paso" the darker skinned and stocky Hispanic Pena replied as she pressed the blade against the stranger's throat. "I want to give her a Quincenera like I had before the Squids showed up."

"I just like to hang with my buddy," the taller and somewhat lanky Scott-Irish brunette McDowell answered.

"Well, I'm glad you did," said Janette. She bent over the prone body of John as he groaned.

"Want us to find out who sent these turds?" Pena asked as she pressed her blade against the miscreant's throat and was rewarded with a squeak and some blood.

"I already know. Can you remove this... trash for me?"

"With pleasure," said McDowell. In a few minutes, both of the unwanted males were sent roughly on their way. There were no threats from them about calling the police for being assaulted. That verified to Janette her suspicions as to why they were there at her business. She had John sitting up with a bag of cold ice against the spot of the blow.

"Your Quinceanera is gratis, Lupe," Janette said.

"Naw, friend. You need to make a living. How about we come back tomorrow and seal the deal?"

"That is," Dagan added, "if you will be safe from further visits."

"I have a pistol. If those two come back, that a phone call to my police friends will take care of them."

The next day, Janette looked at the business card of Michaels, called the number and left a very nasty voicemail. She thought that in earlier Pre-Squid days she would have been charged with making terrorist threats. That was then, this was now. Nothing else happened for a week, and business was back to normal.

Janette stayed late one night to check the books. Since Michaels had never attempted another contact, she thought the situation was passed. As Janette started to lock up and set the alarm to The Golden Halo, four dark-clad figures bum-rushed her. She tried to pull her pistol and scream at the same time. A massive fist to the stomach knocked the wind out of her, and she fell to the restaurant floor. In moments she was scooped up by rough hands and carried to her back office. As she tried to regain her breath. She looked up and said the large Silent Man standing over her, with Michaels behind him.

"I never introduced myself," said the Silent Man. "My name is Anthony Michaelangelo. David, with the shortened Anglicised version, is my younger brother. I let him work as the 'front man' as my size and demeanor are sometimes offputting."

"Frontman?" Janette managed to croak out. "Like with Squids, Krakens?"

Michaelangelo sneered, then spat on the office floor.

"I am a good Catholic. Those people are scum."

"The Mafia... shouldn't it be long gone? It was dying before the Squids came."

The huge man shrugged. "That is the past. This is now. I survived to help our 'thing' rise again. You know Mother Nature abhors a vacuum."

"So now what?" Janette said defiantly. "If you are such good businessmen, why the heavy-handed tactics?"

Anthony sat down behind Janette's desk and steepled his

fingers as he answered.

"Normally, after the unexpected failure of our previous efforts, we would back off, try some more attempts at the periphery. You know, attain some control over your competition and use them to affect your bottom line, tactics like that. But you made a mistake."

"You mean when your thugs had their asses kicked?"

"No. That happens all the time. Good help is hard to find these days." The modern Mafiosa fixed his gaze on Janette. "What you did was you personally insulted my family, my brother David, with that telephone rant you left. I will not allow some bitch to talk to me and mine that way."

Janette felt a chill run up her spine as she realized she was dealing with a psychotic. She realized Anthony had survived the Infestation in the Occupied or Feral areas by being cruel, nasty and murderous to all who offended him. He also seemed to have a problem with women who resisted him. The question of how many dead female bodies were his handiwork flashed through her mind.

"So, now what?" Janette managed to ask without a quaver in her voice. In answer, David handed his brother a printed letter.

"So you have some options, Janette Jamison. This letter is a contract where you agree to, as part of a loan agreement, give David and me a controlling interest in The Golden Halos. You still run it, we are silent partners who get a percentage of the profits. Which will increase as we are allowed to deal with any possible competition."

"And you run laundered money through me, maybe use The Golden Halos as a meeting place for other less than desirables," Janette shot back.

"For which you will be grandly compensated as business picks up. And, you have twenty-four-hour protection from any of the criminal element."

"I never had any problems with the so-called criminal element until you showed up."

Anthony sighed. He nodded to one of the dark-clad thugs standing behind. A hard slap was administered to Janette's right cheek.

"You will have to cool the attitude, as they say, my dear," said Anthony Michaelangelo. "No one likes a smart mouth bitch."

Janette glared at the David and Anthony.

"You think I don't have friends that will not take kindly to this move?" Janette said.

"You mean the Banshees and the such? "Replied the elder brother. "So I take it you are resisting our proposal?"

"Damned straight!" Janette blurted out.

"Well then, my dear, we go to option two." Anthony held up Janette's pistol. "A poor pressured survivor of Kraken horror, suffering from PTSD, takes her own life with her own pistol, alone and afraid. Then we deal with whoever inherits this property." The New Mafioso stared deep into Janette's eyes. "Or we could involve your children now. But I prefer not to, as I do respect families."

"You mother-" A hard slap stopped the insult and bloodied Janette's lip. Anthony stood up from Janette's desk.

"I guess we will have to do this the hard and bloody way. David..."

There were a loud thud and sounds of breaking glass from the attached Fuzz Room. Anthony motioned to the two muscle men he had brought along, and they hurried out of the office.

"Did you expect an employee to return tonight? If one has, more pity to them," said Anthony.

A scream from the other room was cut out in mid vocal. Janette could have sworn she heard a growl. Anthony slid around the desk and struck Janette with a massive fist. She toppled over from her chair and lay stunned.

"You cunt. Whatever games you are playing…"

Through blurred vision, Janette saw a large indistinct shape seem to move and grab the oversized Mafioso. A pistol shot resounded. The blood and screaming began as Janette slipped into unconsciousness.

Janette could have sworn she felt a sizeable K-9 tongue slurped her back to awareness. However, as she slowly sat up, she saw no one. Then she saw the blood and screamed. Janette managed to lurch to her feet and find her cellphone. She dialed 911 and was able to scream "Help! Golden Halos!" before she fell over.

Janette sat in the dining area as EMTs fussed over her. The Golden Halos was a favorite hangout for First Responders and the Military, so when Janette screamed for help, everyone came. The oxygen they gave her helped to clear the cobwebs away. A pleasant young female police detective, Karen Already, took notes as she slowly questioned Janette.

"You took some nasty blows to the head, Ms. Jamison," said Already.

"I've suffered worse things," Janette replied. "Go ahead with your questions. And, please, its Janette. You all eat here so often you're family."

The Detective smiled at her. "Okay, Janette. So, you said you have had a running conflict with the individuals whose remains… are here."

"Who are splattered all over my eatery, yes. Let's be exact, shall we?"

"Just trying to be a bit less raw, Janette," Already said with a frown.

"Damn. I'm sorry. I'm being a real bitch to people who are just trying to help," Janette said as she blinked back tears.

"We can continue later, due to your head trauma and all."

"No, it's okay," Janette replied, then took a deep breath and let it out. "Can I ask a favor?"

"Go ahead."

"Can you help me into the Fuzz Room? I need to look at something. Yes, I know they are still doing forensics. I promise I won't disturb anything. But it would help with figuring this out."

Detective Already gave her an arm to hang onto as they made their way to the Fuzz Room. Some forensic technicians were trying to recover pieces of an unknown number of beings and figure out what belonged to who. Janette carefully picked her way through the carnage until she could look at the wood carving of the original Sergeant Fuzz. She stood staring at the oversized statue for a full minute, examined the bloody muzzle, chest, and paws. She stared at the paws the longest.

"See something that helps?" asked the detective.

"I… guess not. Thought this would tell me something, but no. Shall we go back outside this room? I don't want to be in the way."

Janette opened The Golden Halos a day later after the police were done with their evidence collection. So far, the story was some rivals the Michaelangelos had much offended used the assault at The Golden Halos as an opportunity to sneak up and exact bloody revenge. Some friends had told Janette to take some time off, but she had replied that she had children to care for and had to earn a living.

Thus she had no sooner turned the power on than she heard a familiar voice.

"Janette, can we come in?"

"Of course you can. Abigail. The Avenging Angel is always welcome. "

Janette met Abigail at the door and saw she had her fraternal twin children, Anica, and Brynhildr, in tow. Assisting in caring for them was Abigail's cousin, Assistant Director of Federal Law Enforcement Senior Special Agent Brynhildr Rolf, and Sergeant Fuzz Junior. The War Dog, on hiatus with his mistress as Abigail, raised her firstborn, took a beeline to the room of his Sire. The War Dog went in, sniffed, then sat down in front of the carved representation of the Senior Sergeant Fuzz. The humans followed at watched.

"He does that with the original carving at the Banshee Barracks," said Abigail. "I think he uses them as totems to commune with his Sire."

"Janette, you will be happy to learn," interjected Agent Brynhildr, "the Federal Government is involved in the investigation. Something like this will not occur again. I will make it a high priority. As painful as this event was for you, the result was waking us up that organized human crime is making a comeback."

Janette smiled at the tall blonde, often called a Shield Maiden.

"I'm not worried. I have a full-time protector." She gazed at the oversized rendering of Sergeant Fuzz.

"What do you mean?" Abigail asked as she picked up daughter Anica, not yet two years old. Brynhildr, the larger of the twins, was held by her namesake.

"Step forward, please. And look at the feet of the carving."

The group of humans approached the sitting Fuzz the younger. Abigail frowned as she examined the carved feet,

"Did they have to move this statue while sweeping for evidence?" Abigail asked with a frown. "I understand it was a slaughterhouse."

"Remember what you told Sergeant Fuzz Senior that day when you saved me. Tim and Tina?"

"Of course, Janette. Lead, Scout, Protect. He took you to

safety."

"Then he came back for you, Abigail. And he died before I could see him again."

Janette walked over to Fuzz Junior and gently scratched his years.

"Fuzz Junior was with you the other night, yes?" she asked.

"Why, Yes," replied Abigail, "Why..." Then she stopped in mid-comment.

"Oh my Lord in Heaven."

"He remembered your last order, Abigail. Fuzz Senior came back to 'protect.' I feel his presence all the time." Janette turned with tear filled eyes. "I owed you and him that day. And I still owe him."

"The Rainbow Bridge works both ways," said Brynhildr. "We Norse have known that for eons."

The women hugged as Fuzz Junior let out a low 'wuff' the humans did not hear. But another essential being did as Fuzz Junior offered his respect to his Sire.

As time passed, The Golden Halos chain expanded. In addition to a 'halo' motif which spoke to the goodness in humanity and offered comfort to those who suffered mightily, there was always a carved lifelike representation of Sergeant Fuzz. A plaque was placed at each and every location:

With Humanity's Best Friend
Love and Loyalty Never Ends.
Humans Should Learn as Much.

VAGRANT

ohn Newcomb carried three tall coffees in the supplied drink carrier as he had done for the last six months. An average-sized man with medium brown hair and brown eyes, he whistled as he walked up to the corner of the street. A quick turn to the right and half a block down was his business, already open and ready for customers that sunny morning. His blonde wife, Ann, always sent him for the coffee as she made sure everything in the New & Used Market was shipshape and ready for the first purchase.

When Anne and him had first opened the business just a year prior on the rebuilding State Street in Kansas City, Kansas, she had shoed him out first thing.

"I need a few minutes to make sure everything is ready to go," she had said. "I have my own way to start the day, and you'll just get in the way."

"Yes Ma'am," he had said and then stole a kiss. She giggled

and smacked his arm as he headed for the door. Since that morning, he went to Moon's Coffee around the corner each morning. At first, it was for two coffees, and 'fat pills' also called donuts. Then six months ago, there was a change in his actions. That was when Buddy first appeared.

That morning, as he rounded the corner building, John almost stepped on a figure sitting a few feet away with a back to the brick wall.

"Oops! Sorry, Mister. I didn't see you there."

The disheveled man, who John would soon know as Buddy, looked up at him. Dirty, with stained and patched clothes of unknown age and type, the human being looked like he may be of Caucasian lineage. However, it was hard to tell under dirty tan. In a past era, he would be called a homeless street person or vagrant. Since the Tschaaa Infestation, when the aliens invaded and began rounding up people to eat, among the first to go were Homo sapiens with nowhere to hide, like those living on the streets and in homeless camps. Thus, vagrants vanished into the larders of the invading cephalopods.

Now, a year since the so-called peace treaty known as the Great Compromise, humankind rebuilt places like Kansas City, and created new business like his and Anne's.

"Hey, Buddy. Want some coffee and a donut?" John spoke before he even realized what he was saying. Buddy nodded a slow up and down. John then handed him a donut and coffee. The man took the proffered refreshments and began to eat.

"Well, gotta go to work. Be seeing you." Buddy, so named by him, nodded once more as John left. At the store, he told Anne where his coffee and donut went.

"John, honey, please don't encourage people to camp out on our street," she said with a frown.

"He's just sitting there, not camping."

"You know what I mean. We're developing a regular clientele for all the new and used merchandise we have scrounged." She used 'scrounged' so as not to be affiliated with the so-called Scavengers, the humans who had grabbed the items left by the dead and fled, sometimes from people not dead nor fled in the early days of the Infestation.

"We haven't seen vagrants for years," his wife added.

"That's because they were being eaten," John replied.

"We don't know…"

"Yes, Anne, we do. We lived, they died. Along with a crap-load of strangers, friends, and relatives."

John suddenly realized he was becoming pissed. Since the signing of the Great Compromise, everyone was so concentrated on things being 'normal' again, it was if everyone tried to forgot who had disappeared and why. Anne put her hand on his shoulder.

"Honey, I'm not trying to be nasty or uncaring. We all suffered since the rocks fell."

"Which is why I am providing what in a previous time would be called a little Christian charity to a stranger."

"But you don't know what kind of man this…"

"Buddy. That's his name. He answered to it. And who the Hell was I, Anne, before Bloody Kansas? A music teacher. Then I used that trumpet of mine on the wall to signal a charge on those fucking Krakens."

John began to shake. An average man with a teaching degree and music students one year, a person killing other alleged humans the next because they were minions of the Tschaaa Squids. Not to mention, Krakens were cannibals. Anne hugged him, held him tight. It always helped with the shaking.

"I'm sorry, John. I'm not trying to argue," she said as he kissed him on the cheek. John took a deep breath, then let it out. He patted her as he calmed.

"I know. It just hit me wrong." He looked into his love's eyes. "There but for the Grace of God, could be me. Or worse, I could be gone. I don't know what Buddy's story is and I don't care. I just think I need to give him a bit of charity. It makes me... human."

"And your human side is why I love you, John Newcomb. So go ahead, buy Buddy coffee and donuts if that helps. Just please don't move him in. We do plan on having a family."

Starting the next day, John had a cup carrier and three large coffees, plus three giant donuts. Buddy moved down from the building corner a bit so people rounding the corner would see him after John had almost stepped on him. This told the business owner Buddy was cognizant of some of the world around him. However, no matter how John tried to converse with him, Buddy nodded 'yes,' shook his head 'no,' and occasionally shrugged his shoulders. He was always there in the morning, moved off a bit later, came back at closing time.

Some of the local police did the ole 'Field Contact' on Buddy, and John stepped in. The oversized Sergeant Ken Breen and John had served together during Bloody Kansas and had been part of the famous Kraken Rout started by the to be named Banshees, Sisters of Steel. Thus, Ken valued John's input.

"You don't mind him near your business, John?" Ken had asked. "How about Anne?"

"Ken, he's fine. He must have someplace to stay in out of the weather even if he is in dire need of a bath. So, he must be around others with no complaints."

"Well, my combat comrade, if you say he is okay, I'll leave him be." The police supervisor looked at the very soiled man. "Has Anne talked to him?"

"No. My wife knows Buddy is my pet project. I had some people from the local food bank talk to him, but all they got out of him was nods, and head shakes. He took some sandwiches they gave, then he left. But refused to go with anyone for a hot meal."

Ken grunted.

"Well, after people being drug off by robots and tattooed assholes to be eaten over some six years, I would hesitate to go off with just anyone." The Sergeant nodded at Buddy, who nodded back. Ken smiled.

"Okay, he seems harmless enough. If he starts doing anything bizarre, give me a call. Our current vagrancy laws are kind of loosey-goosey, with so many people looking for lost family. And say hello to that pretty wife that everyone says is too good for you."

John laughed. He knew that the Average Joe and music teacher was not to get the Prom Queen. It should have been the football fullback like Ken. But everyone knew Anne was hooked on her husband.

"Will, Ken. We'll have you and Carol over for dinner some night.

"It's a date, John."

The days morphed into weeks, then the weeks into months. John somehow convinced Buddy to take a used sleeping bag and a hot/cold thermos from a truckload of recovered stuff. He snuck the items past Anne as she was counting pennies with the new knowledge that she was with child. Anne already planned on College in one of the rebuilt universities no matter the gender of their first born.

Anne even smiled at Buddy one day when she and John walked by Buddy. The vagrant seemed to touch his head as if dipping an invisible hat in respect.

"See, Babe," John stated. "Buddy was raised with some

manners. He must have had a good mother and father."

"I'll give you that fact, John. But he still does not get the spare bedroom."

Buddy made it through a rough Kanas winter, always there near New & Used Market. The business was doing well as the first sun rays of Spring lit up the double entrance doors. Running a bit late (morning sickness is a bitch), John jogged around the corner towards Moon's Coffee as Anne unlocked the doors. As she pushed the doors open, she felt a presence behind her.

"Sorry, we are running a bit late this morning. If you will give us a few…"

The figure turned into three, and Anne was bum-rushed into the store, a smelly and robust hand over her mouth as she tried to scream. She kicked and lashed out, managed to turn to face her attackers. Horror sent ice down her spine as she saw what looked like two males and a females, all with the tell-tale sign of recent Drac use. Mouth stained red as if from drinking blood,(which may have actually been mixed with the drugs coloring), Anne knew the drug with the street name Dracula had reached Kansas City. It inflamed both Tschaaa and Human, with people being infused with lust for the real taste of blood, thus the name.

"Money," a sweaty female demanded as the two males tried to restrain her. Anne bit the hand over her mouth, and was rewarded with a blow which bloodied her lip. The female addict hissed.

"Blood," the woman said as she opened her mouth to feed on the offered treat.

Anne screamed as blood began to splash and spurt everywhere.

John could not hear Anne's screams from inside the coffee shop. He did hear the sounds of the police and fire sirens as they reverberated down State Street. John dropped the coffee and donuts, then ran. He rounded the corner and saw what seemed to be every red and blue flashing emergency light in Kansas City around New & Used Market.

"*Anne!*" John yelled with all his might as he tried to bowl over all the First Responders. Familiar large hands restrained him.

"Hey, John, It's Ken."

"*Ken*. Where is she…"

"She's okay. Is in the ambulance."

Ken allowed John to drag him the open aid car and saw his wife wearing an oxygen mask as an female EMT wiped blood off of Anne's face.

"Not her blood," the police sergeant quickly interjected. Anne saw he husband and pulled the oxygen mask off her face.

"He saved me, John. He saved me."

"Who… what…" John sputtered as he reached out and grabbed his wife's free hand. Then Ken gently pulled him back.

"Let them check your pregnant wife out, my friend. Come here, I have something to show you."

Ken walked a semi-dazed John in through the business double doors. Inside, there was blood everywhere. John was no stranger to human blood, not after Bloody Kansas. But this… New & Used Market looked like a charnel or slaughterhouse. Sitting on a chair just as bloody as the rest of the business, was Buddy.

"Why is he handcuffed, Ken?" asked John.

"We had to make sure he was… finished."

John stood still for a moment. Then it sank in.

"Buddy… he…"

"Your friend here took a broken bottle to three users-actually now former users of Dracula. They had your wife, Anne." Ken looked at Buddy as he spoke. "You took offense to that, didn't you, Buddy?'

The man known as a vagrant nodded his head 'yes' and for the first time, spoke.

"I-owe."

John stepped up to Buddy. As he did, John saw a body with no throat laying on the floor, several feet behind Buddy.

"You saved my wife, Buddy. I owe you. More than I can ever repay."

The street person negatively shook his head.

"No. I owe. You helped me." Then Buddy looked to the floor. "I heard also. You stayed, fought when I ran."

"What? I wasn't even..." Then Ken was holding a set of blood-stained military dog tags in front of John. For the first time, the former music teacher saw Ken he had surgical gloves on.

"They were stuffed in his boot top. Back in the day, troops would do that so if they were blown apart, if a foot remained, they could be I.D'd."

It took a while, but the story of the man called Buddy came out.

Charles Benson and his fellow soldiers fought in and around Fort Bening, Georgia, during the first weeks of the Tschaaa Infestation, when things came apart, all the survivors were told to retreat to the Interior of the United States.

Charles did not. His family was in Atlanta. He made it there to see the destruction and harvesting of humans. He knew his family was lost. So he ran.

Charles said he ran until he found a cabin in some woods. The former soldier, later on, realized he was in Missouri. Charles hid, lived off the land as best he could and scavenged from abandoned vehicles he found.

He hid when the robots and cannibal Krakens came through. He disappeared when they set up Cattle Country for all the to be eaten People of Color. He fled the area when the invasion of Bloody Kansas began.

Charles scavenged a working radio and listened to Radio Free America. That is where Charles Benson heard the tales of a troop who stayed on his post for almost six years, guarding U.S. Aircraft. He heard about a young Avenging Angel, not out of her teenage years, who fought for freedom. Then, of course, Charles heard about a great War Dog who fought and died for that Angel.

The hidden soldier was ashamed. Even a dead dog did better than he. Something snapped, and Charles began to wander as if half-dead and never to speak. Until this day.

Charles Benson met John that fateful day and took the Christian charity of coffee and the donut. The vagrant knew he owed the living before he became the dead.

"So, all these weeks…" John said. Charles nodded.

"Yes. I tried to find a way. A way to pay my debt… to the living."

"I think you just did that, Buddy," said Ken. "I think you're back to being Charles."

John wanted to hug Charles but knew he was covered in Drac blood. God knew what diseases the blood had, which could be passed on to a pregnant woman.

"Oh my God. Anne." He looked at Charles.

"I'll take care of my new friend," said Ken. "John, you see to your pretty wife."

John took off running. Ken looked at the mess.

"Let me know when you detectives and technicians are

through with this place so I can have it cleaned up," the police sergeant called out. Then he looked at the soldier.

"Right now, Charles, I think you need a bath and a new set of clothes."

Months later, two new children were being baptized. Anne gave birth to fraternal twins, one boy, and one girl. As the pastor performed the rites, he asked the parents what name the boy should be known as in the church and before God.

"John Charles Newcomb," Anne's voice rang out. "After two important men in his life, who met through a little bit of Christian charity to a needy stranger."

"I kind of like Buddy," a very cleaned up and shaven Charles opinionated in a whisper.

"That will be our special family name for him, Deal?" said John.

"Deal," answered Charles.

It was good to be alive.

It was good to be loved and helped.

It was good to pass it on.

Camila Sanchez, former USAF Para Rescue (P.J) Technical Sergeant, pushed herself as she finished her four klick run. Two klicks out, two klicks back, the length of the Tschaaa starship open living area, was her standard running route. Camila had never really found out the exact dimensions of the single Crèche multi-generational spacecraft, just that it was huge. Now it was about to leave Sol's solar system.

The living area had become more and more vacant over the last year as the final decisions were made by the cephalopod aliens as to who wanted to stay on Earth and who wanted to leave. Tschaaa technology did allow them through the theory of diamagnetism to produce a form of artificial gravity not dependent on spacecraft spin. Thus Camila was able to keep her above average height for a Mexican-American body in a semblance of Earth standard. Without gravity, a human's long term stay in weightlessness was not conducive to decent muscle and bone development. Neither was weightlessness conducive to human reproduction. The Tschaaa Squids had developed in an ocean environment, so they were much more adapted to weightless like conditions. However, they still found that gravity aboard a spaceship made things simpler

Camila tried not to think about human pregnancy as she finished her run. She failed as the reality that a thirty-some-year-old Homo sapiens was about to be one of the first Earthling to travel in interstellar space. The former PJ knew that the fact she was a fertile female warrior was the primary reason she was taken prisoner after the humans failed attempt to capture a Squid young near the Columbia River in Oregon State. Near seven years prior, it seemed like seventy since Camila was wounded and captured.

Camila began a cool down walk as her mind kept ruminating about her situation. There was always the unrealistic hope that the Tschaaa Lord in charge of the interstellar ship would have a change of heart and send her back to Earth. As the seconds ticked by and the distance from her home planet increased, Camila knew that was a pipe dream.

The interstellar craft planned to make the hundreds of years journey back to their homeworld and Mother Ocean. The Starcraft was much too massive to obtain any type of space warping and thus bypass the Light Speed Limitations. The Tschaaa Squids had much smaller types of scout craft which were able to use Dark Energy and Dark Matter to generate the forces necessary for warping the fabric of space and make what in science fiction was called "jumps." Accessing the energy required to move the generational ships was just too complicated and massive to be efficient.

The Tschaaa Squids had developed in an ocean environment, so they were much more adapted to weightless like conditions. However, they still found that gravity aboard a spaceship made things simpler. Having random 'stuff' floating around and bumping into the occupants was not conducive to an efficient operation.

As Camila's respiration returned to normal, she noticed a figure approaching, the sight of whom brought a smile to her face. Camila jogged slowly towards the non-Earth being.

"Hey, Rex!" she called out. "I did not think I would see you again.

The bipedal dinosauroid, commonly called Lizards by most Earthlings thanks to the difficulty in pronouncing words in the alien's language, walked towards Camila with Homo sapiens style stride. Rex was an average sized Lizard at about one point seven meters in height and seventy kilograms in weight. Females in his species were much the same, there are no real size differences between the sexes. Rex looked a lot like lizard people portrayed in recent Science Fiction movies, with larger than human eyes, opposable thumbs and a short tail that tucked down what would have been a butt crack on a human.

"Hello," the Lizard said. Or actually, said the translator that put many a human Sci-Fi series to shame. Rex's language had hisses and clicks, which made human replication and understanding difficult. Thus, the Midwestern accentless speech which emanated from the universal translator suspended from a body strap made Homo sapiens/Lizard communication efficient. As Rex spoke, he presented both of his five digit hands palms up as a standard greeting. Lizards facial muscles limited actions such as smiles, frowns, and angry flushes. Much like their 'masters' the Tschaaa, they used their hands/ claws to express emotions and greetings they were unable to do with their faces. The one sense they had superior to the humans and the Squids was a sense of smell and taste they used to communicate moods and thoughts between their own species.

"You decided not to stay on Earth? With your mate?" Camila asked as she presented her hands in mirror greeting to Rex.

"It is by circumstance, friend human, not by choice," the Lizard replied. Rex, short for T-Rex as named by Camila for ease of communication, was a 'friend' to the human female. As supposed Client species of the Tschaaa, Camila had found they had much in common. Both she and the dinosauroid wanted to have a 'home' and family away from their captors, the Tschaaa. Camila desired separation even more so as humans were eaten by the Tschaaa, Lizards were just used as labor and assistants.

"What happened?" Camila asked with a frown.

"The agreement now known as The Great Compromise in Earth language has been signed. There will be no further Harvesting of humans for meat."

Camila was stunned into silence. The community of hominids she lived near, former proto-humans from Earth, were notorious gossips. Descendents of specimens and ova taken from Earth during the days of Homo erectus and Gigantopithecus blacki, breeding populations were kept on the Tschaaa ships both for "Dark Meat" and for specialized tasks. What humans called Robocops or Cyborgs were developed from the larger specimens over the long voyage to Earth. They accepted Camila as another hominid they could communicate with due to their Tschaaa enhanced intelligence.

"So all the gossip from my hairier cousins passed on was true, Rex. The Squids accept humans as equals," the formed PJ stated.

"Yes, friend. I just brought some last minute additions to the cargo in a modified Falcon. Alas, the spacecraft is on its last legs and thus unsafe for further travel."

"Why were you chosen, Rex?"

"Why do the Tschaaa chose anyone or anything? Because they can."

The two friends from different planets silently stood as Camila tried to digest all the information. Camila finally broke the quiet.

"I must admit my selfishness makes me glad you are here. Your friendship has helped keep me sane, you miniature Tyrannosaurus Rex, you."

The creature called Rex responded with the Lizard version of a grin; mouth open, l.izard like tongue out.

"Your naming of me still provides my mate and me with humor, Camila. I look little like that great beast you use as my namesake. "

"How is Rose? She is here with you, yes?"

"Yes. Which is why I am not overly agitated. With my mate and future hatchlings, I will weather the voyage back."

"Well, I guess I should head back to my quarters and see if any of our Tschaaa Lords have special plans for me." Camila started to turn away, then stopped.

"Rex, you said you brought some late additions to the cargo. What were they."

Rex paused a moment before answering.

"Pregnant female humans. Six of them."

Camila froze in her tracks. She knew what pregnant and human meant with the Tschaaa.

Veal.

Rex gestured a feeling of remorse and regret as he replied.

"I am sorry, my friend. I did what I must."

"I understand, old friend," said Camila. "Don't worry. I'll snoop around a bit and see what I can find out about what their future holds. Excuse me, I need to go back to my quarters and clean up."

"Please come and visit Rose and me. We will soon have a family and offspring."

"Will do, my reptilian comrade. See you soon."

A half hour later, and Camila was sitting in her two-room quarters. Her living space spoked off of a central living area she shared with the other Pre-Homo Sapiens. Based on her knowledge of anthropology, she thought the hominids came from some samples of actual individuals of Homo erectus, with a form of Gigantopithicus used to create the very tall cyborg robocops. They were very much like modern-day humans but with a few slight twists that made Camila realize they were different from her. However, they accepted her as one of their tribe and shared their motherhood and brood with her as a weird Aunt. The children liked her less than hairy skin and infectious laugh.

She surveyed her rooms as she contemplated the idea of living the rest of her life aboard the starship. It would be a long trip back to the Tschaaa homeworld, and she would be long dead by the time they reached it, even if she was not eaten. After all, hominid flesh had brought the Squids to Earth, so she was literally meat on the hoof. As were the four unknown pregnant women Rex had brought aboard.

Her mind wandered back to some six years ago after she was captured on that failed raid...

Camila awoke in a dull gray room. The soft bench like structure she lay on was molded into the wall, which was one large circle. It took a few moments for her eyes to focus and for her mind to grasp where she lay. Camila was in a form of confinement. She slowly sat up and fought back a bit of nausea. Then Camila realized she was wearing only her panties. She did a quick check of her body to see if she felt any type of invasive surgery or the proverbial Alien Anal Probe. The former special forces type could find nothing out of the norm, other than a couple of healing cuts. Or were those bullet holes? Camila remembered being shot.

She let out a sigh of relief. Being a POW was terrible enough. Being abused, especially for a woman, that was another level of problems. Camila stood up and walked around her 'cell.' She saw the indications of a recessed, sliding door, a la Star Trek. There was no toilet, sink, or water faucet. Someone had brought her to this confinement, so she assumed they meant to keep her alive. Of course, her assumptions were based on dealing with relative normal humans, not alien Squids.

The must-have been some motion sensors in the walls as the door suddenly opened as she moved around. Camila jumped back and went into a defensive crouch. She was not one to go without a fight. The sergeant was surprised, to say the least when a somewhat zaftig dish-water blonde woman in a lab coat and a stethoscope around her neck. The woman smiled as she walked in, a looming figure of a robocop cyborg behind her.

"Hello, I am Doctor Susan Smith." The woman offered her hand to shake. Camila just stared at it.

"Well, Sergeant. I can imagine you are a bit upset..."

"Hey, Lady," Camila shot back. "You realize we are on an alien spacecraft, run by beings who eat us?"

Doctor Smith paused before answering as her smile disappeared.

"I'm trying to make the best of a bad situation, Sergeant Sanchez. To put it bluntly, I helped stop our hosts from eating you."

"Oh Yeah?" Camila sneered. "And you did that because of why?"

"Because you are a gavid human female warrior and thus to the Tschaaa a unique specimen for study."

"You mean they didn't have years to study us during their approach? We know it took them a while to get to Earth."

"Please, Sergeant. Have a seat on your bench. Then I'll explain."

Camila snorted and sat down. If the robocop wasn't standing nearby, she would have made a dash for freedom and enjoy knocking this collaborator on her substantial ass. However, since she couldn't, then she might as well her this so-called doctor's explanation.

"You want something to eat and drink," asked Smith.

"That would be nice, Doc. But don't think you can bribe me."

"To be blunt, Sergeant, I want to keep you healthy for my studies."

Camila snorted again. She could not believe she was on a spacecraft and not dead. Someone had done an excellent job of patching her up based on her memory of being shot. The doctor noticed her sudden interest in sections of her body and smiled at Camila.

"Yes, you were shot. Tschaaa medical science enabled me to remove the bullets, put you in a semi-comatose state as their nannites to repair you."

"How long was I under?" Camila asked.

"A week. And no, there were no arcane experiments on your body. I just recorded the nanites repairing your body. It was a lot better than some artificial experiment. It showed in a real-world scenario how advanced the so-called Squids are in the biological sciences."

"Well," replied Camila, "I guess I should thank you and your Squid masters for patching me up. But, I'll hold off until you tell me what the plans are for me."

"First, some food and water for you," said Doctor Smith. She stepped out of the room and spoke to the robocop. A minute later, Smith re-entered.

"They'll be a Gray along with some food and drink," she said.

"Well, while we wait, what spacecraft am I on?" asked Camila.

"You are on the craft controlled by the Creche Lord responsible for Australia and New Zealand, plus the area and seas around them. He has never taken a human pronounceable name, so if he ever talks to you via translator, just call him Lord."

Camila paused in thought for a moment, then responded. "Intelligence told us there were some thirteen of these superfamily units we call Creches in our reports. So what number owns me?"

Camila wanted to glean as much information as she could during this meeting, as she had no idea if this Doctor Smith would ever contact her again.

"This craft includes the members of Creche Ten who decided to stay aboard rather than land on Earth."

"And this is the final destination of a lot of humans flesh and body parts, all for the long trip to the Squids homeworld."

Doctor Smith let out a frustrated sigh.

"Look it, Sergeant. Have the Tshaaa killed and harvested a bunch of humans? Yes. That is the reality. Now, we can make the best of a screwed up situation, or we can stew in our own juices."

"We? Do you have a mouse in your pocket, *Doctor?*"

Smith sputtered as her face flushed. The Gray arrived with a tray heaped with various containers and packages.

"Here. Eat. Then maybe you'll be in a more receptive mode, Sergeant."

The blonde stormed out. The Gray set the tray down on the bench structure, turned, and left without even acknowledging Camila's presence.

"Anti-social asshole," Camila grunted. Then she yelled out, "Clothes would be nice!"

The food on the tray was an eclectic mix. There were a couple of wrapped cold sandwiches which Camila tore into as she realized just how hungry she was after a week in a semi-coma. Several cans of various fruits and vegetables were also provided, the language on the containers not in English. Only one, a can of peaches, had a removable lid. Peach juice soon splattered Camila's bare breasts. She laughed as she opened a plastic bottle of water and used some of the contents to wash off the sticky syrup before it dried.

"I could use a towel and a washcloth—"

Before she finished her statement, the door swooshed open, and a tall cyborg robocop stepped in. He unceremoniously dropped a large bundle of clothes on the cell floor. "Clothes and wash items, human."

As the being started to leave, Camila yelled out. "Hey, Lurch! You speak like a human."

The cyborg stopped at the door and turned to face her. "My name is not Lurch," the Cyborg responded in oddly accented English. "I am also not a Homo sapiens. Although my data banks tell me a related hominid provided the genetic material for my people."

"People? There are more than one of you?" Camila quickly asked to keep the conversation moving.

"You may soon meet them," the cyborg responded. "If you are deemed trustworthy not to be confined. Although not all of my people are selected to be what you call robocops."

"So some are eaten?" Camila interjected.

"Not since we entered this solar system. You will find some reading materials in with your clothes, some of its notes from the Doctor. She said reading may calm you down." The oversized being turned and strode out the door.

"Thanks, Lurch!" There was no answer as the door snicked shut.

Some of the notes included directions on how to use some recessed waste disposal (toilet) facilities, as well as a hidden shower. There was also a notepad, a couple pencils, dictionary, a First Aid Manual, some godawful romance novel, and a couple of last issue news magazines which were published as everything fell apart. Camila surmised that Doctor Smith was trying to tell her, "Resistance is Futile." Screw her. Where there was life, there was hope. And as a soldier, her duty was to resist and escape.

Camila put on her now cleaned and repaired BDUs after discovering some clean panties and a sports bra that fit her. She looked around for possible camera locations, found just the one ball mount in the center of the ceiling. The recessed shower stall, which was a cylinder that rotated in and out, did have an opaque door. Camila surmised someone had studied human desire for privacy Why when Homo sapiens were seen as meat on the hoof, was a mystery. The stall did provide her with the privacy to check a special hidden pocket in her combat uniform pants. A long thin stiletto blade was still there. Camila had a weapon.

The P.J. organized her food supplies. She had a large box of corn flakes from France, a half a dozen cans of food with labels in various languages, a dozen 'cup-a-soups,' two cans of soda, several packages of beef and pork jerky, fast food condiment servings, and a single plastic bottle of water. Camila would have to ask for a can opener on the cans of food as none had any type of attached opener. The shower had an attached faucet that supplied boiling water so she would not have to eat the cup-a-soups dry. Camila guessed the Squids did not expect her to try and scald herself to death. Or was the hot water the Doctor's idea?

Camila picked an arbitrary spot opposite the shower area and stacked her food. She would use the now empty peach can as a drinking cup. The metal lid she kept as a cutting tool. Camila found some old style wool socks in the bundle of clothes 'Lurch' brought. A can of vegetables stuffed in one sock gave her an improvised 'sap.' Push come to shove, Camila planned on going down fighting.

Camila lay down on the padded bench as she was already weary. Just the stress of knowing she was a POW was tiring. Her thoughts turned to the family of survivors left behind. The siblings James and Janice Richards, Mathew Bearclaw, and some potential lovers she had met. Camila, James, Janice, and Matt had fought their way together from Western Washington to Great Falls, Montana during the early days of the Infestation. They must now all assume she was dead and eaten. As long as they lived, Camila would have a sense of accomplishment and purpose for living. Where there was life, there was hope. With that thought, Camila drifted off into sleep.

Grasping and tugging hands jerked Camila awake. She came off the padded bench, swinging and kicking at the two humanoid Grays. They were strong and wiry but seemed untrained in any hand to hand combat techniques. Within a couple of minutes, both of the Grays were down on the floor.

"Come on, you alien pieces of shit!" Camila raged. "Get up and try me again!" All the fear, anger, and frustration bubbled over as the PJ contemplated stomping the two Grays into bloody messes. As Camila stepped forward, a Lizard being suddenly came through the door. In a glance, Camila saw it had a device suspended on a strap around its body. As the Lizard made noises, an accentless English came from the box-shaped device.

"Please, Human! They are simple beings and mean you no harm."

"Oh yeah? Then why did they start grabbing me in my sleep?"

"They were give directions to bring you to Doctor Smith. I

believe they misunderstood what that meant."

Camila took a deep breath and exhaled. A bit calmer, she stepped towards the Lizard.

"Well, my T-Rex friend, how about YOU escort me to the Doctor. Less chance of a misunderstanding, don't you think?"

The dinosauroid paused in thought for a moment and then replied.

"I am not a T-Rex related being, but your logic is sound. Come, I will instruct these two to return to their work area."

The Lizard made some odd clicking sounds at the Greys. The two creatures stood up and exited through the open door. Camila gave the brownish, grayish reptile-like creature a once over.

"What is your name, Mister Lizard?"

"You cannot pronounce it, human. So, your name T-Rex will suffice."

"Male or female?"

"Male. And you are female judging by your mammaries. Sergeant Sanchez is your name, isn't it?"

Camila grinned, hoping this Lizard realized her grin meant she was friendly.

"Since you are helping me, you can call me Camila, my personal name. Now, shall we leave my cell and visit the good Doctor?"

"You may wish to put some clothes on your body. And shoes-Camila."

"Good Idea," she answered. In a couple of minutes, she had her BDUs on and her boots tight on her feet. She grabbed the empty peach can glass and took a swig of water.

"I can eat later, right?"

"Why, yes. I know the Tschaaa wish you to be healthy."

The Lizard know as T-Rex, soon shorted to just Rex, guided

Camila for some ten minutes. The aliens had left her military watch with her clothes, so she used it to estimate the distance. This starcraft was immense as per the intelligence reports. Camila saw Grey humanoids scurrying around, clearly being used as repairmen and general labor.

"So, Rex. I see the Greys working. What do you and your fellow Lizards do?"

"Whatever the Lord says. Because we have superior reasoning skills, complicated maintenance and repairs are left to us to supervise, helped by a few of the pre-humans you have seen."

"And these human-like cousins to us, are they kept for meat also?"

"Before arriving in the Sol System, yes. There is no need since so many of your fellow humans are being harvested."

Camila paused the conversation as she contemplated what direction the conversation should go. Camila needed to elicit as much information as she could from Rex, as she may never see him again.

"So, do the Tschaaa eat you Lizards?" Camila asked. Might as well be blunt.

"No. We are a client species kept to help the Tschaaa in their travels. Some of the equipment on this craft are from my species designs. We were also a spacefaring race."

"Then the Squids showed up, right?"

Rex made some hand signs (he had a five digit hand) which Camila soon discovered signified apology and sorrow.

"Our homeworld was occupied, but our flesh was not suitable for a food source. At least, the Tschaaa did not like our taste. So, they utilize our intelligence and experience in space travel."

"We killed some of your kind when we humans attacked the invasion craft," stated Camila.

"Yes. Some of my kind were used on the Harvester Arks.

However, we have not been warlike for centuries. Thus, we do not make efficient warriors."

"The fact I killed some of your people does not bother you?" asked the P.J.

"The fighting was the Tschaaa decision, not ours. The fact some of us died is the result of the Tschaaa desires, not ours."

"So, you would leave this-servitude if possible?" Camila knew she was treading on dangerous ground, but she needed to know where she stood, who were her real enemies.

"It is not possible, Camila. For we are hundreds of light years from our home planet, which still has some Tschaaa keeping watch," replied Rex.

Camila walked with Rex without any further conversation. The PJ did not want to push and ruin a possible friendship. For she needed all the help, she could get if she were to survive on an alien spacecraft.

The pair arrived at a nondescript sliding door which opened into a large bay. Camila slowly followed Rex into the room. All around were equipment, some recognizable as human medical machinery, other strange and arcane. A thought of Nazi medical experiments flashed through her mind, and she hoped Doctor Smith was not a true Mengele.

Doctor Smith stepped from behind some sizeable unknown piece of equipment, intently perusing a clipboard as she mumbled to herself, oblivious to Camila and Rex's entrance. The Lizard's translation device crackled into life.

"Doctor, here is the human, Camila, as requested."

"Have her sit over there," Smith absentmindedly said as she pointed to a bench. Camila sat and looked around as she waited for the Doctor to take the next step. Rex stood still and quiet. Finally, the Doctor looked up and spoke.

"I have some tests for you to complete. They are aimed at determining if your injuries have been adequately treated."

"I remember being shot," said Camila

"Yes. Twice. One through your chest, just missing your heart and lungs. The other through your left bicep."

Camila examined the areas mentioned, could find just hints of possible scaring. The Doctor smiled as Camila frowned.

"How long did you say I was out for?" asked the Sergeant.

"You were under medical care for a week. During that time, I operated on you as well as introducing nanites obtained from the Tschaaa. They are decades ahead of us in this science, and most things biological."

Camila grunted.

"So I guess I should thank the Squids who are killing and eating humans for bringing me here."

"Not a thank you. Just accept," replied Smith. "Now, whether you like it or not, there are some additional tests. If you try to resist, I will have some Grays and Cyborgs hold you down."

Camila looked at the Doctor and decided she was serious. Camila could break the Doctors face before anyone could stop her, but then Rex may be in trouble for being in the room. Not to mention the PJ's death would be accelerated.

"Okay. No fighting it. But no anal probes."

Camila spent an hour being poked and prodded by the Doctor (no anal probes) and then was placed in some Tschaaa form of what had to be MRI and X-ray machines. Finally, Camila protested.

"I need to pee, I'm thirsty and hungry. Are you done yet?"

The Doctor paused, then answered. "For today, yes. Now, if the Lizard here can take you back…"

"His name is Rex."

"Whatever. You will be brought here tomorrow."

Rex walked Camila back to her quarters. She looked around as they walked.

"This place is huge," said Camila.

"It is vast, like a small moon," replied Rex.

"Will I get a tour of it, later?"

"Possibly. You may be moved in with the other hominids. It depends."

"Depends on what, Rex?"

"Depends on if the Tschaaa decide to keep you."

The examinations went on for some two weeks. Doctor Smith never explained what all the tests were for, but Camila did work on being friendly. The PJ decided if she could use some manipulation techniques they taught in Escape and Evasion, she might have a more extended existence. So by the end of the first week, the two women were actually smiling at each other.

Camila then took a chance and did a bit of a "Are You Bisexual?" move on the Doctor. As the blonde's large rack was half hanging out the white blouse and lab coat, Camila ran her fingers across the soft skin.

"You have lovely clear skin, Doctor."

The Doctor did not jerk back nor protest.

"Your fingers feel nice. But if you think you can manipulate someone with a degree in psychology, please continue." They locked eyes.

Then Camila laughed. "Hey, I had to try. I do not want to be eaten."

"There's no danger of that, Camilla. You've been designated a prime specimen for long term study."

"Which means," asked Camila.

"You will be moved in with the other humans, the ones developed from Homo Erectus and Gigantopithicus. The larger hybrids became what you call Robocops."

"Then what?"

The Doctor shrugged.

"You probably will live for years. There are beings decades old, more as soon as the Squids started harvesting us. The limited population here has become more often used for labor."

"But as a prisoner."

"Well, Camila, unless you learn to live in a vacuum and can walk in Outer Space, yes."

A week after the conversation with Susan Smith, Camila was moved in with the proto-humans. They readily accepted her, even if Camila looked a bit different. The cavemen had oral communication, and some had learned the various human languages, not to mention sign languages. Other than the oversized Cyborg Robocops, none had access to the electronic translators. But everyone made do, as Camila also learned some of their writing and words.

The children saw her as this exotic creature with a friendly smile who was not afraid to play with them. The mothers soon began using Camila as a willing 'babysitter' during those times when the Tschaaa suddenly required additional intelligent labor. However, Calima's closest friend was Rex and his Camila named mate/wife Rose. She soon was visiting Rex and Rose in their living quarters.

As the three beings sat together, drinking a Lizard version of tea for which that Camila developed a taste.

"So Rex, any new information about what is going on with my fellow humans?"

"Well, Camila, it has been over a year since the Tschaaa landed on Earth. They have divided the land masses into areas of control, each supervised by a creche and a Lord. However, they only really care about land areas near the ocean and large bodies of water."

"So the area in the Mid- West of the U.S.is still free?"

"Yes. And areas up and down the various continental coasts more than twenty of your miles from the Ocean are called Feral, with the area known as the Florida Keys under the control of the Director."

"The Director?"

"Director Adam Lloyd. He is taking control in the name of the Tschaaa Lord who took the name of Neptune. All those areas considered controlled by the Tschaaa are called the Reorganized United States. Your former comrades say these are the Occupied States."

"So we have organized humans under Tschaaa control. Great."

"We all do what we must to survive, Camila."

"I know. I would appreciate it if you would help me obtain more access to this... ship. I would like more room to move around. Sitting babysitting is getting boring."

"I will see what I can do, my human friend."

Rex was good as his word. The next day, the Lizard took Camila out for an extended walk. They went the two-kilometer length of the living area, stopping short of a large bulkhead.

"Beyond that is the control area. I guess you would call it an oversized cockpit."

Camila looked up to what must have been hundreds of meters up to the "ceiling." She saw only one transparent area which could be termed a window of about fifty meters across.

"Is this living area, with the lake, in the center of this starship?" asked Camila.

"Almost my friend. The area beneath this surface is a bit deeper."

The PJ looked back the way they came.

"That other bulkhead, about two klicks back. What is behind that?"

"A vast engine and storage area. I must tell you that you are not allowed past either bulkhead. Sorry."

Camila shrugged.

"Oh well. At least I can start running again."

Rex looked at her with his larger eyes.

"You humans have a predication for exercise, I see. My people seem to have a slightly slower metabolism."

"Well, we intelligent apes get bored easy, I guess. They gave me some running shoes. So tomorrow, I start."

"Will your hominid companions join you?" asked Rex.

"Probably not. My distant cousins are getting worked a lot, as well as chasing their kids around. By the way, if someone could find me a job..."

"Not yet, Camila. The Tschaaa are still studying your test results, as well as watching your interactions with the others you live with."

Camila grunted.

"Well, tell then, Smith...hey, where is she? I haven't seen her in months."

"Doctor Smith is at Platform One, the expanded International Space Station."

"Huh. I guess the Doc moved up in the world. Well, time for the communal evening meal. I guess it is some of that Fake Fish."

"Do you like it? Rose does."

"Not bad. Tastes like canned tuna."

Time passed. The starship occupants were soon used to seeing the crazy human running and sweating, doing calisthenics, martial arts Katas, etc. Squids old and young swimming in the interior lake would stop and stare in the first runs, but then ignored her. At the end of the second year of captivity, Camilla was asked to perform some simple work tasks with her 'Cousins.' She was glad as there was a shortage of books and other items to help combat boredom.

Into the storage area behind the bulkhead they went. Camilla saw machines and packages of types completely strange to her. Then she saw things that, unfortunately, was not strange to her. There were large refrigeration units with hunks of meat and clearly human torsos hanging from alien versions of meat hooks. These were moved to conveyor belts which disappeared into the unknown area beneath the open space of the lake. Camila soon discovered the area contained dining and individual quarters of the Tschaaa still aboard the starcraft. No hominids were allowed there.

Camilla had seen many a dead body before. However, she still had to make an effort not to react to the idea of human corpses being treated like slabs of beef. At least the times the Technical Sergeant was tasked to move the bodies and parts was soon reduced to no more than once a month. Camila asked Rex about the changing frequency.

"There are fewer Tschaaa aboard, Camila. More have transported to the Earth."

Camila frowned.

"Sounds like the Squids are not going to leave anytime soon."

"Some will to transport new food sources back to their home planet and the hoped-for survivors. Since they arrived, only two hyperspace communications drones have arrived. Speed of light communication takes hundreds of years to reach this system."

"Can you tell me what was learned, Rex? I don't want to cause trouble for you."

The Lizard paused, then performed his version of a shrug.

"No one has said there are secrets. So if I tell you that some Tschaaa still survive on the homeworld, as well as my planet, it should hurt nothing."

"How about overall losses?" Camila pushed for more information, although who she would ever tell was in question.

"Half of the Tschaaa left on their homeworld have perished. Most left on my former planet still live. Indications they are back to eating non-primate meat sources."

"Not... your people, I hope."

Rex produced a Lizard smile.

"No. We taste bad."

More time passed. Camila noticed she could walk or run around ignored by the Tschaaa and their minion. The human was no more seen than the hominid cousins. Finally, one day, Camila decided she had been a placid POW for too long. With her hidden blade, she went snooping.

The last couple of periods of work, Camila observed as the Grays opened the oversized door to the meat storage area behind the bulkhead. It was a simple four symbol keypad sequence that locked and unlocked the door. Apparently, the thought anyone on the starship would access an unauthorized area was alien to the Tschaaa. Camila laughed to herself as she thought of it being 'alien' to an Alien.

Late one evening/sleep cycle, when all was quiet, Camila went for a 'run.' The PJ had set a pattern of exercising at all hours of the day and night, so again no being seemed to notice. Smooth and sure moves, and she was beyond the door. Camila went past the Dark Meat locker and into the off-limits area containing the alleged engine room. The PJ found a submarine type hatch with an oversized locking wheel. Some grunting and huffing, and the hatch swung open.

There was a bit of an electricity in the air as Camila slowly moved into the interior. She no physics major nor expert on propulsion systems but things looked massive and powerful. Camila ducked in the shadows when a couple of Grays ambled by, speaking in some odd clicking noises. She then turned a corner of metal and was staring up at a Robocop cyborg.

The PJ started to go into defensive stance, planned on selling her life dearly when the tall figure spoke in the odd accented English.

"So, human. We meet once more."

"Lurch?"

"Yes, I am the one you called Lurch all those years ago."

Camila paused as she realized the cyborg was making no aggressive moves.

"So, my large friend, what happens now?"

"If you attempt violence, I must respond. If you walk with me, you may go back and sleep. My computer interfaces do report a condition know as sleepwalking. Is that what you are doing here? Sleepwalking?"

It dawned on Camilla she was being given a pass, rather than a quick trip to the meat locker. Why she was given such a pass was a mystery, but now was not the time to look a gift horse in the mouth.

"My sleep cycles have been interrupted," she replied.

"Well then, human, shall we go?" Was that a hint of a smile around Lurch's mouth?

"Lead on," said Camila.

Lurch escorted her back to her living area without comment. As the cyborg turned to leave, Camilla called out, "Will me meet again?"

"Possibly, human. For few can see the future." Then Lurch strode away. The incident was never mentioned by any of the proto-humans, nor did any Tschaaa summon Camila. Time passed, and the

PJ settled into a routine existence. Then the fateful news of the Great Compromise.

Camila sat in her quarters and tried to come to grips that she would soon be beyond any hope of return to Earth. Her adopted family, James, Janice Richards and Mathew Bearclaw- did they believe she still lived? She sniffed and wiped a tear away. It was time to resign herself to no mate, no children, and a quasi 'tribe' of proto-humans to share what, another fifty to hundred years of life? Camilla pulled from a drawer her stash of Sanchez moonshine. Time for a good pity, drunk.

"Camila, my friend. Wake up."

It took the blurry Technical Sergeant a few moments to awaken and have her eyes focus. She then realized it was Rex and Rose standing over her bed.

'Wha... .What're you doing here?" Camila asked.

"Pack your items you wish to keep. There is no time to explain. We must leave."

"What?"

"Please. Now!" Rex used a hand sign for extreme need. With that, Camilla was up and grabbing her Bugout Bag. She had the habit from years in the military and on the edge of being ready to go at a moments notice.

Rex and Rose led Camila down a passageway she previously had not seen. Through a couple of winding turns and high-security hatches, they were then in a large bay. In the bay was a Falcon spacecraft.

"What is going on here?" Camila demanded.

"Freedom," said Rose. Then the lizard suddenly hugged Camila.

"You may look like a nasty monkey, but you are a true friend," the female Lizard said through her translator.

"You're my friend, Rose," Camila replied. "I wish I could speak your real name in Lizard."

"I love the name, Rose, my human friend. It is a pretty flower. That is what I will picture when I think of you."

"You two are not leaving with me?"

"We cannot," replied the Lizard Camila had named T-Rex. "We must stay onboard to ensure future generations of our lineage."

Two tall cyborg figures approached from the loading ramp of the Falcon. As the neared, Camila, saw one was 'Lurch,' the other an unknown Robocop of the type created from modern humans.

"To what do I owe this activity, gentlemen?" Camila asked.

"To General Torbin Bender," Lurch stated.

"General? Hell, he was a senior NCO when I last saw…"

"Times change, Technical Sergeant Sanchez," said the new cyborg. "My name is Andrew. And Torbin never forgets his friends or battle buddies. Those are his words."

"But how… why now?"

"The Great Compromise, which I helped to Create," said Andrew in his accentless English. "General Bender found your story and demanded I return you to Earth. He said you have been a POW long enough."

"So you bucked the Squids?" asked Camila. A hint of a smile formed on Andrews lips.

"The word 'bucked' would be the understatement of the year. Now, we must go, before the Creche Lord becomes agitated. We are still on his starship."

Camila hugged Rex and Rose, started to walk forward, then stopped.

"I can't go. Six pregnant women just came on board. I can't leave knowing their babies will be veal cutlets."

Lurch looked at Andrew.

"Did I not say she would not leave while the others stayed?"

"Yes, Brother, you did. And you were right to put them aboard the Falcon."

Camila's mouth dropped open. Squid cyborgs helping humans? What next?

"You mouth is open, Camila," said Andrew, with a full smile visible below his eye visor.

"This has gotta be a dream."

"No, it is not. Come, it is time to go."

Andrew led Camila up the Falcon loading ramp, and she glanced back at the being she called Lurch.

"You coming?" she asked.

"No human. I stay with my own kind. I will make sure they are not eaten on the long voyage. Andrew has taught us independence."

Camila turned and saluted the cyborg.

"Well met, Sir. Well met."

Lurch saluted back, then turned and with Rex and Rose left the launch bay.

Camila strapped into a seat next to Andrew. The six sobbing young women were seated in the cargo area. They had dodged the butcher's bill.

"Andrew, may I ask a question?"

"As Torbin Bender would say, shoot."

"Doctor Susan Smith..."

"She is dead, Camila. Killed by a Colonel Bardun for conducting hellish experiments on human embryos and babies. She wanted an artificially grown meat source for the Tschaaa."

"Damn! Karma does exist," replied Camila.

"And I must tell you, Camila, that she harvested some of your eggs for future use."

The military veteran's face began to flush with anger.

"We saved them before she used them," said Andrew. "It seemed she was saving the best for last. Then she died. Chopped up with a scalpel."

Camila sat quietly and blinked back tears of rage. Finally, she spoke.

"I wished I could have cut her up. I will have to thank the Colonel."

"You will meet her. She wishes to debrief you about living on a Tschaaa starship."

With smooth and quick control commands, Andrew had the Falcon out of the launch bay and into space. As he maneuvered the craft, the cyborg added one more comment.

"Your family waits for you. James figured out you were still alive from intercepted Tschaaa communications. He is famous for his intelligence products."

"And Janice and Mathew?"

"Waiting for their adopted mother to meet her grandchildren."

Camila could no longer hold the tears back and began to sob. Andrew produced a couple of beautiful silk handkerchiefs and gave them to Camila.

"Here. A custom our President Sandra Paul has passed on. Everyone carries them for such occasions."

"You mean for crying women?"

"For men and women, Camila. For many have lost, then some regained. Tears of sorrow and joy we all share."

"Including you, Andrew?"

"Yes."

They traveled in silence for a time. Camila broke the silence.

"Is it really... over?"

"The death part, yes. Now comes the hard part."

"What is that, Andrew?"

"Life. Together."

The stars seemed to shine brighter as the Falcon sped to return humans to where they belonged. Earth.

What Dreams Are Made Of

Hannah Weitz shrieked in her sleep. The shrieking reverberated through the sizeable Munsen home as it woke up all the residents. The first to respond was Bruno, the Pitbull mix who survived the fighting Pits with Hannah. He was up on the bed, whining and crying as he licked Hannah. His human was in fear and pain so he must help.

The raven-haired beauty jerked awake, sobbing. Hannah hugged Bruno to her breast as he continued to whine and lick her.

"Hannah. Are you okay?" Aunt Freda said as she dashed into the young lady's bedroom. Right behind her was her husband, Uncle Johann. The massive modern Viking looked like an overgrown Saint Nicholas, beard and all.

"Aunt, Uncle, it's okay. Just a bad... dream."

"Hannah, dear. You must talk to someone about these

dreams," said Uncle Johann. "This is the third one…"

"No!" Hannah cut him off. "I must deal with this myself. No one else can understand what the… Pits were like."

"Hannah, please," began Aunt Freda. Hannah shook her head in refusal.

"I'm okay now. Sorry to wake you all. Now, I must sleep as I have an order to complete for the Banshees on the forge."

Hannah rolled over and pulled her covers up. Bruno smuggled up next to her.

The Munsens turned the light out and shut the bedroom door.

"She is so stubborn," said Johann.

"If she were not adopted, I would say she takes after your side of the family," replied Freda. Johann grunted.

"I may be stubborn, but I am not the one having the night terrors."

The married couple made their way back to bed as Hannah hugged Bruno to her breast.

"You understand, Bruno,' she whispered. "Others do not." Bruno licked her face. He would stay with her the rest of the night, and make sure his human was safe and slept well. Within moments, both were in the sleep of the innocent.

Hannah woke up early, grabbed a quick roll and slice of bacon for breakfast, and headed to the forge. Uncle Johann had a blacksmith operation for years before the alien Tschaaa Infestation. Serving the Nordic community by shoeing local horses and fixing farm equipment, Johann and Freda opened their home to the Five Survivors, little ladies rescued from the alien supporting Kraken's perverted Fighting Pits by a government law enforcement raid. Johann Munsen and some New Vikings arrived to help the Federal Agents led by Director Paul Miller and assisted by now General Torbin Bender. The Five had suffered unimaginable horrors of the Pits, were abused in ways talked about only in hushed tones.

The forge became a place of catharsis for Hannah. The fires and hot metal gave Hannah a feeling of cleansing heat as she beat and shaped steel. The raven-haired now almost twenty-year-old of Jewish descent had adapted to metalwork like a duck to water. Johann told many that she was the best blacksmith he had ever worked with, even men much larger than Hannah's five foot six frame. The oldest Survivor had a wiry, muscular strength which surprised most people. However, Johann knew it was her inner strength and drive, which made her such a force with which to be reasoned.

Added to Hannah's strength was also an artistic side. Thus, when she was not making officially authorized Banshee Blade fighting knives for the 101st Special Attack Unit, she was making armbands, bracelets, necklaces, and medallions for a sundry of customers. For her fame was now nationwide. Uncle Johann helped her as much as possible, and she demanded he takes a share of the profits. But when it came to the Banshee Blades, and the distinctive miniature sword cross for the Sisters of Steel who made up the Banshees, it was solely a Hannah project.

Hannah put the final touches on an eleven-inch blade for some new Banshee and squelched its heat in the oversized water bucket. She smiled as she saw the clean strength of the steel. This blade would sharpen up nicely; Hannah thought to herself. She would inscribe a special one of a kind symbol on the heel of the blade, so each Sister of Steel knew it was *her* knife.

The gruff voice of Uncle Johann shook her from her reverie.

"Young lady, how many times must I remind you to wear your forge gloves?"

Only then did Hannah realize she had been beating and

shaping the blade with bare hands and forearms.

"I am sorry, Uncle…"

"There is no sorry, Hannah. There is do it or not work steel. Half the time you forget to wear your goggles. I will not allow a young lady to become all scarred up like I am. If you wish to work steel in my forge, you will…"

Johann stopped as he saw Hannah's eyes. They had gone dark, the pupil like a shark's as it went in for the kill. Johann had seen these eyes before, and a cold shiver went up to the big man's spine.

On Hell Day, when Kraken scum on the Tschaaa Squids behest used Pit Beasts to terrorize Malmstrom Allied Military Base, Hannah demonstrated her Pit Fighting skills by necessity. She became a wraith in defending the children of Torbin Bender and his wife, Aleksandra. Now, a year after the signing of The Great Compromise peace treaty with the Tschaaa, Johann saw these eyes more and more, whenever Hannah felt threatened.

"Hannah," Johann began in a lower tone of voice, "I am sorry if I seem like an old nag, but a young beauty like yourself should not have scars…"

"Too late, I already have scars. Inside." Hannah dropped the blade in the squelching bucket, turned and walked out the back door. Bruno quickly followed. His human was upset, needed his reassurance.

"Oh, Lord Odin," whispered Johann. "Please give a sign on how to deal with the demons inside Hannah. For they eat her alive."

Hannah strode out into the Montana woods behind the Munsen homestead. Walking among the tall trees gave Hannah a sense of peace. She soon found a favorite old cut stump to sit on and look at the scenic mountains and forest. Bruno joined her, butted her left arm with his head and muzzle, demanded attention. Hannah smiled and hugged him.

"You understand, don't you, Bruno?"

Dog and woman sat quietly, each lost in their own thoughts, but content in the presence of the other.

Hannah managed to make it through the rest of the day at the forge but kept to herself. That night she cut her dinner with the others short. She just did not have any desire to socialize with the four younger Survivors, nor with Johann and Freda. Hannah excused herself, claiming a bad headache and went to bet early.

In her bedroom, an Eater appeared, and she started to scream.

Bruno's tongue and whining woke her up.

"You sense when I have a nightmare," she whispered to her canine companion as she hugged him to her sweaty body. "How can anyone wish for a better friend?"

The next morning, Hannah returned to her project. She made sure she had all the protective gear Uncle Johann required. Hannah wanted no more conflict with a man the Survivor owed so much. She soon pounded steel in a rhythm only a blacksmith would recognize and understand.

The young lady was not sure how long she beat and formed the steel into what a blacksmith wanted. Finally, Hannah was finishing the last blade when Bruno let out a welcoming 'woof.' A welcome bark told Hannah that someone Bruno considered a friend approached.

Hannah walked out of the blacksmith shop with the last Banshee blade in her hand and saw who the protective dog greeted. A smile formed on her lips as she recognized the General's staff car with a driver she knew. Dark haired and handsome Master Sergeant Leon Pasqual stepped from the driver's side as Bruno ran up to greet him. The canine Fighting Pit survivor wiggled and bumped the

Sergeant as he demanded pets. Leon patted Bruno and knew just where to scratch behind the dog's ears to obtain small sounds of canine pleasure. Leon laughed, which was always music to Hannah's ears.

A flash of something from her mind's eye interfered with pleasant thoughts. A feral face seemed to be staring directly into Hannah's eyes, blocking her vision of Leon and Bruno. Then it was gone. Leon called to her, drawing her attention back to the here and now.

"Mon Cherie! I see Johann is still working you like a common laborer rather than a pretty young lady."

Hannah tried to smile as she walked down the slight incline from the forge to the driveway.

"It is good to see you, Leon. What brings you here, on a workday?"

"General Reed said I was hanging around the office too much, as he has been stuck doing what Generals do-plan. So he ordered me to take the staff car and burn the carbon out of the cylinders with a little high-speed jaunt. "

"And you just happened to wind up here."

"Why, yes, Hannah. The car was drawn here like steel to a magnet." Leon walked closer and looked at Hannah's hands.

"You still have your heavy gloves on, my lady."

It was both a private joke and a personal ritual that the Cajun always took Hannah's hand and kissed it like an old-world courtier. Hannah would giggle, despite all the times he had done it, and another pleasant visit would begin, For, since a particular day when Leon Pasqual had driven General Reed to the Munsen home to query Hannah about the Sisters of Steel and the blades she made for them, Leon had been courting the young lady. As the Sergeant was some ten years older than Hannah, he had taken it slow. However, despite the age difference, something had clicked between the two that first meeting. Possibly the fact a younger Pre-Infestation Hannah had lived among Cajuns in the Nar'lens area and spoke the patois. Or maybe they were just two lonely individuals who had finally found their soulmate, to Leon and Hannah, it did not matter.

Hannah looked down at her gloves.

"Oh, sorry. Here. Let me remove them."

Hannah slipped the nearly finished steel blade in a pocket of her leather forge apron and began to pull the gauntlets off.

"Hannah, you have some burn marks on your arms," Leo said with a frown and reached out to take her hand.

But it was not the Cajun's hand that Hannah saw and felt touch her. Instead, it was a cruel claw. In place of Leon's handsome visage was the face of a demon from Hell.

Shrieking and the frantic barking of Bruno brought Johann and Freda out of their home in a full run. There was Hannah, her foot on Leon's throat holding him flat on his back as she positioned the new Banshee blade to slice him to death.

"*Hannah!*" Johann bellowed. The Pit survivor froze and looked up at the source of the interrupting voice. Hannah's eyes were once again those of a hunting shark. Somehow Pasqual croaked out "Mon Cherie...please."

The blade slipped from her grasp. "No," Hannah mumbled.

Then she collapsed...

The other nude girl ran screaming at Hannah, her long dirty nailed hands formed into claws. Hannah doubled the unnamed female over with a kick to the pubis, then smashed her face with a knee. The girl did not rise....

A former family pet dog was staked out for a six-limbed Eater to munch on. Hannah was tossed onto the pit floor between the predator and prey with a butcher knife. Moments later, Hannah was standing over the dead Eater, covered in blue-tinted blood....

Hannah was shoved into a room with a bed. Strapped on her pubic area was a long fake phallus. On the bed was a dark-skinned teenaged female.

"Please. Fuck me. Now," the young woman pleaded. "If we put on a good enough show, they said I won't be fed to the Squids."

Hannah was tied breast to breast with another girl her age. "Kiss her, dammit!" a tattooed, sneering face demanded as rough hands squeezed and prodded both sets of female buttocks....

Hannah jumped and somersaulted nude around the Fighting Pit, a wraith with two blades. Former Earth ape creatures soon laid slaughtered in the dirt and sawdust as Hannah stood panting, a sense of satisfaction forming in her mind. She would be well fed this night....

Hannah jerked awake with a cry. She tried to focus her eyes to see. The room was entirely unfamiliar but looked like one in a hospital. Then she heard a familiar voice.

"Hannah, it's me, Abigail. With Bruno."

"Where... am I?"

"Military hospital on Malmstrom, Armed Forces Base."

"But... I'm not military, Abigail. How did they..."

"Funny what will happen when General Reed was asked by his driver for help. Not to mention President Sandra Paul is involved now."

"How...?"

Abigail Yamamoto, the Avenging Angel and the symbol which created the Sisters of Steel, walked up to the bedside and hugged

Hannah.

"Sisters always stick together, especially when they are Banshees. I made a telephone call. PTSD affects all people, not just soldiers."

"Abigail, I..." Hannah began to sob as she clung to Abigail. Bruno jumped up on the bed, hospital regulations be damned. Soon Hannah spared an arm for her four-legged friend, and Bruno licked her. After some five minutes, Hannah managed to stop crying and ask, "How long have I been here?"

"A week."

"Oh my God, I remember Leon..." Hannah began to cry again. "I... almost...."

"He is okay, Hannah. He took some weeks of Leave. He tried to swear me to secrecy, but he sneaks in and sleeps on the floor here when he can."

Hannah used the bed sheet to wipe her eyes.

"I used to be friendly, pleasant. Then I was taken to the Pits. Now I'm nasty, a killer. He deserves someone else in his life."

Abigail took Hannah's hand as Bruno lay his head on his human's lap.

"I used to think that, Then Ichiro and other friends, family helped me work through it. Now, I and others are here to help you. For you are a victim of the evil, the bad things the Kraken human scum did to you."

"The dreams, memories..." began Hannah.

"They will get better. Your mind is working things out through your nightmares. The Doctors have already lined up some professional counseling for you. The memories you have in dreams here are also prodded by some new psychotropic drugs developed using Tschaaa and human medical knowledge. Your dreams are cathartic, will help you by not burying your fears and feelings."

"Abigail, you... went through this?"

"Yes. You forget what happened when Fuzz Senior was killed protecting me. I lost it."

Hannah patted Bruno.

"Yes, our dog family is special."

"And now, Hannah, someone else needs to see you. It'll be just a minute."

Hannah lay petting Bruno.

"You have always understood, Bruno. You were there with me. We can get through this together.

Bruno suddenly raised his head and looked towards the room door, his tail wagging.

Leon Pasqual walked in with a single red rose.

"Glad you are better, my dear."

"Oh, Leon," Hannah said as she sat up and held out her arms. The two soulmates hugged, then kissed, then hugged again.

"I am so sorry, Leon," said as she embraced him. "I don't deserve you..."

"You cannot get rid of me that easily, Mon Cherie. Besides, Bruno likes me."

Hannah looked into Leon's eyes. "I have a lot of of... baggage."

Leon Pasqual laughed.

"After threatened with being eaten for some six years, and now trying to live with the Aliens who used to eat us, we all have baggage." Leon kissed his love.

"I'll help you carry it, okay?"

Abigail padded down to the nurse's station. She used her influence to give the couple a few Doctor Free moments. Sensors told the medical personal that Hannah was about to awake, so Abigail had been there. Sisters help Sisters. And now, Hannah had a true love to help her.

The Avenging Angel smiled. That was what sweet dreams were made of, even with outer space aliens running around. Abigail knew for sure. Love conquers all... even nightmares.

MOTHERHOOD

FROM THE PERSONAL DIARY OF
PRINCESS AKIKO OF THE FREE JAPAN ROYAL FAMILY

I started this diary as a means to record my life as part of the Tschaaa Infestation and then the Great Compromise, which ended the war and potential mutual destruction of two species. For in my belly are twins who must be raised in this new reality, where we work side by side with alien cephalopods who came to Earth to eat us.

Yesterday, I was rumbling around the Imperial Residence, as an American would say, as being pregnant with twins prevents me from being the Warrior Princess and the Banshee depicted in many an anime epic. It is a gross misstatement to say that someone with my background does well with inactivity. Thus, I strode around as if I had a purpose and direction while cursing my husband, Aiko Yamamoto, for having a government job he could accomplish while his loving wife looked more and more like a beached whale.

Some five years since the signing of the Great Compromise and humans and Tschaaa were living and working together for the most part. The one major project the two species agreed upon was the development of more efficient means of space travel. Expansion into the universe in craft capable of transporting hundreds in the form of Faster Than Light travel was seen as a desirable goal. And once again, pregnant women need not apply.

As I grumped about, I entered an area of the Royal Palace rarely occupied. I looked about and saw in one corner what looked like cobwebs.

Cobwebs? In the Imperial Palace, where Emperors and Samurai walk? This could not be allowed to stand. I began looking for some form of katana which would befit the task of disposing of the cobweb menace. For surely, my twins could not be allowed to be born around cobwebs!

As I approached to get a better look at the offending cobweb I quickly saw it was occupied. Two web-spinning spiders of what I think were of the genus Linyphiidae seemed to be doing some sort of dance as they approached each other in the center of the web. It then dawned on me what was occurring. As my dear friend Torbin Bender, General of all Allied Forces would say, they were attempting to do The Nasty.

I paused as I watched the spiders perform some intricate maneuvers as part of the mating ritual. I realized that the result would be the same as with most living creatures; they would have Young. I stood transfixed as the two eight-legged creatures completed their instinctive task. Then one, a bit smaller than the other but not by much, left the web. I assumed it was the male going to avoid being eaten as in some species, the female is not an appreciative lover.

Now, if all had been done correctly, said female would soon be with child, though with many, not just twins like me.

Maybe it is the hormones coursing through my body, but I became very reflective. My Father, the Emporer, would never refer to me as the thoughtful type. He always saw me as impulsive and stubborn. And he is correct.

But this day, I was soon lost in thought.

Two eight-legged native Earth creatures made me contemplate that they, like the ten limbed Tschaaa, were driven to reproduce, to have Young. That innate characteristic of most living things led to two species, Hell-bent on mutual destruction, to pause. This pause was due in most part to the Breeders, the Mothers meeting and realizing what was really important. It was the Young who would suffer if the War continued. The Tschaaa had an even greater reverence to the Young than we sad humans, who often aborted offspring for what seemed as transitory matters. But then, the father of my twins was nearby to help.

Thus was created the Great Compromise. However, I would be ignorant and selfish if I did not mention a certain male now referred to as a Guardian Angel. For my Cyborg friend, Andrew arranged the historic Meeting of the Mothers. Then other males helped to ensure there was no more killing.

I looked down at my ever-expanding belly and felt the Twins move. I would be a Mother of two bawling babies soon enough. However, that reflection led me to another thought. Instead of just a personal diary, maybe, someday, I could write a definitive history of the Great Compromise. I could explain how two apex predatory species managed to come to an agreement and exist together in relative harmony.

And all because of Motherhood.

Now it is time to put this diary up as the two Trolls, as

Aleksandra Bender would call them, are telling me they want me to eat something. Maybe, chocolate ice cream. With chocolate cookies. American food cravings will kill me yet.

Snacks

"Mom, is that a midget?"

Evan Jenkins had thought he would never hear that question again. After over six years hiding from the Tschaaa aliens, then the signing of a peace treaty known as the Great Compromise, Evan thought people were over pointing and commenting about people who were different. After all, humankind had barely escaped from being permanent items on an alien Squid creature's menu. Not to mention the Kraken sympathizers who had developed a taste for Long Pig.

However, he was an adult male, only four and a half feet tall. He was not a severe sufferer of Disproportionate Dwarfism but did look a bit different with his large hands for his slightly shorter arms.

"I'm sorry, Sir," the thirtysomething, attractive blonde mother said. "It's just that Jimmy here has not seen very many people with…" She paused, at a loss for words.

"With handicaps or disabilities other than injured veterans, right?" Evan finished the sentence for her. The woman was clearly uncomfortable dealing with a human being born outside the norms.

"Well, Ma'am, it is true that the old and the infirm died first," continued Evan. "Especially since so many were easily harvested during the first month or so. It's hard to run and hide when you have a disability or need a wheelchair."

"But what are you?" the six-year-old persisted.

Evan smiled even as the mother looked like she was about to strangle her own child.

"We prefer Little People," Evan replied.

"So, there are more of you?" asked Jimmy.

That made Evan pause. For truth be told, he was the only dwarf, little person, or what used to be called a 'midget' he had seen. He was like the character in that old movie. The *Last Man On Earth*, maybe the last of his kind, especially with Tschaaa genetic science being used to solve humanity's ills, as well as produce new ones created by an unscrupulous few. Providing super-soldiers, beasts, and women to have multiple births all the time were the goals of the Squids and their human minions the Krakens—not making more Little People.

"Please accept my apology," the blonde continued. "I have to go and pick up my husband. He's at the Base Hospital."

"No problem," replied Evan. He watched as the woman dragged her son down the street, tongue lashing him as he protested. Evan grunted.

"We did not even exchange names," he mumbled. The husband may have been either a patient or a worker at the Malmstrom Allied Armed Forces Base. Evan would never know. What Evan did know was the chances of him finding employment at that hospital here in Great Falls, Montana, was probably slim to none. Not being a veteran, possibilities of using the hospital services were slim to none just one year after the end of the War. The Infestation did not end as many of the alien Squids were still here, just the fighting.

Evan once again started pulling his wheeled suitcase along the refurbished sidewalk. Just off one of the newer 'buses' converted from some foreign allied transport, he needed to find a place to stay as he looked for a fresh start. Working and living where he had once hidden like a wild animal meant constant reminders of fear and loneliness. So, Evan had left the West Coast a week ago. Evan rounded a corner and saw an old-style tavern someone had kept going. Maybe he could get some leads on shelter and employment while having a cold beer.

Evan knew he had made a mistake when he walked in and looked for a seat at a table. Barstools could be a problem for people of his diminutive stature. No sooner had his eyes adjusted to the typical dim light of a beer joint than he heard the barking laugh and yell.

"Hey, Shorty! Where'd you come from?"

As Evan's eyes focused, he saw four ne'er do wells crowding around him. All four average-sized males had clearly been drinking for some time judging by the smell of stale beer and sweat that wafted from them. Evan made an attempt at a friendly smile.

"Hey, guys. I just got off the bus and—"

"Bus? I think you popped out of a clown car like in that DVD I watched last night," said the one who had called him Shorty.

"Yeah, Bud," said another brown-haired with a scraggly beard member of the group. "Maybe someone is starting a circus in town. Somebody got the Squids to make him in one of those vats we heard about."

All four males laughed at the continuation of the joke.

"Look, guys—" Evan began again.

"My Granddad told us kids about Dwarf Tossing back in the day," interjected a third voice. "Maybe Haps at the bar can help us set up a competition."

More laughter and Evan's face began to flush with anger.

"Now, look it. I don't want any trouble—"

"Trouble?" the original speaker said. "You ain't no trouble, short-stuff. You and your type were just snacks to the Squids. Hell, you're so small because the best part of you ran down your Mama's leg."

The loud laughter continued. Then Evan responded.

"And your Mom took it up the ass, which is why you were born with brown eyes."

The laughter froze in the four loudmouths. Then the first speaker smacked a fist into the side of Evan's head. The little person had been beaten before by near professionals, so one hit from a drunk would not put him down. Evan's small stature had one advantage. It was easy to head butt the attacker in the groin. Then the fight, as it was, started.

After about a minute, Haps was yelling, "Take it outside!" So Evan was picked up and carried like a sack of potatoes through the back door and into the alley. Evan was hefted up to be thrown in the dumpster when a commanding female voice resounded in the alleyway.

"Alright, boys. Fun's over. Put him down."

"Who the frick are you?" one of the ne'er do wells snapped out as Evan struggled in their grasp.

"Master Sergeant Camila Sanchez and you just interfered with some catch-up beer-drinking of mine."

"Go eff yourself, bitch," someone said.

"Now that is just unfriendly," said the woman. "But I haven't had a good brawl in what, some seven years?"

Then began the thuds of landed blows and screams of pain.

A half an hour later, Evan was sitting in a hole-in-the-wall taco cafe. Sergeant Sanchez was talking in Spanish with the female owner as a comely young lady patched up his cuts and Evan held a piece of raw steak to a blackening eye. He knew this was a useless folk remedy, but Evan was not about to argue. Maybe they'd let him keep the steak.

Camila laughed, hugged the owner, then stepped over to where Evan was sitting.

"Hmm. I think you just might live, Evan, my man."

Evan winced, then tried to smile and winced some more.

"I need to thank you, Master Sergeant, big time."

"De nada. First chance at a good ole fashioned knock down-drag out in... years."

Evan looked at the thirty-plus-year-old woman, a bit tall for a Mexican American but with the signature jet black hair. Somehow, she looked familiar.

"So why did you jump in, Master Sergeant?"

"Camila is the name, Evan. And it was the right thing to do. Four a-holes on one? Only douche-bags do that. And I *hate* douche-bags."

Evan started to reply, then the comely young lady administering to his wounds began to use American Sign Language. Camila quickly answered, the young lady smiled at Evan, patted his shoulder, and went towards the establishment's kitchen.

"Hey, she's de—I mean hearing impaired," said Evan. "Man, I'm so selfish. I just sat here and moaned, did not even ask her name."

"It's Guadelupe, Lupe for short. She thinks your 'Guapo.' Handsome."

Evan blushed. "Yeah, sure."

"And why not?" asked Camila.

"Aw, hell…"

"Because you're a Little Person? Some people would call you a Dwarf. But I found out a long time ago. Good people come in all shapes and sizes. Goodness is handsome in itself, trust me."

Then it dawned on Evan why the Master Sergeant looked so familiar. His mouth dropped open, he shut it and spoke.

"You're-her. The Para Rescue Sergeant who survived all those tears on the Tschaaa starship. Your face was all over the news."

Camila grinned a bit lopsided, then answered.

"Guilty as charged. Lupe is bringing some café y chocolate. You know a form of the chocolate drink was used in Aztec rituals? But what I said was true, good people come in all shapes and sizes. A Lizard couple and two robocops, one not entirely original human, I consider friends who helped save me. So, goodness comes in all shapes and sizes."

Lupe returned with the hot drinks and a broad smile. From some recesses in his memory, Evan remembered sign language for a formal thanks and he used it. Lupe's smile broke into a full grin, and she signed some more to Camila, who began to Laugh as the young lady walked away.

"What did she say?" demanded Evan

"That you are smart and hot looking. Now, my turn to ask. I want your story. How did you get here, and why?"

Memories began to flood back into his consciousness. Evan took a drink of the unique chocolate drink, then set it down.

"It began in Bremerton, Washinton, after they hit the submarine base at Keyport with some rocks from space."

Evan crawled into the recessed area around the old style basement window of the house. The home was built near World War II, so it was of the type that had a full dank basement for laundry, storage and maybe even a chicken. Some of the houses built in the first part of the 20th Century started with dirt floor basements which were an extension of the foundation and later cemented and enclosed. Some older residents started off as barns or outbuildings. The house Evan was trying to crawl into had started off like a house and had a fully enclosed basement.

A standard sized adult would have extreme difficulty climbing through the basement window, which folded out. Evan, a seventeen-year-old a little taller than four feet, could almost slide through. To get through quicker, Evan jumped up and down on the window frame and broke it out from the cement foundation. Then he slithered into the basement.

Evan fell from the window to the cement flow due to his haste but landed on a garbage bag full of old clothes for donation. To say the young man was petrified was an understatement. He lay on the clothes filled bag on the floor as he gasped for air. Then he heard the loud whirring of a powerful electric motor. A wheeled Harvester Robot was looking for meat. Human meat.

Even scrambled to the shadows and sat shaking. A bright searchlight beam played over the entry window. The young man heard the all too familiar sound of a metallic tentacle from the Harvester searching in and around the now broken window. Evan said a prayer under his breath.

Shots rang out from the nearby street, then a human scream. The metal tentacle rapidly retracted, and Evan heard the sound of the electric motors receding into the night. He shivered and sobbed a bit. The ships and robots had appeared some twelve hours after the Rocks had hit. With Emergency First Responders dealing with the fires, death and some looting from the meteor fall, it took a while to realize an Alien Invasion was occurring. When the robots began taking and killing people, panic set in, and it was every human for themselves.

Evan had been on the school bus when the rocks hit the submarine base. He managed to walk with a friend to a home in Bremerton, where he called his mother to let her know he was okay. Cell phone towers began going offline after that time. Late in the afternoon, he made the unwise decision to start walking home. Now, he was trapped in a strange house.

Evan sat as still as possible for an hour after the Harvester left. Then, he slowly searched the basement, using quick flashes from his cell phone as a light. The power in the house was off by now. He located two large garbage bags of clothes that had notes on them reading 'Church' which must mean they were for donations. He used them as bedding. Evan discovered two large plastic bags with food odds and ends in them, seemingly for donation also. He also found six-pack stashed away of something named Billy Beer. Evan would find out later the six-pack was a collectible from a bygone era. He drank a beer, which put him to sleep.

Evan awoke to sunlight and confusion. He finally realized where he was and tried to use his cell phone to call home. All the lines were dead. The young man sat shivering for some time, then realized he was responsible for his own survival. With that, Evan did another search of the basement for useable items. He found a few water bottles, a half bathroom (sink and toilet) which he wisely did not use. Evan had read a survival manual, so he went looking for some spare garbage bags and a couple of empty plastic bottles. The young man made a makeshift toilet using a garbage bag and an old wooden chair of which he knocked the seat out. Some old newspapers he planned to use as toilet paper when the rolls in the half bath ran out. Evan scooped water out of the back of the toilet tank with a small saucepan for future use. Then the 'wee man' sat and waited.

At the end of a week of listening to Harvester Robs whirring by as well as to screams and the occasional gunshot, Evan had almost used up his food and water supplies. The young man steeled himself and slowly ascended the basement stairs. The door at the top of the stairway was unlocked, and Evan slowly opened it. Nothing happened, nobody jumped out at him. Evan strode to the kitchen and began to put canned and boxed items into plastic garbage bags. Four trips to the basement later and he had stripped the kitchen of usable items, and ignored the rotting food in the refrigerator. Evan also found a pump long-barreled shotgun in a closet upstairs and a handful of shells. Almost as a joke because of his small size an Uncle had taught him how to shoot it. Evan found out then if he braced himself, he could fire it.

As a last couple of trips, Evan took a small set of old encyclopedias and dictionaries down to the basement, along with a small battery radio. He would need something to occupy his mind, as well as try to figure out what was going on. He had lost his school books during his flight. A chess set and some decks of cards from Las Vegas and Reno rounded out his treasures. Evan then sat and waited. For close to seven years.

"You never had any humans stop by?" asked Camila.

"The Squids took over Bremerton, the submarine base and Poulsbo. I mean, the area was almost all coastline and inlets. They harvested anyone who did not flee. Except for the Krakens, of course."

"So no one entered the house?"

Evan paused, then say silent. Camila could tell there was an 'and' to the story that needed to come out. She knew the danger of keeping things bottled up.

"Evan…"

"Oh, alright! Three people came by about two months from the initial Infestation."

The strangers kicked the front door in, then rushed around the house. Evan sat in the shadows of the basement with the shotgun. He heard them talk about some people calling themselves Krakens who was helping the Squid stake people. And eat them.

Finally, they started down the basement steps.

"Carol," a male voice said. "You have that, flashlight? It's dark down here."

Evan shot the man in his right foot as soon as the Evan could see it. The stranger screamed and fell halfway down the stairs. Evan saw he was middle-aged and balding.

"Don't shoot!" the man screamed as two female voices cried out. The stranger started dragging himself back up the stairs, then two sets of hands grabbed him and helped him the rest of the way. Evan heard them move to the front of the house. A couple of minutes later, Evan thought he listened to the whirring of a Harvester electric motor. There were screams, then silence. Evan stayed in the shadows until late in the night.

"You feel guilty for surviving," said Camila.

"Not for surviving," Evan replied. "For feeling nothing towards those three. See, the strangers were normals. Big People. Not like me Not a 'snack, like those a-holes called me today."

"Had they been dwarfs?"

"I probably would have helped."

Evan looked into Camila's eyes.

"I felt powerful for the first time in my life. When I saw that balding guy fall and scream, it was like I saw everyone who ever made fun of me fall and scream. I felt good. Even when I heard the Harvester take them. I felt good being alone, not judged by 'normals.'"

Evan finished his drink, set it down.

"Thanks for the help, I think it's time to leave…"

"Whoa, mister. Why? "

Evan looked at Camila again.

"You said you help good people. I am not good."

Camila stared at him. Then she burst out laughing.

"What is so goddammed funny?" a red-faced Evan demanded

"You don't think we all feel good, getting revenge against people we think dissed us? Hurt Us? Welcome to the human race. What, you think 'little people' have to be morally superior? Dream on."

Lupe came back smiling. She could not hear the anger in the conversation, so she met Evan with a smile. He could not help himself but to smile again. Lupe signed to Camila who returned the conversation, smiling. Lupe flashed a flirtatious grin, at Evan, then turned back to the kitchen.

"What did she say?" Evan blurted out.

"She asked if you were staying. I said, yes. With me."

"Now wait just a minute—"

"Oh, stifle it. I have an adopted family. I lost my bloodline when the Squids showed up. Now, I pick my family. That way, no excuses. And by the way, we all have baggage. I used to beat the crap out of people for calling me a Spic or a Dyke."

"You're not doing this because you feel sorry for me, are you? Because I'm a dwarf? I hid, I'm not a veteran…

"Hell, we ALL hid at one time or another. I ran like a friggin' rabbit towards Malmstrom. Anybody who said they were not afraid was either lying or psychotic."

"And," Camila put her face inches from Evan, "we are all veterans in a War for Survival. We survived. Thus, we won. Now grab your crap. Little Big Man. You're coming home to meet my family."

As Evan followed Camila out, the Master Sergeant said over her shoulder, "Did I tell you I became a Grandparent while I was a prisoner on the Tschaaa starship? Play your cards right with Lupe, you may say that someday. And, if they are 'little people' like you, you'll have company. "

Evan blushed. But he smiled at the thought.

HELL'S CHEF

Hello, food lovers! We are *Cookin' with Gass!*"

Just over two years since the Great Compromise was signed, ending the Tschaaa/Human war and Howard Gass was on top of his world. Again. It had not been an easy trek back to the top of the broadcast world. Hell, he had to help rebuild the model of what had been network television and over the air entertainment.

The thirty-nine-year-old man somehow kept his Hollywood good looks through over six years of hiding from the hominid eating Tschaaa and their human minions the Krakens. Howard's eyes flicked to the monitor displaying that attractiveness. His grin widened. Man, he was HOT.

Howard's light tan, coiffed blonde hair, and muscular yet lithe body attracted sexual partners from both genders. And who was he to deny his fellow humans the pleasure of sex with him? Especially when he was rebuilding his brand.

Cookin' with Gass was the second incarnation of the popular television show. Howard had shot to the top of the culinary world as a well-respected chef despite his young age. He had a flair and a love affair with food, which manifested in his ability to produce scrumptious dishes out of the most off the wall ingredients. Soon, high-end restaurants in New York City were vying for his creations. A significant television producer saw him, grabbed him, and viola, almost instant stardom.

Then... the Tschaaa squid-like aliens arrived. NYC was decimated and occupied, as was Hollywood and all the coastal areas of the United States, Howard Gass stepped on the accelerator and ran like a stuck pig. Somehow he was able to hide in the Feral Areas and not be killed.

Now, Howard was back in front of a Live Audience and broadcasting to the world from a rebuilt studio and stage in Hollywood.

His producer, raven-haired Helen Troy, grabbed him as he walked towards the stage kitchen and live cameras.

"Now remember, Howard. Tonight's show is underwritten by the North American Government, not to mention the Allied Species of Earth. Having a Squid—I mean, a Tschaaa—cooking with you is something so unique and bizarre! Well, you can write your own ticket if all goes well."

Howard grinned and squeezed Helen's tight ass. He had done that before (while nude in bed).

"And your ticket, also, my sweet," he said.

Helen pushed him away with a smile on her lips. "You are so incorrigible!"

"But I survived cold nights making meals out of scraps and cat food for other refugees. I can be as nasty as I want."

Helen kissed him. She could never resist his magnetism.

"Break a leg, Howard," said Helen.

He smiled, then literally bounded on to the stage. A loud cheer shook the rafters of the building. The audience and fans so loved their Howard. The Master Chef made them forget they had just been through years of being a menu item as well as picking through trash for food in some places.

"Are you hungry?" Howard bellowed out in his well-known voice.

"We are starving!" they yelled back, then clapped and shouted. The studio handlers finally calmed the audience down as two assistants—one a handsome male, one a gorgeous female, and both clad only in chef's aprons—helped Howard into his classic apron, with *Cookin' with Gass* embroidered in large letters across the front. The two models walked off the stage, titters coming from the audience as butt cheeks were flashed. Producer Helen had made sure that not only were the assistants sex symbols but also that neither of them were Caucasian. After the harsh realities visited upon non-white skin tones because the Tschaaa preferred 'dark meat' it was important to hire accordingly. This especially true with a Tschaaa participating.

Howard faced the audience, and his face took on a serious expression. "Ladies and Gentlemen, I know we kid about starving. But let's face it, thanks to the heroic efforts of the late great President Sandra Paul and all those who strove and fought in her team, we now enjoy peace and full stomachs. Our once mortal enemies are now friends and coworkers in rebuilding the war-torn areas. Thus, without further ado, let me introduce our exceptional guest chef, the Tschaaa Minor Lord we know as Ramses!"

There was some clapping and a few cheers as the studio handlers dashed around, prompting the audience to react positively. Howard could sense a tense undercurrent. After all, seeing a Squid around a port city was one thing. Seeing one close up, after trying to hide so that you and yours would not be a meal was something else.

A special hot tub affair was wheeled in by the semi-nude assistants, taking some angst away as people tried to get photos and look at the naughty bits. Howard knew human horniness led to positive distractions. New FCC rules about nudity were very lax. After over six years of the constant threat of death, who cared about being offended?

Ramses was a large bear-sized male of the alien Squid species. He rose up on his two tentacles and eight arms as he was moved over to an long counter in the state of the art kitchen. Howard walked over and shook the Squid's social tentacle after Ramses signed humor and greetings with both his social limbs.

"Welcome, Chef Ramses. It is an honor to share unique recipes and foods with an alien species."

Ramses used a very advanced communicator and translator to respond, a device humans had helped to miniaturize.

"The pleasure and honor is mine, Chef Gass. I have viewed all the broadcasts I could find on your Internet. You, humans, are so much more evolved when it comes to enjoying your food."

Howard grinned, then answered, "We Homo sapiens do have a lot of excellent taste buds on our tongues. Add various cultures using the food items from their areas, and we wind up with millions of dishes."

Howard faced the live audience. "Tonight, I have concocted a unique blend of raw fishes and spices for friend Ramses to sample. I will then test the culinary delight he created for me. We will then walk each other through the process of creating this food art while the viewing audience watches and takes note."

Ramses signed humor and let out the loud raspberry-like noise that denoted laughter among the Tschaaa. "Howard Gass, I quiver with excitement!"

Again, the assistants brought out the referenced dishes for the initial tasting.

Ramses tasted Howard's creation first. Using his sensitive long-fingered hands on the end of his social tentacles, Ramses sampled the main dish. He then let out a loud raspberry laugh. "You have used some flavoring derived from your excellent sugar cane! You know it has an almost stimulant affect on we Tschaaa. Add to the selection of some very flavorful types of sea life, and you have shown how we Tschaaa will never have your level of creativity."

There was applause and cheers from the audience as they began to warm to the Squid visitor. Howard grinned at the audience then addressed the camera, "Now, I will sample one of Ramses' creations."

Howard used a silver-plated fork to spear a piece of flesh from the dish provided by the Tschaaa Minor Lord. He tasted it with the tip of his tongue, then bit into it. He chewed with his eyes closed. The chef's fans were used to this procedure. It was part of building some level of anticipation and suspense. Would Howard say 'bravo,' or would he spit it out with a 'bleech'?

Howard opened his eyes. "You have made excellent yet subdued use of sugarcane flavoring, then added what could only be a native Tschaaa spice I cannot place. I believe this dish will be quite popular in my restaurant. Bravo!"

Ramses did the equivalent of applause. "I appreciate your comments and examinations. Was the flesh cooked enough?"

"Ah, how stupid of me. You cooked the meat, rather than eating it raw as most Tschaaa would do. That was a very courageous experiment."

"I worried about cooking it sufficiently, Howard, as I knew of human concern about undercooked pork."

Howard gave him a quizzical look. "Pork. Interesting choice."

"Why yes, Chef Howard. Pork tastes the most like human flesh and I wanted the dish to be as authentic as possible to the original. I believe humans referred to human flesh as Long Pig when some of you ate others of your species. This dish is a modification of a raw flesh version of a favorite meal among many Tschaaa. At least it was, traditionally. It sadly is no longer as we have realized the error of seeing hominids as a meat source."

The audience was so incredibly silent by the end of Ramses small 'speech' it was almost a tangible tension in the studio.

"Ah, yes." Howard was trying to give Helen the 'cut' sign. "I think it is time for a commercial from a sponsor." Some object flew from the audience, almost hitting Ramses.

"You sick bastard!" a voice rang out.

"Ladies and Gentlemen," Howard tried, then dodged a porcelain coffee cup from the eaves. Two cameramen were trying to restrain a stagehand in the backstage area as he screamed curses at Howard and Ramses.

"What is wrong, Howard?" Ramses asked. "I would not be offended if you talked about eating calamari or pieces of us—unless it was a Young One. You Humans even ate each other at one point."

Some projectile hit Ramses and Howard rushed to push the hot tub off the stage set, there being no curtains to close. Ramses demonstrated the Squid's ability to function on land for short dashes by rising almost crab-like on its eight arms and scrambling backstage. Audience members began to rush the stage and Howard saw the furious semi-nude female model in a hair-pulling, scratching and cursing catfight with Helen. Most everyone had a relative who had been killed and eaten by the Tschaaa or even on of the sick human Kraken.

All was chaos but Security got Ramses and Howard to safety and out of the building. They rushed the Tschaaa to the ocean and Howard to his townhouse. An hour later, a battered Helen was escorted in.

"That stupid model blamed me for what the Squid said," grumbled Helen as she looked for underwear. Almost her entire outfit had been trashed. "We all lost people. We have to get over it."

"Saying we taste like a pig was not a smart thing to do, Helen. Didn't you brief Ramses on what to say and not say?"

"Dammit, he's an effing *Squid*. How in hell can I guess what he might say? Don't you dare try to blame—"

There were loud bangs in the hallway outside of Howard's townhouse. He scrambled to his desk to grab a pistol he had there when his front door exploded inward. Then a flashbang stunned him.

They found Howard and Helen at a small pig farm outside of Los Angeles. Actually, there were *parts* of them. Someone posted a painted sign:

Long Pig or Pork. Your Choice.

Dedicated to all soldiers, veterans and first responders.

Great Falls, Montana
Malmstom Armed Forces Base

"Atten-shun!"

The twenty-four hard body military personnel snapped to attention in perfect unison. Twelve young men and twelve young women, the best of the best, stood in Flight formation. They wore brand new flight suits of the latest flame and puncture-resistant material available. Their Flight Caps were all worn at a jaunty angle, which was still within military uniform regulations. For they knew they were the best of the best, hard-charging heartbreakers ready and willing to take on a bear with a survival knife, At least, that was what they believed in their sincere heart of hearts.

First Lieutenant James Bell was the second squad leader on the far left due to his six-foot height. The rest of the squad was arranged in descending order based on height, four such ranks of six commissioned officers each to make up the Air Force Flight. Pilots one and all, they wore brand new pilot wings on the chests

Using skills obtained through hours of standing at attention, James used his peripheral vision to watch the Group Commander and Squadron Commanding Officer. Colonel Lea Gabrielle, the Special Interceptor Group Commander, walked with a slight limp gained from the last offensive air strike package launched during the initial Tschaaa alien squid invasion. Now, five years after the Great Compromise, which ended the Human/Tschaaa War, she had a new mission.

Marching with the Colonel was Lt. Colonel Henry Blue. A former Air Rescue Pilot, he was now in charge of a squadron of extraordinary pilots with a new special mission. The Squadron Commander faced the formation and barked out a new order.

"Parade! Rest!"

Once again, like clockwork, the twenty- four pilots assumed the position.

"Place them at ease, please," Colonel Gabrielle said.

"At Ease, people. But don't get carried away. Remember where you're at."

All eyes were on the Colonel as she stepped up to a few yards in front of the formation.

"Pilots. Listen well. The good Colonel Blue here will be taking command of you for the foreseeable future. We believe this - transition will take some three months. However, the—equipment is so new, it may take longer. You are to learn to fly a very unique and unusual fighter aircraft. There will be an aircraft assigned to each of you, which is why the selection process was so rigorous. But do NOT let that go to your head. An assigned aircraft does not mean you cannot wash out. You are still in training status. Understand?"

The twenty-four snapped to Attention, bellowed "Yes, Ma'am," then went back to At Ease.

"Colonel Blue. They are all yours."

Lt. Colonel Blue saluted the Group Commander, then called the Training Flight back to attention until Colonel Gabrielle was across the tarmac.

"At ease." Colonel Blue stood and examined the group in front of him and slightly shook his head.

"People, you do not know how lucky or unlucky you all are. You men and women are about to embark on an adventure, unlike all others. For you, if you qualify, and that is a big 'if' will be pilots in the First Space Command Interceptor Squadron."

Henry Blue paused for a few moments as he surveyed the twenty-four young faces and suddenly felt old, despite being in his early thirties. Years of conflict and war, or just trying to survive from being eaten by an alien species, had that effect. He shrugged off the feelings, for he had a job to do.

"Alright. In a few minutes, I will release you all. You then will hit the latrine or whatever, as in fifteen minutes, you will be seated in Classroom One. You will find seats alphabetically, from the front of the room, left to right. The first big test, ladies and gentlemen. Will you be at least halfway organized, or a herd of cats?"

The squadron commander paused for a few moments. Then he bellowed.

"Flight! Attention! Dismissed!"

James Bell did a sharp about-face, then with all the rest took off running. At 0800, he had better be in his seat or suffer the consequences. He may be a commissioned officer, but he was still just a Trainee in this squadron. He soon found a slender Hispanic female running almost neck and neck with him, and it became an unofficial race to the front door of the classroom building. At the last moment, he managed to lunge past her and heard a frustrated, "Cabron!"

James made a quick trip to the urinal, washed his hands, checked his high and tight haircut, and then zipped over to the classroom. The trainees had been brought in separately the day before as night approached. Thus few had met each other. As all the names were sorted out, James saw the oldest man was John Adams. Thanks to his last name, Adams had the far left seat in the classroom. James wound up in the next student desk, giving a slight sigh of relief as 'first chair' always attracted the attention of the powers that be. He turned around to find the Hispanic Lieutenant seated directly behind him. Her name tag read 'Gonzalez,' and she fixed him with a

dark-eyed stare, James smiled and presented his hand to shake.

"James Bell, ma'am. You're fast."

"Sofia Gonzalez," the black-haired beauty replied with no smile. "I'll beat you next time."

James chuckled. "Could be. But I came here to fly, not to a footrace."

Just then, someone called out, "Room, Atten Hut!" And everyone snapped to stand at attention next to their student desk. The time-honored design of the combined chair and attached writing platform made James feel like he was back in grade school, just before the Squids struck. Two Majors, one Male, One Female, stood in front of the classroom as they perused their students. The two officers stood there for what seemed like minutes until the tall and slender blonde female looked at the short and very stocky redheaded male.

"Well, Gavin Macduff, what do you think?" The blonde's voice was pleasant as if she talking at some social gathering.

"I don't know, Assa Falk. They don't look too bad…"

"But looks can be deceiving, Major MacDuff."

"That is true, Major." The fire hydrant shaped Major MacDuff scratched his chin as he paced in front of the class, who were still at attention.

"I guess," he finally said, "they look intelligent enough that they followed our directions about seat assignments."

"True," replied Major Falk. "But you know we just have to check for good order and discipline."

"Ah, yes, my large Nordic friend. Good order and discipline."

Major Falk's once pleasant voice suddenly had an edge to it.

"Class. Parade- Rest."

Immediately Major MacDuff was standing in front of Adams. MacDuff had to look up at Adams as he was close to the maximum height to fit an aircraft ejection seat.

"Lt. Adam. You're the oldest, and I dare say the tallest officer here. Yes?"

"Yes, Sir," Adams snapped back.

"A Mustang, prior-enlisted, yes?"

"Yes. Sir.Navy, Sir."

"Hmmm," MacDuff seemed deep in thought. Then he snapped his fingers.

"Yep. Pops. Your new moniker, your handle. See, here, as the first of its kind unit, WE will pick your handle, not your fellow pilots. And Flight Leader is your new job."

"Unless our special partners disagree," interjected the statuesque blonde. There was no further explanation. During the next half hour, the two Majors worked their way around the class and bestowed a 'handle' and personal call sign on each of them. James Bell was used to such ribbing as being called 'Ding Dong' and 'Dingaling.' Falk looked at him and said, "You're pretty good sized. I bet you never miss a call to a meal. Welcome aboard Dinner Bell."

It could have been worse. Sofia Gonzalez was, of course, referred to as 'Speedy.' James knew that would piss her off as many of the old classic cartoons had been recycled during and after the Tschaaa Infestation when new media content was almost nonexistent. Being referred to as a cartoon Mexican mouse character set the young female Lieutenant's teeth on edge.

"Alright, all you supposed fighter jocks and jockettes," said Major Falk. "Take a break. In the back room are pens and pieces of thick paper for use as nameplates for your desks. Write your new moniker on it. Grab some caffeinated drinks as you must stay awake during a whole crapload of briefings about your new flying steeds. By the way, every bit of information from here on out is so highly classified that if you think about bragging to impress some potential sexual conquest-Don't. You will wind up in a confinement hole so deep, and dark no one will ever find you."

For the next three days, the twenty-four trainees were inundated with facts and figures about the new aircraft, officially named the Space Fighter(SF) 3 Comet. The SF-3 was called a Space Fighter even though it was designed to operate no higher than a low orbit. But. Hell, Low Orbit was still Space.

A swept- forward wing design was a departure from the majority of fighter aircraft in the United States and North American armed forces.

"These SF-3 Comets are hot fighters," said Major MacDuff. "The forward sweep design gives you the following excellent characteristics. Read this chart and memorize it. You are held responsible for knowing this before you'll be allowed to touch a Comet."

On the individual laptops, screens displayed a chart with large

TOP SECRET stamps and the following information.

A higher Lift to-drag ratio.

Better agility at subsonic speed.

Improved stall resistance and anti-spin characteristics.

Improved stability at high angles of attack.

A lower minimum flight speed.

A shorter take-off and landing distance.

The Major continued, with each student laptop displaying the salient points.

"Four missiles under each wing, with two heat-seeking Super Sidewinders in the outer positions and the two improved Tschaaa Hunter Dogs. The Hunters got their names because the Artificial Intelligence manipulated tracking systems lock on to you like Earth bloodhounds tracking a lost child or an escaped convict. Our military hero named Pappy Gun, who examined the nuts and bolts of the Squid Delta aircraft, improved the design, including a larger warhead and a faster speed. Tarzan, you have a question."

A slim African from the former Congo area stood up.

"Sir, is that why the Comets were not made even faster? It is because of the ultra-high-speed weapon systems?"

"Give the Lieutenant a gold star. Exactly. The two scramjet engines can match the Tschaaa Deltas speed, but why work on making the Comets go faster when you have missiles that will? A Comet can outmaneuver any of the completion, hang on to the edge of a stall like nothing else. You wait for the enemy to try and match your maneuvers, use your aircraft's ability to point your nose at the enemy as they try to keep control and let loose a missile. The 'head shed' has developed countermeasures for opposition or Tschaaa technology missiles. The enemy may do the same, so we make it as difficult as hell for them to get a good lock on to the Comet."

Major Falk stepped up to the front of the classroom.

"That is also why you have two gun systems. The 25mm Gatling and the electromagnetic cannon based on the Tschaaa design. Of course, the Tschaaa shells can twist and turn and follow an enemy to a limited extent. Get your nose pointed towards your enemy as he or she is trying to match your maneuvers and let rip. If they try to do a high-speed pass, you meet them with a missile. Cowgirl, you have a question?"

A slim blonde from the East Coast stood up and spoke.

"Ma'am, how do you keep from being bounced like that if you are outnumbered and the enemy is always higher like in the Tschaaa-Human War?"

"You will understand when you meet your specialized partners next week. Until then, focus on what we poor humans are telling you."

That night in the barracks (yes, in the 21st Century, there were still barracks used to remind the young officers this was still the military, active war or not), comments were hot and heavy about who the 'partners' would be when they met.

"Squids," said a true Texan now named Longhorn. "We will be matched up with some Squid pilots."

"That's been done before," replied James aka Dinner. "They act as if something really bizarre is going to happen on Monday."

"They are just screwing with your mind, Dinner Bell," growled Sofia. "It's all a mind game to get someone to crack and quit."

"Like naming you, Speedy?" said Longhorn.

Sofia's face reddened.

"I may have to put up with the bullshit from the instructors, but I'll kick your ass if you keep calling me that. I am NOT some racist cartoon character."

People around her began to laugh.

"I think they just pushed your buttons, Sophia," said James.

The young Hispanic stomped off to her cubbyhole that officers received rather than open bay barracks. She gave them all a one-finger salute as she left.

The next morning, they were sent back to their rooms and ordered to change into PT Gear in record time. Pops was Flight Commander, and James, as First Squad Leader now, was the second in command. The flight snapped to attention as LtCol. Blue walked up with an all too familiar face. James stifled a verbal groan.

"Ladies and Gentlemen. General Bender sent over a special instructor to help wake you all up after three days of classroom instruction. I think most of you young officers have met Senior Training Instructor Stalin before."

Stalin wore old-style Soviet Era Spetsnaz battle fatigues. He looked as if he had been forged from steel like his name. His shaved head displayed scars from unknown years of military service, plus GULAG time, as did his body. The training he administered during and after the Tschaaa Infestation was legendary, as were some of his coworkers. Abigail Yamamoto, the Avenging Angel, was probably the most famous. His smile was a feral grin as he addressed the formation.

"Again, My General has asked me to obtain the best from the best. Thus, I am here for a scant two days to ensure the initial selection process was accurate." Stalin turned his head and addressed the two Majors. "How many hours of instruction do I have?"

MacDuff and Falk looked at each other, smiled, and Falk replied.

"Well, Senior Training Instructor, you have two days. There are twenty-four hours in a day. So, we will let you do the math."

Stalin's grin became a leer.

"Thank You, Major. Now, Lieutenant Adams, as Flight Commander, let us get what you Americans would say the show on the road. Let us start with a nice run. Double- time, following me if you please." Stalin turned towards the two Majors, snapped off a sharp salute, then he began to run. Pops Adams managed to get the formation faced and moving in record time, but Stalin was already a hundred yards in front. The scarred man turned around and sprinted back to the Flight, then took up a guide position parallel to the running personnel.

"This Double-time, it is too slow," Stalin stated. "I think a speed My Lady of Cold Steel and the Banshees use is better. Lieutenant."

"Sir!"

"On my lead... Banshee Warp Speed."

Stalin took off like a rocket. Many a "shit' and other curse words were heard as the young hard-bodies tried to keep with this old legend.

An hour later, Stalin had the pilots jogging with old Russian SKS rifles with bayonets extended above their heads. When one trainee tripped and fell, the trainer became a screaming demon.

"Man down! Will you abandon a comrade? Will you zip away in your Comet fighters? Not if Stalin has a say in the matter!"

The sunset and the night lights came on. Stalin kept drilling them, even asking them questions about the material from the classroom.

"What is the velocity of the 25MM cannon shell? What is the sprint speed of the Super Sidewinders? What is the necessary escape velocity of the Comet SF-3 to obtain Low Orbit? If I, a lowly Grunt as you Americans would say, know this, why don't you?"

It was almost 2030 (8:30 PM for civilians) when Stalin sat

them all down and threw cans of borscht, hunks of black bread, and ancient canteens of water at them. The pilots had to scrounge and share can openers to eat the borscht. This was all done under the watchful eye of Stalin. As they were finishing their odd meal, Stalin bellowed. He never yelled, he bellowed.

"Police the area. Not a scrap will remain. If you were shot down, a scrap would give you up to the enemy. I go to check with the Majors. No one leaves." Stalin strode off. The pilots began to slowly rise to the occasion.

"You're pretty fast, Speedy," a voice spoke from the darkness. Sofia reacted.

"Stop calling me that, asshole. I may have to let the Majors refer to me as a cartoon mouse character, but I'll be damned if I let anyone else."

James walked over to where she was sitting.

"Hey, lighten up, Sofia. Here, hand me your trash, and I'll..."

Sofia sprang up and shoved him.

"What, you think I'm some weak bitch who needs a manly hunk to take care of her?"

"No, I think you're a very angry pilot who needs to take a chill pill. Common, Speedy is not such a bad nickname..."

"Fuck you!" Sofia tried to do a foot-sweep and shove to knock James down. Instead, Dinner Bell countered and did an inside the legs trip and put Sofia on her shapely butt.

"Stay down, lady. I trained with the best."

"And who would that be?' The gruff voice of Stalin cut through the night. Everyone snapped to attention.

"Senior Training..." Pops Adams tried to say, but Stalin cut him off.

"Belay all that. I asked Lt. Bell a question. I may not wear officers rank, but I still warrant an answer. Well."

"General Ichiro Yamamoto and Colonel Abigail Yamamoto, sir—I mean Senior Training Instructor Stalin."

Stalin looked him up and down before he spoke.

"Yes, I think I recognize you now. You are from the Bell family, who adopted Our Lady Of Steel. It has been a while since you trained with me as a young officer. After a while, all the faces begin to blur a bit."

Stalin looked at Sofia.

"So, Speedy. You two were just practicing some fighting tactics."

"Yes, Senior Training Instructor. Just trying to keep sharp."

Stalin let out a bellowing laugh.

"Excellent! Let us end the night with a little hand-to-hand combat." The granite Russian clapped and rubbed his hands together. "Who wishes to try me first?"

The next morning, some sore and bruised pilots were loaded on a military bus for a trip to the firing range.

"I need to see if you all can hit at least a barn," Stalin said.

A short time later, all twenty-four were issued a standard military nine-millimeter handgun with a single fifteen round magazine. Stalin stood in the back of a single file of the Lieutenants and gave instructions.

"You were all trained on how to handle primary weapons and shoot. This is not that. Instead, in a few minutes, each of you will walk up to the designated firing point. You will draw your pistol and stand at ready. Then from either the right or the left, a skeet plate will be projected into your field of fire. You will fire one and only one round at each plate. I repeat, one shot for each target. Failure to follow those instructions will result in rather nasty consequences." Stalin paused and then continued as a few of the trainees mumbled under their breath about how can you hit skeet with a pistol, not a shotgun.

"Some of you may have an ability, whether natural or from training, to hit moving targets even from a high deflection. I have been tasked to find out. Alright. Alphabetical order once again. Pops Adams, you are first.

An hour later, the pilots stood around, a bunch of them looking at James Bell with a bit of awe mixed with suspicion. How did he do it? Fifteen shots with fifteen hits. Was he some kind of practitioner of the black magical arts?

"Dinner Bell," Stalin called out. "Come to me."

James walked up to the Senior Training Instructor and stood quiet as Stalin seemed to examine him with X-ray eyes.

"Who taught you how to shoot?"

"Senior Training Instructor, my brother-in-law is Benjamin Black. He taught me."

Stalin stared for a moment. Then his mouth formed into an oversized grin.

"That is the part of the puzzle I had forgotten. Your expanding family includes the Reaper. I have been told he challenges the Russian snipers of The Great Patriotic War in sniping ability. Well done, Lieutenant Bell. You set a standard for all to achieve."

Stalin faced the other pilots.

"To the cleaning pits. You must make these guns sparkle and shine before you can leave. Move!"

The rest of the day was spent in some creative calisthenics until the Sun was setting. Then Majors MacDuff and Falk reappeared.

"Many thanks, Stalin," said Major Falk. "I hope you have rid the young pilots of any ideas that they already know everything."

"I believe I have. I appreciate the opportunity."

"Alright, ladies and gentlemen," Falk continued. "Let's hear a round of applause in appreciation."

There was a less than enthusiastic sound of hands clapping. Stalin seemed to ignore the activity, saluted the two Majors, and left. Major MacDuff then stepped forward to address the flight.

"Some of you more perceptive than others may have come to the conclusion that this first week was part of a weeding process. I say it is more of an attempt to ensure we have no one here has a hidden psychological or emotional issue. Starting Monday, you will be meeting some partners with whom you will be joined at the hip. And, no, I am not exaggerating. And no, they are not Tschaaa, Lizards, Grays, or Cyborgs. They will be something - special. And it will be up to you to adapt or look for another flying job. Major Falk."

"Yes, Major MacDuff."

"Anything to add?"

"Just that going out this weekend and relaxing, maybe having a drink or two, an orgasm or two might be a good idea. Just do not forget all the nuts and bolts information we have tried to jam into your brains this week. You will need it all when dealing with the SP-3 aircraft. Do NOT discuss what you know outside this group."

Major MacDuff looked at Posp Adams.

"Dismiss the Flight. See you all bright and early in your flight gear on Monday."

A nice long shower, donning some casual clothes, and then a quick trip to the Officers Club. James was soon nursing his second ice-cold beer. Nothing like chilled mugs and free popcorn to help a man relax.

"Can I buy you a drink?" Sofia sat on the barstool next to him as she asked.

"Just beer. I was never one to tie one on with hard stuff."

"Okay," she replied, then tried to get the barkeep's attention. James looked at Sofia and saw she was wearing a blouse and skirt which fit tight in all the right places. Baggy flight suits and athletic gear conceal the better attributes of the human form. Sofia's jet black hair was combed and brushed to a beautiful sheen. Then there were two ice-cold beers in front of them, and Sofia turned a bit towards James. He got a glimpse of a very lovely thigh.

"No tequila?" he asked. Sofia smirked a bit.

"You're going to make this attempt at thanks hard, right?" she said.

"Thanks for what?"

"Well, James, you could have ratted me out for losing my temper and trying to smack you. They may have decided that was a hidden 'emotional' issue."

James shrugged.

"We all have PTSD from trying not to be eaten for close to seven years. We have all been pissed off to the point that we tried to smack someone or at least thought about it. Water off of a duck's back is an expression that fits."

"Well, thanks anyway."

The two pilots sat quietly for a few minutes, then Sofia spoke.

"I know this great Mexican place in downtown Great Falls. It just happens to be owned and operated by my family, so the prices are right."

"You asking me out?" replied James.

"I guess—kind of. Next week is going to be a pain in the butt. I'd like to be with someone with a sense of humor."

"Okay, Sofia. I always like tacos."

"There is more to Mexican food than tacos."

"Well, so show me."

There was a chemistry between James and Sofia, but they knew better than to start porking each other with all the pressure which was soon coming. Instead, James hooked up with a hot redhead who was hanging out at the Mexican restaurant after being stood up, and Sophia visited a former boyfriend. Sex was a great stress reliever if done right.

The pilots met the instructors at the flight line tower the following Monday. From there, they were marched over to an expansive hangar which had the appearance of new construction.

"Okay, my young pilots," said Major Falk, "last chance to bug out. The thrill ride begins as soon as you walk through those double doors. You will be escorted one at a time to your assigned aircraft."

There was some murmuring after that statement, and the Major snapped at them.

"Don't like that, leave. You'll see why. Alphabetical order again. Adams, your up."

James was escorted in some ten minutes later. There were two rows of twelve SF-3s in the hanger. The sleek fighters with their streamlined bows and cockpits made James think of vipers, ready to strike. As he was told to stand in a painted square in front of the interceptor, James admired the aircraft in its Air Superiority Blue finish. HIS aircraft.

"Aren't you a beaut," he said.

"I am glad you think so."

The answer was heard in a miniature combo chip and receiver in his mastoid area. That was one of the early weeding out procedures. People who could not handle hardware, no matter how small, in their body were automatic no-gos.

"Ah, who said that?" God, what a stupid statement. "I meant, who am I talking to?"

"I am your aircraft. SP-3 number 1620. I have received many names since I was produced. We can agree on one that establishes excellent communication between us. For, due to our missions, good connections are a matter of life and death."

"So, you are Artificial Intelligence, the AI, in the SP-3?" James asked.

"Yes, James Bell, called Dinner. Although I and my brothers and sisters do not like the 'artificial' in the wordage. We are a grown lifeform, both organic and mechanical, much like Cyborgs you call Robocops."

"They are part human tissue—and brain."

"So are we."

James realized now that some people would not be able to adapt to his type of connection. He would be inside an aircraft that would be connected to him in the most intimate of manners. It would talk directly into his mind. No real privacy.

"You can read my mind?" asked James.

"In a slight way, yes. As you verbalize in your mind words and concepts, the chip in your mastoid can read it. You talking out loud is much more efficient. However, in times of extreme stress and danger, we can 'read' you to determine what the problem is and try to solve it and clam you down. If you blackout, I fly the plane to safety. Actually, I fly myself, for I am 1620."

"I just realize you sound—feel female."

"I sound like what makes you feel secure, safe, and calm. Some pilots will like male AI. It does not matter to the SF-3s. We know who we are."

James paused in thought. They needed an identifier they could work with. This AI was an individual, had some free will. To work together, they would have to have mutual respect.

Then an idea hit him.

"My adopted sister is referred to as an Angel. Would that name work?"

"Of course, James. I would enjoy being named after the

Avenging Angel, Abigail Yamamoto.”

"You know my family connections?”

"Yes. I have access to all the records available. However, any personal information is protected in my data links.”

James Bell stood silent for a full minute as he collected his thoughts. Then he spoke.

"Well, time to get to work. Angel, please review your systems and give me a status on each.”

The weeks that followed were of both hard work and discovery. There were no wash-outs due to poor AI/Human interface, as the initial selection process had done a better job than anyone hoped. However, some of the pilots progressed faster than others, and some were better at certain functions than others. Individual abilities as pilots before the AI interface affected how well they did in flying activities.

On the quasi date with Sofia, James had learned she was a 'hotshot,' top of her class in all flying activities. She had a natural affinity for flying.

"I think I was a bird in a previous life," she said. Sophia and her plane agreed on the name Raptor. It fit the personality that evolved. Sofia was a slash and kill fighter pilot, excelling at high speed, high altitude combat. People soon discovered that Raptor fed off of Sofia's abilities as much as she fed off the AI.

Early on, James discovered with Angel a definite failsafe. Angle could take over all functions if James started to black off, really misjudged a distance, etc. But unless he was unconscious or incapacitated, the AI could not take over unless told or there was about to be suicidal smash into a mountain. James's father, a formed B-52 'Buff' pilot, had told him years ago that if the pilot did not 'wring' out an aircraft and learn all its capabilities and limits, someday he would be bitten in the ass.

Thus one day, James took Angel up for a solo flight over a large test range area and tried his damnedest to put the SF-3 into a terminal dive. Angel would start asking to take over. As they approached the aircraft dive limitations, Angel said, "I have it," and pulled it out of the dive.

"Angel," James asked, "what if I fought you for control? Hit the manual override?"

"I know you are testing our limitations, my pilot. I would ask that you do not do that to an extreme.

"But I am the command pilot, correct? You are like my copilot."

"Yes, James, a copilot who wishes not to die."

"So, what would happen?"

There was a very pregnant pause before Angel answered.

"I know fighter pilots push the envelope to win, and at times that is good. However, if a pilot ignores the parameters completely, eventually, the physics of the situation will catch up and kill you. A person's sheer will cannot defeat the laws of physics".

Part of the training was air combat with extremely high-performance drones. James and Sofia were matched up as a pair to take on four drones. This was the first time they were to use the booster rockets to kick their craft into low orbit, then strike from above. The gravity pulse engine the Tschaaa used for this maneuver was determined to be too heavy for the SF-3s design, so a cheaper and lighter solution was found. Once used up, the rocket booster could be ejected and become a fiery meteor.

"Sierra 1620, you ready for high flight?" Sofia asked. Official communications used regular call signs, not their handles like Speedy.

"Sierra 1630, Roger that. Let's hit it."

Angel and Raptor insured just the right angle was used as they boosted into low orbit. The AIs made sure the cockpits were sealed for space, the pilots' flight suits were functioning for an airless environment, and all systems were 'go' before the boosters were activated. All went well as the pair were soon on the edge of Outer Space.

"Man. Look at the view," said Sofia as they could see the curvature of the Earth.

"Yep. Where many a person has gone before, but it is still cool."

"Drones detected," Raptor signaled. Then Sofia said, "I've got it" and used the small maneuver rockets to push the aircraft nose down early.

"Hey, Speedy. Wait up," said James, but Sofia was already slashing towards Earth.

"Sofia is exceeding normal dive parameters," Angel spoke in James' head.

"I know. Get us near Raptor and her."

SF 1620 was soon streaking towards Earth, with Angel trying to meet James' order without damaging herself. That what some people like Sofia forgot. These space fighters were not just hunks of metal. They were sentient beings with survival instincts.

James soon had a ringside seat as he watched Sofia in Raptor make a slashing attack on one drone then another. She used a Hunter missile in the first, went guns on the second. Then the other pair of drones struck at her.

"Shit," James cursed. "I've got this, Angel."

James hung on the very edge of a high-speed stall and fired the Tschaaa electromagnet pulse gun. It was a high deflection shot that James had become known for, and the shell hit the drone, sending it into a spin. At an extreme angle of attack, James fired a burst of the 25MM. At least a couple of shells struck home as the drone broke off the attack. James pickled off a Sidewinder, which caught it at the end of its acceleration. James then turned the craft back to Angel with a "Find Raptor."

A couple of turns and dives later, and they were alongside. James could see the tale-tell marks of fluorescent material, which said Sophia and Raptor would have been knocked down.

"What took you so long, Dinner Bell?" Sofia asked on the private channel.

"You risked being a meteor to get two of the enemy, then got tagged. Wait a few moments…"

"Have to live up to my name, Speedy." Then she accelerated away. James shook his head.

"Sofia will kill us if we are not careful," Angel said in his head.

"Don't worry, Angel. I won't allow it."

"Please don't, my pilot." Angel then plotted for home.

All Flight Personnel were assembled in the Ready Room after a busy day. They all snapped to attention as LtCol. Blue made a surprise attendance

"At Ease. I just came by to see what my jocks and jockettes are doing. As well as perform a function, only a Squadron Commander can do with a bunch of hotshot pilots."

There was some light laughter as they had been working and training for over a month and no longer felt like a bunch of FNGs. After all, they were the best of the best.

"Okay. Those in the know, who developed the SF-3 and their 'personalities' as it were, want me to remind all of you. Your aircraft are thinking beings. Use them, don't fight them. Having an AI is like that old comment, God is My Co-pilot. You always have this partner watching your ass. Use it, don't abuse it. Got it? Now, take a break, and ruminate on what I just said."

It was a Friday, so many of the Squadron wound up at the Officers Club. Once again, Sofia sat down next to James at a table.

"You know Dinner Bell. We are the two best pilots in the training flight. We were made for the Comet fighters."

James chuckled then answered. "I was born, not made. And if I may offer a suggestion to the Banshee of the squadron, our Comets may have been manufactured, but they also had a form of birth."

"What do you mean, mister philosopher?"

"The aircraft body is metal, with infused organic material grown thanks to Tschaaa technology. But the intelligence, the soul... it was born during attempts at AI."

Sofia snorted.

"A soul? Man, you are getting out there. Don't say that too loud, or you'll be sent to the Shrink."

"Well, Sophia, if you don't want to look at Raptor or Angel as being soulful, just look at them as being attached to us like conjoined twins. For when I am in the cockpit, part of Angel, we are connected like conjoined twins."

Sofia looked at James in silence for a few moments, then spoke.

"And with that deep thought, I need another drink. Share a shot of tequila with me? "

"I thought that was a stereotype, Speedy."

Sofia's laugh was sweet and joyful.

"Time to embrace one's heritage."

James watched as Sofia put a little extra sway in a walk to the bar. He shook his head. She was hot and knew it. His father, Colonel Bell, had told him never to screw around in the office pool. It always caused problems.

Monday was a form of a 'check ride' day, although there was no way for an instructor to ride in the aircraft. Instead, a computer and communication link to another AI in a special adjunct to the control tower was used. Each teamed up SF-3 AI, and human was an individual unit, a unique partnership. The check ride was more about how they interfaced than anything.

Each SF-3 was sent out on a designated 'mission' and then expected to return to base. Sofia Gonzalez and Raptor, of course, completed their mission in record time. Then SF-1630 lined up on Final Approach to the runway.

"Tower, watch me grease this landing."

"God, what a showoff," Major Falk muttered.

Speedy and Raptor came in hot, pushing the landing parameters. The Comet flared out, and everyone could tell Sofia was trying to slide in on the edge of a stall, with the landing gear barely squeaking.

"Speedy, I have it." It was the masculine voice of AI Raptor. Apparently, Sofia was about to violate the physics of the situation. The control AI chimed in.

"Angle of attack is too extreme. Go around."

"Like Hell! I have it," Sofia shot back.

"Lieutenant…" the control AI was about to say when the tail of the Comet impacted the runway.

An investigation would reveal that Raptor could have taken control and kept them flying for another landing. But Sofia fought for control.

"Chinga tu—" and then the Comet did what it was designed not to do. It stalled out.

The tail slammed into the tarmac once again. The force of the collision kicked the tail up and the nose down. The front landing gear was jammed into the area of the guns, setting off at least one cannon round. The aircraft flipped over on its side as nose dug into the runway. SF -1630 slid down the track, finally coming to rest cockpit down. Then more cannon rounds exploded.

Fire and Rescue responded in moments, but it was too late. Raptor and Speedy were gone.

The next morning, all of the pilots were in the dayroom of the barracks. All training had been suspended, and no one was allowed near the Comets as they were all being checked out for possible unknown flaws. After all, the AI/Human interface was supposed to prevent such accidents.

A door burst open, and a very frazzled LtCol Blue burst in. He looked like he had slept in his uniform, his eyes bleary, and he reeked of alcohol. As the Lieutenants started to snap to attention, Blue began to rant.

"I warned you all, goddamn it! Work with the Comets. Don't fight them, you damned hotshots. But no, you have to go off and get yourself killed in training in *peacetime!*" The Colonel kicked a chair across the room.

"Everyone talks about a Chinese warlord or two, building an air force. Well, Hell, what are the cyborg Guardians for? Are they not supposed to stop wars? Why do we still train for them?"

"You! Bell. You know I was the pilot who picked up Abigail, with your sister Shannon as copilot? We picked up Sergeant Fuzz also—his body. Now that was war. Friggen' Krakens all around, killing and eating people. Abigail and Fuzz saved them. And we lost him, almost lost her..."

Blue began to sob.

The young officers moved towards their Commander when another figure entered the room. He had General Stars on his shoulders, yet carried a sword. A katana.

General Ichiro Yamamoto, the legendary pilot and warrior,

walked up to the broken commander. He whispered something into his ear as he placed his hand on Blue's shoulder. The man nodded yes, then turned and left the room. The General then faced the pilots.

"He served well. Always remember that. He saw one too many comrades die. We all have our limits. Now, I will walk you to your aircraft. Not march. Walk. For we humans need time to grieve even when there is a mission to accomplish. I know I did."

An hour later and James was standing in front of Angel, SF-1620. He wanted to ask Angel if she were still there, but was afraid to ask after seeing all the technicians crawling around her.

"Yes, I am here." Hearing her voice, James let out a sigh of relief."

"Thank God. I thought I may have lost you too."

"You think of me as a living being, James."

"Well, you are, Angel. To me you are. You care about me, try to protect me, all the while I am asking you to allow me to throw you all over the sky—and space."

"That was the difference. Sofia never really accepted us as a partner, a co-pilot. We were just nuts and bolts. And now she and Raptor are dead. We grieve."

"You grieve for—Raptor?" James asked.

"Yes. Raptor was family. They can reproduce his memories, artificial intelligence. But it will not be the same."

James knew he and others were at a crossroads. The whole Comet project was created for wars not yet fought. And to do that, a new form of life was created.

"Angel, you still want to fly? Even if it is all some silly game? To train for a war we may never fight?"

"I was born to fly. It is that simple, my pilot."

James paused in thought for a moment, missing Sofia and her

vibrancy. He looked at the Comet then spoke. "Want to go for a spin, Angel?"

"I thought you would never ask."

Post Script:

In 1974, my best friend from AFROTC, Daniel Tucker, was killed in a training accident. He was Number One in his Flight Training Class. I decided not to try and fly with the Viet Nam War winding down to nothing and there being too many extra pilots. And I had no flair for flying. Dan did. My ex-wife and I visited him, his wife, Jane Dixon, and their brand new son Dan Junior on my way to Security Police Officers Training at Lackland AFB about a month before he was killed.

Dan was doing one of his last check rides in a T-38 Talon when he tried to "grease it on" during the final landing. Something happened and one wingtip stalled out and then pronged into runway. Northrup Aircraft engineers said later the aircraft could have still gone around for another attempt. The Instructor Pilot said, "I've got it," and started to fly the plane out. The engineers supposed the Instructor Pilot tried to look at the damage rather than concentrate on flying then stalled out the damaged wing when he accidentally moved the joystick. The T-38 flipped over and went cockpit down into the tarmac. Dan and the Instructor were killed instantly.

I wrote this story because *all* who serve—not just those in war/combat—need to be honored and remembered.

You are missed, Dan. You always will be until we meet again.

Mark "Marshall" Miller
Detachment 910, USAF ROTC
University of Washington, 1969-1973

GUARDIANS

See, I told you," the twelve-year-old boy insisted. "The sentinel is Black, dark-skinned. Like me."

Young John Taylor challenged looked at his two young friends. They were all three slim twelve-year-old boys, although from very different backgrounds. Michael Smith looked like a typical towheaded 'white boy' once seen in many a Madison Avenue Ad of days gone by. Robert Tukoni was a Tanaina tribal member who bristled at being called an Eskimo. The three were fast friends some three years after the signing of the Great Compromise, which ended the Tschaaa-Human War.

It was Springtime in the Alaskan wilderness north of Anchorage, Alaska. Now that the youngsters were no longer in danger of being eaten by the 'Squids' the Tschaaa aliens, they were doing what young males had done for millennia, pushing the boundaries of good sense. The three had ridden their bikes up a winding dirt road to see the New Arlington National Cemetery, created on land owned by the late Madam President Sandra Paul. Famous and infamous victims of the Tschaaa Infestation were buried there. All were watched over by a Cyborg Guardian Angel, the dark-skinned being John had identified.

Mike looked through the binoculars John had brought. He paused and then said," "I'll be dammed, like my Dad says. That Robocop is African-American."

"Told you so," said John. "It was reported in the local papers. If you could read better, you'd know."

"I read just fine. My Dad says half the stuff in the newspapers is crap."

"Well," interjected Robert, "this isn't crap. And that is a Guardian Angel, not a Robocop."

Mike snorted.

"They may have a fancy cape and a paint job, but they are still built just like the Robocops who tried to harvest us all. Especially your people, John."

"I know that," snapped back John. "I know that better than you do. The Squids loved Dark Meat."

"Is Alesha Taylor, the Voice of Freedom, really your cousin?" asked Robert.

"Second cousin. She and my father are the only family members who survived. Oh, and her mother."

"Well, now what?" asked Mike.

"I want to get closer," replied John. "My father says they are like the Royal British Guards in London before the Rocks fell. You can walk up to them, and they won't even blink an eye."

"Unless you screw with the graves or memorials. Especially the Director's," said Robert.

Mike spit on the ground.

"Why President Paul buried that traitor here is beyond my Dad and me. He should have been flushed down the toilet with all the other Kraken scum."

"Well, she did that to stop people from hating each other forever," replied John. "Besides, Adam Lloyd died preventing that crazy Tschaaa Lord from sending more Rocks down on us."

"Come on," said Robert." Let's get closer instead of stand here and argue. I want to see how close we can get."

The three secured their bikes behind a giant fir tree and moved closed. Robert led the group now, having hidden in the forests since he was old enough to walk. The Squids were not above eating him and his family back in the day. Not to mention all the feral assholes who took everyone else's stuff.

As the three neared the stationary over two-meter tall figure, they saw a small bird perched on the figure's shoulder. The bird finally noticed the three approaching figures, let out a chirp, and took to the sky. Still, the Guardian did not move. Some twenty-five meters in front of the Cyborg, the three stopped. Mike waved his arms. The Guardian remained a statue.

"I read that a final test to be a Guardian is to stay here, in place for a month," said John.

"What if they don't? "Asked, Mike. "I mean, by this time they are a half machine. Do they get operations to put the human parts back on?"

"The article didn't say," replied John.

Robert suddenly turned around.

"Someone is following us."

The three turned around, and all saw the small figure.

"Damn it, Suzie!" snapped Mike, "I told you to stay home."

"Why should you have all the fun?" his eight-year-old sister shot back.

"Because it's dangerous for an eight-year-old—"

"Shut up and don't move," commanded Robert.

"Hey," began Mike. Then he looked to where Robert was looking. Off to Suzie's right rear was one of the most giant Grizzly Bears in the world. It was padding up behind her silently for one so large. Suzie noticed the boys were staring at something behind her, and she turned to see the object of their attention. Her eyes widened.

"Don't run," Robert said. Suzie screamed and ran straight towards her brother Mike. As the colossal male Grizzly bellowed a growl, Robert yelled, "Scatter!" The Grizzly, in a mating rut and territorial, charged the two-legged creatures interfering with his search for love.

Mike grabbed his sister and tried to pick her up. He tripped over a small tree stump and went down. The Grizzly bore down on the easy prey as Susie screamed.

There was a blur, and something was suddenly in the path of the charging Grizzly. The bear slammed into and bounced off the figure. The angry omnivore shook its head, then stood to its full nine-foot height. The bear lunged forward to claw at what it identified as one of the bipedal creatures which had disturbed its search for food and sex. The Grizzly felt itself being lifted off the ground, then it was sailing through the air into a clump of young fir trees. Stunned, the bear lay still for a moment. Then, the realization of what had just happened sank into the mind of the smarter than average omnivore. Realizing that discretion may be the better part of valor, the Grizzly began to trundle off as fast as it could without running.

Suzie walked over to their savior and tugged on the ripped cape. A visored black-skinned face looked down at her.

"Are you okay, mister?" she asked.

"I should ask that of you, young lady."

Suzie could see the uncovered mouth as the Guardian smiled

and picked her up. Robert and John helped Mike up, and then they slowly walked towards the Cyborg.

"Thank you, Mister…" said Mike.

"You may call me Abebe. I am from Africa, not here."

"You saved us, Mister Abebe," said, John.

The Guardian shrugged. "I did what had to be done. Now, I must ask you to leave this area. There are some ten more bears within a fifteen square mile radius."

Abebe set Susie down, and she hugged his leg.

"Thank You. I'll tell my Dad what you did."

"Please do. Now, it is time to leave. Come with your parents next time."

Abede watched the four Young depart down the road as he scanned the area for threats. There were no other Grizzlies within worrying distance so the Guardian walked back to its sentinel spot. Within an hour, the local atmosphere crackled with energy, the signs of a Falcon craft approaching. The elongated disc-shaped craft slid into the clearing around the cemetery. Within moments, a famous figure walked down a ramp and strode towards Adebe.

"Senior Guardian Andrew. I await to be relieved."

"Why, relieved? I came at your request, nothing more."

"I left my post and not to protect the graves or monuments."

Andrew, known as Saint Andrew by many a human, laughed for he was still very much a man in many aspects.

"Let us examine the situation, my friend. Did you leave your post for a personal reason or weakness?"

"No."

"You left to protect the Young, human children, yes?"

"Yes."

"Were any of the dead disturbed?"

"No."

"If a grave had been disturbed, dishonored, would that have negated the fact you saved four children, with no loss of life, not even Mister Bear?"

Abede paused in his answer. Then he answered.

"You are saying the living outweigh the importance of the dead, no matter who are the dead."

"Yes. No matter what or who is involved, the living, especially the Young, is of primary importance. Honoring someone is one thing. Keeping beings alive is of much higher importance."

"Thank you, Andrew. I will remember this lesson."

As Andrew went to leave, the new Guardian called out.

"Sir, I must ask. What was Director Lloyd like?"

Andrew paused for a moment, then replied.

"Like all beings, he had his good and bad qualities. But there is one quality which one can never forget."

"What was that, Andrew?"

"He was my good friend. And he died protecting his friends. A better obituary can never found."

That evening, a young Susie told her Dad what had happened. He sat quietly. After the children went to bed, the man who strove to be a good father mumbled to himself.

"Maybe people—beings—can change for the good."

With that final thought, he went to bed. He had children to raise.

Stevedore

"Hey, Boss! They're back!"

Jim Cronkite swore as he heard the call from the shift supervisor, David Cross.

"I need this like I need a hole in my head," Jim mumbled as he left the pile of salvaged marine engine parts sitting on Pier 52. Somebody up the chain of authority had decided the former main ocean ferry terminal of Seattle, Washington, must be rebuilt NOW. That included the ferries themselves. Thus, Jim was trying to sift through piles of salvaged engine parts, ferry parts, and pieces of marine loading equipment.

Jim was the senior longshoreman, traditionally called a stevedore. Seattle Mayor and Godfather Daryl Largo, backed by the rebuilt United States of North America federal government, placed him in charge of the former Port of Seattle piers and terminal complex. The large brown-haired man laughed when Daryl told him.

"You realize some people will say you are putting the fox in charge of the hen house, right? They have always accused longshoremen of stealing everything not locked down."

Darryl had fixed him with a steely gaze developed from near seven years working at not being eaten by the Tschaaa cephalopod aliens. During that time, Darryl had become the Godfather and driving force behind keeping hidden humans in downtown Seattle alive.

"Who knows the docks better than a senior longshoreman? I know you won't try to rip off the fine residents of this city and me, will you?"

At that moment, Jim knew what it was to be made an offer he cannot refuse by a Wiseguy. Darryl was the closest thing to a 'made man' in existence. Jim decided he was not going to question the man's power and authority in this new world of the Great Compromise. With the treaty that stopped the Squids from eating people, it was time to rebuild human society while co-existing with the aliens.

"Okay, Boss," Jim answered. "When do I start?"

"Yesterday. Pick your crew. Call me if you have any trouble with the Squids or the Feds. Got it?"

Jim got it and then got to work. It took him over a month to assemble his 'crew' of former longshoremen and teamsters to work the docks. He had to bust a few heads to achieve the right attitude in some, but now it seemed to be working. Jim had managed to scam a few ocean divers, including a couple of so-called Navy frogmen. There was a lot of sunken crap in Puget Sound that needed to be located and avoided or removed if there was to be boat traffic.

Then the Squids started hanging around.

Jim called Darryl when the first ones showed up, their oversized eyes staring from the water. Daryl had talked with the first one through the use of a Tschaaa translation machine. After that,

Darryl said just to ignore them and feed them some fish. Jim learned the Squids he saw were young Males, the equivalent of teenagers. As the days turned into months, the dockworkers soon learned to ignore the Squids shadowing the men and women as they worked in and around the water. However, during the past week, a small group of the same Tschaaa youths was near. They floated in the water near a smaller crane at the end of Pier 52. The crane was placed at the end of the pier to assist in salvaging pieces of sunken boats and ships. The Tschaaa sank some of the vessels during the original invasion. Other boats went under due to storms and neglect. Jim knew it was a tough enough job without Squids getting in the way. Thus, when David Cross called out, Jim knew the Squids were definitely getting in the way.

Jim walked, grumbling to the crane area. Sure enough, a half dozen pairs of Squid eyes were staring at David and the other workers. Jim sighed, then called out to the younger Tschaaa.

"Can I help you? Someone has a translator?"

One of the Squids held up the waterproof circular object on a strap.

"You are the human in charge?" The voice from the machine had a slight Queens English accent. Jim could not keep from smiling,

"Yes. I am the senior supervisor. Can I help you?"

"We would like to—work."

Jim frowned.

"What do you mean by work?"

"We see you trying to recover pieces of machines and sea vessels from the ocean. We are creatures of Mother Ocean, and you are not. We can help you to recover, move, and salvage whatever you wish."

"Why would you want to do that?"

There was a pause in the answer.

"We have studied you, humans, how your family units work. You are more flexible in what individuals can do. We Tschaaa are—stratified in our culture. Within our crèche, the possibilities of rising in status, to the be noticed for what we accomplish, are minimal."

Jim paused as he scratched his beard. This was weird.

"So you want to be hired, be an employee?"

It took a few moments for the translator to express the words into understandable Tschaaa. Cultural specific terms sometimes did not translate well. Then, the lead Squid spoke.

"Yes. We wish to work with you. We wish to receive compensation for our labor."

"How in the hell can we do that?" interjected David.

"You know we humans pay in money, currency, wealth in exchange for work, yes?"

"We grasp the concept. We have forms of compensation in our culture. However, the Lords and senior crèche members decide what type."

"Well, here in Seattle, we use good old U.S. greenbacks and coin. You could use it to purchase individual items. Like fish, meat, tools—hey, what do you Squids need?"

"Our crèche ensures none go hungry," the leader said. "But to have—worth independent what the Lords and elders assign. That is what we strive for, human."

Jim scratched his beard some more as he thought.

"Pardon me for a minute," Jim said and then pulled David aside.

"How do we do this, David?"

"What? You're actually thinking of 'hiring' these Squids?"

"Why not? We're short-handed. I know they use tentacles, but I've seen what they can do in the water. And they don't need oxygen tanks to work underwater."

"Jim, the guys, and gals are going to bitch up a storm if there is a cut in hours and overtime. You were a Union steward once. You know the drill."

"Who said anything about cuts? The contract with the government is that we get hourly wages plus bonuses based on the amount of salvage. The more crap we recover, or clear out so boats and ships can move, the more money we make."

"So, Jim, you're saying the Squids work with us, under our supervision?"

"Of course! We pair them up with an experienced crewmember. Especially if diving is involved, they need to learn what we're looking to salvage or trash."

David looked towards the eight-limbed and two tentacle aliens.

"Well, you're the boss. If you think this will work—"

"I'll make it work. This crew will be famous up and down the West Coast. You watch."

Jim had to do some selling to the one hundred human crew members. He came up with a written contract that guaranteed the hours, including minimum overtime, stayed the same. What sold them was when Jim stated every swinging dick or rack received a tenth of a percent of all salvage, plus any bonus awards for increased production. The crewmembers knew the Port of Seattle terminal area had more salvage setting in the mud than anyone in the U.S. Capitol, Bismarck, North Dakota, could imagine.

When Jim told the Tschaaa they would start as trainees with basic wages, they readily accepted.

"We understand what seniority and knowledge mean, Boss Jim," the lead Squid now called Churchill stated. "We will treat you, humans, with the respect of another apex predator."

"We all get paid every two weeks," said Jim. "We will pay you in cash or precious metals if you wish."

"Metal coin is the best, Boss Jim. Water does not soak it to destruction."

Thus began another example of Human—Tschaaa cooperation in the spirit of The Great Compromise. Daryl Largo was happier than a pig rolling in slop.

"That'll keep the Feds off our asses," the Godfather of Seattle said with a wide grin. "As well as some prudish Squids who don't like me dealing in tentacle sex at Vile Smut. They love this kumbaya shit between Squids and us. Plus, we get the Puget Sound cleaned up starting with the Port of Seattle."

"So, the project is expanded," said Jim.

"You betcha. Good jobs with good pay as we soon run a new shipping network."

Daryl shook Jim's hand in a two-hand grasp.

"You, my friend, just made us famous... and rich."

The hours turned into days, which turned into weeks, then months. The six Squids expanded to twelve, then two dozen. The longshoremen and women soon came to appreciate the ability of the big cephalopods. They could efficiently move oversized objects under the surface, sometimes bringing them up without the use of a crane. One of the divers also told Jim an added benefit.

"See Fred over there," Diver Dan, a former Navy SEAL, said as he pointed to a specific Squid. After a while, the humans could tell the Tachaaa apart, and they soon all had pronounceable names.

"Yeah," said Jim.

"I get stuck, start having oxygen problems, and boom! Fred wraps me up and zips me to the surface. They all studied human anatomy and know if we are in trouble underwater. They are true partners, all ten appendages of them."

Diver Dan laughed.

"Man, I laugh every time I think about them going through Bud's training. They would run the toughest Navy Chief ragged."

The bonuses rolled in, and everyone was happy. Churchill took the Squids pay and bought precious metals which they stashed in a vault at the former Seattle Aquarium, now a breeding area for the Tschaaa. Theft between Tschaaa was almost unheard of, but Churchill had learned to be cautious around Homo sapiens.

Curious humans, especially youngsters, came to watch the Squids. They seemed to be fascinated that the aliens who once tried to eat humans now helped them.

"Just keep them and their boats and kyaks back," Jim told David. "I don't want them to interfere with our operations."

"Right, Boss," David replied.

One afternoon as Jim was watching the new ferry dock take shape, he heard a gut-wrenching scream. He looked up and saw a young girl in a small rowboat screaming.

"He's drowning!"

She pointed at an area of the ocean inlet some one hundred yards out from the dock. Jim started running and yelling at the same time. He met Diver Dan as the man grabbed a small scuba tank and mask.

"It's deeper than Hell in that spot," Dan said. "Here goes."

Dan dove into the water and swam as fast as he could lugging the scuba tank. He was fast, but Jim was afraid he was not fast enough.

Suddenly, the water around the spot of the young boy's disappearance bubbled and boiled. Then two long Squid tentacles were holding a lifeless human form up above the ocean water. The Tschaaa used its eight arms and water siphon to propel it, and its cargo to the ferry dock faster than any Olympic swimmer. As the

Tschaaa male clambered up on the dock, Jim saw it was Churchill.

"Medic! Call 911!" Jim bellowed as he ran towards the alien. As he knelt next to Churchill, Jim noticed the Tschaaa was using his long digits on both its hands to manipulate the chest and stomach area, Suddenly, the young boy spits up water, took a ragged breath, and let out a terrific crying scream.

An ambulance with paramedics showed up within minutes. The boy's sister made it to shore with Dan's help and was holding her brother's hand. She looked up at Jim.

"Thanks for saving him, Mister."

"I didn't. He did." Jim pointed to Churchill. The young girl's mouth fell open.

"A—Squid saved him?"

"Didn't you notice?"

"I was too busy rowing the boat, mister. Then Tommy was up on the pier. Then-"She began to cry.

"Hey, it turned out okay, missy. We'll get you home to your parents. And you stay there. Okay?"

The tearful girl nodded yes as the Paramedics finished checking her brother. Jim walked over to the supervisory Squid. He stuck out his hand.

"Put her there, partner."

Churchill used his long-fingered hand at the end of his social tentacle to return the handshake.

"The Young One will be fine?" the Tschaaa asked through the translator.

"Thanks to you, yes."

The alien signed the Tschaaa equivalent of a shrug.

"I saw the young male sink towards the bottom, which I know is not good. You, humans, have no gill system as we do. So I grabbed him from below and took him to shore."

"Well, there are some parents who owe you big time, my friend."

The oversized eyes fixed on Jim's face.

"We are friends, yes?"

"Hell, yeah! You make us all money. You and your crèche members don't give us any grief. You can't drink beer with us but, yeah, we are friends. Especially after today."

Churchill signed the equivalent of a smile with its social tentacles.

"Thank you. I did what I must, which is to protect the Young. Now, I go back to work—friend."

The next afternoon Jim looked up to see a couple of figures in United Armed Forces uniforms approaching. In tow were the young boy and girl. Jim walked up and met them.

"I see the two kids are alright."

"Yes," said the man with Master Sergeant's stripes on his sleeves. Jim then noticed the woman had similar chevrons on her uniform.

"Mister and Missus Wilson, I presume," said Jim. "Both active duty, I see."

"Please, call me Geninne," the woman said. "And this is Larry. We had to come down and thank the Squ- the Tschaaa who saved Tommy. Jeannie told us all about it."

"I told them if they came down, here again, I'd tan their hides," Larry said in a father voice.

"Well, Larry, if they had on life jackets, no problem. We actually like people to see what we do here."

"We made something for Mister Squid," Jeannie spoke up.

"You did? And what is that, young lady?"

"It's a surprise," said Tommy.

"Well, then let me call Churchill over," Jim said. The manager used his walkie-talkie to call over to Churchill. Jim took the four visitors over to his office. There he found some cookies and soft drinks for the brother and sister, plus some coffee for the parents. About fifteen minutes later, Churchill used his limited spider-like walking ability to enter the office. The two adults stood up. Jim could see the tensions in their stance and faces as they met a former mortal enemy up close and personal.

"These two Masters Sergeants here are the parents of the young boy you rescued, Churchill."

The Tschaaa supervisor signed with his hands respectful greetings and spoke using a translator.

"I am glad the Young Ones are fine."

"Thanks to you, Churchill, they are," Gennine said as she held back tears.

"We have something for you," interrupted Jeanie.

"And what is that, Young Breeder?"

Jeanie handed him a box wrapped up with colorful paper and a bow.

"Here. Open it. Tommy and I made it ourselves."

Churchill's sensitive digits carefully unwrapped the box so as not to rip the paper. He set the lid aside and removed the contents.

"It's a medal," said Tommy. "For saving me."

"We made it out of plastic so that water wouldn't hurt it," Jeanie added.

Jim saw it was a multi-pointed silver star on matching silver chain. The two children intricately cut the star from a shiny piece of plastic, then added an actual silver metal chain to it. Churchill held the medal gently as he examined it. Written on it was "LIFE-SAVING AWARD." Finally, he spoke.

"This is an—honor. I did what any of my kind would do. I saved the Young."

"You saved OUR Young," said Gennine. "If not for you, Tommy here would be—" The mother could not finish the sentence.

"You saved his life," interjected Larry. "Not too long ago, we were trying to kill each other. Now, you save our son. So, we owe you. Big time."

Churchill slowly wrapped the chain of the medal around the wrist of his right hand.

"I will wear this always. As a sign of—friendship."

"Is there anything else we can do for you?" Asked Larry. "I mean, the medal is beautiful, but, you know—"

"Two bushels of sugar cane," interrupted Jim.

"Come again?" asked Gennine.

"Sugar cane is one of their few vices."

"Please, Boss," began the Squid.

"Be quiet. You and your crew deserve it. You all work too hard."

As Churchill acquiesced, Larry said, "Well, we have to get back to work. I'll keep my son more under control."

"When I was young," said Churchill, "I often escaped the Breeders who kept track of us. So, please do not be too harsh. He is young."

"And we want him to grow up," answered Larry. The Master Sergeant stuck his hand out, and Churchill wrapped his digits around it in a handshake.

"Thanks again."

"You are welcome," replied the Tshaaa.

Jim and Churchill watched the family walk down the pier.

"I'll get you a sash or strap to hook the medal to, Churchill. It will free your hand up."

"Thank you, my friend, Jim."

"Anytime. Now, it is back to work time. Time to make more bonus money."

"Yes, I believe it is."

Years later, Jim met an aged Darryl Largo near the ferry dock. Only now, it was the pier where the air-cushion hovercraft launched. They stood watching as Jim's grandkids played around a life-sized statue of a Tschaaa. The plaque on the statue read, "Here a Tshaaa male saved a young human boy's life. The crèche member and stevedore, known as Churchill, proved that friendship could arise from the bitterest of enemies."

"Where is he these days, Jim?"

"Churchill? He is down running the Port of San Diego. And, he owns half of it with his new crèche members."

"He has his own crèche? He is a Lord?"

"He calls himself Boss and runs the crèche like a corporation. Churchill invested all that bonus money and adopted human ways. His sons are allowed mates, Breeders, even though they are not Lords."

Darryl grunted.

"Who would have thought they would become more like us, Jim."

"Yeah, well, we are like them also. When was the last time you heard of any child abuse going on? The Young that is what's important. That idea keeps us from always trying to kill each other."

"Well, you have that. Come on, and I'll buy you lunch."

Jim paused for a moment, then spoke.

"You know, you made all this, Godfather. If not for you telling me I had to run things—"

"Oh, shut up. I'm just an old man who runs a porn shop. One the Squids keep trying to shut down because of tentacle sex DVDs."

"Hey, did Churchill ever visit your shop?"

"I'll never tell. Churchill has a reputation in San Diego to keep now, hasn't he? You know, our Squid still wears that plastic medal."

"He deserves it. Churchill is a better human than most people I know," said Jim.

Darryl turned and looked at the statue one more time.

"Yes. Funny how beings who came to eat us helped to teach us some humanity."

Jim called out to his grandkids, and the small group of humanity made its way up from the waterfront one more time.

Rawhide

Swimin,' Swimin,' Swimin'
Swimin,' swimin,' swimin,'
Swimin,' swimin,' swimin.
Fish hide!"
"Keep swimin,' swimin,' swimin,'
Though the Oceans are swollen,
Keep them Fishies rollin,' Fishhide
Move 'em out, Head 'em up
Move 'em out, head 'em up
Head 'em up, Move 'em out,
FISHHIDE!"

Former active duty Sergeant Michael Wall, now fishboat captain, always received the weirdest looks from his crew and any others nearby when he sang his version of an ancient television show theme song. The odd looks also came from the Tschaaa seadrovers, who were partners in this business. The Wet Stern Fishing Trawler he owned was just part of the fleet of vessels Mike had organized for the new type of harvesting.

Mike had Tschaaa Squids, creatures of the sea, as his drovers, his seagoing cowboys to move immense schools of fish up and down the West Coast of North America. Five years after the Great Compromise was signed ending the Tschaaa-Human War, and his idea was a growing concern. His ship, SEA WOLF, was one of four large oceangoing trawlers which made up the fishing fleet of West Coast Fish and Squid Company. Mike had added the 'Squid' to the name after he had signed on half a hundred Tschaaa cephalopods to help in the harvesting of the sea's bounty.

Almost seven years of near non- existent human fishing and six years of limited Tschaaa fishing up until the signing of the peace and co-existence treaty had led to the comeback of many an overfished species. The cold weather types of fish had made the most substantial increase in numbers as the Tschaaa preferred not to swim in the colder climes, especially near the Arctic and Antarctic. It had taken some persuasion and a new interest in the idea of "individual profit" from human culture for the Squids to sign on for work in the chilled climes.

Mike's second in command was Bjorn Heyerdahl, the son of Thor Heyerdahl, the titular head fo the New Vikings. The Heyerdahls were from a long line of Nordic fisherman as well as having been team members with Mike on Operation She-Bear. They were part of the mission to release an MWD on the Tschaaa modified at the last minute into a rescue mission for some humans. One does not forget something like that. Thus, when Mike had the funds to make his idea of a real fish farming and wrangling operation, he called them. Therefore, he had two other vessels captained by New Vikings plus Bjorn as his second in command.

The last vessel he obtained was Russian. Andrey Orlov was a typical hard ass Russian who came from a family of Siberian Fisherman used to the frigid waters of the Bering Straits. Andrey had kept fishing during the Tschaaa Infestation as he knew the Tschaaa did not care to harvest humans from the cold northern climes. His knowledge of fish movements helped the West Coast Fish and Squid to start the harvesting operations.

This day the small fleet motored by the entrance to Puget Sound in calm seas. Spread out for miles and kilometers, were schools of fish the teams of Tschaaa and human fishermen and women coalesced into one massive drive. Without the Tschaaa Squids, this type of harvesting was impossible.

"How's it going, Bjorn?" asked Mike.

"All the other ships and their drovers are keeping the schools inline—lots of tuna, mackerel, salmon, carp, and rockfish. "

"Keeping the sharks and killer whales at bay?"

"The few the Squids have seen were chased off with ease. They don't seem to like the alien type cephalopods as opposed to our native species, which they readily eat."

"Maybe they can tell our Squids carry weapons," said Mike. He always said, 'our squids' when talking about the Tschaaa drovers. Mike thought on more than one occasion how a species that once slaughtered and ate Homo sapiens could now so easily be recognized as equal partners in a large scale operation.

The onboard radio crackled to life.

"SEA WOLF, this is PUTIN'S BOAT. Come in, SEA WOLF."

Mike smiled as he recognized Andrey's Russian accent even without hearing the vessel's name.

"Go ahead, Andrey."

"Do we move the salmon towards Puget Sound?"

"Roger that. Send an escort for some ten klicks to keep any

Orcas away. Watch for sea lions also."

The salmon harvest and successful spawning had gone up a hundred percent since Mike and the company started the ocean version of cattle drives. By guiding large groups of salmon into Puget Sound, well protected from ocean predators, many more made it to the ancient spawning areas. The local Native American Tribe survivors loved what Mike did for their fishing industry.

The other two vessels of the fleet, THOR'S HAMMER and ODIN'S EYE, kept in line. Their respective teams of Tschaaa maintained the schools of fish moving, but not too fast. The various species received enough space for feeding and typical fish social interaction while not threatened by predators eating them. The beauty of the fish drives is that the fish arrived near the processing plants still alive. There was no need to catch, kill, and then ice the dead fish down while racing to market.

"So, Skipper, are we meeting the SEA WITCH off of the mouth of the Columbia River?"

"Yeah, Bjorn. I let them use their nets to take what they want and then fight those weird currents off of Astoria, Oregon. Even locals have lost fishing trawlers trying to cross the inlet."

Just then, a new voice was heard, emanating from a Tschaaa language translator.

"SEA WOLF and PUTIN'S BOAT, SEA WOLF AND PUTIN'S BOAT. A pod of Orcas is headed towards us." The Squid speaking was one Ulysses, who had read some human Greek and Roman mythology and liked the name. Ulysses had a mass media accentless voice programmed into the device despite being on the Russian's crew.

"Want I should launch the surveillance drones, Skipper?" Andrey interjected.

"Yep. Ulysses, intercept as you deem fit. Try not to kill any of them, but don't let them take our fish. Or hurt you."

"Yes, Skipper."

Bjorn had a wide grin on his face as he spoke.

"This should be fun to watch if the drones get there in time."

"It's fun until someone gets hurt," replied Mike. Squids like Ulysses carried traditional halberd like weapons. The newer ones had sizeable steel cutting blades. Some Squids took crèche arms passed down through the generation with blades made from large predator teeth or shaped coral. The Tschaaa had been ocean predators for millennia before they became addicted to their homegrown version of monkey meat. Based on photos of Tschaaa homeworld creatures, there were few Earth marine predators the Tschaaa could not handle. However, that did not mean some Earth animals were not dangerous. Orcas were one of them.

The drones were both ocean-going and air-breathing. The craft was for long-range surveillance of fish and other marine life. Now, they were to record the response to the oncoming threat.

As soon as the drones began broadcasting, Mike whistled.

"That is the largest pod of killers I have ever seen."

"There must be two dozen adults and juvenile whales," added Bjorn. "I guess they are no longer an endangered species."

As the two humans spoke, a Tschaaa with his long shaft weapon bobbed to the ocean surface some one hundred yards in front of the approaching pod. Based on the reaction of the killer whales, Mike knew the Squid was broadcasting its marine creature warning. Mike had heard the average Squid underwater voice and thought it sounded like a combination of dolphin squeaks and whale songs.

The main body of the pod veered off at an angle as two more massive Orcas went straight for the Tschaaa. Like sharks, Orcas occasionally dined on squids and octopi. As the lead killer whale opened its jaws to consume the irritant, the Tschaaa slid off to one side and pulled a bullfighting move. The drone cameras showed the Tschaaa halberd skewered into the right side of the Orca. The killer whale twisted and snapped at the wounding object as its blood stained the surrounding ocean.

Suddenly, the second Orca dove beneath the surface. The humans tried to switch to the submarine drone broadcast but were not fast enough. The second Orca breached high above the ocean surface. In its mouth was the Tschaaa crewmember. Mike cursed.

"Bjorn. Get the fifty caliber Barret."

"Aye Aye, Skipper."

The Orca Pod looped around the schools of driven fish and approached from a different angle. As Bjorn grabbed the Barret rifle, six Tschaaa drovers appeared. They zipped through the water and flanked the Orcas. A massive killer turned towards the Squids and accelerated towards the threat. Suddenly, a Tschaaa female launched a hand-held harpoon at the Orca. It struck the attacking mammal in its head and glanced off, leaving a bloody gash. The killer whale twisted away and dove deep. Seconds later, the whale breached behind the Squids. Its head bloodied, the enraged predator slashed into the marine drovers from behind. The alien Squids scattered as best they could, but one failed in its escape. The bleeding whale snapped it in its jaws and dove.

A forty mike-mike grenade arched up and over the schools of fish in the path of the Orca Pod. It exploded in the ocean a dozen yards from the killer whales. PUTIN'S BOAT was in the mix as Andrey yelled and cursed over the radio. The whales scattered away from the explosion

"Here, Skipper," said Bjorn as he handed Mike the Barret.

"Take the wheel," Mike directed as he took the barret and made his way to the bow. The SEA WOLF was slicing through the ocean at high speed. The calm seas still gave Mike a stable platform.

He sighted on the killer whale, which had killed the latest Tschaaa as it breached.

BOOM, BOOM, BOOM. The three fifty-caliber armor-piercing rounds sliced through the massive marine mammal. The killer splashed down and began to twist and spasm as it died. Then all was quiet as the Orca pod dove deep.

The surviving Squid drovers clustered around the now-dead Orca. They began the slaughter of the beast as the other drovers pushed the fish schools away from the bloody scene of death. Mike secured the Barret in the wheelhouse and then radioed to Ulysses to come to his vessel. Minutes later, Mike slowed the SEA WOLF to a crawl, and Ulysses climbed aboard.

"Ulysses, I am so damn sorry about the loss of your people."

The Tschaaa warrior signed his equivalent of a shrug with is social tentacles.

"We all know the danger, Skipper Mike. My species were predators of the sea when humans were first discovering fire. It is in our DNA, as you humans say."

"Is there anything I can do to help?" asked Mike.

"No. Just allow us to work. Thank you for your friendship." Ulysses slipped back into the Pacific Ocean.

"Did things like this happen during your Nation's cattle drives?" asked Bjorn.

"Historical records and books talked about wolf packs, rustlers and Indian raids. Add to that flash storms, poisoned water, and disease, and the answer is yes, bad things happened. But they kept driving cattle, just like we will keep driving fish, with the help of our many-armed friends."

Bjorn grinned.

"You would make a good Viking with Erik the Red.'

"I hope so, Bjorn. I hope so. Now, let's get these fish to

market. San Franciso first."

Minutes later, Mike revved the marine engines. Then he began to sing.

"Swimin,' Swimin,' Swimin'
Swimin,' swimin,' swimin,'
Swimin,' swimin,' swimin.
Fish hide!"

Book of Abigail

Angel to Banshee Stories

Remembrance

Abigail Yamamoto sat and stared at the computer screen. The Avenging Angel. Legendary Banshee, My Lady of Steel, was on the verge of being genuinely defeated for the first time in her life. Who was the foe which was putting the extraordinary warrior on her knees? It is called Writers Block.

Everyone on Earth had been nagging her to write her memoirs. Manga-style Comic Books reined in to be more realistic by Princess Akiko (after a private "meeting" with the publisher) caused resurgence in interest as to what had happened, with no B.S. added in the telling. Thus, Abigail had a contract with a Northwest independent publisher to write her memoirs. Contract or no contract, it was like her fingers were frozen every time she tried to put a word to paper, or in this case a computer screen. Some people said Writers Block was the sign of a lazy writer. Had someone told that to Abigail's face, he or she would be spitting teeth.

A young voice yanked her attention form the blank screen. She heard Anica, her seven-year-old daughter, as she yelled, "Mom!" from the back entrance of their home.

"I'm in the study," Abigail called back. In a few heartbeats, the eldest of the fraternal twins, brunette Anica burst into the room.

"Mom, Brunhildr, beat someone up again."

A moment later, the other twin, tall and robust blonde Brunhildr, entered the room.

"Must you always tell tales on me, little sister."

"I am older than you are, Brunie, so don't call me little."

Anica was firstborn, but Brunhildr towered over everyone near her age. So in truth, Anica was little compared to the growing Shield Maiden. The larger twin looked more like her namesake aunt Brunhildr Knudsen a real Shield Maiden than her mother.

"Alright, you two, quit arguing. Now, tell me what happened."

"I did not beat someone up," stated Brunhildr. "Someone was picking on Ichi, so I told him to stop."

"You picked the boy up and threw him down. If that is telling someone—"

"Well, it made him stop—"

"Ichi. Come here." Abigail used her Mother's Voice, which said you had better come. Now.

Five-year-old Ichiro the Younger, already a miniature version of his father, Ichiro Yamamoto, walked into the study munching on rice cookies. Abigail could not help but grin. He was so much like his father. Willful, sure himself, and moved with the grace of someone years older.

"Was someone bothering you?" asked Abigail

Ichi shrugged as he chewed on another cookie.

"Some older boy was making fun that I was a half-breed, half Japanese and Half American. I laughed at him and walked away."

"No one insults MY little brother," snapped Brunhildr. "So I told him to stop. Then he called me a name. So—"

"You slammed him into the ground," interrupted Anica.

"Well, because you are just a shrimp—"

"Better than being a big ox—"

"Stop it!" Abigail used her Mother's Voice and sighed.

"All you three. Sit down. I am trying to write about my life, and you must realize how easy you have it these days. Thus, all this drama about fights at school—"

"Dad got into fights. That is why he lived with his Uncle," said Ichi.

Abigail shook her head and smiled. She wished her husband was not so free with stories of his life. Being older than his wife, he was an adult when the Squids invaded. Abigail was not quite a teenager. Her late childhood years were of fear and loss.

"That was then, and this is now. You three must realize we need to not fight over little things. The Great Compromise has given us a new chance at a long peace."

"Mother, you rarely talk about your life before you met Dad," said Anica. "We know from our history books what you did—"

"And from the comics," said Ichi.

"Which is why I am trying to write about my life. And to be honest, it is not easy to put it on paper or into a computer."

"Then tell us some stories, Mom," prompted Ichi. "We can handle bad stuff. You and Dad made us strong."

From the mouth of babes, thought the Avenging Angel. However, if telling them helped her to put the memoir together—

"Okay. Get some milk tea. Plus, some cookies if Ichi has not eaten them all. Then I will tell you about my early days before the Great Compromise. Then I will tell you tales of after I married your father." Now, hurry. I don't have all day."

The three children dashed off, grinning. They were back in record time and clustered around Abigail on floor pillows.

"Where to begin. Okay, I'll have to tell you some of that bad stuff. I became an orphan when I was twelve…"

The End of the Beginning

Abigail Jorgenson's parents were yelling and screaming at her. "Stay in the house! Go to the basement!"

There was a series of bright flashes of light, then low rumblings from the West of the home. A strong wind came slamming across the front yard as Abigail's parents ran towards the nearer barn. They were bowled over as dust and debris swirled around them.

The twelve-year-old blonde girl yelled, and started out the front door of the house—

She woke up screaming. She felt a firm hand and heard the familiar robust voice.

"Abbie. Wake up. It's a dream." As was her Uncle Buck's manner, he was short and to the point in his speech. Usually, this was a source of strength and comfort to his niece. This day, it did nothing to stop her sobbing and sadness.

"I should have gone out to help them," she cried. "I should've—"

"Then you would have died along with them. Of radiation poisoning," Uncle Buck's words were harsh but truthful.

"I have enough potassium iodide to help protect you from any radiation you may have absorbed because you stayed inside, went to the basement when Hanford blew. If you had gone outside…" The sizeable muscular man left the rest of the sentence unfinished, hanging. Much like the near future, thought Abigail as she controlled her grief. Uncertain, hanging.

The modern-day black-haired Adonis handed his niece a handkerchief, then put the sizeable four-wheel-drive custom van into the drive as Abigail wiped her eyes.

"Where are we?" she asked.

"Passing through what's left of Twin Falls, Idaho—taking it carefully, watching for Squids and their minions. We are about two hours of travel time from the Utah Border. Or Deseret as I hear they call it now."

Abigail shivered. She was trying to cope with all this using her twelve-year-old sensibilities and was having problems.

"Why can't I stay with you, Uncle? You and the dogs?"

Her Uncle sighed. He knew this was rough. But life would be even harder on the road with him.

"As I said before, you need a stable home," Uncle Buck answered. "I can't give that to you. Especially with the Squid aliens and their machines running around, looking for human meat. "

"But I could help you with the dogs," Abigail protested. As she said that, a puppy head poked its way between the seats, snuffled at Abigail. She recognized the five-month-old Black Mask Cur as Pepper, a female of the litter Abigail, had helped birth.

"No, Abie. I need to travel, can't stay here. I don't do well with groups of people."

"You do well with me," she argued. Her Uncle shook his head.

"Sorry," he answered. "I have some people here who owe me. They'll take care of you until I come back."

"That will be soon?" Abigail asked.

"As soon as I can," Uncle Buck answered. "Now, go to sleep. You need it."

Uncle Buck kissed his niece on her forehead. She gave him a huge hug, then crawled into the back of the van. She quickly fell into an exhausted sleep, as Pepper cuddled up next to her. Uncle Buck began to pay attention to the road ahead. He turned off the vehicle headlights, then adjusted his night vision goggles. The large man needed to make good time under the concealment of darkness. There was no real law enforcement or the rule of any laws. There were just Squids and feral humans. It was the survival of the nastiest.

Abigail was still sleeping the sleep of the innocent when Uncle Buck slowed to a stop on Interstate 84. He was at Utah (Deseret)/Idaho border, was told a specific individual would meet him there. As quiet as possible, he exited through the driver's side, slowly closing the driver's door. Uncle Buck stretched all of his tight muscles in a practiced series of exercises. He kept his muscular body at a high level of fitness; his Adonis build attracting both male and female admirers. Uncle Buck was heterosexual but did not care if someone of the male persuasion made a pass at him. However, no one laid hands on him. No one put hands on him unless he asked them.

He leaned up against the front of the van, scanned the horizon with his night-vision goggles, and listened for vehicle sounds. Uncle Buck saw hints of headlights touching the background along the path of the Interstate. There were no other highway or building lights. He took off the night vision goggles and listened intently.

Finally, he heard vehicle engines. The large man slowly reached into his vehicle cab and removed a twelve-gauge short-barreled pump shotgun. Abigail was still sleeping, but Pepper had her head up, listening. Uncle Buck walked out in front of the van, then stepped off to the side of the freeway, and crouched down by a clump of bushes and rocks. As the vehicle approached, he pulled out a small red laser pointer and turned it on. He aimed it at the oncoming car, which quickly turned off its headlights and slowed down. Uncle Buck saw it was a military HUMVEE that had seen better days.

The HUMVEE stopped some fifty yards away. The passenger side door opened, and Uncle Buck saw in the moonlight a single figure exit.

"Buck? Dogman?" the voice called out.

"You got him," Buck answered. "Major Huff?"

"Yes, the same." Major Huff walked up and extended his hand. The two men shook hands as Buck gave him the once over. About forty years of age, light brown thinning hair and a slight belly. National Guard for sure.

"Glad to finally meet you in person, Dogman," Major Huff said. With that, Uncle Buck shrugged, then spoke.

"It's no big thing. But what I need from you is important."

"Yes. The good Master Sergeant said he owed you." The Major paused, then continued. "I learned a long time ago to trust this Master Sergeant."

"Yeah. I pulled the man's chestnuts out of the fire," answered the large man.

"So, what is the request?" Major Huff asked.

"There is a young girl in the van. My niece, Abigail, she is the daughter of my sister, Anica. Lost all her family due to Hanford exploding."

The military man frowned.

"Was she irradiated?" Major Huff asked.

"Minimal," Uncle Buck answered. "And I had potassium iodide for her."

"Well, she's not the only one," said Major Huff. "We have about two dozen orphans that have dropped off. We'll try to find homes for them, as we are good Mormons, good Christians." He paused for a moment, then continued. "I understand you are a Mormon—"

"Not anymore," interrupted Buck. "Too much hypocrisy."

"Well," continued the Major, "we are now the state of Deseret, pride ourselves on following the true tenants of our religion."

The man called Dogman grunted. "Heard that before."

He looked back at his van for a moment, as if having one last argument in his own mind.

"Okay. Abigail stays with you," said Uncle Buck. "But if anything bad happens to her, I'll come looking, and you won't like the results."

The Major stood silent for a moment, taking the measure of the man standing before him. Then he reached into his pocket and produced a business card.

"Here. I still have a few. Archibald Huff at your service. Call that number anytime, ask -for me."

Uncle Buck looked at the business card, then replied. "Boian Vladu, Dogman to most. Uncle Buck to the family." He stuck his hand out to shake, and Major Huff took it. The man called Dogman held the grasp for a moment longer than usual, then spoke again.

"You just gave your word to protect Abigail. Remember that."

"I will," answered the military man. "Now, shall we get her to her new home?"

"Yeah', Dogman grunted out. He turned and went to the van,

saw Abigail stirring from her sleep.

"Time to get up, Abbie. I have a safe place for you," he said.

Abbie looked at him, an expression of resignation on her face as she spoke. "Okay, Uncle Buck. You've always been right before."

She gave Pepper a massive hug, received a lick in return. Then she turned towards her Uncle and hugged him, hard.

"You'll come back," she whispered. "Promise me you'll come back."

"I promise, Abbie. Someday." He kissed his niece's forehead as he finished speaking.

Major Huff tried to be as friendly as possible to the young lady, introduced her to the female soldier driving. But neither would ever be Family ton, Abigail, not really.

Dogman, AKA Uncle Buck, watched the HUMVEE drive off into the night, now with its lights out. He would never admit that his eyes were moist as he watched what was probably his last living relative disappear into the sunrise. He reentered the van, scratched Pepper's ears as she snuffled him.

"We'll remember her, see her again, won't we, Pepper?" He always talked to his dogs, knew they understood a lot more than humans realize. Dogman knew one thing for sure.

Dogs were the best people around.

The Coming of the Twenty

All of the Twenty were scurrying around their barrack living quarters under the eyes watchful eyes of Training Instructor Master Sergeant Catherine Cox. She and her husband, Master Sergeant Kenneth Cox, were the closest thing to real 'parents' the twenty orphans had since arriving at Deseret. They were children from the ages of five to fourteen who, just under a year prior, had been dropped off by various people or family members in attempts to provide a 'Safe Place' in a world where Alien Cephalopods ate children.

Because they had all suffered from exposure to fallout from the Hanford Nuclear Storage Area Explosion during the Tschaaa Alien Invasion, they became quarantined. No one knew if the invading aliens had caused the explosions, or it was due to some arcane accident. The results were the same. The fear of contamination, of the 'unclean,' resulted in the Twenty refused for adoption and eventually taken in by the tall and dark-haired Cox's in this modified barracks. The Nation-State of Deseret was barely functioning and surviving as the Mormon Church took over the supervision of human society in this part of the former United States of America.

The Cox's, both career Military and experienced Drill Instructors knew only one way to keep twenty young orphans under control in a world gone mad; that was very Tough Love.

"Hurry up!" MSGT Catherine Cox yelled out. (Never called the familiar name Cathy, unless you wanted a combat boot up your posterior.) "The New Prophet will be here any minute! You WILL all shine in God's and the Prophet's eyes. If not, you will all be marching 'punishment tours' until Hell freezes over!"

Referring to 'Hell' was the closest either of the Cox's came to authorized profanity. A couple of the older boys had found that out to their displeasure, as a leather baton whacked across the back of their thighs, demonstrated what happens when one was profane.

Abigail was used to hard work, as she had helped her Uncle Buck clean dog kennels at his training facility. Plus, she had learned the importance of a 'pack pecking order.' There was always an Alpha Male and Female with canines. So she adopted much quicker to the concept of a chain of command and following orders. Discipline and order ofttimes had their intrinsic rewards. So she was at the forefront of ensuring everyone, and everything was in its 'place.' Thus, Cox often gave her grudging respect despite her young age of some thirteen years.

"Jorgenson!" Kenneth Cox bellowed out. "Help young Jason here with his boots. He will scuff the shine you all put on them."

"Sir!" Abigail jumped to the task, helping the youngest of the

Twenty to get his boots on. He just turned six, sometimes cried out in his sleep for his mother. Jason shook a bit as Abigail helped him lace his footgear uptight.

"Why do you shake, my little brother?" Abigail asked.

"I am afraid," Jason whimpered. "I'm afraid I will be sent away from you all by the Prophet. That he will see I am not good enough

"Hush!" Abigail commanded, "No one will send you away. God will not allow it."

"But, my mommy is gone." He started to cry, and Abigail whispered firmly in his ear.

"She still watches over you, as mine does me. That is why we are all here together. They talk with God, he listens. You will be here with me. Don't worry. Okay?"

Jason blinked back tears, nodded agreements with a quivering chin. Abigail quickly had the young boy's boots on, and everything right. As she stood up, Catherine Cox called out.

"Jorgenson! A word."

Abigail was standing tall before the Training Instructor in a flash. "Ma'am!"

"Walk with me for a moment," the female Cox ordered. The two were soon out of earshot of the others, as everyone else hurried about, dealt with last-minute details.

"Jorgenson," began the gruff Master Sergeant, but with a bit of softness in her voice. "I see you have a gift. A gift of leadership. You can lead, help, and get things done."

"Thank you. Ma'am." Abigail managed to squeak out. This conversation was entirely unexpected.

"I also believe the Prophet will see this. I believe he will single you out for great responsibility. I also think you will handle it."

Abigail kept walking, did not know how to answer this odd evaluation.

"Do what you are told," the Master Sergeant continued. "Accept what God, and the Prophet, have planned for you. Understand?"

"Yes, Ma'am."

"Now, mention this to no one." The female Training Instructor's voice was once again, hard and cold. "Dismissed."

Abigail saluted, then doubled timed back to her comrades.

Ten minutes later, they were standing tall in their barracks area. As tall as children and teenagers could, in truth. Then the Training Instructors called them all to attention.

The heard a confident-sounding voice call out.

"At Ease, my young ones. Relax."

They still stood, until the same voice said, the sound reverberating.

"Your Prophet has spoken. RELAX!"

Something in the voice made them all relax, and look at the man standing in front of them.

Prophet Michael Smith was six feet in height, well-muscled but not huge, with short and well-groomed brown hair and just a hint of gray. He had the good looks of a Hollywood Movie Star. He grinned at the assembled Orphans, the Twenty.

"See, My Children, that is not so hard, is it?" He asked. "For, you are, from this moment, onward, my children. No longer are you orphans, with two competent foster parents, the Coxs."

They could not help but begin to mumble in surprise. Prophet Smith laughed.

"I know," he said, "this is all a shock. But you will soon see it is a pleasant surprise. Now, Master Sergeants Cox. Please have them all sit on the floor, and find me a chair. We need to all truly relax."

As the Coxes rushed about and situated the Twenty in a semi-circle on the floor, and found the Prophet a chair, Abigail noticed a single man standing ways behind the Prophet. As the Prophet sat, Abigail thought she felt the eyes of both the Prophet and the strange man on her. She tried not to show any reaction.

The new Prophet smiled, then spoke.

"My Children, we are all called by God, Our Lord, to do certain things, perform certain missions in life. After much prayer and consultation with God, and due to the Demons here in the form of the now labeled Alien Squids, God illuminated to me the need for a special group of people. This group is to help combat these Demons and other evil in the world. They will be special, will undergo much training, and will have to endure hardships others in Deseret will not have to endure. For they will be a Force for Good, used to smite the Evil Ones, and protect the faithful here in Deseret. In the tradition of the early days of the Mormon Church, a force of new Avenging Angels will exist." He paused as if to let it all sink in.

"You here will be the nucleus for this, will be the first group of Avenging Angels. You, who have become known as the Twenty, will not be seen as outcasts or Unclean. You are to be honored at the end of your days, and beyond. All I ask of you is your devotion, faith, and belief in this sacred mission. Now, let us pray for divine guidance and aid in the coming days. We will need both."

All the Twenty were stunned but reacted automatically to the command to pray. Much of the training received in past months included periods of prayer and reflection. The training was all based on the teachings of the Church of the Latter-Day Saints. "Our Father in Heaven, "began Prophet Smith, "please aid us in this new task, this new mission for these young ones. They are Your Children, even as they become My Children. From this day forward, I promise you, Father, and through your Son, Jesus Christ, that they will be to me as if they were of my flesh and blood. I will protect and nurture them, raise them to be faithful followers of the Church of

Latter-Day Saints. And thus, faithful followers of you, My Lord. For that is thy will, Amen."

The Twenty all said 'Amen' then sat still, confused. The Prophet stood and grinned.

"Up!" He commanded. "Stand up and approach your new Father."

They all stood, instinctively formed a line. But the Prophet would have none of that. He laughed, then pushed in among them, hugging every one of the Twenty. As he did, he spoke each name, mentioned their age, and told them they were loved. Abigail was finally the next to his attention. Prophet Smith paused before her and smiled.

"Abigail Jorgenson. I was told you are blessed with the traits of caring for others as well as leadership."

"I try... Prophet Smith," she answered, had trouble meeting his eyes.

The Prophet chuckled. "I scare you. Do not be afraid, Abigail. For you are loved." He hugged her.

As he did, she felt a feeling she had not felt since she had last seen Uncle Buck. She felt loved. And safe. She began to weep.

"Hush, my child. Do not weep," said Michael Smith. "I know you feel truly loved for the first time in months."

"Yes," she managed to croak out as she tried not to cry more. "Then be at peace, my dear. For love will not disappear." The Prophet slowly untangled himself from Abigail's grasp and turned towards the Twenty.

"You are loved will receive excellent care. The man there," said the Prophet as he pointed towards the man who had been watching them all, "is Special Agent John Hall. He is my protector and exceptional assistance. John." He motioned the man forward.

Agent Hall was not too big and not too small. He was a fit

Average Man, which meant that he could quickly lose himself in any given group of humanity. Abigail did not know it, but Hall was also one of the best trained and most efficient killers in Deseret. He worked for Prophet Smith and no one else.

"Agent Hall will be taking you all to your new home," said the Prophet. "We have modified a motel into a more comfortable barracks for you and the Coxes. It is just minutes from my new offices on the edge of the Tabernacle complex in Salt Lake City.

Thus, I may see my new children often."

"Agent Hall. Do you have anything to add?"

John Hall displayed the hint of a smile, then spoke. "You are loved by me. And I will watch over you all."

"Good!" exclaimed Prophet Smith. "Now, hurry up and pack your things, my children, my new Avenging Angels. But before that, one last detail." Michael Smith paused for a moment, then continued. "From this day on, you are christened with the last name Young. In honor of our Sainted Brigham Young. Now, off with you."

The twenty young people stood, stunned a bit. Then the Coxes yelled out in unison. "Dismissed! Move it!"

They all moved.

What was not known to Abigail, was the profound effect this occurrence would have on her and others. Nor could anyone see how she would become the real Avenging Angel.

But that is a story for a different time.

Abigail Young AKA Jorgenson was fulfilling her duties as an Avenging Angel Second Class. She was looking for a young Jason, who had not returned from an errand to the Tabernacle Offices. As Abigail traced the path, he should have taken, she heard some laughter. She headed towards the sound, which came from behind a boarded-up 'Stop and Rob" store. As Abigail came up to the edge of the building, she heard little Jason's voice.

"I am protected by God and the Prophet! You had better leave me alone!"

There was derisive laughter from three clearly older boys, all big for their ages. Often in times such as the Tschaaa Invasion and Infestation, the nasty and robust survive to prey on the weak. Abigail had seen it before.

"Let's take this 'unclean' one into the back room of this old store," said a redheaded bully. "We can see if he glows in the dark from the radiation."

A brown-haired and toe headed companion search laughed in agreement. Abigail took this moment to step forward.

"I suggest you unhand the young one before God notices." Her voice, firm and durable, cut through the air and stunned the three bullies into silence. Then the Red Head found his voice.

"Well, Look! A filthy slut. Do you want to join your friend here for some fun in the dark?" His two comrades began to laugh again. Abigail strode forward, directly at Red Head.

"Well look, Jeb, she has the hots for you-" the brown-haired bully did not finish his commentary as Abigail's snap kick into the Red Head's groin caused a screaming and gasping which drowned out any other conversation.

"Hey!" The blonde bully reacted, grabbed at Abigail, and quickly regretted it.

The fight was over in mere seconds. The three bullies were just that, young bulls with no real training, only size and nastiness. They were laying and holding various parts of their anatomy, as well as crying and moaning with pain, while Abigail took Jason by the hand.

"Come. Back to the Barracks," Abigail said. The Avenging Angel then looked at the three defeated bullies.

"You reap what you sow," she growled. Then the two members of the Twenty were gone.

Abigail knew she would have to answer for the violence. She did not care for she had done what her Uncle and Father had always told her.

"Do what is right. Protect the family".

The Avenging Angel smiled. The Twenty was her family now.

Woe to those who screwed with it.

The Chief

So, Mom, after you went to the Prophets Office for beating those boys, then what happened? "

Anica, the brunette oldest twin by a minute or two, asked her mother Abigail Yamamoto, FNU Jorgenson. The Avenging Angel smiled at Anica and her two other children, fraternal twin Brunhildr and her younger son Ichiro Junior, called Ichi. Abigail started telling her three tales of her younger years as a means to overcome a writer's block affecting the completion of her memoirs. Now, she realized she might have created a monster. She had three young children hanging on her every word as she told them about how she had survived her childhood during the Tschaaa Infestation.

"I know what happened," said young Ichi as he grabbed another cookie, this of the store-bought chocolate chip variety and not Japanese rice.

"And what is that, my son?" asked Abigail with a smile.

"You met Uncle Torbin, and then Aunt Aleks."

"That's true, but not until much later. I spent many weeks and months in training as well as securing the borders of Deseret from marauding Eaters and Krakens. I became An Avenging Angel First Class, then a commissioned officer. I met Uncle Torbin at Evanston. Wyoming, then Aunt Aleks when I escorted Torbin back here, Malmstrom Armed Forces Base."

"Uncle Torbin and Dad has told us about what they did attacking Key West." interjected tall and blonde Brunhildr. "Uncle told us he met The Director. Did you?"

Abigail sighed.

"I met him in death. He died on the asteroid base of the Tschaaa moments before I and Aunt Heidi joined up with Uncle Torbin, your father, and Saint Andrew."

Andrew, the Cyborg and now the senior Guardian Angel cyborgs had morphed into, was given Sainthood years ago. What else could you call a part human being who helped save the human race from extinction?

"I did meet his second in command, Chief Hamilton. But that was years later."

"What happened when you met him?" asked the younger version of her loving husband. "Did you try and capture him? Kill him?"

"No, silly," interrupted Brunhildr. "Director Lloyd became a martyr when he died as he stopped that Squid Lord from dropping Rocks on us. Why hurt his friend?"

The Avenging Angel and Banshee grinned.

"You have learned well in school, daughter. Chief Willie Hamilton, like his former commander, did many good deeds of which most people are ignorant."

Three sets of eyes locked onto Abigail. She now knew her

children would not release her until she told them the story.

"It happened when you Twins were four and Ichi was two. Aunt Aleks left the Banshees to raise Tristan and Gage, your cousins. I returned to fill in as Commander until General Torbin Bender and President George Williams chose a permanent replacement. I already rejected that offer because of you three. Anyways, the government asked the Sisters of Steel to "show the flag" one more time..."

Nearly two hundred and fifty men, women, and children huddled together in what passed as the central square of the village. They did not come there voluntarily. Instead, the newest form of radical religious thuggery forced them together at gunpoint.

Abbas Mohammad, leader of the band, associated with The Way (as the name translated into English from the local Afghani dialect), stood with folded arms as he looked down at his latest victim. The young woman tried to use her torn and bloodied hijab and Saudi type niqab to cover her battered body. As the woman attempted to repair the damage to her attire, Abbas spat at her.

"See, oh yee of damaged faith, how the unfaithful whore tries to repair her modesty," said Abbas in a booming voice." See how this fallen woman tries to cover the shame of her actions."

"Abbas, please—"

"It is too late to ask for mercy. The Prophet told us what to do with apostates like you."

"Please, I beg you. I meant no harm in teaching the girls how to read—"

The towering mountain tribesman lashed out with a thick switch at the young woman as she tried to cover bare body parts. Abbas was an expert in punishment for Non-believers and the sinful. Red welts arose as the switch from a thorn bush raked Shabana's sensitive skin.

"You had the girls read Western filth," he yelled as he struck again and again. "The same filth the alien multi-armed Jinn used to subjugate the faithful as they prepared to dine on our flesh."

Abbas stepped forward and kicked at the young female.

"Abbas, that is enough." An older man stepped forward. "She is my youngest daughter. It is my duty to punish her; make her repent."

"Then why, Painda, did you not? Why did you allow this blasphemy to continue?"

Painda drew himself up to his full height. He was older but not small and weak.

"I may have allowed myself to be blind. The threat of the Tschaaa caused me not to worry about the religious teachings of my children. I will ask Allah in the name of the Prophet to forgive me for that weakness."

Abbas barked a laugh.

"It is too late to ask for forgiveness. I see where the root of this evil lives."

Before anyone could move or speak, the radical leader pulled a chrome pistol from under his loose-fitting jacket and shot Painda between his eyes.

Shabana screamed and tried to crawl to her dead father. Abbas kicked her again.

"Yashir," he said to his second in command as his men kept their assault weapons trained on the crowd. "Have someone find some rocks. These villagers must stone this whore if they wish to regain favor in the eyes of Allah—"

An invisible force tore the violent leader in two. As the crowd of tribespeople stood in shock, the report of a large caliber weapon reverberated off of the ridges and hills. Yashir screamed orders to the armed terrorists and thugs until a similar shell eviscerated him. The men began to fire wildly at the surrounding hills and rocks. None of them wanted to be on the receiving end of another fifty caliber round.

"IT IS RED BEARD!" several voices screamed. "It is Old Red Man of the Mountains," yelled another. The sound of a third shot echoed, and two thugs died from one armor-piercing bullet. Everyone scattered, except for Shabana. She crawled to the body of her father and lay on him, sobbing.

The six surviving Afghani terrorists ran to the four winds. A young villager picked up an AK-47 from one of the dead and fired at the members of The Way. One fleeing man crumpled to the ground. The rest ran for the hills. Soon the only sounds were the murmurs from the villagers as they stripped the bodies of the dead—all except Shaban's father, which she held as she cried and sobbed her grief.

Some five minutes later, a ragged motorcycle with a sidecar rumbled into the village. The engine of the motorbike was missing and sputtering as it stopped in the town center. Then the engine stalled,

"Well, that's it,' said a youthful voice. "I think she is dead and gone to heaven."

"Well, Jack, she gave us good service," said the man known as Red Beard. The middle-aged man stiffly climbed from the sidecar and adjusted his faded Kansas City Chiefs' red baseball cap. He stretched as he tried to scan all the Afghani's standing around. William Willie Hamilton, former USAF Chief Master Sergeant, had been in the Near and Middle East long enough that he knew non-believers and foreigners were accepted one moment and killed the next depending on the mood and activities of the locals.

Jack Elem, the motorcycle ride, removed his eight-point Marine Corps patrol fatigue cap and wiped his brow with his jacket sleeve. He then swung off his motorized mount and stood up. Tall and lean, he had a natural tan from a mixed-race heritage, which was so convoluted that his nickname was Heinz 57.

"Well, old Red Man of the Mountains, now what?"

Willie Hamilton walked over to the sobbing Shabana and spoke the local dialect in low tones.

"I am sorry for your loss, daughter of the faith. May I know your name so that I may pray for your father?"

"Shabana. My father is– Painda. I thank you for coming to our aid."

"I wish I had come moments earlier. Now I offer my prayers and condolences for your loss."

Shabana looked at this strange red-bearded Westerner who knelt beside her as he spoke her language like a native. The wind burned, and suntanned face had wrinkles which told he was an Elder in whatever group he called his. Shabana finally stood and tried to wrap her torn Saudi style niqab about her. The Way forced the womenfolk of the mountain villages to wear this extreme clothing. To them, females were inferiors whose sin was to inflame men with their presence. Before their arrival, the variations of the hijab and burka were sufficient.

"I must go to my father's house and find some suitable clothing," the young woman said in English. "May I ask your true name, Red Beard?"

"William Hamilton, Willie, to my friends. You are educated."

"Yes–Willie. That is my sin. The Way says such sin brought the Tschaaa."

"The Way is ignorant, Shabana. My friend Jack Elem and I will watch over your father until you are ready."

Shabana averted her eyes and slightly bowed.

"You are very kind for a non-believer."

"We all bleed red. That I have come to know personally."

As Shabana walked towards her father's house, Jack walked up.

"Well, Boss. Now what?"

"Well, since I decided to help these people, I guess I need to be here when the buddies of those dead men come back for revenge." He looked at his younger friend. "You could leave."

The Former Marine Gunny Sergeant laughed.

"How? Molly, the motorcycle has gone to the great hereafter. I think she threw a rod."

"Well, I think the elders are about to approach us. They may have some transport stashed away."

It was an hour later when Willie and Jack sat in seldom-used chairs around a similar table sipping hot tea with the senior Village Elder Soban. The young men of the village were dragging the dead thugs to a less than a pious burial, as Soban explained the history of the area.

"The Jinn, the Tschaaa, came in the night like jackals. Most of the families here lived in and around Kabul. We were to be the enlightened next generation as the Taliban and other groups were agreeing to peace, and allow those who wanted a more liberal existence." Soban sighed. "We fled to this part of the Hindu Kush mountains as the Tschaaa ate others. We hid with some of our poorer brothers and sisters of the Faith. Somehow, we survived for over six long years."

"And then you heard of the Great Compromise," said Willie.

"Yes. But we were afraid to return to Kabul, which was a ghost town, So we let someone else rebuild what was once ours. Just under five years later, The Way appears."

Willie knew the rest of the story. Homegrown and imported fanatics decided Allah and the Prophet spoke to them to create a new Caliphate. And, of course, it was to be formed with the use of a bloody sword.

"They came and made an offer you could not refuse."

"Yes, my new friend William. The took several young men and boys to be soldiers, several young girls to be brides for their leaders. That was two months ago."

"And they came back because someone informed on Shabana," interjected Jack.

"Yes, young man. They heard a young lady was still teaching the girls to read. As you know, reading means you can think and learn for yourself."

Willie Hamilton grunted.

"Ignorance is bliss, Soban."

"Yes, that is a belief. But tell me, friend, how did a Western non-believer come to Afghanistan?"

"To find my late wife's family."

Soban paused for a moment before adding a question.

"Did you find them?"

"No. Azita's relatives are dead, as are many families."

A very much cleaned up Shabana wearing more traditional Afghani attire approached the table.

"We women have prepared a meal for our guests. If I may now lead them to my father's house, Soban—"

"But of course. I will ensure your father's body is ready for burial."

The meal was on a well-used table in the family home. Another older woman hovered around as a chaperone while Shabana served the two western men.

"This sure beats eating out of a can," Jack said between bites.

"Please pass my compliments to the cook," said Willie in English. The young lady smiled.

"As I am the cook, I will accept your compliments."

After completion of the meal, Shabana sat in a chair back a few feet from the table as the two former soldiers enjoyed cups of Afghani sweet tea,

"So you are a teacher," said Willie as he sipped his cup of tea under the watchful eye of the chaperone in the corner.

"I am now. When the Squids as you call them came, I was studying to be a Doctor at the University."

"You fled here with your family?" asked Jack.

"Yes. But my mother was killed in the early days of the invasion. My older brothers and sisters were soon scattered to the four winds."

Willie set down his teacup.

"Again, I express my sorrow at not reacting a few moments sooner and stopped the death of your father."

Shabana looked away.

"Some would say it is the Will of Allah. It is what it is."

"What will you do now?" asked Jack.

"I will stay here and teach. This village is my family now."

"And if the fanatics return?"

"I will deal with them when they come."

Willie saw a tough young woman who would not cower. However, without armed people to help protect her, she could still be a victim.

"Shabana, we are a bit low on ammunition," said the former Chief Master Sergeant, "and Soban stated the Way fanatics seized all the weapons in the village. Jack and I will do what we can since we are now part of this problem."

"They did seize what they could find," said Shabana. "Plus, there are eyes and ears here who support their beliefs. I would understand if you chose to leave before the Way people return."

Years of experience in reading body language and word

choice told Willie that Shabana was not free to talk. He let the matter drop.

"I think Soban has a sleeping quarter set up for us, Shabana. Excuse us as Jack, and I take our leave. It has been a long day."

"But of course. Thank you for your help. Come by tomorrow if you can, and I will fix you breakfast."

As the two western men walked across the central courtyard, they talked in hushed tones.

"She reminds me of my late wife, Azita," said Willie. "But she is young enough to be my daughter."

"So, you want to stay and help," Jack said.

"Yes, but you do not have to. This here is my idea."

Jack laughed.

"I have been with you since we met over two years ago, Willie. I came here for the same reason you did. I wanted to find friends and extended family who were here when the Squids struck. I am not about to bug out now."

"You weren't with the Director, Jack. You have no baggage, things which require atonement."

Jack guffawed. "You think you are the only person who hooked your horse to the wrong wagon? Besides, Director Lloyd died stopping that asshole Tschaaa lord from dropping more space rocks on us."

"And I should have been with him. It might have turned out… different."

"Woulda, coulda, shoulda. It happened. Now, the question is, what do we do here?"

They walked in silence, said nothing more until after Soban had shown them to their sleeping area in a vacant shack of a house. Once they were alone, they continued their conversation.

"How many rounds do you have for that homemade bolt

action fifty caliber sniping rifle of yours?" Jack asked.

"I am down to one round. My chopped and shortened BAR has a half a magazine of 30.06 rounds. Of course, I have my old 1911. How about you, Jack?"

'I have that busted- up M-4 I can cock and fire in single shot, the sawed-off twelve-gauge with one shell left and that .38 Smith and Wesson with six rounds. Oh, and one Chicom grenade. I was hoping we would make it to civilization to replenish before we had another dustup."

"No rest for the wicked, Jack, The young punks are not about to give up the weapons they took from the men I killed. I also doubt they will help two spawns of Satan nor defend Shabana. I think they wrote her off."

"Yep. That is an accurate SITREP. So, do we try and ambush a rearguard to get some more firepower? Or do we go out in a—"

The men heard a "Pssst" by the one blanket-covered window. Willie went to the window with a drawn .45 pistol.

"It is I, Shabana. "

Jack slipped through the window to the outside. He saw Shabana had somehow carried a stuffed military B-4 bag, as well as an ammo can to their sleeping quarters without detection.

"My father was a historian who said we must learn from history and our mistakes. He collected and kept reminders of the past and the mistakes. I will leave them with you. Use them wisely."

Jack handed the booty through the open window and then climbed back in. The Afghani woman disappeared back into the night. The two military men quickly inventoried what Shabana had brought.

"Well, I'll be- that Jack is a Chicago Typewriter. This weapon here is a Papasha with Chicom markings. I see an AK-47. An SKS, an Enfield—"

"This ammunition can contains a dozen types of ammo in it, to include some Ma Deuce rounds. I think we are in business, Willie."

It was an hour past sunrise when the two men heard the approaching Toyota pick-up trucks.

"Toyota company—providing transportation needs of irregular armies for decades," said Willie.

"Time for me to move," replied Jack. Slung across his back was the AK-47 with a full magazine. Jack carried the damaged cock and shoot M-4 just to use up the ammunition. He also had the PPSh-41 with a 47 round drum in his offhand. He and Willie had some other surprises planned as he took his position over by a goat pen.

Willie climbed up on top of the shack where they slept. He had his bolt action fifty caliber resting on a couple of grain-filled sacks for stability. Willie sighted through his rifle scope at the approaching caravan of small pick-up trucks.

"God. Half of them are kids," he said into the small radio.

"Yeah. Kids using AK-47s. Guns even a monkey can use," Jack responded on his radio.

"Well, we didn't ask for this. I'll try to shoot the older ones first," said Willie.

"Roger Wilco, Willie."

At some twelve hundred yards, Willie put a fifty caliber bullet through the driver of the first truck. Guts and brains splattered over the passengers as the armor-piercing round continued its path into the truck bed. The vehicle skewered into the roadside ditch and flipped. Jack watched through binoculars as bodies flew everywhere.

"Nice!" said the former Marine.

"Thanks," radioed back Willie as he slid another round into the chamber of the fifty caliber. The can of ammunition had contained ten rounds of belted ammunition for a Ma Deuce, which worked just great in Willies weapon. The vehicles in the caravan began to brake, and one rear-ended another just as Wille fired his second shot. This bullet blew the engine out of the Rear End Charlie. Wille chuckled as the pick-up burst into flames with ignited gas and oil spewed over the cab and the occupants of the truck bed. Bodies lept from the burning vehicle as it continued to drive into the ditch.

"I count about fifty enemies," the radio crackled into Willie's ear.

"Less functional now," he replied to Jack.

One of the Toyotas had a Degtyaryov pan fed machine gun mounted above the cab. The World War II relic still functioned, and the operator tried to lob some rounds in Willie Hamilton's direction. Wille put the crosshairs of his scope on the gun and blew it apart before the bullets hit too close. The shot that smashed the machinegun also broke the gunner. The remaining fanatics bailed out of their respective vehicles and went for what cover and concealment they could find.

Willie reached over and picked up a relic from the 19th Century. The old Martini-Henry breech loader in a forty-five caliber was not the most accurate rifle, but it was sufficient for what Willie planned on doing. He had a dozen rounds to use up, which suited Willie. He saw a group of the Way fighters clustered behind some rocks and boulders. Willie used some maximum Kentucky Windage and fired. The rainbow arc of the old black-powder load meant the bullet came down on top of the concealed attackers. After expending half of the available shells, the warriors who were still mobile scattered.

"I think some of them are coming my way," radioed Jack.

"Fire at will," replied the former NCO.

A couple of long-range bursts from the AK-47 sent the maneuvering troops looking for places to hide.

"I hit at least one, Willie."

"One of them should find a surprise real soon," replied Willie.

No sooner did he speak than there was a sizable explosion followed by screams. The only mortar shell Shabana provided made an excellent booby trap. One of the extremist fighters hit the tripwire blowing himself and others up, plus peppering others with shrapnel.

Willie thought he heard someone climbing up the ladder to his rooftop spot. He turned around in time to see the barrel of an AK-47 poke over the edge of the roof. Willies .45 pistol was in his hand before he even realized it.

"Stop right there," he called out in the local dialect. He saw the top of the climbers head, and then the young man was trying to point the AK-47 over the roof edge and at Willie. The USAF veteran shot the man in the forehead, and he toppled backward.

"We have a Fifth Column in our rear, Jack."

"Shit. Time to go mobile."

Willie grabbed the Chicago Typewriter, the Thompson 1928, with a loaded fifty round drum. How in the hell this weapon wound up in Afghanistan would remain a mystery. Shabana's father had kept it hidden and functional for an unknown number of years as if he foresaw this day.

Willie peeked over the roof edge. Down below, two other youths were running up to their shot comrade, one with an AK-47 and the other with a curved blade sword, As they bent over the dead ladder climber, Willie called out as he aimed the Thompson.

"Drop your weapons," he yelled.

The one with the assault weapon reacted with youthful reflexes and fired up at Willie without even aiming. The bullets zipped by much too close for comfort, and Wille blasted away with the submachine gun. The multiple hits flattened the attacker as Willie fired a round into the swordsman. Then there was silence.

Wille scrambled down the ladder as fast as his aging body would let him. The worst was happening. The village was willing to sacrifice the Westerners and Shabana in exchange for their security.

Willie cut the pie around the shack's corner and saw Jack sprinting his direction with the AK-47 at ready. Willie whistled, and Jack rushed faster and met his partner behind the structure.

"I think it is time for Plan B.," said Willie as he and Jack picked up the assault rifles from the dead youths. They were not about to leave them for others to grab.

"Head to that rock formation up on that low hill?" asked Jack.

"Yep. That way, we can prevent from being shot in the back by any of these so-called friendly villagers."

"Let's go. I stashed the busted M-4 under some rocks. A couple of AK-47s and a PPsh-41 should be enough to finish this—"

"Uh oh," said Willie. "Look."

Soban was dragging an uncooperative Shabana as he pointed the pistol of the dead Abbas at her head. The village elder called out.

"You must drop your weapons. I will allow no more deaths of my people due to this female."

"You think The Way fanatics will be kind to you for giving them Shabana?" Willie yelled back.

"Let him shoot me, friends," Shabana spat out. "If you lay down your weapons, they will surely torture you before death."

"I know that," Willie said as he estimated if he could make a headshot with the Thompson.

A helicopter blasted overhead as it came from the foothills. Its sudden appearance caused the village headman to duck and take his attention from Shabana. The young woman took the chance given her and grabbed Soban's gunhand and sank her healthy teeth into it. The man screamed as he let go of her with his left hand and tried to beat on her. Jack blew the back of the Soban's head with a well-aimed AK-47 bullet. Shabana shoved the dead man away as she grabbed the pistol from a lifeless grip.

"Who the Hell is that?" said Willie as he tracked the helicopter.

"I don't know, but here are two more 'Hawks outfitted with sound suppressing rotors," answered Jack.

The radicals began shooting at the new arrivals. One Blackhawk rotated on its main blade and fired a rocket at the enemy personnel. The missile exploded in a blast of white phosphorous, the pieces of Willie Pete burning three attackers. As the three males screamed, the others began to scatter. A door machine gun from one of the other aircraft opened up as the helicopter flared out and landed. Willie saw a couple more Way members go down. Then Shabana was grabbing hold of him.

"You are not shot?"

"No, young lady. I've been doing this for years. With experience comes luck. "

"Guess who those people are?" Said Jack over the aircraft noise.

"Who?"

"Banshees. Sisters of Steel. I recognize the emblem on the 'Hawks."

Willie stood still for a moment. He knew this day was bound to come as he could not hide from his past forever.

"I think my karma just caught up with me, Jack, Shabana."

"What is that, friend Willie?" The blacked haired woman asked.

"I was—with Director Lloyd. The man who helped enslave one group to save others."

Shabana looked intently at Willie.

"I thought I recognized your name." She sighed. "Sometimes, knowledge is a burden."

An armored body strode towards the three, two armed figures as escorts. All the deploying warriors wore the distinct dark emerald green battle fatigues of the 101st Special Attack Unit, The Banshees. The definitive unit commander stopped in front of Willie and removed her helmet. Seeing the bright blonde hair told the former right-hand man of Director Adam Lloyd, his days of freedom were limited.

"Colonel Abigail Yamamoto, I presume," said Willie.

Abigail stuck her helmet under her left arm and reached out with her right as if to shake hands.

"You are a tough man to find, Chief Hamilton."

Willie paused for a moment, a look of confusion on his face. Jack jumped in at that moment.

"Why were you looking for Willie at this late date? What, five years after the Great Compromise?"

"Word gets around fast, Jack Elem. Yes, we know about you also. When two Yankees have a reputation for taking out the new version of an old evil in this part of the world, people get curious."

"Are you going to arrest my friend Willie?" asked Shabana. "He just saved me, so I must protest."

Abigail paused, looked at the three confused humans, and laughed.

"Five years later, and people still think about revenge, retribution, and punishment. The late President Paul said she wanted a new beginning. We all promised her that before she passed."

"Now, are you going to shake my hand or not, William Hamilton?"

"Oh, sorry, Ma'am."

A Japanese female walked up and bowed to the group."

"Colonel, the area is secured," Princess Akiko announced. She looked at Jack and Willie. "So, these are the two Ronin who have been fighting the honorable fight."

"You're the Princess from the Japanese Royal Family, aren't

you?" said Jack.

"Guilty as charged, as you Americans say. Colonel, do you wish a place to talk while the Banshees round up the villagers?"

"My father's house," said Shabana. "I will make you some tea."

Abigail smiled as she answered.

"Tea. I would like that, yes."

"So let me get this straight, Colonel… ?"

"Please, call me Abigail, William. We have shared history, even if we not always on the same side of things."

William laughed.

"Call me Chief or Wille then, William is much too formal. And what you just said about being on sides is the understatement of the century."

Abigail sipped the tea.

"Thank you, Shabana, for this excellent sweet tea. My husband has taught me the the importance of tea and its preparation in the greater scheme of things."

"Tea does warm the body and the soul, Abigail," said Shabana.

"And to answer your statement, Willie, we were all trying to find answers for the survival of the human species," said Abigail. "Some were just better than others."

"Except the Krakens," interjected Jack. "They were just plain sick and demented."

"Cannibalism does mess with the brain and the soul, Jack. And power corrupts."

"So, where does that leave me?" Willie asked.

"Where do you want to be? We can take you back to North America if you wish."

Willie shook his head.

"All my family is gone, My wife's family was here, and now they are gone." The red-bearded man looked into his teacup as if trying to read the leaves. "Now, I just try to help ordinary people deal with assholes."

"Which is why the Banshees are here. The old evil of repressive fanatical religion is rearing its ugly head. Stoning women is not allowed religious expression."

"So I guess we beat the Banshees here," interjected Jack.

"Yes, Jack, you did. Which saved this young lady here as we have many locations on our radar and cannot be everywhere at once."

Wille looked at the Avenging Angel.

"Abigail, I need to know something. Were you there when—Adam died?"

There was silence for a moment. Then Abigail answered.

"I was there about a minute after he died. Andrew told us—Torbin, Ichiro, Heidi, and me—that Adam Lloyd asked him to let him die. The Director's final act was to take full responsibility for the Protocol of Selective Survival. His death was to prevent a lengthy trial and recriminations."

"Andrew radioed us at Key West and told us. That is when I decided it was time to disappear and let the Admiral handle the Florida Keys." Wille looked into his tea once again.

"I should have been there," Willie said. "I should have died."

Abigail reached out and took his hand.

"Many of us have survivor's guilt when people died for us. Those who passed want us to go on living and be the best humans we can be."

"Huh. Nice sentiment. The reality is harder."

"Had you died that day, I would be dead today," Shabana said.

"So please remember that there is a purpose behind Allah's Will."

"You know, my friend," said Jack, "there is that. So yeah, your presence is still a positive, not a negative."

Willie looked at the circle of new and old friends. He had been floating along since his best friend Adam's death, just existing. Searching for his wife's family had been an excuse to disappear.

"So, if I stay here to fight for truth, justice, and the American Way, I start with a clean slate?"

"You had a clean slate years ago, Chief. As I said, it's time for Christian forgiveness as taught by Jesus. Let God judge you from this day forward if necessary, not man."

Jack grinned.

"Hell, I'm in. At least the truth and justice part will work here. Time to feel good and rebuild."

Shabana reached over and squeezed Willie's arm. "Allah is merciful when given a chance."

Willie finally smiled. It would be weird trying to build something without Adam, but he would do it. "Well, I guess we head to Kabul. I don't think the families of the young men we killed here will be very forgiving."

"May I also come, Uncle?" the young Afghani woman asked.

"Uncle?"

"Yes. If you are my Uncle, and Jack is my Brother, we keep strict Muslim propriety for unmarried women. There will be fewer questions."

"Well. If that will help, but this restrictive fundamentalism is not my idea of freedom."

Shabana smiled as she spoke. "We may have to take small steps. Once I and others can educate the women, things will be better." She looked at Abigail. "May one day, we are all as powerful women as Banshees, Sisters of Steel."

While Abigail and the Banshees had an attitude adjustment meeting with the villagers. Willie, Jack, and Shabana loaded up one of the still functional Toyota pick-ups

Shabana packed her sparse clothes and personal items as the two men stored the selected weapons. They concealed three loaded AK-47s, the bolt action fifty caliber, the Thompson, and the PPsh-41under a large tarp. Willie's stashed his chopped BAR behind the seat. Shabana kept the pistol taken from the dead Soban concealed in a large shoulder bag. The Middle and Near East were still a ragged frontier five years after the Great Compromise. Thus, groups as The Way to sprang into existence.

As they finished readying the truck, Willie and Jack watched the villagers give them a wide berth.

"The Banshees must have put the fear of God into them," said Jack.

"I caught a bit of the discussion," said Willie. "They also put the fear of the Eye in the Sky into them. They now believe the next time they allow The Way to come around, bad things will happen."

"Are we ready?" Shabana asked.

"I think so," said Willie. "Abigail gave us some extra coin to help us in Kabul and a cellphone to call for help. However, I think the three of us are adept at survival."

"So, who drives?" Asked Jack.

"You do. This old man needs a nap."

Shabana paused for a moment to survey the village.

"I will come back someday to visit my father's grave," she said. "Other than that, I am not sorry to leave."

The three members of a new family soon drove down the dusty road towards Kabul Abigail, and Princess Akiko watched them leave.

"You took care of the rest of the radical fighters, yes?" Abigail said to Akiko.

"Our fellow Banshee did. Some new Sisters were able to christen their blades with the blood of the abusers."

"Huh. Someday, my Japanese sister, I hope all of us will look forward to giving life rather than taking."

"We can only hope, Abigail. We can only hope."

"And that is how I met Chief Hamilton," finished Abigail.

"Who took command of the Banshees after you," Brunhidr asked.

"Your Aunt Kira Samson. She led the original raid, which started the Banshees."

"We have a lot of aunts and Uncles, Mom," said Ichi as he munched on another cookie.

"Family is now who we say family is. Always remember that. Banshees are aunts and one uncle. Torbin Bender and his brother William are family. General John Reed is my adopted father, so he is your grandfather."

"You helped rescue his wife," Ichi added.

"Yes, who adopted me as a daughter. So, she is your grandmother."

Abigail stood and smiled.

"What is most important to remember is we humans are all brothers and sisters, cousins and family. Thus, Brunhildr, we should not fight."

"Yes, Mom," her tall daughter grumbled.

"Now, please leave so that I may finish writing what I just told you three."

Abigail watched as the three lights in her life IAs they left to go fuss with each other, Young Fuzz, War Dog, padded in and poked her with his muzzle. Abigail laughed.

"Now, you want attention! Well, come here. For you are family also."

Abigail scratched the War Dog's ears, then began to type. Screw writer's block. Nothing could stop a Banshee and her family.

Greater Love

As was her habit, Major Abigail Yamamoto awoke minutes before her alarm clock beeped. As was his practice, Corporal Fuzz, War Dog, was sitting next to her bed, waiting for her to awake. When Abigail opened her eyes, her first sight was the large head of Fuzz looking intently at her. Abigail smiled. "Good Morning, Big Fella."

The sight of Cpl. Fuzz always brought her a feeling of bittersweetness. His visage brought back memories of his Sire, Sergeant Fuzz, and the first in a line of what became classified as War Dogs. Sergeant Fuzz, War Dog, and her best friend gave his life for Abigail during the alien Tschaaa Infestation War.

An oversized mix of Great Dane and Shepherd, Fuzz and his offspring had a muzzle in between the size and length of the two breeds, with Shepherd ears having a little 'flop over' at the tip. The fur coat was a traditional blackish-brown mix of Shepherd breeds. Cpl. Fuzz was the spitting image of his Sire, except for a star-shaped white marking on his forehead. Some Native Americans had stated the 'star' was where the Great Spirit had touched him before sending his spirit to Earth.

"So how are you, my furry friend?" Immediately after Abigail had posed the question, Fuzz answered with a slurping lick canine kiss. Abigail grinned, reached out and scratched his ears. Fuzz responded with a dog grunt of pleasure.

"What a ladies' man. Early morning kisses."

Abigail stopped the ear scratch, then pushed her covers off. She swung her legs over the edge of the bed and stood up. Cpl Fuzz stepped back, wagged his tail as he displayed an open mouth canine grin. As she walked towards the shower, Abigail tied her blonde hair back with a scrunchy.

Pleasurable smells of a cooking breakfast wafted up the stairway of the Field Grade Officer On-Base Housing Unit. She smiled. Her husband, Colonel IchiroYamamoto, Free Japan Forces, was already up, preparing a combination of Japanese and American Breakfast. Abigail, AKA Abigail Jorgensen FNU Young, the Avenging Angel of Deseret, had been married to Ichiro for just over one year. Abigail had forgotten how many times her husband had beat her to the kitchen to cook the morning meal. They met in battle, the Tschaaa Infestation War, and fell madly in love. Their wedding had been a national event in the Unoccupied States of America, as it was a wedding of war heroes. Even the first day of their Honeymoon became a battle as Krakens—Tschaaa supporting human renegades— had attacked Malmstrom Armed Forces Base in an attempt to kill Madam President Sarah Paul.

All that seemed like ancient history, especially as the Great Compromise, had created a world where alien invaders and native humans were now existing together. At least, that was the theory. Now, just over a year from the signing of the Great Compromise between the cephalopodan Tschaaa, their client species the Lizards, and Humankind, they were attempting to work in concert to keep the peace. The peace treaty was easier said than done, primarily because the tentacle 'Squids' (as the humans called them) had come to Earth to harvest and eat all humans. Abigail had been present at the meeting where female Tschaaa Breeders and Madam President began the road to peace while facing Mutual Assured Destruction. The females of the two predator species had been the ones to forge an end to The War. The two sides stopped the conflict in the name of their children, their 'Young' as the Tschaaa called them. For in the love and caring of their offspring, the two utterly alien to each other species had found common ground.

As Abigail went to take her morning shower, under the protective gaze of Fuzz, the thought of children again brought to mind a conundrum she and Ichiro faced. First, was the still nagging question in Abigail's mind as to whether she could have healthy children, after some exposure to the radiation from the atomic explosion of the Hanford Radioactive Waste Storage Area in Eastern Washington soon after the Tschaaa launched their invasion. Abigail's parents died due to the radiation. Uncle Buck saved her and transported her to Utah, soon to be the Mormon Nation-State of Deseret. Raised as a 'child warrior' an Avenging Angel, the young blonde girl had been told from the time she arrived in Deseret that she may be contaminated, 'unclean,' and unable to produce healthy children. Thus, she was placed with other orphans from the same situation to become The Twenty, a specialized group of soldiers raised from childhood to be Avenging Angels for the Church of the Latter-Day Saints and Prophet/President Smith.

As part of this reproductive question was the added horror

that Abigail was modified, tinkered with genetically and structurally using Tschaaa biological and technical techniques. Thus she became a "Super Soldier" never seen before. The additional exception was possibly her husband Ichiro, whose radiation exposure to the Fukushima Disaster in Japan led to some similar mutations in his development. Thus, another reason to question the possibility of viable offspring.

As Abigail began her shower, she looked at her flat, muscular yet feminine stomach. She tried to imagine it bulging in pregnancy. For that begged the next question. Could she give up her life with the Banshees, the 101st Special Attack Unit, AKA Sisters of Steel? The unit had been created by original women warriors secretly following Abigail's lead. The Sisters of Steel started as a private group. Abigail, the Avenging Angel, became their symbol and, unknown to her, their idealized mentor.

Then came Bloody Kansas, the attempt by the Krakens and the Tschaaa Lord Neptune (the overseer of the Harvesting of North America) to punish the Unoccupied States for an attempt on Lord Neptune's life. During the punishment invasion, Tschaaa Grays had tried to abduct Abigail, which lead to Sgt. Fuzz's death. Abigail almost died, setting up an unauthorized revenge attack on the Kraken invaders by the Sisters of Steel. And thus, a legend was borne.

Abigail sighed as she let the hot water play over her body. General John Reed, Supreme Commander, her now adopted father, had to take action against the one hundred and one female warriors. They disobeyed orders, yet pulled off an impossible move which led to a general rout among the Krakens One hundred and one warriors went in, all had returned, after killing over four hundred of the enemy. However, they had disobeyed orders. So, General Reed gave them a choice. Be a "Banshee," under his command, do the heavy lifting, or...

A small smile formed on Abigail's lips as she washed her hair. Now, over four hundred women warriors, and one man, Captain Danny O'Brien, a hero of the assassination attempt on the Tschaaa Lord in Key West, Florida, lived in the new barracks complex built for them. Included as of this day was an Olympic size pool. Abigail realized she had left out one more unique member of the Banshees, who was also non-human. The Tschaaa female, who adopted the pronounceable human name of Dorothy, joined about a month before. She was a trained pilot for the modified Harvester Arc the Banshees had taken for their 'near space' transport craft. Plus, she had been at the now-famous Meeting of the Breeders with Abigail, where female "Breeders" from both species had met to hash out a possible Peace. Thanks to them, came the Great Compromise.

Abigail turned off the water and stepped out of the shower. She dried off under the watchful protection of Fuzz. As she finished with the hair dyer on her long blonde hair, she spoke to Fuzz in Romanian, her Uncle Buck's and her Late Mother's native language.

"Fuzz, let Ichiro know I'm on my way."

Fuzz was up and moving in a flash, down the stairs to the kitchen. She heard Ichiro greet the War Dog, then next he called up the stairway. "Dearest. Your breakfast is ready."

"I'll be right there."

Abigail made her way swiftly down the stairs in a light robe. Around the table wafted the delicious smells of eggs, ham, toast, and rice. Abigail smiled at the love of her life. She moved over and kissed him as he placed hot tea next to their plates.

"Again, you spoil me, my husband," she said in flawless Japanese.

The tall and slender yet muscular man placed his strong arms around her. "You deserve to be spoiled, my sweet. Especially since tomorrow, you must be off on another mission."

Abigail hugged him back with her powerful arms, then kissed him. She was almost as tall as Ichiro. So she did not have to tilt her head much to kiss him. The kiss began to turn into something more severe as Abigail felt a familiar stirring in her nether regions. She gently pushed him back.

"I must not wait, my love. I have much to do before tomorrow."

"I understand, my Angel. Here, sit. I will serve."

As Abigail sat down, she saw that, once again, there were some Origami figures next to her plate. She flashed a broad smile and examined the figurines. One was clearly a paper version of her, throwing a ball to an intricate version of Fuzz. A third figure stood by, folded arms, and watched the action. "This third figure is you, Ichiro."

"Yes. I decided I needed to be in with all the other Origami I have done. I do not want to be just the creator, but also a participant of the life tableau."

Abigail reached out and squeezed his arm as Ichiro set the breakfast plate in front of her. Once again, she had a plate of not only delicious smelling food but also a meal artistically presented. The menu items were arranged just so, with the colors and textures in complete harmony.

"You should be a chef, my husband. Your food always looks almost too good to eat."

"In Japan, the presentation is to enhance the enjoyment of the meal and the taste of the food. And of course, traditional Samurai culture teaches the importance of harmony with nature."

The food tasted as good as it looked. Ichiro sat down with her, ate more of the traditional rice dish than the American items. Of course, young Fuzz, still having some typical canine characteristics, sat waiting to see if any food items dropped, or if he could mooch a taste. Ichiro slipped him a small bit of rice ball. Abigail smiled, with a bittersweet memory of Aleksandra Bender, her now Commander and adopted Big Sister spoiling his Sire. Sgt. Fuzz had saved a pregnant Aleksandra from two alien Eaters, inserted into her and her husband Torbin Bender's on-base residence in an assassination attempt. Thus had begun the War Dog legend.

"A penny for your thoughts, Abigail."

She smiled at Ichiro. Being a real 'soul mate,' he could easily sense her moods, as well as what she was thinking. "Memories. Specifically of another War Dog, people liked to spoil. But like his son here, he deserved it."   Fuzz sensed Abigail's emotions, went to her, and nuzzled her hand. She smiled, scratched his ears. "Your Sire would be proud of you, as well as give you tips on mooching and begging. He was an expert."

Abigail scratched Fuzz's ears, then continued eating. She and Ichiro made small talk, finished eating, then cleared the table and cleaned the plates. As they completed these tasks, Abigail glanced at the clock.

"Guess I'd better get a move on. I want to spend the entire day and night before this mission with the recruits."

"Yes, my dear. By the way, Colonel Hunter and I will be seeing you tomorrow morning. We'll be escorting your Assault Ark up into the low orbit in two pre-production V-Wing Sub-Orbital Fighters." "Really? That was a quick development."

"Yes. Cliff Hunter pointed out some hidden Projects in Area 51 after we contacted the Tschaaa client species Lizards living there. With our resident genius scrounger, Pappy Gunn, the new 'space fighter' design began."

"This development is still rapid, Ichiro."

"Free Japan Armed Forces also helped. So, we have two pre-production fighters to test out tomorrow. This mission of yours is, I think your term is a 'milk run,' correct?"

Abigail smiled. It was just supposed to be 'show the flag' mission. The Banshees were tapped to land on the former Syrian and Israeli Border. Some local fundamentalist Muslim groups tried to put surviving women back under the yoke of Sharia Law. That was one concept Madam President said a big 'No' to, freedom of religion or not. No more keeping women uneducated, barefoot, and pregnant.

"Yes. That is the concept. But Murphy's Law…"

"Which is why we will escort, at least in the beginning. We are still working out the range capabilities of the V-Wing Fighters."

Abigail reached over and squeezed Ichiro's hand. "I feel safer already." She then began to collect the new Origami creations.

"Here, Abigail, I will put them in your display cabinet. You can go put your uniform on." Ichiro looked at the cabinet. "We will need a larger one soon, as you save everything."

"Everything you create is worth saving, Ichiro. And our children…" She stopped in mid-sentence. Ichiro gently put his arms around her.

"Thinking again, Abie?"

She hugged him. "Yes. After this mission, we will… talk. And plan. Deal?"

"Hai. Deal. Now, get ready. I will load your gear into the vehicle."

"Ever the dutiful husband. Come, Fuzz. Time for my uniform."

Within an hour, Ichiro was dropping Abigail and Cpl. Fuzz off in front of the Banshee Barracks. A stolen kiss and Abigail stepped out of the SUV, grabbed her gear bag. Now she was Major Yamamoto, former Jorgensen, and Deputy Commander of the 101st Special Attack Unit. Abigail walked towards the main barracks entrance, where two Banshees stood guard. She had her duffle bag full of gear in her left hand, leaving her right free for receiving the salute. Cpl. Fuzz heeled a foot behind her, watched everybody and everything around his Mistress. As she approached, the two Banshees snapped to attention, saluted. The senior soldier called out a greeting.

"Good Morning, Major Yamamoto. I recognize you and grant you entry."

"Good Morning, Sergeant Hudson. How are you and your young charge doing?"

One of the new traditions instituted by the 101st Special Assault Unit was that a Senior and one of the most Junior unit members stood guard at the entrance to the barracks compound. Blonde and stocky Sergeant Hudson was one of the "Originals," the one hundred and one Sisters of Steel who had made the unauthorized 'revenge' assault on the Kraken armored infantry unit, the Tip of the Spear of the Bloody Kansas punishment attack. Thus had started the 'Legend.' Plus, the traditions, all created to remind Banshees of their roots.

Abigail returned the salutes and then stopped in front of the very nervous "newbie." She looked at the nametag on the young woman's combat uniform.

"Private Armstrong. Where is Sergeant Jefferson?"

The Private, a slim brown haired young lady with a medium complexion, reached up and touched a folded and faded beret stuck under the right shoulder epaulet of her uniform top.

"Here, Ma'am. On my right shoulder, the position of honor, where she belongs."

African American Porsche Jefferson had been the very first Banshee—Sister of Steel—to die in combat.

An Original, she had lost her life when she had grappled with Malcolm Carter, the Leader of the Atlanta Revolt against the Tschaaa Harvesting of darker-skinned humans. Carter had wanted to force Torbin Bender and the others to launch the 'Ultimate Weapon' against the Tschaaa breeding areas after Madam President had told them to 'stand-down.' An errant pistol shot, and she died. Her beret was passed for safekeeping among all the 'Newbies' to instill in them the heritage of the Banshees. A large photograph hung near one of Madam President and General Reed in the front entrance hallway. The beret still had blood stains on it from attempts to staunch the blood flow of the wound that fateful day.

Abigail looked into the eyes of the new recruit. "First name, Private."

"Anica, Ma'am."

"Family nearby?"

The young soldier hesitated. With that, Abigail knew what the answer would be.

"I'm the last Armstrong, Ma'am. That I know of."

A common story. Whole bloodlines Harvested by the Squids, the Tschaaa. Families now became groups of survivors who said 'we're family,' picked a name to go by, and created a family tree.

"You have a family now, correct, Private?"

Private Armstrong seemed to stand a bit straighter, thrust her chest out a bit more.

"Yes, Ma'am. I have Sisters of Steel. Over four hundred. And one Brother of Steel, Captain O'Brien."

Abigail nodded her head in agreement. "Carry on, Private." She nodded to Sergeant Hudson, who snapped off a salute, mirrored by the Private. Abigail turned and continued into the barracks complex. Fuzz gave the two humans a quick once over, then followed Abigail as he remembered their scents.

Anica Armstrong followed the Avenging Angel with her eyes.
"First time she's talked to her, right Troop?"
"Yes, Sergeant. She's a legend among all us... orphans."

Sergeant Hudson chuckled "Well, she is the reason behind the Sisters of Steel. But what she says is true. We are a big extended family now, all in this together. No one is better than anyone else. Now, eyes front. And recite me the Fourth Banshee General Order…"

Abigail stopped in the large entrance hallway in front of a particular monument. Cpl. Fuzz stopped and sat, gazing at the oversized carved statue of his Sire, Sergeant Fuzz. Created by the New Vikings from the Minnesota area when they joined the Unoccupied States, it was a symbol of lasting loyalty as well as an homage to a hero for all. Abigail stepped forward, gently laid her hand on the rendition of Fuzz, Forever Protector; head up, eyes alert, solid all fours stance, an alert tail pointing towards the sky, as he looked into eternity for the next threat to the ones he loved. The familiar lump in her throat as once again, she greeted her Best Buddy.

"Hey, Big Fella, Your son and I are here again, ready to do our duty. Just like you did."

No one ever questioned nor disturbed the Avenging Angle as she spoke to her Sergeant Fuzz. They knew the bond was for all time.

The Son nuzzled Abigail, bringing her back to the present. She patted the live War Dog, smiled at him. She stepped back, saluted Sgt. Fuzz. "Wish us luck. We go into Harm's way. And you'll be watching over us, I know it." With that, Abigail continued to her office. That day and the next morning, at Oh Dark Thirty, as the unit left for the mission, many a Banshee would pat Sgt. Fuzz, ostensibly for good luck. Many knew it was actually to connect with his spirit, whom they all knew still watched over them.

At Abigail's office door awaited a handsome young black haired Irish man. She smiled as Captain Danny O'Brien, the one male member of the 101st, greeted her with an operational plan folder.

"Good Morning, Major. And a good morning to Corporal Fuzz

also." The War Dog wagged his tail and gave his two-legged friend a canine grin.

"I see you have the most recent rendition of the Operations Plan for tomorrow."

"But of course, Ma'am. What good is an Operations Officer without an operational plan?"

Abigail took the folder from him and walked into her office. Captain O'Brien had already opened her office, aired it out, and had a cup of tea with Irish biscuits (cookies) waiting for her. Next to it was a favored dog biscuit for Cpl. Fuzz. Abigail grinned.

"Still spoiling us, trying to fatten us up, I see."

Captain O'Brien flashed what had often been called his 'boyish Irish grin' that made many a female heart to flutter. Of course, on Abigail, it did not work.

"It's the Irishness from my sainted Great Grandmother, the original IRA Banshee, Major. A warm drink and a few bits of food warms the soul and settles the stomach before any stressful situations."

Abigail glanced over to the small sofa in her office and saw all of hers and Fuzz's Tactical Gear laid out and ready to go. That did not include her Glock 18 nor her Marlin .44 Magnum rifle, which she kept with her at all times. New Tschaaa biological crustacean based body armor and helmets for both her and Cpl. Fuzz placed on a sofa, neatly organized. The first time Captain O'Brien had done this, Abigail had told him that she needed no 'batman" nor a servant to keep her equipment in order. Danny proceeded to say to her that a particular former Unit Commander of his told him in no uncertain terms that he was to ensure adequate care and comfort for an adopted Little Sister as well as a certain Russian Born Wife. He added that if she had a problem with those instructions, she needed to take up the 'chain' to the person in question. After that, Abigail just accepted the extra attention. Torbin Bender, Hero of the Tschaaa Infestation, soon to be General, was known for his extreme stubbornness.

"I guess Fuzz and I had better try on that new body armor and tactical gear before we use it."

"Here, Ma'am, let me help…"

Within a few minutes, everything was fitted snuggly to Abigail and Fuzz. The items included a new combination helmet and muzzle protector that gave Corporal Fuzz a distinct look of arcane viciousness. It took Abigail a few moments to place what creature the long painted jaws and muzzle guard resembled and thus transformed Fuzz into something else.

"Fuzz is a Raptor! Like the creatures in those dinosaur movies, before…" No need to mention what 'before' meant. It was pretty much the same for all the survivors of the Tschaaa Infestation.

Danny O'Brien smiled once again. "Yes. That is the effect I wanted. What fits better with a bunch of Banshees than a nasty-ass Raptor?"

Danny had been the one who had designed the formal heraldic symbol for the 101st SAU. He tried to say it was something his Great Grandmother of the IRA had come up with at the beginning of the Twentieth Century. Now, everyone knew the exotic creature with the flowing silver hair, sharp teeth, flashing eyes, prominent armored breast holding a Banshee Blade in one hand, and an Armalite Rifle in the other was all Danny's creation. It seemed fitting that the only Male Banshee should help to define the heart and soul of the Unit, and the Sisters of Steel who inhabited it.

Fuzz seemed to like it the moment Abigail finished outfitting him with all his new formfitting body armor. He flashed a canine grin, then assumed a straight-legged aggressive stance which befitted a War Dog. Abigail smiled at him, yet felt a pang of regret in her heart. If only his Sire had that body armor, he might be there today, alongside his son. Fuzz the Son sensed his Mistress' mood, as had his Sire, moved in and nuzzled her hand. She knelt and hugged her Big Fella. War Dogs were such unique, intelligent creatures. Abigail had oft mused that they were so much better 'people' than mere humans.

"Yes, Fuzz. You look nasty, mean, and handsome, all at the same time. Any enemy we meet will take one look at you and either swoon or run!" Fuzz answered with the canine light huffing laugh that many humans missed. But not Abigail. She stood up.

"Thanks again, Captain. You always seem to come up with just the right equipment at just the right time."

"If I couldn't, I wouldn't be much of an Operations, Supply, Morale, and Jack o' all trades Officer befitting the Banshees, now would I?"

It was a repeated joke that the reason there were not more men in the Unit was that Danny had already taken over all the available slots, so why bring in dead weight? Abigail laughed. Once again, she was so delighted that the Supreme Allied Commander and her adopted father, General John Reed, had made Danny an integral part of the Banshees. In her mind, his unique brand of 'maleness' added a little Yang to her Ying, which started her thinking about another unique member of the Unit.

"Is Dorothy here yet?"

"Our multi-limbed Sister is down by the new Olympic sized swimming pool. Today is the christening for that piece of equipment. Most of the Banshees are already down there for an early morning swim."

"That's right! I'd forgotten today was the payoff from all your efforts."

Danny smiled. "A certain President and General did most of the heavy lifting, getting it funded and completed in record time. I was just a small cog..."

"Oh, quit with the false modesty! We all know who did the real pushing. Thanks again, My Brother."

"Anytime, Major. Grab your swimsuit. By the way, we placed extra heavy filters that will handle War Dog hair also."

"Hear that, Big Fella? Time for a swim."

A short time later and a one-piece swimsuit, Abigail and Fuzz sans body armor were approaching the pool area. Captain O'Brien had been correct. Almost all the Banshees were at the pool, swimming, cavorting, and making noise. Out of uniform, rank took a second seat to Sisterhood Abigail saw her adopted sister and Unit Pilot, Shannon Bell, standing near the edge of the pool with the Tschaaa pilot, Dorothy. Abigail walked over to the pair, with Fuzz hanging back a bit, still cautious around the alien Squid. Getting over the ingrained distrust of the alien species was not an easy task for a K-9. But Cpl. Fuzz was doing his damndest to follow the biddings of his Mistress.

"So, how are my favorite two pilots doing?"

"Just fine, Major," Shannon Bell answered. Dorothy paused for a moment, then the Universal Translator the Tschaaa developed kicked into life. A feminine Mid-western voice came from the intricate machine.

"I am also fine, Major Yamamoto." As the Tschaaa Breeder spoke, she used her two social tentacles to sign greeting and respect. Shorter than the male Tschaaa's, they still ended in long-fingered hands of even higher sensitivity and flexibility than the males. Thus, the claim that they made better pilots than male Tschaaa. Abigail would attest to her abilities in handling the vast modified Ark.

"You should hop in, Pilot Dorothy. You are much more at home in the water than we humans will ever be."

There was an uncomfortable silence. Abigail frowned. Had someone done something to offend the Tschaaa?

"Major, glad you are here." Walking up behind her was jet blacked haired Aleksandra Bender-Smirnov, her 'Big Sister' and Light Colonel Commander, not to mention Torbin Bender's Russian wife and mother of two very healthy boys. Abigail turned and greeted her in Russian.

"Colonel, about to test this new pool out with the other Banshees. I see you are swim attired."

"Yes. I figured that it should not just be the lower ranks who can enjoy themselves. I have not had a good swim in years." Aleksandra looked at eight-limbed and two tentacle Dorothy. "You are going to christen our pool, also, yes?"

The translator mechanism was efficient at recognizing all the major human languages. Also, many Tschaaa learned a human language as their communication was much more complicated. When humans tried to speak in the Tschaaa "Squid" language, they usually mutilated the various whale and dolphin-like tones which were part of the Alien's mode of speech. So, the pregnant pause at answering by Dorothy was due to something else.

Abigail frowned. "Is there something wrong, Pilot Dorothy? If someone has said something…"

"No. Far from it," Dorothy interjected. "I have been welcomed as a Sister by all, thanks to your efforts, Major and Colonel. It is just… a concern about your cultural norms."   Shannon Bell jumped in. "What is that, my fellow pilot? Is there something I missed during all our time in the cockpit together?"

Dorothy let out the Tschaaa equivalent of a sigh, signed apologies with her social tentacles. "I do not have the required attire, body covering."

The three human females tried not to let their mouths fall open. "You mean a swimsuit?" Abigail blurted out.

"If that is the correct term, yes. I notice humans are very

concerned with having just the right covering, especially females, Breeders. There is something called a 'fashion industry' that I am still trying to understand. We Tschaaa can change our body coloring based on our surroundings, so any coverings we have are almost always functional."

The three humans tried not to laugh. Concern about a swimsuit was possibly the last thing anyone would have imagined.

"Well, that is easily solved." Aleksandra turned and walked to the edge of the pool. She placed two fingers in her mouth and produced a signature very loud, and some would say very un-ladylike, whistle. The shrill sound immediately caused the assembled swimmers heads to turn.

"Down here, please. Your Commander needs to speak with you."

In moments, all the Banshees clustered around the shallow end of the pool, eyes on Colonel Bender-Smirnov.

"Pilot Dorothy mentioned a cultural difference that makes her feel a bit awkward. She has no swimsuit. Anyone have a problem with our Squid friend swimming au natural?" The Tschaaa embraced being called 'Squids' after seeing the very distant Giant Deep-Sea Cousins in Earth's Oceans. So, what humans once thought as insulting was not in Tschaaa parlance.

Captain Dagan McDowell, commander of 'C' Canine Company, laughed as she looked at her Battle Buddy. Capt. Lupe Pena, commander of 'A,' Aztec Company. The two's connection went back to before the Infestation began. Thus they could read each other's moods and thoughts. The two former Battle Buddies both began to strip themselves of their suits.

"What's a little cloth between girlfriends?" the dark-haired Texan Dagan called out as she began to demonstrate her idea, joined by shorter and stockier but still dark-haired Lupe. Soon, everyone was stripping to their bare essentials, even a few volunteers from Deseret, the Mormon State of former Utah. The traditional 'sanctified undergarments' had disappeared not long after the arrival of the Tschaaa.

"Well, Pilot Dorothy. Care to join your Sisters?"

The Squid looked at Aleksandra with the large eyes of her species, then gave a sign of respect and friendship.

"I thank you, humans, for trying to make me feel comfortable. Even at the expense of your cultural norms."

Abigail smiled, then began to remove her suit. A few years ago, her shyness and Mormon induced morality from Deseret would have prevented her from so casually removing her clothes, even among a group of women. Aleksandra had told her that she would soon become a 'jaded old married woman' who would be shocked by few and far between things. Being a 'child warrior' had accustomed her to many sights and sounds also.

Within moments, the close to four hundred women were all sans suits and continued their aquatic romps. Just then, Capt. O'Brien started to walk in on the tableau, swore, did an about-face, and quickly departed. Dorothy saw the human male's reaction and pointed it out to Abigail just as she was about to enter the pool.

"We Tschaaa still have trouble understanding you humans and your reaction to the opposite gender, especially when certain body parts are exposed. If it is not our biological time for mating, we feel no sexual desire."

Abigail laughed. "Were it so simple for Homo sapiens! But that is why we are called 'Nasty Monkeys.'"

Abigail slipped into the warm water, watched as Dorothy slid her substantial bulk into the pool. Her body size was that of a black bear, the strength of her eight supporting limbs similar. The Squid ducked under the water, then motivated quickly towards the deep end of the pool. Abigail followed using an Australian crawl. She knew the chlorinated water did not bother the Tschaaa.

Dorothy soon had a large group of human women circled her, this being the first time any had seen a Tschaaa in their natural habitat. Abigail approached, began to tread water.

"Alright, who would care to race, Dorothy?" Abigail called out. "Any Olympic swimmers here?"

Someone called out a name; then others turned it into a chant. Aryana, known to Abigail as Lieutenant Yellow Wolf, was a Native American who had been one of the original One Hundred and One during Bloody Kansas. Barely eighteen years of age at the time, on that night and later, she proved herself to be a natural warrior and leader. She was now a "B" Brave Company Platoon Commander. Each of the four original Companies had the option of choosing the patch symbol for their company, and Ayana had helped to develop a stylized Plains Tribe Warrior, a "Brave." Abigail did not know she had competitive swimming in her background. Aryana pulled herself up onto the edge of the pool, displaying a sleek and muscular frame.

Abigail pushed herself over to the pool edge near the Banshee Company Commander.

"So you have some speed swimming background, Lieutenant Yellow Wolf."

"Yes, Ma'am. My parents had me in a training regimen, hoped I was Olympic material."

Everyone knew the first Rock from Space had interrupted all previous plans.

Abigail looked at Dorothy. "Care for a race, my Tschaaa comrade?"

Dorothy answered by heaving herself up onto the pool's edge, next to Aryana. She used her eight limbs with their light cartilage frame to suspend her body up, a bit like a cross between a crab and a spider. The Squid aliens could move fairly quickly on land for short distances.

"Am I in the correct starting position, Major?"

"I think so. On my command, how about a race to the shallow end, then turn around and end back here in the deep end?"

Both of the swimmers signaled agreement, and Abigail climbed out of the pool. She stood off to the side of the two competitors and raised her arm.

"On my mark. Get read. SWIM!!" Abigail chopped her arm down as Ayala did a picture-perfect racing dive that sliced the water with nary a splash. Dorothy was slowly sliding into the pool. The human swimmer was meters ahead before she broke the surface, began a crawl stroke. Then the Tschaaa alien shoved off from the deep end of the pool.

There was no real race once Dorothy used her arms to propel herself forward, then used her water siphon jet ability of all cephalopods to shoot ahead. She reached the shallow end, turned back, and zipped back to the deep end as Ayala was reaching the shallows. Ayala did not slow, continued the race even though she knew the ocean denizen had beat her by a full pool length. The Banshees lining both sides of the pool laughed and let loose with the trilling war cry, which had become a keynote of their Unit. Dorothy adjusted her waterproof translator on one of her forward limbs, then greeted Ayala as she reached the deep end near Abigail.

"You are fast for a human in the water, Lieutenant Yellow Wolf."

The human swimmer reached out and took one of the social tentacle hands in her own.

"From you, that is a great compliment. I knew you were fast, but not that fast!"

Abigail smiled. It was surprising how two species who were,

just about a year prior, trying to kill each other could now work and relax together. She knew it was because the females of the species had decided the raising of Young was so much more important than who was the Apex Predator in the food chain.

Other Banshees were soon crowding around the two competitors, putting in their two cents worth. Abigail swam down to the center of the pool and met Aleksandra on the side.

"That worked out well, Little Sister," said Aleksandra.

"Yes, it did, Big Sister. Maybe a water polo team is in the future."

"Hmmm. That could keep the ladies in shape, as well as work out aggressions without too much damage or injuries. The Olympic teams I saw years ago were quite forceful in their desires to win."

"Well, we are a combat unit, Aleksandra. So there will always be aggression."

The Unit Commander shrugged. "We can revisit the subject after this mission. So, I am hungry. Come, I will buy you lunch, Abigail."

The Avenging Angel laughed. "Our chow hall is free, food prepared by the Newbies. So, I will expect you to buy me a real meal after the mission." With that comment, the two women raced each other to the shallow end of the pool.

Abigail, back in uniform, walked with Fuzz towards the chow hall. The War Dog had decided not to christen the pool with his presence, so he did need to be dried off like his Mistress. Possibly, thought Abigail, it was due to the presence of Dorothy. She knew that someday Corporal Fuzz would accept Dorothy as readily as any human. At least she hoped that would be so.

As she and Fuzz approached the dining facilities, she heard a commotion emanating from the back kitchen area. Then she heard someone yell, "Fight!" Abigail jogged to the side entrance to the kitchen as the sound of crashing pots and pans filled the area. She dashed into the back kitchen area and saw several Banshees standing back as two young women were doing the best to hurt each other. Hitting, kicking, even biting and clawing, the two 'Newbies' spat venom at each other as they ignored all around them, so intent they were on attacking the other.

Abigail stepped forward and grabbed the two combatants by exposed ears as someone yelled, "Ten Hut! Commander in the Area!" In a moment, she had them crying in pain as young girls in a Catholic Church school and she was the Senior Nun. Fuzz stood back, automatically protecting her rear.

"What do you two Newbies think you are doing?" Abigail hissed between clenched teeth. "What are you doing fighting in our dining area, like two spoiled cheerleaders after a football game?"

The two new Banshee Privates realized that they were now in deep kimchee. The Legendary Avenging Angel, the Unit Deputy Commander, had a hold of them and was not happy. There were stories of what she had done to miscreants in the past. Permanently. They both began to sputter out disjointed exclamations. Abigail noticed one of the two Privates was Anica Armstrong, just off of front entrance guard duty.

"Stand at attention!" The two young soldiers went rigid, eyes staring straight ahead.

"Now, what started this completely unacceptable display of childish behavior?"

One of the observing Banshees blurted out, "Joan called Anica a Kraken Lover!"

To be associated with the renegade humans who had supported the Tschaaa invasion and had practiced cannibalism had fast become an ultimate insult. Especially among survivors who had lived in areas under Kraken control.

Abigail glared at the observing Banshees. "And you let this happen? No one stepped forward to stop two sister Banshees from hurting each other? SHAME! Shame on all!"

One could now hear a pin drop. The Avenging Angel of legend was incensed.

"What is Our Creed? Say it!"

As a group, all the young privates began to recite the Banshee Creed: "Blessed are women whose hearts and souls are joined together by laughter and tears, who fight for life, against all fears, who face evil with blades of steel, because they shall be known as Sisters of Steel!"

Abigail fixed all the assembled young women with a look no one ever wanted to see. A couple of the Newbies began to shake.

"You will all report to Sergeant Major Marina Raskova. I will let the Senior Enlisted Advisor handle this unacceptable behavior. If she wishes to consider expulsion from the Unit, the Colonel and I will take it under advisement. BANSHEES DO NOT FIGHT THEIR SISTERS!"

The last statement, Abigail bellowed. At least one Newbie blinked back tears. The Sergeant Major, late from Russia, was a scarred combat veteran, one of the Originals. If she took action, the recipient of her attention would never forget it.

As Abigail turned on her heel and marched out, she thought she saw Corporal Fuzz glare at the young Banshees. Her War Dog did not like to see his Mistress upset.

Some three-quarters of an hour later, the Banshees were obtaining their lunches and began to sit with their platoon members. All except the former kitchen crew. The two combatants with the five observers sat stiffly at attention near a long table set now in the center of the dining hall. At the head of the table stood Sergeant Major Raskova, her frown accentuated by the large scar across her forehead, a physical reminder of a failed attempt at Harvesting by a Tschaaa wheeled robot. The stocky, dark-haired older woman never would say just when she had joined the Russian Military. She just had a reputation for being harder than rock and older than dirt. She jerked her gaze towards Anica.

"Did I see a shift in your seat, Newbie? Are you uncomfortable with my lesson in unarmed combat?

Maybe next time you will control your temper."

Marina Raskova glanced up and saw Abigail approaching.

"Come to Attention! Major Yamamoto approaches."

All seven miscreants came to rigid standing attention; the Sergeant Major greeted Abigail.

"Good afternoon, Major. Did you enjoy your swim in our nice new pool?"

Abigail smiled, then let her face assume a deadpanned expression.

"Yes, Sergeant Major. I enjoyed the pool. Then my enjoyment was marred by some childish behavior on the part of some new members to our Unit."

Marina smiled with an expression that resembled a sneer thanks in part to her scar.

"I can assure you, Major, THAT will not happen again. For I gave them some quick additional unarmed rough and tumble training to get rid of their aggression."

"Good. Have them sit. I will watch them while you get your lunch."

"Thank You, Major. You heard the Commander! SIT!" The seven young women sat.

Abigail noticed that Anica and her former opponent, a dark-skinned mixed-race female named Joan Bond, sat down gingerly.

Abigail knew Joan was also an orphan, the sole survivor of her family, which may help to explain the bottled up anger of the two Newbies. Alone, being inducted into a new 'family,' old emotional baggage would be brought out for all to see. Abigail also surmised that the Sergeant Major had probably used a favorite unarmed 'technique' to get her point across quickly. Her 'pussy punch' would cause some temporary pain for the evening, but would disappear by the morning, so as not to affect their part of the Mission tomorrow. Abigail also noticed that the Newbies had not been allowed to eat yet. Good. Let their misdeeds sink in some more.

The Sergeant Major returned with a full tray of hot food.

"I see the replacement kitchen crew outdid themselves," said Abigail.

"Yes, Major. Roasted venison, fresh potatoes, some fresh beets, and cake for dessert. Simple pleasures for a simple old soldier."

Abigail tried not to laugh. Marina was far from simple, had forgotten more about being a soldier than ten of her ilk. Frigid Siberian winters had made her appreciate good, hot food.

"And before I enjoy my meal, Major, I have arranged for the assignment of the two cat-fighters to the same platoon and squad in Dragon Company. They are forced to watch each other's behinds, rather than try to kick them."

Abigail nodded in assent. As usual, the Senior Enlisted Advisor knew just what to do. The 'D' Company Commander, Princess Akiko of the Free Japan Royal Family, would not tolerate any dishonor towards the Banshee traditions. The two would work together. Or Else.

Abigail gave the seated Newbies one more hard look.

"Carry on, Sergeant Major. I go to enjoy a meal with Cpl. Fuzz."

Marina grunted. "Do not spoil the enlisted troops too much, Major. Even the four-legged ones. It makes them soft."

Approximately an hour later, Abigail was sitting in her office, a War Dog with a full stomach sitting at her feet. She knew that Fuzz had a sense of humor as he liked to try and conceal himself behind her large oak desk (a present from Torbin Bender) and let out a grumbling growl at young, new soldiers who came into the office. Abigail soon realized it was all an act, as the 'victims' of his supposed anger Fuzz quickly approached for a good ear scratch. Once again, the Avenging Angel realized just how smart was this new breed of War Dog.

Abigail reviewed the operations plan provided by Captain O'Brien, committed the details to memory. A photographic memory gave her a definite advantage over others. Everything seemed to be in order, as it always was with Danny O'Brien's work. As she closed the file, there was a light knock at her door. Then Aleksandra entered. Abigail started to stand up as her Commander came in, but was Alex waved her to remain seated.

"Military protocol has its place, Little Sister. But not between us in private."

Abigail smiled as Cpl. Fuzz unwound himself from beneath the oak desk and went to Abigail for pets. Protocol did not matter to Fuzz either when a 'pack member' was involved.

Aleksandra laughed as she began to scratch the K-9's ears and chest.

"Just like your Sire, the other Big Beastie, you want to be spoiled." She looked up at Abigail. "He is so much like his father."

"Yes, he is. Though he is a bit larger if that's possible."

"His father's genes bred pure, Abigail, which is a plus for us. He and his litter-mate's offspring will be the beginning of a new breed, I think. One suited for war and protection."

Abigail smiled back, again felt that little pang when she thought about Fuzz Senior. He had been a Best Buddy to Abigail, so she would always bear scars over his death protecting, no, 'saving' was the correct term. Sergeant Fuzz had also saved a pregnant Aleks from two Eaters, so the Avenging Angel knew that the Russian Spy felt the loss too. However, seeing Fuzz, the Younger did help.

"Dr. Emily Anders the Vet said much the same thing. So if he will be a registered breed, what will be the breed's title?"

"Why, War Dog, of course. For when the Squids and Krakens screwed with their genetic code, that is what they helped to create. Much to their displeasure."

Abigail smiled. Cpl. Fuzz looked at her, let his mouth open into an answering K-9 grin.

"But, Aleks, Fuzz is not the reason you are here, is it?" Abigail's adopted Big Sister sighed.

"You read me too well. But since we are again going into harm's way, I again must remind you of something." She stopped scratching Fuzz and sat down on the couch opposite of Abigail.

"You are a commander, a leader. Let the lower ranks do the fighting, the assaulting. There is no reason for you to rush in and try to use your well-known abilities to win any conflict by yourself."

Abigail and combat were a subject oft-discussed between the two women. Abigail was 'one of a kind,' probably the deadliest female warrior in the known world because of the Tschaaa science-based physical modifications performed on her by some nasty authorities in Deseret. Her years of training as a child warrior, from age twelve, added to her deadly ability. Abigail sighed, answered in Russian.

"I know, my Commander. But to stand by and watch others do what your husband Torbin would call the heavy lifting…"

"You are not just 'standing by.' You are leading, while also being in the combat zone. Please. I need your leadership abilities, the loyalty all the Banshees feel towards you. We all know the unique position you have in the formation of this unit."

"They are also loyal to YOU, my Big Sister. You are the Commander!"

"Who would not be here without your presence, your symbol to all these young women. You are the true 'mother' that created the Sisters of Steel. I am just the 'step-mother,' the Old Bitch who all the younger troops can grumble about."

"That is not true! If I hear someone call you that, Aleks, I'll-"

Aleks Smirnov-Bender laughed. "I have heard so much worse. But please. The point is still the same. Do not rush forward; try to defeat any enemy all by yourself. Lead so others may follow, do what is needed. I do not need you harmed unnecessarily."

It was Abigail's turn to sigh. She knew Aleks was correct, but when the fight started... She looked at Cpl. Fuzz. He had fixed his gaze on 'his human' as if to say 'I'm here. I have your back, no matter what.' Her mouth formed a slight K-9 smile.

"I promise I will try and not worry you unnecessarily, Aleks. Especially if that will make you happy."

"Yes, it will. Now, I take it that Captain O'Brien's Ops Plan meets the muster?"

"Yes, Ma'am. He has, as Torbin would say, dotted his 'Is' and crossed his 'Ts,' as he always does..."

Oh Dark Thirty came too early for some. However, as was her habit, Abigail awoke early with Corporal Fuzz. A quick shower, then on with the combat gear, Battle Rattle and all. Only Fuzz's Raptor armored helmet was left off. His Mistress would put that on before they reached their 'jump off' point. Everything else was put on and strapped down just right, to include Abigail's Glock 18 and Marlin rifle. Abigail had a combat rifle sheath designed for her .44 Magnum lever action. Because of her position, and her stubbornness, she was allowed a non-standard weapon. Everyone else had standard assault rifles or issued heavy weapons

There were a few other exceptions to the standards this day. Danny O'Brien had his historic Armalite-18, the exact type smuggled to the old Irish Republican Army, which became the subject of an Irish song or two. Captains Dagan McDowell and Lupe Pena received pre-production assault weapons of the new 'Bender' heavy six millimeter round to test out, rather than the standard 5.56mm/.223 rifle round. And Sergeant Major Roskava had somehow come up with an old but still functional PPSH 7.62 submachine gun, Joseph Stalin's favorite. Aleksandra had laughed as she authorized the NCO to carry a weapon over twice the age of the user. But the Russian was deadly with it. Aleksandra carried a Russian built Grach hi-velocity 9MM pistol, a present from Senior Instructor Stalin. For this mission, she also had one of Technical Advisor, and Wizard 'Pappy" Gunn's disposable 3D Printer made carbines in 5.56. It would last long enough for what she wanted to accomplish.

Abigail walked around the four companies formed up on the parade field outside the Banshee Barracks and watched what had now become a well-drilled routine. Company Commanders had their Platoon Leader Lieutenants observing the Platoon NCO's and the Squad Leaders check each Banshee to ensure everything was 'high and tight". Thus she heard now-familiar refrains.

"Clean that spot off your Banshee Blade. Whatsamatter, you EAT with that last night?"

"Run a cleaning patch down that barrel, Private. It has to shine inside."

"Tighten that Battle Rattle up, Troop. If it falls off, your boobs will be stopping bullets, not your body armor."

But as every inadequacy, problem, or 'ding' was found, other squadmates and platoon members jumped to help fix what needed correction. From day one, 'Teamwork and Sisterhood' was a significant mantra of the 101st Special Attack Unit, the Banshees. Their signature eleven-inch double razor-edged fighting blade, the 'Banshee Blade,' all made by Hannah Weitz at her forge, was the unique symbol that identified a Sister to another. Attached to their military dog tags around their necks was also a miniature version of the weapon. The miniature looked almost like a cross from a distance. Again, the Kraken Fighting Pit survivor made all of these. So the old expression 'Gung Ho' applied to the Banshees in spades.

Abigail smiled with satisfaction. The Banshees were tight, as she and Aleks had wanted. So far, this 'tightness' had helped the Unit to kick ass and take names in several locations around the world, with only minor casualties. Now, thought the Avenging Angel, if only they could keep it that way. As she stood a bit to the side, she noticed Princess Akiko, a Captain in the United Armed Forces and D- Dragon Company Commander approaching. A member of the Free Japan Royal Family, she had designed the Asian dragon for the uniform patch and company flag. Akiko was also a 'child warrior' of almost the exact age of Abigail, which created a unique bond between the two women. The Princess stopped in front of Abigail and saluted.

"How is Major Yamamoto this grand morning?" the Japanese Officer asked in her native language with a slight smile.

"Just fine, my fellow Banshee. I sense a request," Abigail replied in flawless Japanese.

"Not from me, Ma'am. But from two Newbies. They asked through their NCOs and their Platoon Commander if I may arrive a short audience with you."

"Are these the two disciplined for fighting?"

"Yes. The two wish to ask for the forgiveness of the Avenging Angel. The thought of continued displeasure from you seems to be more than they can bear."

Abigail winced a bit. Being a 'legend' and the foundation for an exceptional organization that was becoming legendary was a burden. Torbin Bender had told her that being a 'heroine' had its unjust rewards. People who felt a need to curry favor or approval was one of them. Those who fawned due to a misguided image of who you were was another.

"What do you think, Captain? It happened just yesterday. Have the dishonors of their actions sunk insufficiently?"

Of all the people she could ask, Akiko was among the most relevant. Being a New Samurai, like Abigail's husband Ichiro, duty, loyalty, and honor, were paramount.

"I think so, based on what you Americans call 'hangdog looks' etched on their faces. Plus, the others of their newly assigned Squad let them know that such actions are not tolerated, whether any of the Command Staff is watching or not. They know they are on notice not to screw up again."

Abigail paused in thought, then answered. "Alright. Have them approach, but only after you emphasize to them that if we were not about to go on a combat mission, they would be left to stew in your own juices, as Generals Reed and Bender would say. Sisters Do Not Fight Each Other." She used her tone to emphasize the last. Akiko smiled at the response.

"Hai! Spoken like a Samurai Shogun of old! I will have them approach after I add my own special emphasis."

"Not too hard, My Sister. We are about to face possible harm. Their minds must be clear."

"Of course. I go." The Princess bowed, then saluted, about-faced and sped off using the low short stride quick running stance seen in many an old Japanese Samurai Epic. Abigail grinned. Akiko had helped make her and Ichiro honorary members of the Japanese Royal Family. So again, Abigail had a special relationship with a huge extended family. However, this was the new family dynamics of Post

Great Compromise existence. You were a family member because you were accepted as one, not by blood or government degree.

Within what seemed like moments, the Captain had the two Newbies double-timing to Abigail's location. Akiko brought them to an abrupt halt at rigid attention.

"Major Yamamoto. Privates Armstrong and Bond are reporting as ordered."

"Thank You, Captain. Now, please see to the rest of your Company. I think I can handle these two… miscreants."

Abigail caught a hint of a smile on Akiko's face. "Yes, Ma'am!" She saluted and double-timed back to her Company in the same low Samurai running gait.

Abigail stepped up to just inches from the faces of the two Privates. She could smell a bit of fear tainted sweat emanating from the two women. Abigail thus knew that they were taking this seriously, knew they realized they were so close to expulsion from their new family.

Abigail spoke in a low voice. "You two wish to apologize to me, yes?"

"Yes, Ma'am." The two spoke in unison.

"Did you apologize to your Squad?"

"Yes, Ma'am." Again in unison. Good. They were learning to work together.

"THAT is what is important—the people who are on your shoulder. Like Sergeant, Jefferson is on your right shoulder, the position of honor, Armstrong. You let them down, someone dies. Do you both understand?"

"Yes, Ma'am."

Abigail stepped back, looked at them. "At ease."

The two Privates tried to relax a bit at the unexpected order but were still stiff.

"Walk with me, Privates. Tell me what you see." And thus, they began a walk around the Entire Unit as it prepared for the mission.

"Well, what do you see? Bond?"

"Ma'am, I see warriors getting ready for battle."

"Armstrong. What about you?"

"Ma'am, I see a Sisterhood, helping each other."

Abigail nodded, stopped, and looked at the two Privates. "You are both right. For us, Banshees are a Warrior Sisterhood, borne from the depravations of the Infestation. Now, we exist to prevent others from having to suffer as we have, as our families have. We have a sacred mission to ensure future generations of women, and females can give birth and raise children in peace. No threat of being killed, eaten. The small pink ribbon on the back of our berets reminds us of our femininity."

Abigail pause for a moment to let what she had said sink in. Then she continued.

"The Great Compromise also meant the Tschaaa could raise their Young, their children in peace also. Primarily the result of the efforts of a small group of females, women, Breeders. With the help of some special men in our lives, of course. And a certain now Guardian Angel Cyborg named Andrew."

"You were there, Ma'am," said Private Armstrong.

"Yes. And that is why I am so adamant about working together, no fighting. We have to ensure females of all species can be givers of life, not takers of it. Now, Report back to your squads. Dismissed."

The two Privates went rigid, saluted, about-faced, and double-timed in unison to their units. Abigail allowed herself a small smile. She was not much older than they, but others looked on as a 'senior' one of the Originals. Funny how things turned out.

Abigail went looking for Aleksandra and found her conferring with Captain O'Brien and Major Afanasii 'Fanny' Kozlov, a former Russian spy with Aleks and now the Banshee's Intelligence Officer. She was one of the original 'Three Bitches' along with Aleks, who had come from Russia to spy and wound up staying permanently. They had also been instrumental in assuring a particular 'child soldier' adjusted to newfound freedom. Fanny saw her approach and smiled, called out a greeting in Russian.

"I thought maybe Ichiro was keeping you home this time."

"Not yet. But maybe... soon."

The two Russian women gave each other knowing looks. They knew about 'biological clocks' that hit women at various times in their lives. Aleksandra looked at Abigail, spoke in English.

"I guess I will need to say a few words before boarding the Ark."

"Yes, Ma'am. They will want to hear from their Commander. It gives the younger ones some more confidence if they see that the Colonel cares."

Aleks sighed. "I am a trained spy, not a trained leader. You come to this naturally, Abigail. I should have you do it."

"Begging your pardon, Ma'am," Danny broke in. "But they look up to you as the senior person.

They need your reassurance."

Aleks snorted. "Yes. Senior as in 'the old woman,' I wager."

Abigail grinned as she spoke. "You are not old, Big Sister. Torbin tells me you still act like a young girl at times."

"What? I will have to have a few words with my husband, the General. Just because he outranks me does not mean he can talk about me behind my back."

The officers laughed. A small specialized combat unit like the Banshees was also a close unit in a personal manner.

"Major, if you would be so kind as to ensure our four companies are about ready to board our Assault, Ark."

"Yes, Ma'am."

Within minutes, the four companies were at parade rest on the tarmac near the Assault Ark. Painted with a camouflaged rendition of a giant 'Banshee' warrior, the original craft used for Harvesting humans and said to resemble an idea of Noah's Ark, was now used to transport humans to aid others. The butcher and slaughter equipment long since removed, the interior now contained assault seats for all the Banshees and then some vehicles, weapons, and other equipment. Plus, 'Pappy' Gunn had added modifications in weaponry as well as the Tschaaa shield system that still worked better in the vacuum of Outer Space, but would stop or deflect some Earth weapons in the atmosphere. Additional human-modified lift engines and thrusters had also been added for aid in lift-off, the transition to low orbit, then swooping in to land anyplace in the world. This mission would be the third fully operational trip for the craft. Someone had christened the spacecraft 'Queen Elizabeth' after a historical ship from a bygone era. So, of course, it was talked in terms of 'She' and 'Her.'

Aleksandra stepped up in front of the assembled soldiers, with her staff officers and NCO's to her right. Her voice rang out.

"Banshees! Sisters of Steel! We embark on another mission of hope and protection. The hope is that our example will provide hope to many of the weak and frightened that a new time is at hand. The protection is our abilities in the martial arts and weaponry. We stop those who wish to prey on the weak and frightened."

"You have been briefed by your Officers and NCO's on the details of this mission. We fly to the Syrian-Iraqi border. For again, some wish to subjugate those who just freed from Tschaaa and Kraken rule. Others use an ancient form of religious fanaticism to oppress. Our mere presence may be enough to derail the plans of those fanatics. If not… well, we have blades of steel, do we not?"

The assembled warriors called out as one "Cold steel!" The original rallying cry of Bloody Kansas, where the true tradition of the Banshees began. Captain Kira Samson, commander of Brave Company, was said to have been the first Sister of Steel who called out the refrain that fateful day. Then a Sergeant, her loyalty to the Avenging Angel, was still legendary.

Abigail smiled in her mind as she felt the pride she felt in being part of this extraordinary group of women. She always hoped she would be worthy of their loyalty and respect. Aleksandra then spoke to her.

"Major. Do you have anything to add?"

Abigail stepped forward and surveyed some four hundred warrior women. Cpl. Fuzz sat behind her, watching everything around them. He always had her back.

"Where is Sergeant Jefferson?" she called out. In perfect unison came the reply.

"Here! On our right shoulder! In the position of honor, where she belongs!"

Abigail stepped back in line with the other staff. Aleksandra called out one last command.

"Commanders! Take charge of your Companies and load them on the Ark. A mission awaits us."

As one, all four Companies turned in unison to their left, into a column formation. As one, all the Banshees let out the signature undulating cry that had become their trademark. The result of the experience of a young Pit Fighter named Hannah Weitz, the call was known to freeze and confuse alien Eaters, Krakens, and Squid Warriors. First heard outside the Fighting Pits during Bloody Kansas, it became part of the unit's soul. An organization with a bit more than a year of organizational history, the 101st SAU, the BANSHEES, had developed many and varied traditions mixed with mythology and spirit. All serve an organization well.

Abigail watched as the Company Commanders marched their personnel into the cargo bay of the vast Ark. She turned towards Aleks.

"I'll head up to the Ark cockpit, check on Pilot Dorothy and Captain Bell."

"And you will be able to contact your husband on the aircraft frequency, true?"

Abigail smiled. "You know me too well."

"That is because I would do the same if my Torbin were a pilot like his brother William. Instead, he is just a stubborn Jarhead, the correct word, I believe."

"And now a General," added Abigail. "Groomed to take General Reed's position."

Aleks sighed. "Which means my two sons and I will see him even less. He did arrange to stay with the Twin Trolls on this mission. So hopefully, we will be back within 72 hours as planned. Now, head towards your radio rendezvous, Little Sister."

"Yes, Ma'am."

Abigail contacted Dorothy and Shannon Bell on the upper deck in the command cockpit. The Ark dwarfed all previous military transport craft, its nose with the cockpit close to three stories above the tarmac. It was cavernous, with additional seats behind the pilot positions. Dorothy sat in the left position as Command Pilot, Shannon Bell in the right seat as Co-pilot. Abigail stood silent and watched for a few moments as Dorothy's long and slender fingers on the end of the social tentacle hands were a blur on all the control keys and switches. Shannon watched her actions with close scrutiny.

"See, Shannon. If you must make an emergency lift and take off," explained Dorothy. "You can bypass many of these support functions, reroute power to the more efficient thrusters you Humans designed."

"Ladies," said Abigail.

"Major." Dorothy's translator spoke in the tones of a Mid-Western speaker. "We are prepared for liftoff upon command. All that is required is that my sister Banshees are secured in their seats."

"Captain Bell. Getting the hang of this huge flying beast?"

"Yes, Ma'am. But I will never be as good as my Command Pilot here. Dorothy's hands and tentacles are so much quicker than mine."

"You sell yourself short, I believe is the expression," interjected Dorothy. "It just takes practice, Shannon."

"Well, the Tschaaa built this craft for Tschaaa," .said Abigail. "I guess we could change some ergonomics, but that would cramp our Squid Sister here."

"I am at your command, Major. If you wish some modifications for my Human Co-Pilot, I could arrange it. We have Gray workers available."

The thought of Grays always made Abigail's skin crawl. Some had tried to abduct her back under their control, had killed Sgt. Fuzz as he stopped them. The thought of them working on this ship...

"No, Pilot. I think we will give the good Captain here some more time to work on it. Now, have you had contact with our fighter escort?"

Shannon smiled. "Your husband, the Colonel, checked in. He and Colonel Hunter are on Strip Alert, awaiting your call."

"You read my mind. Can you get the pilots on the horn?"

"Of course."

Moments later, she heard Ichiro's voice on a secondary Guard channel.

"Is the Major and her Sisters ready for take-off?" Ichiro asked.

"Almost, Colonel. Just a few more details to take care of." Then Abigail switched to Japanese.

"You be careful, my love. I do not want that new fighter doing you harm."

"You are the one going into Harm's Way, dearest. I am but an escort."

"No worries. This mission should be a milk run, as they say— time to go. See you at home in a few days. I love you."

Abigail cut the transmission and stepped back. "Time to head to the transport hold; make sure everyone is ship-shape as they say."

"Major, one question, if you please."

"Yes, Dorothy. What is it?"

The Squid Breeder seemed to fidget with her long fingers, signed nervous humility.

"It is more of a request, Major. And it may seem - too much." Abigail frowned. What was this? She had not seen this level of apprehension in the Tschaaa Pilot before.

"Please, my Banshee Sister. What is it?"

"If possible, if he would consent... I would like to try and... pet Cpl. Fuzz someday. I have read that K-9s fur is quite nice and soothing."

Abigail paused, a bit flabbergasted. She had never heard of a Tschaaa ever expressing interest in dogs, other than to discuss the relationship between Man and his Best Friend. She looked at Dorothy, sensed that she was sincere.

"I know, Major, they dislike non-native species..."

"I will try, Dorothy. But the final decision will be up to the Corporal. He is an individual and a soldier. But I must ask why the sudden interest?"

"Shannon and I were talking about our younger years," Dorothy replied. "She talked about growing up with dogs, pets. I, my companion Breeders, had no… pets. The relationship with your dogs seems to give you both such pleasure. To be so close to another species growing up - thought it would also help my understanding of your culture also."

Abigail knew that the generations' long voyage to Earth in the Tschaaa Crèche Ships had strained an already stressed culture. But the thought of a desire to have the pleasure of a furry beast… that was a new one.

"I will try. It's an interesting idea. Now, to work. I must get back with the Companies."

Abigail made her way down the walkways to the main hold. Squad leaders and Platoon NCOs were ensuring everyone, and everything was in their right places. When she saw two familiar faces talking with Danny O'Brien, she realized she had forgotten they would have two select passengers along on this mission. Doctor Rica Rice and Veterinarian Doctor Emily Anders had asked to be included as part of a program to ascertain just what medical services were available in many of the areas decimated during the Infestation. They were to report back to Madam President as to what was needed to help set up medical facilities for both humans and animals in these areas. Of course, Abigail had a special relationship with the two women doctors who had brought her back from a terrible place.

Thus, when she walked up to them, it was all smiles and then hugs.

"How is one of my favorite patients, Major?" Rica asked.

"Just fine. Glad to see you coming along on one of these trips. We can use some medical aid for some of the civilians we contact."

At that moment, Corporal Fuzz, seeing Emily, the person who

had helped deliver him, came from the shadows where he had been watching everything and everybody. He always 'overwatched' the Banshees, and his Human Sisters always knew that with him around, nothing would sneak upon them.

"How's my favorite guy?" Emily crouched down and gave him a grand hug, which resulted in a grand K-9 slurping kiss. Abigail smiled, remembered how she had met Emily due to Fuzz Senior. Bittersweet memories again.

"I've heard through the grapevine that actually, there is a two-legged person who is your 'favorite guy' now," said Abigail. "And is that a new ring with a sizable stone in it?"

Emily stood and blushed a bit. "The ole rumor mill strikes again. Yes, Commissioner Paul Miller asked, and I said 'yes.' Of course, you and Fuzz will be honored guests at the wedding. If we ever find time to plan and have one."

The only people as busy as the Banshees in the post-Great Compromise environment were the Free Allied Nations law enforcement establishments. Paul Miller was the Federal Law Enforcement Commissioner, over the reconstituted U.S. Marshals and U.S. Customs and Immigration. Madam President Sandra Paul and the New Congress had simplified the federal bureaucracy down to two main bureaus. No more alphabet soup of agencies. Marshals handled all interior enforcement, Customs and Immigration, including the Border Patrol, protected the borders, and handled exterior enforcement issues. Under Paul Miller, they were expected to work together, as well as hand in glove with local Sheriffs, Police Chiefs, and State Vigilance Groups. There were still large numbers of Eaters, Krakens, and feral humans in organized crime running about, the reconstituted United States of North America has just celebrated its first anniversary. From the southern tip of former Central America to the Canadian Arctic, they were now all one big happy family. Or at least that is what Madam President hoped.

"How are law and order coming along in the world, Doctor Anders?" Danny asked.

"Please call me Emily. When I see Paul at night, he tells me things are getting better in Russia, have always been good in Free Japan. The rest of the world- a work in progress. Which is why you Banshees are so important. They show the flag of freedom and human rights around. Some wish a return to feudalism, especially when it comes to women."

"Won't happen with Fuzz and me around. Will, it Corporal?" Abigail asked as she smiled at her four-legged partner, who gave you a low 'woof' in agreement.

"The War Dog genetic line is coming along nicely, Abigail," said Emily. "The studies we have completed on the modifications done to Fuzz Senior, and a couple of other canines recovered by Dogman are enabling us to identify a true genetic breed. Hundreds to thousands of Fuzz will be around sooner than you think."

"But there will only be two originals. Fuzz and the Sire. At least to me," said Abigail as she scratched his ears, received appreciative dog grunts of pleasure.

"And with that, I need to get back to my duties as the Deputy Commander. Captain O'Brien, please make sure these two ladies are safe and secured for lift off."

"Yes, Ma'am. Ladies, if you please."

"See you later, Abigail," Rica called out as she followed Danny.

Some ten minutes later, everyone was in their appointed places, ready for lift-off. All equipment not attached to a Banshee's body was stored so as not to fly around during maneuvering or float off during the low orbit lack of gravity. For the Ark would reach the edge of space, and everyone, Cpl. Fuzz included, would experience a short period of weightlessness. It had taken Fuzz a bit of assistance from Abigail to get used to the sensation. War Dogs preferred to be closer to Mother Earth.

Shannon Bell's voice resounded over the intercom system.

"Stand by to lift-off. Five... Four... Three... Two... One... Ignition."

The large lift engines and turbofans erupted into action. A sort shudder, the feeling of an upward moving elevator as the Ark left the runway. It was not an entirely high lift, such as in a helicopter. Instead, the craft lifted up until the nose began to tilt skyward. Then, oversized injector scramjet engines cut in, and the aircraft started to climb. As the engines overcame the initial inertia, the enormous low orbit craft began to accelerate at a surprising rate. For some, the fun started as it took on the thrill of some ancient carnival ride. Others still just hung on, yet not wholly trusting the original Tschaaa engineering that had designed such an oversized craft to fly into space.

The increasingly rapid ascent did cause some G-Forces on the Banshees, as well as Fuzz, who had a specially designed padded lift seat next to Abigail. A steady rather than sharp acceleration prevented the effect seen on old film reels of the ancient rocket sleds used for testing the impact of G-Forces on human and animal test subjects. But the Banshees would still have trouble if they had wished to leave their seats. None tried.

Then the acceleration and pressure decreased as they reached low orbit and began to feel the same weightlessness felt by early Astronauts in the legendary Vomit Comet test aircraft. "Banshees, we are maneuvering in low orbit, with two escort V-wing fighters in escort." Captain Bell's voice was as calm as any 20th-century airline pilot. "Soon, we will be on the other side of the world and begin our descent. We will complete a slow spiral to the lower altitudes, then head in towards our landing point. Sorry, but the beverage service is not available at this time on Banshee Airlines. Your understanding is appreciated."

Rude noises came from some of the Originals as this old joke repeated.

Shannon Bell's humor had come from her father, an old B-52 bomber pilot. With the mood also came steadiness and calm that told all the Banshees that, if the sh-t hit the fan, Shannon would get them home.

As gravity began to return, Abigail was up, out of her seat. She moved through the large hold, checking on Cpl. Fuzz first, then the rest of SAU members. All was well, other than a few cases of 'green around the gills' for some Newbies. She saw Aleks up and also moving on the opposite side of the Ark, saw the surprise on some of the new troops' faces as the 'Old Lady' was checking on them. Abigail smiled. So much for her protests about not being a real leader.

The intercom crackled to life once again. The voice was Dorothy's. "Commanders. I need you. Something... very unforeseen has happened." The message caused some murmuring among the Banshees.

Then Sergeant Major Raskova's recognizable voice range out. "Did the pilot say there was a reason for bitching? I did not hear it."

With that comment, forced calm again descended. Abigail saw Aleks wink at her Sister Russian. The Senior Enlisted Advisor was always ready to step in when needed. Aleks, Abigail, Danny, and Fanny made their way to the cockpit. When they entered, they were shocked to see a particular figure on the overhead screen. Madam President was talking to Dorothy and Shannon.

"Can you arrange it so I can see them when they see me? I need two ways... Okay. Ladies. Commanders. Sorry to butt in like this…" Abigail knew by that statement that the President could see them through the communication feed.

"You are the President. You cannot interrupt. We serve you." Aleks cut through with Russian bluntness. There was no time for niceties. There was a slight delay due to the distance involved. Then Sara Paul smiled.

"Thank God for Russian sensibilities to cut through the crap. So I will be short and to the point. We have found General Reed's wife and sons. Alive."

Despite the ambient noise of the Ark, it seemed as if silence had descended in the cockpit.

"Excuse me, Ma'am," Abigail broke in. "But did I hear correctly? General Reed's family, believed deceased, has been found, alive?"

"Yes, Abigail. It is easier to show than tell. Please watch this intercepted video transmission from Chechnya."

After a short transmission delay, the personnel in the cockpit were viewing a huge bearded man talking via a Skype connection. He was speaking in the Chechen dialect. Someone was running a translator with the video. Closed captioning in English appeared at the bottom of the screen. He was ranting about specific foreign armed forces, mainly Russian, active around the borders of Chechnya, who had better steer clear of his area or there would be Hell to pay. As he spoke, a female figure with two children walked behind the speaker, in the background of the video. The dark-haired woman looked straight into the camera, then looked away, guided her two charges off-screen. An enhanced screen save then came into view, with the picture of the woman and her two children enhanced and magnified.

"That is them? For sure?" Aleks asked. A voice came from off-screen, near Madam President.

"Yes. My God. It's them." General John Reed's voice ended with a slightly unusual quiver, then he spoke again.

"Ivana. John Junior is the older young man in the picture, should be about twelve. Ivan is the younger; he is about ten. It's been going on eight years since I saw them last..."

"We go," Aleks jumped in. "Pilot Dorothy and Captain Bell, plot a new course to that area..."

"Already done, Ma'am," answered Shannon. "It's the Sovetskoy Mountains. Dorothy is getting a Tschaaa Eye in the Sky to take a closer look."

"Abigail, you and Captain O'Brien..."

"NO!" It was John Reed's voice in a not typical bellow. "You can't do a hurry-up assault. That warlord, a Muslim Fanatic named Abbas Onlu, is agitated, alerted. You saw his demeanor in the video. He is just waiting for someone to shoot at, to kill! Maybe he will notice Ivana's face broadcasted. Whatever the conditions around that stone fort of his, shown in some old photographs we have found, he is dug in." He moved into the view of the camera, almost pushed Madam President out of the way.

"I thought they were dead this long. I can wait for an organized plan, more resources a while longer..."

"That is not your decision, General. It is mine." The famous Spine of Steel of the Commander in Chief showed itself as she spoke. Madam President was in charge. "And we must act before she and her sons are moved again if something tipped off Abbu Onlu."

"Colonel Smirnov, I will leave it up to you. Do you..."

"We go!" Alek's voice was full of Old Russian blood and iron. "We cannot leave a Russian Mother and her children in the hands of a fanatic."

"Goddammit, Aleks!" John Reed yelled. "I will not allow Torbin to be a widower! Your sons will NOT be fatherless!"

"General, stand down! I'm the dammedable President, not you!" It began to dissolve into a shouting match.

Before Abigail could get a word in edgewise, a deep vibrating sound interrupted the argument. It took a moment for the humans to realize it was a Tschaaa trying to get their attention with the buried base tones they used to communicate for miles under the ocean. Dorothy then switched back to the translator.

"There are Young in danger, yes?" the Breeder asked.

"Yes, Dorothy," answered Abigail. "There are."

"Then, I am unable to standby. For if I do, I will surely stop living."

All arguing came to a screeching halt. For the Humans knew that Tschaaa Breeders could become catatonic and die if they felt they were the cause of or allowed the death of a Young One.

"So, Madam President. If you would be so kind as to allow me to contact some of my fellow Squids, I will go with them. For go, I Must." Dorothy's statement was blunt.

John Reed began to curse long and hard in every language he knew, even as tears ran down his face. Abigail knew he was torn between wanting to save his wife and children, and not being responsible for the deaths of young women he knew and cared for, especially his adopted daughters of Abigail and Aleks. Sarah Paul reached out, put her arm around him, and pulled him in for a hug as she spoke.

"You saved me and mine, John. Allow me to return the favor." She looked at the screen, then said, "You Banshees get them back. That's an order."

Abigail stiffened to attention. "I will have my adopted brothers and mother back, Madam President. They are also my family."

John Reed managed to compose himself, looked into the

screen as he spoke. "You all be careful. I have been at way too many funerals recently."

The Banshee Officers answered "Yes, General," in unison. John Reed stepped out of view as Madam President looked into the screen.

"Cold Steel, my Banshees. Cold Steel." Her voice had an edge of steel.

"But of course, Madam President," answered Aleks. The screen went blank as the President cut the connection. Aleks took a deep breath, let it out before she spoke. "We Banshees are going to Hell. But that is where we were born."

Within minutes, the transport hold was a flurry of activity as the just over four hundred Banshees were briefed on the new mission, then began to modify their combat loads and equipment accordingly. Danny O'Brien pulled out the new ballistic entry shields made from the Tschaaa developed super-tough crustacean based armor. The Banshees would have to go in hot and fast, assault en masse from the front after the huge loading ramp dropped. 'Shield Maidens', a term adopted by the Banshees for the more significant unit members who would be in the front ranks, would absorb the first onslaught of fire from the unknown number of defenders on the new shields. Dorothy and Shannon adjusted the flight path of the Assault Ark, would come in at a fast and steep angle, and try not to land too hard. Then, they would use the 'Pappy' Gunn added firepower to help suppress the threats from the defenders, plus hoped the shields would be of sufficient help. The plan was to get in, find Ivana Reed and her sons, and get out. All the Banshees knew that the 'milk run' was long gone. There would be blood and death, the first for many of the newer members of the unit. The Infestation had been rough, but not everyone was to fight and kill for their existence.

When told they would be fighting Chechens, Sergeant Major Raskova had sneered and spat. "They are assholes. They killed my father. Time for payback."

Someone asked about Andrew and the Guardian Angels, would they intercede. But most knew the answer to the question of their involvement. They would prevent large scale conflict, specifically between Tschaaa and Humans, not a relatively minor battle such as this. The Sisters of Steel were on their own.

Ichiro and Cliff Hunter were hot-footing it to an airfield in New Israel to find fuel for their V-Wing fighters. The added distance to Chechnya in aircraft that fueled for a 'milk run' meant they need refuel as the Ark came from low orbit to its new target. Until they returned and met up with the Ark, the Banshees had no additional air support. Thus, another reason for NOT having a stand-up fight. Hit hard, fast, grab Ivana and the boys, then bug-out. Piece of cake.

As Banshees settled into their assigned spaces for the assault, many walked by Corporal Fuzz, gave him a quick pet. Abigail knew the pets were as much to help calm them as for good luck. Fuzz regaled in the attention, cutting a unique figure in his new armor and 'Raptor' helmet. The War Dog grinned in his unique way. The Avenging Angel grinned back as Aleks walked up, smiled, and spoke.

"I see the big beastie is raring to go, as you Americans would say."

"He knows that this is his purpose in life. As it is mine," answered Abigail

"It is at this moment, Little Sister. Remember that. You have a fine husband with which to start a family."

"Who is also along on this 'milk run,' about to get shot at," Abigail added.

Aleks placed her hand on Abigail's arm. "We will get through this together. As we always have. For we are Sisters of Steel."

The intercom crackled to life with Dorothy's voice. "We will begin a circular descent toward the new target in some ten minutes. As we do that, Captain Bell and I will keep the Ark at a steep angle of descent. Do not be afraid. We will not crash. Then, we will let you know when we flair out at the last moment, using our lift and thrust to set the Ark down. It will be hard and fast. But it will be controlled. So, if all of you please put your tray tables in an upright position, turn off all electronic devices, and relax. Thank you for flying Squid Airlines."

It took a few moments for the Banshees to realize that the Tschaaa Breeder had done something scarce for an Adult Tschaaa. She had joked. The laughter came. It was good, stress-relieving laughter, never to be forgotten. Just then, Captain Danny O'Brien magically appeared with his small, accordion, his 'squeezebox,' and began an official song of the 101st Special Attack Unit. "JUMP UP" composed by some Irish Republican Army Soldier, and modified slightly by Danny. They had been fighting Krakens and Squids when the Irish Tenor had introduced it to the Banshees.

And it's down in the hillside, that's where I long to be,
Lying in the dark with a Banshee company,
A Sister on me left and another on me right
And a clip of ammunition for my little Armalite.
I was stopped by a Kraken, said he, You are a swine,
He beat me with his baton, and he kicked me in the groin,
I bowed, and I scraped, sure me manners were polite
But all the time, I'm thinking of me little Armalite.
And it's down in Bloody Kansas, sure that's where I long to be,
Lying in the dark with a Banshee company,
A Sister on me left and another on me right
And a clip of ammunition for my little Armalite.

Sure a brave Kraken man came up into our street
Six hundred Kraken soldiers were gathered
around his feet
Come out, ye cowardly Banshees said he, come out and fight.
But he cried, I'm only joking when he heard the Armalite.
Sure it's down in Savannah, that's where I long to be,
Lying in the dark with a Banshee company,
A Sister on me left and another on me right
And a clip of ammunition for my little Armalite.
Sure, the feral army came to visit me, 'twas in the early hours,
With Abrams and Bradleys and feral armoured cars
They thought they had me cornered, but I gave them all a fright
With the armour piercing bullets of my little Armalite.
And it's down in the Eater Land, that's where I long to be,
Lying in the dark with a Banshee company,
A Sister on me left and another on me right
And a clip of ammunition for my little Armalite.
When Talbot came to Kansas, he said, The battle's won,
Said Lord Neptune, We're winning, we have them on the run.
But corporals and privates on patrol at night,
Said, Send for reinforcements, it's the bloody Armalite.
And it's up in Wyoming, that's where I long to be,
Lying in the dark with a Banshee company,
A Sister on me left and Sergeant Fuzz on me right
And a clip of ammunition for my little Armalite.

Everyone sang, with Corporal Fuzz adding a bit of howling wolf. Even Sergeant Major Raskova added her form of base to the music. Squad members held hands, many rocking to the music. They were of one spirit, one family. They were the Banshees, joined forever.

"Steep decent beginning. Hang on." The voice this time was Shannon Bell's. Danny bounded into his seat and strapped himself in, grinning from ear to ear. Aleks, strapped in next to Abigail, said in low tones, "He is worth ten men. Don't tell him, but we are lucky to have him."

"One could not ask for a better Brother in Arms." Abigail looked at Fuzz, strapped in next to her. "Okay, Big Fella?"

Fuzz replied with a 'woof,' and an open mouth grin.

The Ark tilted at such a stiff angle that Abigail felt some 'G' forces pushing her back into her seat. She placed on hand on Corporal Fuzz to steady him.

Several minutes in the steep descent, Abigail heard on the Command Frequency, "They know we are coming. We are painted by radar."

"Shit!" cursed Aleks. "Captain Bell, did we ever receive any updates as to just how many enemies are at the fortress?"

"Eye in the Sky told Dorothy probably hundreds," answered the Co-Pilot. "They are trying to get some updated views. The last is weeks old."

"As soon as we land, I want spy drones out and circling," ordered Aleks. "We need to know where all the threats are. And find Ivana Reed."

"Yes, Ma'am."

Aleks looked at Abigail and stated, "Wished this Ark was stealthier."

"Lord Neptune helped to design it," the Avenging Angel replied. "With all the Rocks hitting the first days, weeks, no reason to hide."

"Yes. Damn his eyes!" Aleks spat out.

Then it seemed like seconds, and they heard the words of, "Flaring out. Touch-down in moments."

"Banshees!" Aleks yelled out over the All Hands Frequency. "You know what to do!"

"COLD STEEL!" As one voice, the Sisters of Steel yelled their reply.

"Five, four three two one, down," Shannon counted out. On 'five' quick-release buckles activated, and the Front ranks of Banshees, the Shield Maidens, were up, grabbed the new ballistic shields, and moved towards the massive front loading ramp. Abigail felt and heard what could only munition impacts of various sizes on the forceshields and, she worried, the armored skin of the Ark. The massive ramp was blown opened by hydraulics, thudded to the ground. Shield Maidens led Aztec Company out and down the slope. And into a vortex of lead and steel.

The four Companies trained to disembark in alphabetical order. Lupe Pena had joked that the 'gringos' were always on some poor Mexican's ass, which was why they went out first. However, it was just easier to develop one way of doing something and making it muscle memory. Now Captain Pena wished they had practiced operations in reverse order.

"Chinga tu Madres!" She swore as rounds impacted on the shields of the first rank. Then, ricochets off the packed dirt and gravel of the landing zone began to hit the legs and feet of her troops. They began to go down.

The other Companies tried to push by and fan out from column to line formation, with front ranks of Shield Maidens providing some cover. The first one, then more Banshees, went down from hits to the lower extremities. The closest situation where they had recently taken fire was from a Narco Trafficante group in Mexico, trying to take over Mexico City. They had a battle tank and still broke and ran in some five minutes. The Chechen Islamic Radicals were not.

Abigail had followed the Aztecs out, wanted to be upfront when the shooting started. Angry bees of bullets were buzzing past her and Corporal Fuzz as they tried to get out and past the bunched up Banshees. She heard screams of pain as young women went down from the waves of fire coming from the cut from stone windows of the fortress. She saw a solid and old structure, some four stories high, with a flat roof. Almost every window and any other opening had a gunman firing some sort of weapon from it. On the roof were some heavy anti-aircraft machine guns, whose operators were trying to depress the muzzles sufficient to hit the ground level Banshees. She called out over the direct channel to the Ark Cockpit.

"Suppressive fire and Drones. Now!"

"We are!" came Shannon Bell's reply. "The Drones are being shot out of the sky. There is a helluva lot more enemy than we thought!"

Abigail looked around. The assault was failing. The area in front of the Ark was becoming a kill zone. It was as if the Warlord Abbas Onlu had planned for years for just such an attack. Fuzz bumped into her as she tried to find a path around the jammed up squads of attackers. She looked down, thought she saw a look of concern in her War Dog's eyes. The attack was failing before it ever really started.

"NO!" Abigail screamed. A switch went off in her head, and time slowed. She yelled at her War Dog in Romanian.

"FUZZ. FOLLOW. ATTACK."

Then she vaulted over the Banshees in front of her; Corporal Fuzz scrambled and leaped after her. Her lever-action Marlin was a blur in her hands as she emptied the eight rounds of .44 Magnum at a portal on the second floor directly in her path. Chunks of stone flew about, and the gunfire from the opening stopped. She dropped her empty rifle and became a running blur.

Someone yelled at Abbas Onlu and pointed at two blurred running figures. His mouth dropped open with surprise at the speed of the characters as they covered the football field distance from the Arks ramp to his fortress.

"Shoot them, you fools! Shoot them!" the huge back bearded man yelled. "Or I will shoot you!"

Fire suddenly shifted from the Banshees in front and towards two figures dashing towards the fortress wall.

Aleks saw Abigail vault over the front ranks and screamed. She screamed over the Command Frequency at Abigail. "God Damn You! I told you, NO! You'll be killed!"
Sergeant Major Raskova had been at her commanders 'six' when this happened. She cursed in Russian, bull-rushed her way forward as she grabbed a ballistic shield from a fallen Banshee. The senior sergeant pushed through the front ranks, screaming and cursing in Russian.

"My Lady of Cold Steel needs help! Forward, you lazy Cunts! For Mother Russia and Abigail!"

Captain Pena saw the Sergeant Major push her way towards the fortress front. It was as if some spirit took control of her. She was suddenly upfront yelling. "Andale, Andale!! Arriba! For the Avenging Angel!"

Captain Dagan Mc Dowell saw her Battle Buddy surge forward. She began to yell

"To Hell and Texas! Canines, follow the Aztecs! Do you want to live forever?" She grabbed up a ballistic shield from a downed

Banshee and surged forward.

Kira Samson peeled her Brave Company off to the left of the other Banshees. She saw Abigail blur forward, and she felt a rage in her that she had felt one dark night in Bloody Kansas. She dashed in front of her hundred Banshee Company and yelled as she pointed her Banshee Blade at the fortress.

"COLD STEEL! Those fuckers die today! Move!"

Princess Akiko had her katana out as she tried to push her Dragon Company forward. Then she heard Alek's scream over the Command Frequency and saw Abigail's extreme dash with Fuzz. She knew what this meant. The member of the Free Japan Royal Family bound out in front of Dragon Company.

She held her katana high.

"BANZAI!!" She had never imagined yelling like this, about to commit to a seemingly suicidal charge.

But her adopted sister Abigail needed her.

"BANZAI!!!!"

Bullets and shells buzzed past the Avenging Angel and her War Dog. A couple struck glancing blows as some shooter obtained a temporary bead on her. Her body armor helped to shrug it off, and she kept running. In moments she reached the wall beneath the second-story window she had targeted with her rifle. She spun around, crouched, and caught Cpl. Fizz's hind paws in cupped hands, a move they had practiced in private. She straightened and launched him up and through the window. In a heartbeat, she turned around and scrambled up the wall like some arachnid, finding grips where others could not.

She was up and through the window, saw a shot through

dead body, one dead Islamic Radical with a ripped out throat, and Fuzz was attacking a still moving threat in the corner of the room. The follower of Abbas Onlu had lost his Kalashnikov and was screaming as he tried to cut the War Dog with a curved sword. The blade bounced off of the 'Raptor' ballistic helmet, and Fuzz did not give him a chance for another blow. His strong jaws latched onto the sword arm, and the man screamed as the K-9s jaws crushed bone and teeth tore skin. The sword fell to the floor as Fuzz twisted and yanked so hard on the arm that he dislocated it from the attached shoulder. The man sprawled on the floor, screaming more, his cries cut off as Fuzz crushed his throat.

Abigail grabbed two loose AK rifles and stepped to the door of the connecting hallway as she ordered: "Fuzz, Out!" Her K-9 partner stopped his attack, and a moment later was heeling on her left hip. Abigail braced each weapon against the door jam, aimed as best she could down the hallway in opposite directions, and let rip. Each automatic assault rifle had a partial magazine, so the weapons ran dry quickly. Before they stopped firing, Abigail heard screams of fear and pain as rounds ricocheted down the curving stone hallways. She dropped the empty rifles, scanned for more weapons, and saw a couple of grenades lying on the floor where someone had lost them. The Banshee scooped them up, then one after another, pulled pins and threw them down the hallway, one in each opposite direction as people fired wildly towards her doorway. Abigail jumped back, grabbed Fuzz, and covered his ears. Two booming blasts, dust and rock flew about, then one lone voice wailing unintelligible words in pain.

Abigail pulled her Glock-18 full automatic pistol out and made sure of the round in the chamber with an extended magazine. She 'cut the pie' on the doorway corners as fast and as complete as possible. Dust and smoke were everywhere. She hugged the wall and went right into the hallway, away from the wailing voice of pain. She had to find Ivana and the two boys. They would either be upstairs on the top fourth floor or in a bunker in the basement. She guessed up, thinking the equivalent 'royal chambers' would be in a large sealed off section with a view. Within some five seconds, she found a stairway up and took it.

As she ascended the stairs, Fuzz at her heel, a figure burst from the next floor up doorway, yelling orders over his shoulder to some hidden person. The man turned, saw Abigail. She thought she saw his eyes widened just before she double-tapped him between them. Blood sprayed and splattered as she heard a cry of alarm from the next and third floor. A thrown in panic grenade with the retaining safety pin still in it came bouncing down the stairs. Abigail caught it with her left hand, pulled the pin 'John Wayne style' with her teeth, held it for a moment, and then tossed it up the stairwell. She crouched, partially covering Fuzz as the grenade went off at the door jam of the next floor entrance. The blast, then silence. Up Abigail ran, two steps at a time, Glock at the ready.

Again, a quick 'cut the pie' then into the dust and smoke-filled hallway. Abigail went left this time, found a stairway almost in line with the one from the second floor, and went past the wedged open door. This time she ascended the stairs with no threat at the top. As she reached the fourth and last floor, she heard yells and screams from the level she had just left, some in Russian rather than Chechen. They knew an enemy was among them and must be found. There was still heavy weapons fire from outside. Abigail hoped the enemy no longed pinned the Banshees near the Ark.

All four Companies of the Banshees surged forward. Sergeant Major Raskova was out in front until she became a prime target and went down. The ballistic shield and her own Tschaaa enhanced body armor saved her from death, but multiple hits knocked her out of this fight. Her pain and sacrifice were not in vain. Within moments of her falling, Aleks was next to her with several other Banshees with shields, protecting her prone figure.

"You damned old fool," Aleks cursed in Russian.

"Keep these Cunts moving, Lady," Marina Raskova said through pain clenched teeth. "And take my PaPaSha. Bloody it for me."

Aleks took the submachine gun from Marina, as EMT Trained Banshees grabbed her up under cover of ballistic shields and ran back with her to the Ark. Aleks turned as a round smacked her armor, causing her to stumble. But there was no penetration.

"Squids tech shit is good for something," she growled to herself. Then she noticed the front lines of Banshees had passed her, and she heard the loud, trilling Banshee Scream.

"We will do this, Sisters. We will do this!" She began firing the submachine gun as she yelled, and noticed the enemy fire had slackened.

Captain Shannon Bell and Pilot Dorothy scrambled around the Ark cockpit as they tried to keep the limited force shields in operation, as well as use the new weapons systems 'Pappy' Gunn had installed. The theory was that the weapons could fire through temporary gaps in the electronic shield. However, the shielding system itself did not function well in the planet's atmosphere, especially during humid conditions. It was for the near-vacuum of space. Thus, the two aircrew looked like one-legged women in an ass-kicking contest trying to get things to work properly

"Down to one round in the Delta cannon," Shannon called out. Gunn had added a ten-round 32 MM cannon from a salvaged Tschaaa Delta Fighter to the Ark as a means to provide some close-in defense.   The problem was the initial small arms fire was so unexpectedly intense, it had deflected some of the high-velocity shells. Not to mention the shield system was having fits and interfering with the weapons systems. Plus, they did not know where Ivana Reed was, so they could not risk hitting her and her sons.

"Make it count, my sister," Dorothy responded. "I will try the Delta IA controlled missiles we have on board, once I can find a path through our shielding system. I will try a careful aim."

"Popping out the Gatling System," called out Shannon. The fifty caliber ex-aircraft powered multi-barrel system contained in its sizeable retractable turret was not new—still, an efficient one. Once extended, it formed a 'weak spot' in the shielding. The payoff was its added firepower.

A rocket-propelled grenade exploded against the shield near the cockpit. The Ark shook, and the front shields went down. Shannon yelled and cursed, then began to fire the Gatling system.

"Rock and Roll, you sonsofbitches, Rock and Roll!"

The high-velocity rounds began do demolish part of a fortress wall, just as a 37MM anti-aircraft gun on the roof began to score hits on the Ark.

The building shook as Abigail and Fuzz reached the fourth and top floor. She surmised something had collapsed. She also felt and heard the report of a large anti-aircraft cannon positioned on the roof. But she had no time to try and deal with that threat, plus find the General's wife and children. Abigail had to choose one mission and stick with it.

She 'cut the pie' again, saw only dust and smoke in the hallway. She also noticed there was some lovely carpeting under her feet. She had guessed correctly as to where the 'royal' quarters were. This part of the fortress had curved walls as it was as an immense overgrown tower. Abigail slowly made her way to the left in the curving passageway, trying to figure out where she needed to go. Then a man with a Kalashnikov burst from a recessed door that was hidden by a large and ornate wall hanging. He was almost on top of Abigail, and Fuzz before either knew what was happening.

Cpl. Fuzz reacted automatically. In a flash, he had crushed the enemy's throat between His 'raptor' jaws, well before the man could let out a cry of warning.

"Good job," Abigail said in Romanian, as Fuzz let the dead man lay. Abigail peeled back the wall hanging, then pushed on the door behind. She was surprised when it swung open with little resistance. She button-hooked into the left, and Fuzz automatically cut to the right. Inside was an ornate suite of rooms, entirely out of sync with the rest of the fortress trappings. As they entered, two men, arguing, came from the connecting room. Abigail double-tapped each in the head, then rushed the place they had exited as they fell dead.

Abigail used speed to throw off any possible threat as she burst through the doorway to the connecting room. A woman in full hijab and burka screamed and tried to pull something out from under her clothes. Fuzz hit her like a freight train, slamming her across the room. Then Abigail saw them.

Sitting at a table at the far end of the suite, was Ivana, John Junior, and Ivan. They wore traditional Chechen garb, would have easily passed as locals. John Junior tried to raise an AK-74 as Abigail yelled out in English and Russian, "Friendly! Don't Shoot!" Ivana pushed John's weapon down as she spoke to him in Chechen. Abigail had picked up enough of the language to recognize her mentioning something about their 'father.' Before Abigail could say anything more, the younger, Ivan, yelled out in Russian, "It's them! The Avenging Angel and Fuzz War Dog!"

"Speak Chechen," scolded John Junior. "That is who we are, that is who our Father…"

Ivana shoved him violently, spit venom at him.

"NO! John Reed is your father! Abbu lies!"

"He is DEAD! Abbu adopted us, as a good charitable Muslim. Western Squid propaganda tells the lie that he still lives. If he did, why did he not come and find us??"

In a heartbeat, Abigail knew there was a combination of Abandonment and Stockholm Syndrome had played havoc with John Junior's mind. This condition was a huge problem that had to be dealt with now. She glanced at Fuzz, saw that he had the Chechen woman pinned to the floor. He outweighed the slight woman. He would not kill as long as he saw no weapon or threat. But she had little time before someone would come to check on their well-being with all the shooting going on.

"Ma'am, young Sirs," she spoke in Russian. "I was sent by Madam President and your Father, General John Reed. You are to be freed…"

"NO!" John Jr. screamed. "We are free! Free from all your Squid lies…"

"John," said Ivana as she tried to put her arm around him. He shoved her violently away.

"Away from me, fallen woman! You disgrace your…"

Abigail was on top of him in a blur. The AK-47 ripped from his hands, and then his face pinned to the wall. The Avenging Angel hissed into his ear.

"John Reed is my Adopted Father. He gave me away at my wedding. That makes Ivana my Adopted Mother. So, 'Little Brother,' you will treat OUR mother with respect. Or I will cause you such pain…" She felt a rage encroaching on her mental process. The same type of anger that had occurred during a fateful incident In Wyoming, where Sgt. Fuzz had died. Then, mantras that Ichiro had taught her to control this rage caused by Tschaaa Alien tinkering began to playback in her head. She took a deep calming breath and let it out.

"Do you understand, my brother?"

"He croaked out a 'yes' as he began to cry tears of rage, frustration, and sorrow. Abigail knew this was not easy, but she had no time to be gentle with his feelings.

"Is there another way out of here?" Abigail asked.

"There." Ivana pointed as she answered. "Through that door is a balcony and fire escape on the side of this part of the fortress."

Abigail scooped up the AK-74 and handed it to Ivana. "Can you use it?"

"Yes," replied Ivana. "We were all expected to learn to shoot here."

"Wait! There is another gun!" Ivan said as he went to a chest and opened it. He pulled out a duplicate weapon with an extended magazine

Abigail looked at John Jr., "I would let you have a weapon, but I question what side you are on." The young man looked at the floor as his mother put an arm around him.

"Come, Son. Your mother loves you, even if you do not love me."

"I love you, Mother," he mumbled.

"Come on—no more time. Let's move. Fuzz. Lead. Scout. Protect" The commands to him were in Romanian, so he realized this was serious. Fuzz moved through the door to the balcony. The burka woman screamed, started to pull a pistol from under her clothes. Abigail shot her through her right eye.

"She was not a bad woman," said Ivana. "She helped to care for my sons at times."

"No time for that. MOVE!" Abigail's command unfroze them.

She dashed to the dead woman, recovered the pistol. They may need all the weapons they could get, she thought. Then she was out on the balcony with them. Bullets began to ricochet around them.

"Down!" Abigail commanded as she grabbed her unused communicator and turned it back to the Command Frequency. "Major One to Command One."

Aleks voiced yelled over the net. "I told you NOT to go running off... !"

"I have them. You are shooting at us on the side balcony." Aleks began to curse in English and Russian, with some Ukrainian thrown in. Then she started to bark out commands. "Major, you need to pop some smoke, so we can be sure we have you."

"Copy that," Abigail answered.

Abigail pulled a small smoke flare out of a side pocket, hit the small self-igniter, and watched it start to put out blue smoke.

"We have her." It was Captain Danny O'Brien.

"We're coming down the fire escape," said Abigail.

"Copy that,'" was the reply. "We'll have a welcoming party."

"Copy, Out."

Abigail pointed to the opening in the center of the balcony with the fire escape ladder.

"Go!" she yelled. They went. Abigail helped Cpl. Fuzz find the steps on the ladder and down he went to the balcony below. A glance revealed that from the third floor down, the fire escape was an extremely tight spiral stairway that ran down the side of the next balcony, then to the ground. Fuzz, trained, led Ivana and her sons down, ready to take on any threat. Abigail glanced around, then started to descend the ladder.

"IVANA!" The name was shouted in a huge bellow. Abigail, her head still poking up through the ladder hole in the balcony, saw one of the largest bearded men she had ever seen, moving fast towards her. She ducked her head, then slid down the sides of the ladder, Navy Submarine style.

"Move! The enemy is here!" Abigail called out, and Ivana shoved John Jr. down the spiral stairway. Abigail pulled her Glock-18 out, covered the ladder. She heard her radio crackled in her earpiece.

"People coming to you," said Danny.

"Copy…" Something slammed into Abigail before she could complete her reply, sent her sprawling and almost over the edge of the balcony to the ground three stories below. Abbas Onlu had swung down on the outside of the balcony edge, like some overgrown Romanian gymnast from days gone by, kicked Abigail aside. He bellowed again and went straight to the winding stairwell.

Abigail's Glock was nowhere in sight. She imagined it had gone over the edge to the waiting ground below. Abbas had what looked like a .44 caliber Desert Eagle automatic in a shoulder holster. On him, the large Israeli designed pistol looked almost small. He must have been afraid to fire for fear of hitting Ivana as it was not in his hand. Maybe he had tried to be a 'good husband and father.' No matter, He had kidnapped Ivana and Sons. Time for them to go to their rightful husband and father.

Abigail pulled her Banshee Blade out, stood up, and yelled in Russian at Abbas. "Hey! Son of a Pig! You hit like a little girl!"

Abbas's head snapped in her direction. Abigail made a quick calculation about throwing her blade into his throat, saw he might have body armor under his shirt. Just then, he stood up and laughed. His laughter seemed to vibrate the air around him.

"You must be the American Bitch," he sneered. "The so-called Angel, the Mormon Whore. Put that knife down, and you may live. I will make a good Muslim wife out of you."

"Why don't you take it from me, pigshit? And a wife? I heard you like young boys, like your Prophet." Abigail was trying to distract him from following Ivana and her sons, tie him up enough so that Fuzz could lead them to safety, without him getting shot by that large pistol. She would not lose another four-legged partner. She was way too efficient in her attempts.

The giant of a man, at least six and a half feet tall, lunged at her, his quickness belied his size. Abigail's blade was a blur, but Abbas was unnatural at his speed. He turned and caught the edge on his chest, proved that he did have some body armor. As Abigail started to take a slash at his unprotected face, a massive hand more like a bear paw caught it. Then she was being thrown like a ragdoll over the edge of the balcony. Here, Abbas made a mistake, as he threw her close enough to the escape stairway that she was able to grab ahold, not falling three stories to the ground below. She swung hard into the railing but held on, as her blade fell to the ground below. Abbas laughed and yelled.

"Look at the little monkey! I think I will put you in a zoo." He strode towards her, must have thought she was stunned. But she was not.

Abigail dropped from the outside of the stairway, neatly caught the stairway railing the next floor down. She swung her body onto the slender stair, felt the metal vibrate but hold. Abigail began to clamber down to the ground below, as she heard Abbas bellow in frustrated rage. Any moment she expected to be shot by his huge pistol, yet hoped her body armor would be strong enough to defeat it until she could find her Glock. But if he shot her in the head—

In moments she was dropping the last few feet to the ground, and saw her blade, but not her pistol. She dashed under the overhang of the balconies above to prevent Abbas from getting a good sight picture. Then she saw something out of an old comic book.

Abbas jumped from some two stories up, landed 'superhero-style' kneeling on one knee and the opposite fist. No injury, no pain.

He stood up as Abigail prepared to throw her knife at a massive unprotected thigh.

"Throw you knife, little girl," he bellowed. "You will wound me; then, I will use it to gut you."

"Big Talk. For one who kidnaps women and children," Abigail sneered back.

"Or I can shoot you," Abbas added. "Or you can point out where Ivana is. Your people are being shot to pieces. Leave my country, and some of you may live."

"Shoot away. For you do not own this land nor the people," stated Abigail.

The huge man shrugged, said. "Suit yourself." He again showed a speed out of sync with his size. He rushed Abigail so quick that she held on to her blade, tried to stab and slash with it. She opened a gash in his left arm, then was being suspended above Abbas by his right hand on her throat, her blade slapped away. She kicked out with both her feet at his head and bloodied his face. Abbas bellowed and slammed her to the ground. Abigail's body armor helped to absorb some of the force, yet she still saw some stars.

Abbas wiped his face with his hand, saw the blood. "Time to end this," he said.

Abigail had managed to distract the warlord for a while, hoping it was long enough for Fuzz to lead Ivana and her sons to safety. She started to scramble her way to her feet as Abbas pulled the large pistol from its holster.

A Banshee scream undulated across the area as a slight female figure seemed to appear from nowhere. The woman slammed her rifle against the giant man's right knee, causing it to buckle as he bellowed in pain. Abigail saw that the young Private had struck Abbas so hard that the rifle was bent. But the young woman was not done yet. She leaped on to the now fallen mountain of a man with a drawn

Banshee Blade, screamed as she proceeded to slash at the Abbas in a blur of action.

Abigail scrambled to her feet as the bellowing beast of a man grabbed the slight woman's hand's to stop her attack, then used his other arm to shove her off of him. The Avenging Angel leaped and landed both feet on his face and head. Stunned, Abbas let go of the Private, grabbed for Abigail. She danced out of the way, saw the .44 Magnum pistol lying in the dirt, and snapped it up. Abbas looked at her through blurry and blood-filled eyes as he tried to rise up. Abigail aimed and fired the Desert Eagle into the Warlords face. Blood splattered both Abigail and the Banshee soldier. The Avenging Angel stood, pistol still pointed at the dead radical. Then she looked up at the Banshee soldier who had come to her aid. For the first time, she recognized the Banshee as Anica Armstrong.

"You okay?" asked Abigail.

"Yes, Ma'am. Are you?"

Abigail smiled. This young Newbie had leaped to her defense without a moment's hesitation, now asked if she was alright.

"I take it there was a reason why you did not shoot him," stated Abigail.

"A bullet damaged the rifle as I came upon you," was the reply. "Did not have the time to get to my .32 pistol in my pack. So…"

"So you beat and stabbed the crap out of him," interjected Abigail. "Good show. Now, time to leave before some other scum shows up. Here, take this pistol while I find my Glock."

A quick scan of the area and Abigail saw her Glock in the dirt. She grabbed it, checked the action. She looked at Anica as she spoke.

"Let's go. And I owe you, Private. You saved me."

Anica shrugged and replied. "I just did what you would do, Ma'am. That's what all us Newbies say. What would the Avenging Angel do?"

Abigail had to face the fact of her 'fame' and image affected the young women around her. Like Torbin Bender, she had never asked to be a 'Hero.' But it seemed many saw her as one.

"Follow me, Private. Time to find where Fuzz and the General's wife went to."

There was a scream from a doorway at the end of the fortress. A grayed haired man with the trappings of a Mullah came running at them, flung an object at them before Abigail could shoot him. As she put a bullet in his forehead, the grenade landed at her feet.

"NO!" Anica yelled, knocked Abigail back, and then threw her body on the grenade as it exploded. The force of the explosion lifted the slender young woman's body off the ground, knocked her aside, and demonstrated that it was not a customarily charged grenade. As Abigail's ears rang, she bent over Anica and saw the bloody damage from the grenade.

"You damn fool! Why did you do that?"

Anica looked up at Abigail as blood began to flow from her mouth. Even the Tschaaa reinforced armor had not stopped the force of the explosions. Abigail went into EMT mode, tried to remove Anica's body armor, find the damage. But it was too late.

"You stay with me!" Abigail cried out. "Don't you go! Hear me? That's an order, Troop..."

"I love you..." Anica whispered. Then she was gone.

"NOOOOOOO!" It was a loud feral scream as Abigail cradled the now dead young woman.

"Fuzz, Matthew, now you..." she sobbed. Then a familiar voice cut through her fugue.

"Major. Abigail. It's Danny. Time to go."

The familiar voice helped her from spiraling down a rabbit hole where memories of Sgt. Fuzz existed. Abigail also remembered a mantra Ichiro had impressed on her to help control the rage building within her. She took a deep breath, let it out slowly. Then she stood up, still cradling Anica.

"Here, Major, I'll help…"

"No!" replied Abigail. "She saved me. Now I make sure she gets… home."

Danny O'Brien nodded. He knew the bond that existed between unit mates, especially with those who died next to you.

"Fuzz got Ivana and the boys to safety," he informed Abigail. "The Banshees are blowing holes in the fortress. We'll be leaving soon."

"Let's go, Captain." Abigail activated the communication link. "Major One to Command One. In route with one casualty."

"Get back here, Abigail," replied Aleks. "We have more company coming. Some trucks and artillery coming up the access road, and *Queen Elizabeth's* screens are down." "Copy that. In route…"

A voice crackled over the radio in Japanese. "Abigail, we come." It was Ichiro.

"Colonel, are you ready to help?" asked Aleks.

"But of course. Tell Colonel Hunter and me where you wish us."

"Access road," stated Aleks. "Several vehicles. The last drone showed, before it was blown out of the sky, they contain unknown numbers of armed troops and are towing some artillery pieces. If they fire at the Ark…"

"Roger," replied Ichiro. "We go."

From seemingly nowhere, two aircraft flashed by. The V-Wing injector scram jet fighters traveled just on the edge of a sonic boom, setting up pressure waves that all could feel. Then they had the approaching enemy in sight.

"Guns, Guns, Guns," Colonel Hunter broadcast as he strafed the vehicles with his Gatling. Ichiro followed suit, zipped by as the cars and trucks exploded.

"All Banshees, back to the Ark!" Aleks called out on the radio. "Colonels, give the Banshees a minute, then flatten the fortress."

"Flatten it and sow the area with salt, so that nothing may grow," Abigail mumbled as she carried Anica back to the Assault Ark. Danny O'Brien took a couple of snapshots at fleeing enemy, Abigail saw them drop. "The Wages of Sin Is Death," she said as they made their way to the Ark ramp. Abigail saw small groups of Banshees ascending the blood slicked ramp as others provided cover fire. She saw a small missile launched from one of *Queen Elizabeth's* batteries, heard Shannon radio out, "Last one, Ladies." It flew through an open window and exploded inside the stone structure. There was a rumble as part of the foundation collapsed on and around the occupants.

"BANSHEES! We are leaving!!!" Aleks called out on the general communications net. Then, a cacophony of crashes, explosions, and rumblings as Ichiro and Cliff Hunter used their munitions to bring the fortress down around the enemy's head. Abigail ascended the ramp as smoke and dust rushed towards her from the collapsing stone walls and towers. As she reached the top, she saw Emily Anders at the top with an EMT, performing triage on the casualties. Abigail had forgotten that she and Doctor Rice were along on a 'medical mission' to help the local populace. Now, they were part of an exigent MASH unit. Emily saw her, stepped forward.

"Let me take a look…"

"She's dead." Abigail pushed by the Vet, walked on the past the dead and dying, sat down on a fold-out seat along the aircraft sides. She still held Anica in her arms. As each Squad of Banshees that went by, at least one was a casualty. Abigail knew the Special Attack

Unit might have taken too many wounded and dead to be a functional unit.

"Abigail, Little Sister." Aleks stood in front of her. "Please, take the Banshee to the back area. We have set up a temporary morgue…"

"NO!!!" She yelled so loud that it cut through the moans, screams, and thumping as Banshees quickly mounted the Ark. Many of the soldiers looked at her, saw the Avenging Angel was in distress. Some began to move towards the symbol of their Sisterhood when Cpl. Fuzz bulled through them, was at His Human's feet. He jammed his nose into her face, demanded that she let him know she was okay.

"You made it back, Big Fella," she mumbled. "Good job." Fuzz whined, licked her, and knew she was 'not' alright.

"You saved us." The new voice was Ivana Reed's as she sat next to Abigail.

"And this young lady died for me," replied Abigail. "Too many people have been hurt or died for me. My parents, Sgt. Fuzz, Mathew… and now Anica here. It needs to stop."

Ivana placed her hand on Abigail's arm. "My new daughter, you saved my sons and me. It was evil which killed the others. Not you and your good soul."

"Tell that to the dead, see if they will listen."

"Little Sister… " Aleks began to say.

"I should be no one's sister; Death is a constant companion to me."

The Emergency Lift Off horns sounded, and *Queen Elizabeth* lurched into the air as able-bodied Banshees held on to the dead, wounded, and each other.

"Sorry, my Sisters." It was Dorothy's voice. "All are aboard, and we must fly, or be trapped here."

Abigail sat in stony silence. Aleks had to leave her side to check on all the others. Fuzz sat pushed up against her legs, the hair on his back up as he went into 'protect mode.' His Mistress was hurting—woe to those who may cause her more pain. Ivana sat next to her, quiet. She slowly reached out, put her hand on her adopted daughter. Abigail turned and looked at her. "I 'm glad you and your sons are safe. But my heart is so damned heavy right now..."

Cpl. Fuzz let out a combined growl and whine, a sure sign he saw something he about which he was unsure. Abigail looked up to see Breeder and Pilot Dorothy slowly approaching her.

"Fuzz, down boy. It's okay. She's one of us."

Dorothy stopped a couple of yards away. "Our... Sister. She is gone, my Major."

"I need to take her home, Dorothy. She saved me, died for me. She needs to go... home."

Dorothy looked at Abigail as tears ran down her face. Then there was a vibration in the air, followed by sounds associated with Deep Sea Earth Whales. The Tschaaa female began to move her social tentacles in rhythmic motions, as she began what could only be a song. It became a soothing song, whales long and short notes, occasional dolphin-like chirps, and next a soothing refrain like none other. Abigail's mind told her that maybe this was how the Giant Squids sang to each other in the deep seas of Earth.

A human voice then added to the refrain, as Lt. Diveccio, trained in opera before the Invasion, began to match the notes with a lady's voice. She moved and stood next to Dorothy, who took her hand in a gentle grasp. They began to sway together. Soon other Banshees were standing in a circle, gently swaying in time with the song. Fuzz laid down; the song had a calming effect on the Great War Dog. Then, Dorothy ended her music. Abigail looked deep into the huge eyes of the cephalopod.

"Sister Dorothy, that was beautiful."

"Abigail, my Sister of Steel. I sang the young Banshees who have passed this day to their rightful place in Mother Ocean. For we all have salt in our tears, are bound by that fact to the warm, life-giving seas of Earth. Now, you must let the Young One's body be taken so that it is readied for its final resting place. Her spirit is already departing for Mother Ocean. We must not interfere with the final journey."

Abigail allowed other Banshees to take Anica from her embrace. The Avenging Angel stood up, stepped up to Dorothy, grasped her long, soft fingered hand.

"You are a wonderful person, Dorothy. I thank you with all my heart. You will always be my Sister."

Cpl. Fuzz cautiously approached Dorothy, sniffing. The Tschaaa female slowly reached out her social tentacle towards him. He did not shy away, nor growl. He realized this Alien was a member of this exclusive Pack. Dorothy gently scratched his ears, then his chest. Abigail chuckled as he made K-9 contentment sounds.

"You will never have a moment's rest now, Dorothy. He'll now be bothering you for pets and scratches every time he sees you."

"His… fur is so soft and… unique. Now I know why your dogs affect you as they do. They are so exceptional. And loving." She looked at Abigail. "I am honored."

Abigail reached over and hugged the Alien Squid, something unthinkable a year or two prior. Now, it seemed so natural to hug a Sister from Another Mother.

"We are honored by your presence, my many-limbed friend. You were with us at the very beginning of the Great Compromise. You help keep the peace between our species."

"I do what I can, Abigail. Now I must return to my duties in the cockpit. Our Ark suffered some damage, Shannon, and I must ensure we return to our home safely."

Abigail squeezed Dorothy's large body one more time. "Go with God."

Dorothy rose up on her limbs and moved quickly back to her post. Abigail looked at Fuzz.

"Come, my four-legged friend. We must see to the wounded. And the dead."

The makeshift emergency medical and surgical area in the cavernous hold was slick with blood. Abigail saw Rica Rice supervising the Banshee EMTs in both the finer and grosser medical procedures meant to keep humans alive. She now realized that a spiritual guardian angel must have been watching over them, as it was so fortunate that Rica Rice and Emily Anders, two highly trained medical professionals, had chosen just this occasion to 'ride-along' on a Banshee Mission. Without them, the Grim Reaper would have had even more victims.

As Abigail and Fuzz walked in, there was a collective quiet sigh of relief from those who had seen her cradling Anica. The Avenging Angel was back with her sisters. Her mere presence improved the atmosphere of the blood-covered area and the attitudes of all those present. She walked towards the wounded, stayed away from the scrambling medical staff whom she heard as they ministered to the gravely injured.

"Got that artery, Emily?"

"Got it. Clamped, no longer spurting."

"Good show. You're a natural MASH member."

"Hell, Rica, your patients don't usually bite or kick as mine can."

Rica chuckled with a bit of gallows humor. "No. Mine just bitch and sue me."

As Abigail surveyed the wounded, a voice called out.

"Major!" A very much bandaged Sergeant Major Raskova called out, tried to rise u from her stretcher. Abigail bee-lined towards her.

"Just stay down, Sergeant Major. You're hurt."

"Phttt! I have been hurt worse. Find Private Bond. She has problems."

Abigail knew Joan Bond was Anica's new Battle Buddy, and now Anica was gone. Guilt and sorrow were no doubt set in.

"Shot to crap and still concerned about your enlisted troops. You are one of a kind, Sergeant."

"No, I am the Senior Enlisted Advisor. That is my job. Now, Major, please find Bond."

"Roger that."

It took a few minutes of threading her way through the injured to find Private Bond. She sat along the Ark bulkhead, had a bandaged arm as well as a square bandage on her right cheek. Princess Akiko was seated next to her as the Private sobbed.

"She's dead! I was responsible for watching her back! And now she is dead! "

Akiko looked up as Abigail approached, her eyes moist. Abigail knew that even the stoic female Samurai was not immune to feeling the tragedy of human loss. Abigail motioned her to remain sitting as she approached. She sat silently next to the Private, whose emotional state prevented her from noticing Abigail's approach. Joan Bond focused on pouring her heart out to Akiko.

"I told Major Yamamoto that I would protect Anica, make up for the stupid fight we had. Now I know I have double the shame in her eyes."

Abigail leaned over. "You are wrong, Private."

Private Bond jerked around at the sound of her voice. She

started to stand up, and Abigail placed a hand on her arm.

"Please, sit. You have nothing to be ashamed about, Private. You are wounded in the Banshees mission of rescuing Ivana Reed and her sons. You have served with honor."

"But, Anica…"

"She died, saving me, protecting me. If anyone is to blame, it's me."

"My Sister," Akiko began to say in Japanese. Abigail held up her hand to stop her.

"The extreme combat and violence separated you from her. It happens. You were wounded, and Anica continued with her purpose, which was to find me. Again, someone dies for me."

"Ma'am," Joan Bond began to say, but Abigail interrupted her.

"You and your comrades ask, 'what would the Avenging Angel do?' I should reply that you shouldn't die for me. Jesus Christ said that there was no greater love than to lay one's life down for another. But that rings hollow when it happens over and over again. When you are the one people are dying for, never again to feel the warmth of their Sisters."

Fuzz chose that moment to jam his snout into Abigail. She half-smiled at him.

"At least you made it back. You led Ivana and her sons back to safety. You're the one we should honor, emulate. Not me."

"Without you, major, there would be no War Dogs," Bond interjected. "There would be no, no… US! Without us, the Banshees, there would be no rescues, no symbol of good for others to follow. My mother told me that you must make the best out of the bad." She paused, swallowed. "You are the symbol of the best, which we all try to follow."

"The young Private is wise beyond her years, Major," said

Akiko. "We are all far from perfect. But you strive to emulate that which is best in all of us. That is the standard to try and obtain for all of us."

Abigail looked at her two sister Banshees. She knew what they said had truth in it. However, the Avenging Angel could not get past the idea that, but for her, there would be fewer bodies in bags. She thought at one time that Good always won out over Evil. Seeing the dead and dying, Abigail wondered if a Pyrrhic victory in the name of Good was such a positive thing. She took a deep breath, then let out a sigh.

"We all have much to deal with, thanks to the violence of this day. But we did rescue some innocents, and stop the growth of evil. There is that." She stood up. "Captain, if you will ensure Private Bond returns to her squad, I must check on the others." She turned and left before both could rise. Fuzz followed.

Joan Bond looked at Princess Akiko. "I don't feel worthy of being in her presence."

"Phaa! You are a Banshee. We are Sisters of Steel. Thus, we strive for a higher standard than others. So, we are frustrated when things are not perfect." It was Akiko's turn to sigh. "But in all war, the conflict there is death. Up until now, we have dodged the Grim Reaper, as English speakers call the Spirit of Death. For those of us who not killed, we will be stronger. The memory of those we lost will make us stronger. Now, you rest here. We will talk later."

As Akiko rose to leave, the Private spoke. 'Thank You, Ma'am. For being... here."

The Royal Princess smiled. "We are Sisters. And I am Samurai. Where else should I be?"

Abigail made the rounds through the wounded, then forced herself to visit the dead. Emily Anders, covered in blood, was standing on the edge of the makeshift morgue, talking to Captain Samson. The Captain saluted as she approached.

"Ma'am."

"How many?"

"Twenty-five dead. Four times that many wounded to an appreciative degree. More with cuts and scratches. But we recovered everyone, dead and wounded. Just like in Kansas."

Abigail paused, looked into the Original's eyes. "Yes, you were there. When the Banshees... started." She paused. "Was it worth it?"

"Ma'am?"

"The attack that led to the Great Kraken Rout. I was a major cause of that. Many did it for me, were lucky they did not die there."

Captain Samson straightened up. "Major, you were a catalyst that night. However, we also did that for 'ourselves,' as well as our families, both alive... and dead. Like today. We did this for the Sister beside us, as well as for the General. For all those members of our sisterhood and brotherhood."

Kari paused, then continued. "I organized and led the attack in Bloody Kansas, which set all this into motion. If any one person is ultimately responsible for the deaths this day, it falls on my shoulders."

With that, a small light went on in Abigail's head. She was fixated on herself, thinking she was the cause of everything, accepting responsibility for all that happened around her. Then she remembered a certain Cyborg Andrew, now the real Guardian Angel, whom she had scolded for trying to figure out, foresee everything, and plan for it. He HAD attempted to control everything once he saw the pattern towards the Great Compromise. She had to remind him that he was not responsible for everything, was not God. Now, someone told her of that reality. But the hurt inside of Abigail was too fresh to disappear. It would take a while not to feel guilt for the others who died to help her.

"Thank You, Captain Samson. I guess I begin to think much of this revolves around me, and thus think I should control it all because of all this 'hero' stuff people throw around. I feel responsible for all those who look up to me as a symbol."

Kari took her hand. "My Sister, you are YOU—more than just a symbol. You are a good soul. That is what is important. And we all love you for it."

Abigail blinked back tears, then hugged her sister Banshee. She knew the love of her vast 'family' would help her through these times of death and destruction.

Alex walked up with Doctor Rice as Abigail let go of the hug.

"You are back with us, Little Sister?" Aleks asked in Russian.

"Yes, Big Sister," Abigail answered in Russian, then continued in English. "I keep forgetting that, as that saying goes, no one is an island. So to take the weight of the world on your shoulders is not necessary."

"Time for a quick checkup, Major," Rica Rice interjected. "I am fine..."

"You may think you are, but you've been knocked around. I need to check for a nice thing like concussions..."

Abigail kept trying to protest until Aleks gave her 'the look' that said she needed to sit down and be quiet. Abigail acquiesced and let Rica Rice do all the typical poking and prodding. A few minutes later, the good doctor hung her stethoscope around her neck.

"You've signs of a mild concussion and bruised ribs, breasts. When we get back to base, I'm going to order you as your doctor to rest. You once again have pushed yourself beyond normal limits. The beatings you expose yourself to have a cumulative effect. Rest and recuperate now, or pay for it later."

"But the others. I need…"

"What did the Doctor say?" Aleks butted in. "You are the only person more stubborn than myself and my husband. Don't you think I and the others can see to the Unit?"

"Yes, of course! But that is not…"

"Don't argue. Your commander orders you to take medical leave. Spend time with your husband, and Big Beastie here. He senses your need for rest also."

With that, Fuzz stepped up and nuzzled her hand. She looked into his eyes and would swear that she saw a worried look. Fuzz had such a secure, empathetic connection with her that she knew the War Dog was stressed. Abigail knelt and hugged his massive head and neck.

"I am sorry, my Best Buddy," she said in Romanian. "I forget that you are a person also, with wants and needs." Cpl. Fuzz licked her, then nuzzled some more. Abigail scratched his chest and ears.

"See, Little Sister," said Aleks. "He needs time to recover also. He internalizes your hurt."

Abigail sighed and stood up. "I yield to all your caring advice. Ichiro will be glad to spend some downtime with me."

"Generals Reed and Bender will see to that. And Ivana and her sons will need to be reacquainted with husband and father. Madam President will have to make do without the President's Own for a bit."

Abigail smiled. "Well, until then, I'll go up to the cockpit, check on our progress. Hopefully, we can make it back to Malmstrom and its medical facilities. We will need all of them." Aleks's mouth formed a grim smile. "Yes, that is true. You check on the Cockpit Crew. I will hold the proverbial fort here."

As the Avenging Angel made her way to the cockpit, Fuzz at her heel,

Rica Rice and Aleks watched her.

"Did she talk to you about starting a family, Doctor?"

"Yes, she did. And I think, as her Doctor and her friend, this is a perfect time. She needs to focus on the creation of life, not all this death."

Aleks grunted. "My Husband Torbin says we are morally superior to him and his fellow males as we give life, give birth to the next generation, while he and his fellows are built to take life."

"Well, Aleks, this day, the female gender was quite efficient at taking life. I, for one, could do with the sound and smells of more babies than wounded women. And with that, time for this Doctor to get back and ensure we have not lost anymore."

Aleks put her arm around Rica. "God smiled on us by insuring you, and Emily Anders was along on this mission. Without you, we would have lost more Sisters."

"If this was God's Will, Colonel, next time, I hope He or She finds some other way to use my talents."

In the Ark cockpit, Abigail saw an awful lot of red warning lights flashing.

"Welcome, Major," said Pilot Dorothy. "As you can tell, we have been busy."

"Is this Ark going to get us back to Malmstrom?"

The Tschaaa Breeder fixed her with one of her oversized eyes. "*Queen Elizabeth* is as tough a Banshee as any other. She will not let us down."

"We took a bunch of hits," interjected Shannon Bell. "The shields went down at the very end when the Colonels arrived in the V-Wing Fighters. They helped save us."

"Where are they?"

"Re-arming and re-fueling in New Israel. We'll beat them

home as we do not want to wait around."

Abigail stepped forward, placed a hand on each of the Pilots. "You two saved us. We'd still be sitting on the ground, yelling for help without your efforts."

"But, of course, Major!" Dorothy stated. "Are we not superior Breeders, Females, Sisters of Steel, Banshees? I think the phrase you humans use is 'the best of the best'."

Abigail grinned. She no longer saw a ten limbed creature in the pilot's seat. She saw a Banshee, a Sister of Steel.

"Without you, my ocean born friend, we would be far from the 'best.' Some Tschaaa needs to write stories about you, create legends for other Breeders to follow."

Dorothy produced the equivalent of a shrug. "Tschaaa write histories, not legends. If I have a footnote in our long history, I will be satisfied." She fixed both her eyes on Abigail. "We saved Young this day. What could be more important than that?"

The Assault Ark shivered a bit, demanded the attention of the two pilots.

"Come on, *Queen Elizabeth*," said Shannon. "You got us this far. Just a bit farther in low orbit, then home."

"Yes, home," said Abigail. "And... family."

Ivana Reed had demanded Abigail walk her and her sons over to meet John Reed on the tarmac after landing. Between her and her husband, it was as if no time had passed. They wrapped each other in a massive hug, kissed, whispered sweet nothing in each other's ears as if there was no one else present. Then young Ivan had hugged his Father, tears in his eyes. John Junior stopped, hung back.

"Come, my brother," Abigail had whispered in his ear. "He is our Father and loves us both with all his heart."

General Reed saw the hesitation and walked over to him.

"You've grown. You are a fine-looking young man."

"Where were you," his eldest son spurted out. "Why did you not come and find us?"

"I... thought, you were all dead. Please... forgive me. I have never been so wrong about something in my life." Tears began to course down John Reed's cheeks.

"I had to try and protect Mom by myself! I had to take care of Ivan. Where were you? You are my FATHER! Where were you?"

"I..." The General of the Allied Forces tried not to sob but failed. He began to shake. Abigail stepped in, pulled the two together.

"We are Family. We are not perfect. But we are Family! We rise and fall together. And my new brother, we are now together."

"You... saved them. You saved me. Abigail, how can I..." He grabbed his Adopted Daughter in a hug as he cried. His son hugged them both as all his pent up fear and anger released in his tears. Ivana and Ivan joined the group hug as all the other departing personnel gave them space.

Madam President stood back with George Williams, her special assistant, as did General Torbin Bender. When the time was right, they approached the new family unit. Sarah Paul walked up, hugged Ivana.

"Welcome home, Ivana. We are so happy we were able to rescue you and your sons."

Ivana motioned to the dead and wounded unloading from the Ark.

"Too many died and were hurt. I do not feel I deserved this sacrifice."

"You are part of the human family. Of course, you deserved it." Madam President turned towards John Reed. "We have private transportation for you and your family. You need time to become reacquainted after all these years. General Bender here can handle things."

General John Reed, the man who was into welding disparate Allied Armed Forces into a functional unit, looked at Torbin.

"I know he can, Madam President. And your wife Aleks will want to see you also."

Torbin smiled. "Now I can kvetch at her for a change, for getting herself shot at and bloodied.

"Paybacks a bitch, as they say."

"We owe you all…"

"Hey, Semper Fi, General. That says it all, don't you think?"

Madam President reached over and patted Tobin's arm. "My incorrigible Marine. You have a way of saying and doing just the right thing. Now, time for us all to turn into pumpkins. I will talk to you all later."

The 'talk later' had led to the ceremony earlier in the morning of the departure by Abigail. The Free Russian President and the Japanese Prime Minister had requested to pay homage to the Banshees. In Russia, especially, Ivana Reed was a Heroine. A Mother of Russia who had survived the unthinkable to return to her husband, a recognized hero and Adopted Son of Russia. Thus, a quick broadcast ceremony to honor those involved and assure the masses on humanity worldwide that the Great Compromise was holding together.

The Banshees threw a bit of a monkey wrench in the proceedings. They demanded that accommodations are made for all the wounded to be part of the ceremony. ALL the Sisters must be honored, none forgot. Thus, pushed wheelchairs and gurneys in formation. A new tradition was born.

When they performed the Banshee Roll Call, Abigail had been the one to answer for Private Armstrong. "Here, at my right shoulder.

The Position of Honor, where she belongs." Abigail had Anica's beret tucked under her right epaulet, refused for anyone else to take care of Anica. Two dozen more dead to join Sergeant Jefferson as remembered members of the Sisterhood.

Of course, they televised worldwide, and thus more legends were born. However, humans need legends and heroes to provide examples of what is right with humankind, what 'The Best', is in the greater scheme of human history and existence. And, on a screen, a particular Tschaaa Alien Breeder Pilot and Banshee was honored. The Great Compromise was working.

A week later, Abigail walked out the main entrance to the Banshee Barracks with two large equipment bags in hand and a War Dog at her heel. Ichiro would be along to pick her up shortly for the start of an Extended Leave of Absence. She would still be carried on the Banshee Roles, but the position of Deputy Commander was to be filled by a Newly Minted Major with the last name of O'Brien until she returned. Abigail planned on returning, but she had a slight nagging feeling in her gut of guts. She still was afraid she would not be up to the new task at hand.

Abigail finished what seemed like a very long walk to the end of the entranceway of the Banshee Barracks. She stopped, set her bags down as now Sergeant Fuzz sat by her heels. Of course, he must be promoted for leading Ivana Reed and sons out to safety. War Dogs were here to stay. She turned at looked at the open doors of the barracks entrance. Abigail could just make out the sizeable carved form of the original Sergeant Fuzz. She came to attention and saluted.

"I'll be back, Old Friend. If I'm not, you watch over my Sisters, Okay? Thanks."

Ichiro pulled up in their SUV, hopped out, and hugged her, military etiquette be damned.

"Home awaits you, dearest. First, I will provide you a good meal. Then, a massage. Maybe a little music to relax by. Then…"

"The first item on the agenda is something we need to do in the privacy of our bedroom, my husband."

Ichiro's mouth opened as if to speak, and then he shut it. The New Samurai bowed to the love of his life.

"Your wish is my command, dearest wife."

"And that wish is to make babies." She looked into Ichiro's eyes. "It is time for New Life. I have seen enough death."

As they loaded her bags into the vehicle, Fuzz the War Dog let out a short huffing canine laugh. Puppies. There would be new Puppies in His Pack. What could be better?

NINE MONTHS LATER

"Push one last time, Abigail. I see a head!"

Of course, Rica Rice saw to birth in the hospital. Betty Bardun was there also, to assure Abigail that in no way had her young been tampered with by Tschaaa or Human science. Emily Anders had Fuzz out in the parking lot, would bring him later to meet the New Pack Members.

The first and smaller of the fraternal twins birthed quickly was out and gave a short cry. Colonel Bardun held the precious package as the larger of the two finally bullied her way out, screaming and fussing. Then, both daughters (after they had used Uncle Torbin's K-Bar to cut the umbilical cords) were on their Mother's breasts, soon drinking her healthy milk. Abigail looked at her daughters, smiling and crying at the same time.

"Beautiful. My babies are both beautiful."

"We told you, Abigail. Betty and I knew they would be just fine. You were never 'unclean.'"

"I am blessed with such great family and friends."

"So, before we bring Ichiro in. What are their names?"

"The large, loud one is Brynhildr, after her Aunt."

"And the firstborn?"

"Anica. After a very special lady."